Elsewhere....
II

TALES OF FANTASY

ELSEWHERE

Vol. II

**EDITED BY
TERRI WINDLING &
MARK ALAN ARNOLD**

**INTERIOR ILLUSTRATIONS
by Terri Windling**

FANTASY
ACE BOOKS, NEW YORK

The editors would like to thank the following for their help, suggestions, and/or moral support in the editing and illustrating of this volume:
Susan Allison, Nancy Fiedler, ''Rabbi'' Richard Freeman, Lisa Hauck, Allan Jones, Barbara Jordan & John, Ellen Kushner, Robin McKinley, Beth Meacham & Tappan King, Michael Moorcock, Sydni Moser, Mimi Panitch, Kenneth Peck, J. Michael Reaves, Alastair Reid, Sue Stone, Theodore Sturgeon, T.C., Reg Wells & Joyce Abrams, Jane Yolen, and Ace Production Editor Nancy Wiesenfeld.

Cover art by George de Hoff

ELSEWHERE Vol. II

An Ace Book

Published by arrangement with the editors

ISBN: 0-441-20404-X

First Ace Printing: November 1982
Published simultaneously in Canada

Manufactured in the United States of America

Ace Books, 200 Madison Avenue, New York, New York 10016

Acknowledgments . . .

TABLE
OF
CONTENTS

INTRODUCTION

"Had I the heavens' embroidered cloths . . . I would spread these cloths under your feet; but I, being poor, have only my dreams. I have spread my dreams under your feet—tread softly, for you tread on my dreams."
—*William Butler Yeats*

This is a sampler of dreams—tales shaped by the craft of our authors, yet derived, directly or indirectly, from the collective dreams of humanity. In this lies the appeal and importance of fantasy: more than any other form of fiction, fantasy draws upon the cumulative power of human history, experience, yearning, and vision. The most important task of a fantasy tale is a humble one: to entertain. But because fantasy draws upon our universal heritage of myth and folklore, at its best it possesses the magic to transform the substance of our lives into visions of fever bright clarity.

To some, the word "fantasy" conjures saccharine images of prancing unicorns and butterfly-winged fairies, and fantasy has been condemned not only for the sin of being escapist, but for being trite. These critics have never traveled to the lands of faery, where the pearly tip of a unicorn's horn can tear out the heart of a living man, where the price for watching the fairies dance is to have eyes turned to wood, heart turned to stone. Fantasy is, of course, the oldest form of literature—predating, throughout the world, written language; it is also the most enduring, the most pervasive. Fantasy wells up from myth and legend to resonate throughout music, dance, art, and drama. And it seems that whenever certain critics forget that fantasy is the liqueur distilled from myth and dream, others are about to rediscover it; in the past decade, many interesting new terms have been coined—neofabulism, magical realism, mythic realism, visionary surrealism, mystic visionary-ism, post-rationalist remythification (!); but these are not even new bottles, just new labels for the most ancient, and current, vintages of the fictional vineyards.

Fantasy aficionados may find this introduction overly familiar stuff (and readers rejoining us from Volume I may notice that we've already made these points); however, as booksellers we learned to recognize certain readers who came in to our shop looking for new magical realms and stopped, bemused by the scope of the library of the fantastic; readers who talked (sometimes abashedly) about their fondness for Middle Earth, Camelot, Earthsea, the Hidden Lands, Islandia, but were surprised to find on the same shelves works by some of this cut-and-dried social realist century's awarded and distinguished authors: Miguel Angel Asturias, John Barth, Jorge Luis Borge, Isak Dinesen, John Gardner, Herman Hesse, Isaac Bashevis Singer, James Thurber, Amos Tutuola and many others, all of whom have written of magic or mythic quests or hidden lands or imps or the wondrous passing strange. We learned to recognize that some readers, though insatiably hungry for worlds of magic, had learned (perhaps too well) to beware the shoals beyond their island genre, the oceans of "mainstream" fiction sometimes haunted by dragons of atrophied imagination and claustrophilic self-obsession. But there are as many sorcerers in Tierrapaulita as in Amber, as many weird corners in the Bellefleur mansion as in Castle Gormenghast, and it is the rewarding role of both a specialty bookstore and an anthology like this one to serve as a guidepost to travelers in all of fantasy's myriad realms.

Tolkien has stated that it is impossible to define Faery, for one of its properties is to be elusive; the borders of fantasy—regarding style, purpose, theme—are equally phantasmic. Keeping that in mind, we seek, in ELSEWHERE, to explore, not define. Thus, these books are not intended to be an historical survey of fantasy—excellent volumes of such are already available.* In collecting stories we have followed no rigid theme, agenda, nor aesthetic ideology; the tales come from a variety of sources and were chosen in an admittedly idiosyncratic fashion because something within each one struck one or both of us to the heart. (It has been pointed out to us that while the first volume con-

*The Fantastic Imagination, edited by Robert K. Boyer and Kenneth J. Zahorski; A Treasury of Modern Fantasy, edited by Terry Carr and Martin Greenberg; Dragons, Elves and Heroes and The Young Magicians, edited by Lin Carter; Phantasmagoria, edited by Jane Mobley.

tained many stories about love, many of the stories herein deal with death or transformation; one contributor who published a romantic story in Volume I and writes now about death recently offered to write a new story for Volume III—about taxes. Some authors use fantasy to simply (not merely) entertain; some to retell the old tales; some to examine the modern world; some to reexamine our attitudes toward the past; some to hold a mirror to the heart.

Herein a sampler of dreams. Tread softly.

—Mark Alan Arnold
Terri Windling

St. George, New York
Fall 1982

In the Very Earliest Time

In the very earliest time
when both people and animals lived on earth,
a person could become an animal if he wanted to
and an animal could become a human being.
Sometimes they were people
and sometimes animals
and there was no difference.
All spoke the same language.
That was the time when words were like magic.

—*Eskimo Chant*

Junction's Pleasure

Richard Englehart

"I'm ready to die."

"You can't," the cave said.

He was old. His long hair, curled and silvered, burnished now with the sun, flounced in a gentle breeze. His face was an etching of his experiences. His eyes were glittering blue jewels, deeply set, twinkling in the catching of the brilliant morning.

"You know too much," the cave said.

Yellow smoke fumed thickly, pulsing with the energy of a cut artery. "You have taken," the cave said. "Now you must give."

The magician coiled his pride and his dusty robes around him. "I *have* given," was all he said, though his face shadowed.

The hole, time-hewn out of a purple granite skrag, belched sulphurous fumes around the kneeling man. It rumbled again. "You have given," the cave spoke clearly to the man, "of your energies, given to aid and thwart."

"So, I have *given*. Then what?"

The rock around the cave entrance seemed to flex and form as a mouth speaking. "You must hand your knowledge on."

The magician stood in frustration and anger. "I have no successor."

"Are you not a powerful mage?"

"You know I am."

"Then where, old man, is your progeny?"

"I have a child," he mumbled, leaning against a dead, ancient pine.

"A girl," the cave said.

"Where is my son? I am weary now of this life and want to leave. Yet I may not go without passing on my knowledge. I am tired. Listen hole, this gray hair has been earned. There are none who can match my power." The man touched the ground at the base of the tree. Above, a raven watched as the scant humus caught in the rocky folds shifted and the fresh tip of a new pine shrugged through the dirt.

"I am *so* impressed," said the cave, its sarcasm lost on the raven but not on the man. "So," the rumbling continued, "where is your progeny?"

"When first I stood here and we pacted," the old man said, his nails absently flaking bark from the dead tree, "you said you would give me a son."

"*When* we pacted, I said that I would be a source of power and knowledge for you; that I believed in you; and that, if you learned well, if you learned the ultimate, I would give you progeny to whom you would pass your knowledge."

"A magician may pass knowledge only to first born males."

"And the penalty?"

"Immortality. Doomed to live with superior knowledge, different from all, forever alienated."

"Conclusions—with your limited ability?"

"We pacted. You promised progeny. I have waited."

"How is your daughter?"

"Vermillion?"

"You have more than she?"

"I suppose she is well," said the old man.

"You suppose?"

"Since she is not to be my successor, I have spent little time with her. Magicians must not be involved. Our powers are paid for with loneliness, for none can understand us."

"Yes . . . I have heard so. Do tell me more."

"Must you always be so condescending?"

"No," this time the rumble seemed to be a laugh and the smoke puffed jauntily. "But, at times, it is difficult not to be. Consider the circumstances."

The old man began to pace nervously, kicking at the dust. "We cannot really touch even our wives—for they are women and can understand even less."

"Indeed!"

"So, why have you broken our pact?" the Mage dared.

Silence.

The magician challenged: "Well?"

More silence.

The magician's eyes lost patience with this smoking hole, but wisely he held his emotions.

"Well, yourself," the cave echoed—a statement that boomed across the high pine valleys, vibrating the distant peaks and shaking the raven from his lethargy.

The old man's shadowed face ebbed and the tide of his mind prodded him. "You're saying that I have something yet to learn."

"How deeply perceptive. I knew my time was not to be wasted on you. Oh, great mage, you who create pine trees, why don't you create your own successor?"

"This power is not given to me." It was as close to bitterness as he could allow.

"Does it keep you humble?"

"Yes."

"Good. Remember always of powers greater than yourself.

"Junction!"

The use of his name set the importance of what was to follow and he allowed his emotions to dissipate like butterflies in the mountain air.

"Yes."

The mountain thundered as the ochre smoke churned. The cloud enfolded the man and he stood bathed and listening.

"Junction, you know more than any man. But be aware there will always be contenders for your position. Nothing is as sweet to youth as the fall of an old man. There are many who would happily dance on your grave.

"Especially," the cave seemed to drop to a confidential tone, "beware of Castigo."

"Castigo?" The old man blinked, surprised. "How can he be a danger? He was my student, the best. Yet, he doesn't possess near the necessary knowledge . . ."

"You taught him enough. What he has learned from darker sources is what makes him dangerous."

Junction clouded. "I will be prepared, but I assume there is more."

"Continual brilliance. When we pacted, I said that you must learn the ultimate. You have learned all that men have to give you, now you must learn one thing more. This last is an occult from the dawn, from before thought, from a time of Eden. Yet the answer has never been hidden. It has always been around you. It is, indeed, the most fearsome, the most difficult lesson." The cave puffed and seemed to smile. "Old man, you need a teacher. This one does not know what he is to teach; take him with you now. Learn from him and be companion to each other."

Junction looked around as the enfolding cloud diffused to a trickling puff and sunlight fell upon him. He could see no one. A shadow spiraled down from the height of the dead pine; the raven flapped to the man and grasped his shoulder through maroon robes as though shaking hands.

Hello, Junction. There was no sound. The words formed intelligibly, deep within the man's mind.

"Junction, this is Agapis. Until this moment, when I bid he do otherwise, he had no interest in things human—just as you had no interest in things raven. Agapis will be a guide in your learning. Neither he nor you now understands how. Be of care lest the lesson slip by."

And a wind sprang up pushing the smoke and drifting through the man's robes as he looked at the bird on his shoulder. The raven seemed to shrug.

Don't look at me. I know less of this than you. But I'll do it.

"I will also," said the old man. "I've been equally perplexed before, but in the end all made sense."

"I am glad," the cave said, "that we are all in agreement. Well, Junction, Agapis, you had better get started."

"Where?"

"That will take care of itself. You certainly are not going

to learn any more here. I suggest home. Home is always a good place to start."

The raven pulled from the man's shoulder and settled onto the canyon updrafts, a flower opening, rising out over the valley.

I will see you at the valley entrance, Junction. Enjoy your climb.

The man started down, feeling the exfoliations of granite crumble and slither from under his feet. "I really wonder who gets the best part of all this," the magician muttered. "Somehow none of this seems fair."

"Nobody ever said it was supposed to be," said the cave.

Junction reached the foot of the mountain, he retrieved the items that he had stored there prior to his climb: his cloak—collared, sheening black; his shoulder-strapped pouch—leather, containing herbs, potions and talismans; and finally, his heavy staff—black, smooth, a deep natural grain. He strode through the valley, towards the hidden entrance; sifting through the dwarfed shrubbery at the edge, he seemed to fade into the face of a cliff as he entered a niche which became a narrow, twisting canyon. It emptied the magician into a scrubbed wood. From this outer entrance, he looked across low, rolling hills and could see the dusty road to his home looping through the low areas.

Junction! The raven's voice floated softly through his mind and the old man scanned the stunted trees, finally discerning the space in shadows filled with the bird.

"Agapis?"

Would you care to assist a peasant being robbed or is your way home of more importance?

"I'd prefer to continue home; but I suppose I must."

Must? Agapis cocked his head. *My new instincts tell me that you do only what you want and call it 'must'.*

"Do your instincts speak of a magician's duty? 'Power is a double-edged responsibility.' No matter. Philosophy later, Heroics now. Where?"

Watch me and follow. His sheen glided among the mushrooms of trees, a black fan wafting.

The peasant, terrified, speechless, stood cringing against a rock, held by one of the toughs who had twisted the poor man's tattered chemise against his throat. The other stood, laughing, holding a cocked crossbow, relaxed. The bowman spoke, his voice like straw burning. "Fargus, stop playing with him. Take his poke and stand aside so I can put him out of his misery." He gestured casually, but meaningfully, with his crossbow.

"Fargus, rather, just stand aside. Leave his poke and leave the territory. Also, take what's—his—name with you."

At the foreign sound, the two turned and the one called Fargus released the peasant who crumpled to his knees, bonnet askew. The robber reached into the blousing of his cote, producing a small, broad-bladed dirk. He laughed amiably. "San San, how lucky it is we are! Here we are, two poor wayfarers, contenting ourselves with meager pickings from a poor worker. And now, see what has been sent us: an old man, to be sure, but his robes have a richness."

The bowman flipped his rough surcote over his shoulder, freeing his arm. He laughed, "True, Fargus; pickings from him should be good. Shall I shoot him first or the one sniveling by your feet?"

"It's a long time since I've slit the throat of an old man. You take the cryer there, I want this pleasure."

The evening sun deepened the shadows to a purple. Somewhere a thrush bounced through a hidden tangle and warbled sweetly. Fargus held the knife carelessly as he moved with mock respect towards Junction.

"I am compelled by unwritten law to warn you. I am Junction, and I would strongly suggest that you let the peasant go. I dread the taking of lives. Even two such as yours."

Fargus' grin, beard-hidden, lifted his voice and he

laughed, "Well, old one, I do not have difficulty in that area. So watch me. I'll give you a lesson."

The old man unclasped his cloak and allowed it to drop. He spoke quietly, "I dread it, but I can and will do it. Let him go and we will part alive."

As Fargus approached and the banter continued, the peasant scrambled like a mole around a rock, gained his feet and ran. Before San San could raise his bow, Fargus said, "We'll get him later. He can't outdistance us. He'll only prolong his miserable life. Watch the fun here."

The magician leaned easily on his heavy staff as the robber sauntered in, humming a light madrigal, his knife conducting the tune. The rotted-tooth grin stumbled into a startled grunt of surprise as the staff flicked like a frog's tongue. It snapped bruisingly from its resting place into his groin with a dull *thwacking* sound. Junction shifted, delicate as a dove, and the shaft spun like a disc, breaking the wrist bone, the knife clattering into the pebbles.

Junction raised his staff. The next swing would break the man's neck. The magician's pivot saved his life as the squared shaft thudded into him. He spilled backwards, the impact and jolt of pain rolling him into a sprawl. San San's hand, proficient as a striking snake, leapt to his belt quiver and he began to nock the quarrel. Junction, dazed, attempted to clear his head. Fargus, holding his broken arm across his body, had retrieved the dirk and was skulking towards the fallen magician. Through the gauze of shock, Junction saw a black blur fall out of the trees and scramble among the bowman's arms; hands waving, San San swung viciously at the churning feathers but grabbed only air as the bird arched and worried him from a different direction.

The magician rolled, dust clouding. Fargus was only a few feet from him, spitting curses that became his last words as the end of Junction's staff caught him, a slamming piston between the eyes. His head dropped, eyes staring, blood spurting from his bitter tongue. San San cleared for a shot and the Mage, on his back, made a gesture with his hand coupled with a slurred word that did not come from earth. The bowman pressed the trigger and, impossibly, the arrow shot backwards, bluntly tearing through the man's throat.

The magician sat on the ground, the arrow's shaft protruding like a driven stake from his left shoulder. That there was pain was obvious. Yet, as he sat, eyes closed, his mind going somewhere, doing something, the expression deep in his face changed to the softness of silk as he gained control. He grasped the wood shaft and, as though he could see the wound's channel, slid the arrow out.

Agapis understood pain and winced in his fashion as he tried to follow the magician's cool objectivity. The man slid the robe open, baring the bloody pucker. He reached into his pouch and, with the dexterity of a surgeon, cleaned the wound and inserted a thick white ointment on the tip of a probe.

Your bag is a provider.

"I've had enough experience to know what I'll need most."

Will you be well?

"Soon. It will heal rapidly and I can control the stiffness." He returned the items to his bag, organizing them. "This is far from the worst I've had—though it was all easier when I was younger. I am aware that you saved me from worse harm. You have my thanks and I owe you a life."

I did only what seemed sensible. Since we are now companions and I'm finding the experience interesting, I could not bring myself to watch it terminate.

Junction shifted his robe over the wound and wrapped his cape around himself. He smiled. "Of that, I'm glad. I wondered why the cave gave me you. This was a good start. Though I'm supposed to learn something through you—I can't fathom it. Do *you* know what the lesson is?"

I'm a stranger here myself, the raven cackled. *I had no interest in any of this. I just do what I'm told.* A breeze trundled through the clumped trees and the black bird's feathers frayed. In annoyance, it ruffled them into place and modified its position. *You almost gave your life for that peasant. Yet, at the first opportunity, he ran. That is hardly a mode of thanks. Humans can't be trusted much, can they?*

"They can be trusted to be human. We must all admit to a weakness. He owed me nothing."

You saved his life. That's nothing?

"If I can help, then I must. My knowledge gives me responsibility."

He had none?

"His ignorance forgives him."

Ravens consider natural instinct—aiding one who has aided you as mandatory.

"Humans have drifted far from what is 'natural'. Once, perhaps—but now—"

And you? Does your knowledge put you in touch with what is natural?

The old man tested his shoulder, gave an honest grimace but felt his strength and said:

"We should continue. I have an uneasiness concerning my home and something the cave said about a one-time student of mine."

The bird stretched two black silk fans and lofted to an easy hover. Junction pulled himself up on his staff, a maroon vine bursting a silver flower. Though Agapis was overhead, Junction heard him as if the bird were perched on his shoulder.

So ignorance absolves responsibility in humans?

"Perhaps not, but knowledge tolerates ignorance better than ignorance tolerates knowledge."

The umber dust exploded with each of his sandaled steps and he followed his staff feeling a strange urgency, one that he had felt before, one that had demonstrated its validity many times.

Before the sun pinked the highest peaks, Junction stood at the crest of a long slope. His home nestled near the bottom, around several looping bends. He paused only a moment—as he always did at this hill. His childhood was in this valley, and he allowed himself the nostalgia. The black bird rolled out ahead of him, disappearing in the direction of the cottage. *I will announce your arrival and be back soon to allay your fears.*

The magician could not disperse his apprehension, and as he came into sight of the white stone cabin he could see a window broken, no one in sight, and the bird reaching towards him.

Stop, Junction! The bird flapped in a braking arc.

The magician, breathing hard, paused.

Prepare yourself.

At this, the old man brushed at the air and moved towards the house, the bird lifting and following. The threshhold, heaped with the shattered remains of the door, gaped at him. He struggled over the splintered wood. Inside, Junction recognized the trademark of Castigo: the odor of charred timbers, sandlewood and an edge of death. He used it, the magician remembered, the way an animal uses urine.

A window had been blasted and its beam hung across the opening, blocking the sun. Light leaked across the threshhold into the dark, ruined room and, in the shaft, lay a body, female, disheveled, sprawled.

"Mara." The old man knelt, gently gathering his robes, and raised her head, settling it on his knee.

The raven fastened himself to the darkness near the collapsed windowbeam and studied with curiosity this superior man reduced to a tremble.

"Mara." He reached a weathered hand into his pouch and removed from the clutter two phials of amber liquid. He unstopped one and, tilting the container, wet his finger. Forcing her mouth open, he touched his finger to the woman's tongue. The other liquid he daubed under her nose. She coughed, stirred and squirmed. Seeing him, she folded him to her, biting her lips to keep from crying.

When she calmed, he made a pass at an oil lamp which flickered into life, bouncing a bit of the darkness back. She looked at him. "I thought we agreed—" she said through swollen lips,"—no magic in the house."

He shrugged. "It seemed expedient," he said, and he carried her to the bed, softly nestling her into the heavy furs.

"Mara, was it Castigo?"

"Castigo. A rather brash young fellow, don't you think?" Her voice shook and she punctuated it with an attempt at a smile but ended by biting the knuckles of her fisted hand.

"He's an infant."

"Hardly."

"Did he . . . harm you?"

Her blood and her bruises made the question rhetorical. She looked away, then gazed directly into his eyes, watching for his reaction to her words. (She was disappointed, but his lack of concern wasn't unexpected.)

"He is fierce. He raped me. Do you consider rape harm, my husband?"

"Where is Vermillion?"

"He raped *me*."

"You spoke clearly. I heard. What would you have me say?"

"Speak, Magician, of your concern for me."

"You know of my concern."

"I would hear it."

"Then damn, woman, hear. He has forced you. He will pay. But to speak on it further is futile, what has been done cannot be undone by sympathy."

"Sympathy will not harm me."

"It will, however, consume time. Tell me of Vermillion."

She paused, frustrated, her fingers digging into the furs. "It was she for whom he came. He came with his necrasses, black flapping forms. They held Verm while he forced himself on me. I called you. You did not hear. The while, he muttered in my ear that she would be superior stock."

At her pause, he stood and moved away towards the lamp, staring at its subtle shifting. "Stock," he said.

She lifted her head. "He is going to use her with his son, Mordant. Castigo assumes your daughter will give him a powerful grandson."

"Indeed, he is correct. If there were such a union, the offspring would be awesome."

"There will be."

"There will not be."

"How will you prevent it?"

"I just will."

"Does she mean that much to you?" The words were molten lead, dropped slowly from a crucible.

The old man could not hold her eyes. He moved from the bed to the canted beam, assessing its repair.

"She is my daughter," he said with his back to her. His voice was heavy.

"She has been such for twelve years. It seemed little concern till now."

He faced her and saw her beauty, black hair sprayed over the white fur pillow. Her face was wrinkle-free, her age indeterminable. He fought back his human emotions and merely said: "Till now."

The magician, her husband, sat at the edge of the bed to explain that he would stay long enough to seek aid from a couple in a near cabin. And, using his magic, he undid the damage Castigo had inflicted on the cottage. It stood white and sweet again, all trace of Castigo gone. When she was cared for, the magician kissed her. "I will return," he said. "I will bring your daughter. She will be safe."

"*This* time," she answered him, looking at him through swollen eyes. "She is beautiful and—with her bloodline—she will be a prize. How will a magician's daughter protect herself? Especially when her father is never here."

He grunted, gestured to the raven and they started towards a mountain peak that was several ranges and days away.

"Castigo's mountain," said Junction.

The terrain had shifted several times, becoming more dismal as they traveled. They were perhaps a week into their venture and resting in a desert region with deepening night no comfort in the desolation. The breeze fanned the sand in a dry spume over the lips of dunes and the grit penetrated everything. They sat uncomfortably before a fire culled from the straining shrubs.

The magician sat staring into the fire, watching the flames gambol like young orange deer. Agapis had been speaking for some time before his words nuzzled into Junction's fantasy web.

. . . so disturbed?

"What?"

Your intensity and anxiety is disproportionate to your personality and your beliefs. All that you have told me of yourself does not add up to this deep concern.

He gestured to his chest. "Much is carried here. I have a tremendous decision to make. To be involved causes only difficulty and pain."

Your concern for your daughter surprises you.

"It is dangerous."

The bird bounced a bit away from a fire that had grown too hot. Junction turned his attention from the flames and looked at the raven. "Do you understand any of this?"

The more I am acquainted with humans, the less I understand. You are amusing in the ways you deceive yourselves. And if you, a magician, a man close to the understanding of nature, are an example, it will be hilarious to meet others.

"Must you insult? You sound so like the cave."

The bird bounced to Junction's knee and fanned its tail towards the warmth. He cocked his head sideways.

Perhaps I've been around the cave too much. Nevertheless, inconsistency seems to be your only constant.

"I don't need your chiding. I can't expect you to understand, but I have a true human quandary."

It has to do with your daughter?

The magician stood and shook his leg, which had fallen asleep, and the raven squawked its surprise and flapped to the ground. "I have," Junction said "ignored her for twelve years. When she was born, I had expected a boy—someone to whom I could pass my knowledge."

What of parental love?

"I cannot involve myself with human frailties. It is a price that one pays as a magician. You gain the knowledge, the ability to help others; but to be proficient, you must stay apart."

The raven mustered his most sarcastic tone. *Is that to say that you are now objective?*

"I am now confused."

Agapis chuckled and hopped a few feet beyond the rim of the firelight, his blackness melting into the night. The raven looked up at the sky and thought that a flight prior to sleep would be invigorating and soothing. As his muscles tensed, and his wings spread, the sand beneath him suddenly gave way and something slithered and wrapped vise-like around him. He had only time for a brief squawk before he disappeared beneath the surface.

Junction. I don't know what has me, but I'm in trouble. You'd better hurry.

The magician rushed to the depression in the sand, lighting the area with a flickering firebrand. He asked, "Are you being pulled deeper?"

No, I've stopped. It's hurting. Hurry! Please!

Junction said, "I haven't done this one for a while . . ."

He shoved the brand into the sand, and concentrating on the small crater he held his hands above his head, fingers pointing towards the sand . . . *Junction—Help me!* . . . a vicious downward thrust and sparks leapt arching into the ground. A burst of sound and a cloud of sand blasted into the air. Twisting in a feathered frenzy, the bird was catapaulted into the darkness and shook pieces of brown stringy substances from it. The black flapping wings stopped their panicked beating and the bird settled to earth a respectful distance from the crater. In the center of the hole something heaved and pulsed. Liquid spilled into the sand. The something seemed to draw into itself and it pulled into the depths and was gone, leaving pieces behind, twisting and curling.

Agapis alighted on Junction's shoulder, cradling tightly against his neck. He was shaken. There was no bravado. He looked at the bare patches on his body and said, *Was that the best you could do?*

"It seemed expedient."

If you would have blasted a foot closer, there would have been pieces of me lying there instead of that thing.

"Don't worry. I don't eat crow."

Now who's insulting?

"Don't call kettles black."

Thank you, Junction. What was that thing?

"I have no idea. There are many such things here."

Before, I was playing with your weakness. I am sorry— truly so. I guess that makes us even?

"I've never been good at keeping account. Let's just say that we're always even."

You were talking about your confusion . . .

The magician held the raven on his forearm and close to his chest, stroking the soft feathers, soothing. "When a magician dies, all his magic dies with him, unless he passes it on to his first born son."

And you have but a daughter.

"If he does otherwise, he is condemned to immortality."

The bird spoke, calmer now: *I thought humans enjoyed long lives.*

"To live forever, superior in knowledge and powers, unable to be close to another human, unable to regress and be like them—condemned to continue to learn, to continue to grow. My pact was that I would learn what the cave would teach, use it for the betterment of people and pass it on. Before I can die, I must have a son that I do not have and must learn something from a bird and I do not know what that something is."

Well, I don't either. Don't stop, by the way, that feels good. If I had any idea, I'd let you know.

Junction smiled. "How alike we are. Who will judge the judge and to whom does a magician go for strokes?"

That night passed, and two more, with Agapis complaining of stiffness from his encounter. What sun there was faded like roses wasting on a windowsill and the sky slipped to a dull white. They climbed into a rocky, treeless realm, deprived of their shadows. As they rounded a jagged shoulder, the stony path pitched into open space. Below, far below, they could see pines, green fields, an emerald lake, in stark contrast to the gargoyle barrenness around them. Jutting from the center of the lake, a rock spine island struggled until it reached their height. It shrugged solidly as though it were some decapitated beast; and sitting, hunched on the flat top: Castigo's castle.

The structure was linked with the path by a narrow swinging bridge, a thread between two worlds. *Neither of them worth much,* was Junction's thought. *Rather fort-like in appearance,* was the raven's thought. Earthen in color, bulky and powerful, it challenged all to penetrate its squatting coldness.

It seems, thought the bird, *that a magician could do better; more charm, grace, magic-like, you know. It's not ominous, just isolated and daring somehow.*

"That's Castigo. Should he continue along this bent, he will be very dangerous."

Might he change?

"Change is always possible as long as the soul is green. When the bark hardens, even then it's *possible*, but much more difficult. I don't want to kill him."

How do we meet him?

"We just walk across this suspension bridge and into the web. He knows we're here . . . has known for some time."

You're going to walk across that abyss knowing that he knows?

"Castigo must test himself on me."

Junction took two steps up to the wooden ties that stretched intricately woven into the rough hemp-like rope that formed the only path to the castle. He started across and the bridge began a trembling sway. As he walked, concentrating on balance, he continued, "No student is content just *believing* that he is better than his teacher. He has to prove it." Nearing the castle, Junction scanned the structure. Its front walls and battlements leaned forward like a toad supported by flying buttresses shaped like dragons.

What are those, Magician?

At the far side he could see several elongated, flattened black beings, something like an eel with appendages, standing beside the bridge's support ropes. "Those are necrasses—creatures of this area that Castigo has taken a liking to. They have some intelligence and he's trained them."

They have knives. They could cut the support ropes.

"They will. Those are their orders. The imp has sent some underlings to test me, for his amusement. They won't cut the ropes until I get close, and that will be their mistake."

Agapis flew near the creatures. They paid no attention to him; their small, hard eyes were fixed on the magician approaching. Moving almost in unison, as he drew near, their knives sliced at the ropes. Junction waved his staff, shouting three words that sounded like barking. Again he waved the staff over his head, discharging a pulsing wind-like sound. The noise whipped through the air and wrapped the black things in it like an invisible shroud, pulsing and vibrating against them. They squirmed and emitted a white slimy fluid, a natural protection. Their vacant mouths opened and a dismal wail oozed into the sunless air. Yet, the pulsations continued, compacting the sound into pressure, and the necrasses were squeezed, their insides popping from their mouths. As the noise faded, they lay wrung, wasted, their body juices dribbling over the edge of the cliff.

The old man gained the ledge and was met with a booming voice from the main turret to the left of the closed doors. "Nicely done, Noble Master. A simple enough technique. One that expends little energy. It took you some time to get here. You are slowing down."

"Speed, Castigo, is not always essential. At times propriety, class, a certain impeccability of manner, something that comes with wisdom . . ."

"No more lectures, Old Man. I have all of your wisdom."

"You have some of my knowledge and none of my wisdom. The two aren't the same. Mara was right; you have grown quite brash."

"Ah, Mara. And how is your wife?"

Junction chose not to respond.

Castigo gestured behind him and two necrasses wriggled out, dragging Vermillion. She stood there, his daughter, in a thin white chemise, her head up, hair—amber as mead—whipped by the colorless breeze. Junction was struck by her beauty. Perhaps it was the contrast. Perhaps the stress had touched the inner magic power that would be natural in his offspring. Yet she glowed, radiated a pride, a defiance, that sparkled in this sunless land.

Next to her stood Mordant, smiling like his father, slighter in build, obviously not as athletic as the dark powerful man, his teacher. The son smiled, but there was a nervousness there. He glanced at his father.

Castigo swung his legs over the edge of the turret and sat, his legs dangling some distance above Junction. His grin danced, framed by shoulder length coal hair swirling like a shattered spider web. "It's not brash to want one's due. Look, Old Man, let's set this straight. I don't want to take over the world. I am not an evil magician." He smoothed his shimmering black surcoat. "I have my mountain. This is all I want."

"All you want *now*," Junction interrupted.

"Well, *now* is what is important, isn't it? Somebody taught me that. Anyway, *now* is enough." He reached back and brought the girl to the edge, his arm around her. "She is a fine girl, Junction, beautiful, strong. She carries your bloodline. I wish her to be my son's wife. She will bear us both fine grandchildren, don't you think?" He caught her chin between his thumb and forefinger and tilted her head, appraisingly.

Junction leaned against the main buttress directly under Castigo's dangling legs. "What of her wishes?" Junction said, nodding to the girl in the thin white chemise.

"What of them? You didn't seem to care much about them for twelve years. What of Mara's wishes? How many of them did you cast off? Come on, Old Teacher, I know you. We've talked. How is this so much different? You really lose nothing and gain a fine grandson. We don't have to fight."

"Your problem, young one, is that you don't ask, you take. While my own responsibilities may not have been fully met, as you've noted, I've never taken by force. I've never coerced."

"But, Junction, you're forgetting that that's the way nature's set up." Castigo laughed gleefully. "The fittest survive."

The old man grew calm, trying to fathom his adversary's strategy. He noticed that the buttress he was leaning against was supporting the turret which overhung the wall. "You've forgotten the final step of nature. There is survival, yes—but the goal is harmony. Without harmony, nature doesn't exist. You know nothing of nature, little man." As he spoke, he felt that the turret was tied into the wall. He traced his finger along the dragon's tail. He said, "Vermillion, are you well?"

"Father," her voice flowed there in that cold place like sunlight and she was calm. "I have not been harmed and have been provided for. I do not want to be here but I do not wish you to endanger yourself."

Junction threw a sudden, vicious pass at the stone dragon, swept the flying buttress over the precipice, and the turret, itself, began to crumble. Castigo shouted and scrambled back into the turret. Chunks of dark mortar and chinking dropped out as cracks ripped through the wall like the branches of some stone tree and hewed rocks fell, the face of the castle beginning to crumble.

Castigo and Mordant leaped to an adjacent battlement while the turret fell forward, carrying the girl with it. The two necrasses disappeared into the rumble of dust that spewed from the churning stones. Vermillion was falling forward with the wall, with the turret, and Junction, dancing from the tumbling chunks of granite bouncing around him, pushed at the ground—and he levitated, meeting the plummeting tower, picking his daughter from its crumbling floor and, guiding his movements, alighted in front of the palace gate.

The wall of the castle wavered and Castigo and Mordant ran for the stairs, the wall collapsing behind them. Though the rumbling roar clouded his vision, Junction could see Mordant scrambling down the shaking stone steps; behind him, his father slipped as the stairs gave way. The boy turned and looked up as the wall pushed Castigo out from the edge and away. He watched as his father fell on one leg. The splintering sound could be heard even where the old man stood. Castigo rolled on the ground, the rocks crashing, shattering, dust burying him. He lay still, pinned by several stones, his leg splintered, the pain great. He shouted to his son, "Mor, call the necrasses on him."

Mordant ran to the side of the gate, turned and screamed, "Father, they can't. They're trapped. They're behind the gate but the courtyard has collapsed behind them. They're penned in."

Junction had gathered Vermillion to him and was backing towards the bridge as Castigo gestured and the great gates buckled and splintered. Freed, the necrasses surged forward, slithering, a high-pitched moan from a thousand black throats. Almost mindless, the leech-like things wriggled, thousands of webbed feet scraping, dust clouding. Junction roared and threw his staff into their midst as the tide stumbled towards him. The old man backed onto the bridge, keeping himself between the necrasses and Vermillion.

For an instant the staff lay there, kicked by hundreds of slithering feet. Then it shuddered and began to belch clouds of blue smoke and its shaking grew more violent and the ground under it wavered, jaggedly splitting. A growling, grinding sound began building and the gap grew violently, grating the rock, shattering and pitching huge boulders into the air and the crack grew deeper with stumbling black forms falling through the blue smoke, down, lost in the darkness. The gap grew into a chasm and from its bowels a brimstone sound and a blast of heat spewed from the released entrails of the mountain.

Mordant, seared in the red fire glare, had freed his father and was dragging him under an overhanging ledge. Castigo shouted, "Junction, you'll pay for this, pay highly. Old Man, you will die! Both of us cannot live in this world!" He threw several passes at the magician; they spattered aimlessly into the gorge behind Junction and his daughter. "We'll meet again. Soon. There is no use in hiding from me."

"I have no intention of hiding," said the old man. The inner blasts of the mountain were splitting it in two, the palace crumbling in on itself, the flames scorching the necrasses, driving them over the lip of the gorge. A thousand burned and dying wails pummeled the mountain.

You haven't much time old man. You'll never get across.

"Well, where have you been?"

Watching. You didn't seem to need much help. This, I assume, is the fabled Vermillion. The bird alighted delicately on the girl's shoulder and there was a pause.

"Father, he's beautiful. Who is he? Where did he come from?"

"Daughter, this is hardly the time for introductions," said the magician, and he made a gesture, knocking two other black creatures into the lake far below. "We are not out of this yet. I don't know how many necrasses are left. We have to re-group; Castigo still possesses a deadly energy pass and he's not finished.''

What's your plan?

"I'm going to cut this end of the bridge loose, ride it down and drop into the lake. I can break most of the fall with levitation. It will still be rough. If I can't kill him now, I will have to meet him again. Listen, Agapis, I'll be most vulnerable as I swing out. Do you understand?''

Completely. You will not be vulnerable. I will see to it.

The magician pushed his daughter down, urging her to hold tightly. Sparks jumped from both hands and he cut the two ropes simultaneously. The bridge shook precariously, its stability gone. Castigo realized the strategy and dragged himself out into the open, the rumbling, the glare, flashing around him. He watched, shielding his eyes, as Junction cut the final base rope and the bridge dragged from the edge and swung free. The old man pivoted and held both himself and Vermillion against the swinging bridge as it seemed to hang for an instant and then started its long, wavering loop. "When I yell, let go!" he shouted into his daughter's ear. Her obedience was crucial.

The slow, swinging target was an easy one for Castigo and he took his time. He smiled in spite of his pain and extended his index finger—pointing at the magician's back as it drifted away from him. He laughed and was about to release the energy just as Agapis dove in a long looping arc.

Be of care, Junction. I'll take care of him. Your daughter is beautiful and worth any price—as are you.

The black blur hit the young magician just as he heard his son's shouted warning. He yelled in pain as he moved his leg and his energy blast splintered the boards near Junction's head, singeing his hair, driving slivers into his cheek. Vermillion whispered in his ear, "Father?"

"No matter. Get ready to drop."

The pendulum, swinging in a graceful arc, gaining momentum, reached its nadir and Castigo was set for another try. Again, Agapis swooped in. Castigo, annoyed, blurred a pass at him and the bird struck the energy wall that was waiting for him. The shock threw him violently into the air and he bounced back to the earth.

Good bye, Junction.

Junction heard the words as he released his grip and called for his daughter. As they plummeted towards the lake, the old man pointed at Vermillion and their fall became a flutter. They dropped into the cold blue of the lake as two snowflakes.

Mordant stood at the cliff's edge, watching. "They survived, Father. All because of this," and he kicked the black heap of frazzeled feathers over the lip, watching it bounce from ledge to outcrop, finally to splash softly and sink.

"It's all right, Son. We will have our chance again. God, what a master! What power!"

"I don't understand, Father. You admire the man, yet you fight him."

"That enmity has anything to do with admiration is a fallacy. He is a beautiful man. It is too bad that I must kill him."

It was a green place where he carried her: a cavern of trees, heavy-moist, the roof leaf-layered, interlocked filigrees of Thujas, Sassafras, Quassia and Balsam. Humid purple shadows hung like hovering birds, beaten back to niched recesses by shafts of sunlight. Filtered, it cast a delicate green on everything. On the quaggy floor, vervain and orchids dappled the fragrance of hyacinths.

He laid her on a flourish of feathered moss, heavy green. He undressed her gently at the edge of a pool that was turquoise, placid, and pure. The magician looked at his daughter and his heart jumped, aware, perhaps for the first time, that twelve years had indeed passed—that she was a little girl no longer. The soft beauty was muted by bruises and contusions. With care, he applied an amber balsam and a thicker white cerate. His hand cradled her head and he pressed a crystal cordial to her lips, the tonic vitalizing.

He watched the rose creep under the skin and as her eyes began to flicker, he draped the chemise modestly over her.

"Father, are you all right?" She looked into his eyes, concern first for him and only a slight wince as she shifted her position.

"Better now. And you?"

"A bit tired, but very well. We won, did we not?"

"In a battle, there are no winners, only survivors. We lost Agapis." His voice was heavy.

"I am sorry. He was so beautiful." Her eyes shone and the tears were dew on roses, her innocence jolted by the raven's sacrifice.

"He chose to die."

"Why? Why would he do such a thing?"

"For me to learn and for you to live. I was a stranger to him, as different from him as possible, yet he had no hesitation in doing what he knew was necessary."

Her brows knitted. "I don't understand."

"No matter. I do."

"You say that he died for me to live. I don't feel that important."

"In his decision, you were—are. You must not minimize his action. He *was* beautiful. So now you have a gift of life and you are responsible."

Tears streamed and her body trembled. "It's a frightening gift."

He allowed his ancient hands to melt through the shining gold of her hair. "Responsibility is indeed so."

The old man looked up through the holt's canopy at the fractional white of sunlight, holding her for a long time, for a very long time. She stopped sobbing and there was a silence: no wind, no animal rustle scuttling under the betony, not even the sonorous insect purl. He listened to her bruises and the murmur of her wounds. Something untangled inside him and the old man felt his lips lilt into a gentle smile.

"Father, how long will we stay here?"

"Soon, you will be well. You are young and are mending quickly. We are here because you will need the strength from this place when we once again deal with Castigo. And because I want you to meet someone—someone important."

She looked up, a delicate shudder wafted through her, like a seagull. "Must we meet Castigo again?"

"Yes."

"Why?"

"Castigo doesn't know how to let anything go. It's why he was my best student. He learned well and he's at a crossroads. At another time, his brilliance would have made him my successor. Well, even Mages make mistakes and Castigo was mine. Castigo did that human thing—he made a choice. One that I cannot live with. It's going to be such a waste."

She looked down at the water and saw herself reflected there in a shimmer. "My feelings towards him disturb me."

"You are entitled to your feelings. Mine, too, are disturbing. I've taken any number of lives—never without cause. Rarely, though, have I looked forward to it. It is difficult with Castigo for me. I do not want his death, for I understand him too well. I know what he wants, and, from his stance, it's not evil . . .

"Yet, I will do what must be done. With him and you."

She brightened and asked, "You said, Father, that there was someone I was to meet?"

"He is near now. He has been aware of and watching us since we've been here. This place is his. Over there, the other side of the pool—that's where he is."

She glanced over at the green jumble and, through the graced vines of the white jasmine, Vermillion saw him appear. He stepped through a coppice drape and stood near the slender white camphor trunks at the edge of the pool. He was watching. His whiteness was different from the flower-white that dappled the covert. His whiteness did not hold the green cast that all else here held, rather, it flouresced in a primitive purity, a glow that came from within.

He was not very large, perhaps slightly bigger than a pony. In him, though, was a rippling strength, a leanness of defined muscles, that separated him from other animals. His mane and tail were longer than Vermillion would have thought, flowing silk, sheened like the iridescence of milkweed pod flax. And though his fetlocks were sunk into the betony and camomile, she could see that the hair there was longer and tufted. The horn, though, was right. Golden, ribbed, delicately arched, gently proportioned, it exuded a strength that demonstrated this animal to be formidable. The awesome power of the horn gleamed its statement in silence.

Her father interrupted her assessment when he said, "He does not speak. He does not communicate his thoughts as did Agapis. He just is. He accepts or rejects. If he rejects, he is never seen again. He has accepted me and we have ventured together many times. I have never brought another human here, to his home. I had hoped, by bringing you, that he would understand my urgency."

Junction waited, anxious, barely breathing. This was one of those times where his magic had no place; whatever happened would depend on the will, on the needs, desires, of two independent beings.

The unicorn still watched. It tossed its head and the mane swirled like the curling eddies of a deep river. It took a few steps around the pool.

Vermillion's attention shifted from the awesome beauty of the animal to its eyes. She was startled. The glitter of knowledge that danced there was incongruous with its setting. She read eternity there, a song that trilled in an unknown key. He was a lion, an antelope; he was an eagle. Vermillion realized then that the descriptions she had heard of unicorns were not built from physical actuality but from an amalgamation of the *essence* of animals, birds, even plants. He seemed, somehow, to be everything; to be combined extremes without being reduced to a median; to be beauty, joy, ugliness, suspicion. He was male, but his intuition, grace and beauty had the flowerhead of femaleness. No description seemed adequate.

Vermillion smiled and the unicorn snorted gruffly. He approached her where she sat bathed in the incense of jasmine and hyacinth, sunk in the heavy green of the moss. He lowered his head to nuzzle the aroma that honeyed her hair.

Vermillion stood, her fingertips tracing a pattern on the unicorn's muzzle, and she whispered, "You are so beautiful." She touched the golden spike with one finger. It was as the susurrus of a gentle rain and the animal, soundless, gave himself to her. It was a forever thing.

Junction inhaled deeply, his relief tangible. He thought to himself: *She has the magic of the unicorn; the magic and the fury, the grace, the love, the power, the myth—But is it enough?*

He knew it wasn't.

"Father, does he stay here always?"

"This place, this pool, is his. It exists only because of him. He came down from the mountain for me one time and created it. Here he stays." Junction stroked the lean neck, his hand soft on the white. "Unicorns do what they will for their own reasons. Every unicorn must have a pool of pure water or be near purity. Without purity, unicorns die."

Vermillion drifted to the edge of the turquoise pool, her young legs long and slender. Her bare feet sank deeply into the moss. She looked to the animal as if for permission and touched the water with her toe. The unicorn watched, but it made no move. She waded delicately into the cool, perfect pool.

The unicorn looked at the magician.

"She is beautiful, isn't she?"

The unicorn looked at him.

"You are aware that she is in danger?"

The unicorn looked at him.

"It's not right that she be in danger simply because I

helped to bring her into this world . . . You think that I've
gotten soft, that I've lost my detachment."

The unicorn looked at him.

"Well, that's not it. It may seem like that, but . . . you
see . . . it's merely a matter of practicality. After all, I do
have some responsibility."

The unicorn looked at him and nibbled a comfrey leaf.

"I have to maintain my status as a magician . . . I'm not
going to show her everything—just enough to protect her.
Still, I don't believe that the cave will see it my way."

The unicorn paused. He seemed to smile.

And so, there, among the citrus scent of the bergamot
trees in the drifting humid haze, the girl sat draped in her
chemise; the unicorn lay on the deep piled moss, eyes
closed, content, his delicate head resting softly in her lap.

Her father began in detail, touching first the very basic
levels of magic: the apparent split of man from nature, the
sympathy of nature for man and his needs, the develop-
ment of individual strengths—not to the control of nature
by supernatural forces but blending the respect of the two
powers.

"Father, I don't know if I can remember all of this," she
said frankly.

He turned to her and rested his hands on her slender
shoulders. His eyes were intense, bluer than she remembered them.

"Verm, I'm so proud of you. You know, it took me years
of mistakes before I was able to do even some of the
simplest things."

"Really? Somehow, I guess I thought you could do it all
from the start. I can't picture you confused like this."

"Ha! I'll tell you some stories as we go along. Mistakes
are awfully important. They give us measuring sticks . . .
show how much we're growing . . . see? Here, try this
. . . get this comfrey to bend away from the sun. Watch."

He touched the angular hairy stem, pushing it towards
the shadows. It stayed.

Gently, she moved another the same way and it sprang back, some pale purple flowers dropping. She looked at him, disappointed.

"Sometimes," he laughed, "the cave would get so angry with me, I thought it would give up. Often, *I* wanted to quit. Here, just keep trying—talk to it."

Again, with a touch light as a moth, she coaxed the plant—and this time, it obeyed.

Junction stood, laughing, and took her hand in his and they walked through that magic place. He explained and demonstrated subtle, almost obvious concepts. He told her that it was the will of the magician more than the correct secret words that caused things to happen—that it was the magician's wisdom and not the proper ritual that was important. "Yet," he said, "linking will and words— wisdom and ritual—we're able to tap into the forces of eternity." His look and smile swung back to the past, a lone bird flying, and his throat tightened. There was a welling in his chest. He said, "When you were born and were only this big, I never thought I'd see you working with the forces of eternity . . ."

One day Junction said, "We have to leave now."

She asked, "May we return?"

"Your question will be answered by the result of our confrontation. Castigo and Mordant are nearing and I want to face them away from this place. They are coming over the ridge. We will make haste and meet them in the mountains above the timberline."

"We will win—I mean, we will be the survivors . . . won't we?"

"That, indeed," said the teacher, packing his simple goods skillfully, "is my intention. However, Castigo is no fool. He has strengthened himself since our meeting. When two magics contact, the outcome cannot be predicted—only assumed. And assumption is the staple of fools. Come, let us go quickly."

"Father, what of *him*?"

"What of him?"

"Will he come with us?"

"Unicorns do what they do. They remain unattached—like magicians."

She donned the purple surcoat of a mage that he had brought for her. He appraised her sharply and nodded his approval. "As we leave here, the weather will change. Come now."

The unicorn stood watching as they crossed the small stream and waded through the flimsy threads of ferns and nasturtiums. The girl glanced back. "Good bye," she said simply.

The unicorn watched. They left the bowered region and hiked through a galaxy of green springing grass, waist high. The vibrant blue of the sky was tufted with patches of fluff and they could see the dark peak ahead of them sheathed in heavy strata, layered with ominous grays, and, from there, the jagged silver threads of lightning glared at them, warning like a pointing finger. Junction paused and gestured, "It is from there that he comes. We'll meet him near the top." From that darkness, thunder—muffled by distance—rolled at them, a giant ball forcing a path through the gentle fields. And still they climbed.

The meadows wound through pines and the pines, grudgingly, gave up; the ground became rocky, jagged. Vermillion looked up, watching the clouds meet, fold, lock in a glowering canopy. They rolled, colliding with the sheer granite face towering above, and the wind spilled out, tumbling down on them. She followed her father, watching his cloak swirl and lash, his stride powerful.

The gray, soft underbellies of the clouds swelled and spewed a burst of rain. The wind warped across the strewn boulders, glancing off them like shattering ice, whipping their soaked clothing, the rain streaming across their faces. Vermillion's golden hair poured butter-like down her back and she, aware that her father had halted, looked ahead—past him.

The shifting curtain of water parted and she could see that Castigo stood above them on a flattened bare rock crest, Mordant by his side.

Three necrasses weaved near, the black slack skin rippling and glistening. Castigo laughed, water dribbling from his beard. "Hah! Old friend, good to see you again. It gives me happiness to see your daughter looking so well. If I had any part in your injuries, little lady, I do apologize."

The old man squinted against the drilling of the driving rain. "Apologize? Fool! Are you prepared to die?"

"Die? Old man, does that mean that you haven't brought your daughter for my son?"

Junction stood, legs braced, twenty yards from his student. He couldn't look at this man he had known for so long and wish him dead. "I do not desire to kill you. I will yet give you room to leave . . . if you leave with promises."

"I will leave only with what I came for." Castigo's words were soft, deadly. As the two men stood, face to face, the darkness gathered deeper. The rain pelted. Junction focused his complete attention on Castigo who began to step sideways like a crab, moving in a closing arc. "Junction," he said, "this is not necessary. Let it be over. Let it end. It is not so big a thing; my son is good. It will be good for them."

"It was not my permission you had neglected to ask, but my daughter's," replied the old man. Junction stood with his back to a rock face. "To get to the end," he said, "one must pass through the middle and learn as one passes. Are you ready to die without learning?"

As Junction slid along the wet rock, a black loop encircled him. Another loop, and then one around his throat, and with a garbled moan that mixed with the wind's keen whine the necrass oozed from the rock crevass, throwing its weight against the man. They tumbled, splashing, lashed together, tangled, thrashing on the granite surface. On scurrying, webbed feet the three black things squirmed from Castigo's side and swarmed over the man.

Rain blinded, Vermillion glanced to her father as Mordant leapt from the rock ledge and grabbed her from behind, pinning her arms to her sides. He was very strong. He slung his left arm around her chest, locking onto her shoulder, pinning her to him. The boy whispered harshly above the thunder and wind into her ear, "It is my father's doing. This is not mine. Don't hate me."

"Then let me go. It can't work. Not this way."

She watched, fixed on the thrashing black beings that enveloped her father, as somehow a black head screamed and tore loose of the squirming pile, bouncing across the rock shelf. The body jerked to its feet gushing a dark substance and ran in a macabre dancing shuffle, seeming to be looking for its missing part.

Mordant spoke in pain and urgency, his words almost blown away by the slashing wind, punctuated by the garbled thunder. "He is my father. I have no choice." He looked at the man who stood above them, dark hair streaming, casual in his confidence.

Castigo laughed, "You have no more to teach me, old man. There is more magic than yours. I will give you a demonstration."

The dark, fetid bodies parted and Junction, on his back, could see his student sweep his arm in a circular motion. Sparks flew, hissing in the driving rain, and the flashes built into flames that encircled the man in a churning firewheel. Blinding clouds of steam built and rolled, torn by the wind.

Mordant tightened his grip, shifting his arm to the girl's throat. He said, "Junction will be injured. My father will send the fire on him. I've seen it. Tell him. Please. Ask your father to stop, because mine won't."

In his urging, the boy tightened his arm across her throat and she gasped. She couldn't breathe. She struggled as she felt darkness coming, aware of the rain on her face, aware of his frantic voice in her ear. His sounds faded as she fell into the gathering darkness. Suddenly he stiffened; his grip loosened. Gulping air, she slid to the ground, looking up at him. Mordant stood, reflecting the glow of his father's fire; his expression was of surprise rather than pain and he held his position sculpted, as though afraid to move. He lowered his eyes to his chest. Protruding from his brown jerkin: a ribbed, golden spike, itself stained red, the color spreading across the material. His legs weakened, and his body, gently arched backwards, laid soft against the head of the unicorn. The animal flipped its neck and the boy was tossed through the air, thudding dully against a rocky outcrop. He slid into a crumple, a marionette, leaving a smear on the cliff's face.

The unicorn trotted to the girl and lowered his head. She looped her arm around the radiant white neck and gained her feet. Castigo, intent on Junction, was oblivious to his son's still form. Tongues of fire were flipping from the spinning wheel, hissing near the old man's head. The necrasses were shifting him to expose his body to the flames. Still the old mage did nothing and Vermillion didn't understand. She stood shakily, supported by the unicorn, its head pink-stained, the pastel dribbling in a spreading feather-edged fan across its chest. Her father was waiting. Either he did not want to kill Castigo—or he was waiting for her to use what he had taught her. He was held securely by the necrasses; she moved her hand at them but no words would come. Her mind was a jumble. She couldn't do it.

She knew it. It was in her mind. The word. A fire spurt rolled across her father's chest and sizzled against his wet garments, leaving his robe singed and steaming. Panicked, the girl fought the child of her mind but still the word wouldn't come.

Something flowed. She felt a warmth. Something was building inside her. Not the word. Not this time. But these words: *Not the words but the will; the wisdom, not the ritual . . . She is worth anything, as are you.*

This time her gesture was firm and there was no word; only intent. The rocks blasted and sprayed a black thing into the air. It squirmed, heaved, and lay still. Junction rolled as a second necrass released him, writhing, charred into a sizzling mass. The third grasped at him and died as both father and daughter turned on it.

Junction shifted to his feet, ready, turning to face his student. But the younger man was kneeling at the crumpled body of his son, his own body limp, anger and pride gone, the fire gone. His face was pain. The tears blended with the rain, with the agony of a father. He held his boy tightly, rocking gently. Slowly, he lifted his face to look at his old teacher.

"This wasn't the way."

"No," Junction said. "Most likely, it never is. But we do it—and enjoy it—most of the time." He gestured in the rain to the fallen necrasses. The old man walked slowly to his daughter. She stood, her hand resting on the glistening flanks of the unicorn.

Looking at Castigo she said, "You were right, Father. There are no winners."

"I am afraid that you are learning. It's time for us to go. There's no danger here anymore." He touched a necrass with his toe.

She said, "Should we not aid him? He seems so . . ."

"There is nothing that can be done for him." Junction surveyed the desolate land. "Nothing will heal his wound. No ointment, no words, not even time will let this go from him. At his best moments, he can hope for a certain numbness, a deadness of mind that allows rest."

The three of them turned and started down the mountain. The thunder had stopped; rain reduced to a trickle.

"Junction."

The old man halted and turned. His daughter and her companion stepped back, curiosity studding the air.

"Yes?" The old man asked.

"It's not done."

"It's done."

"It is not finished. Don't walk away from me."

"Castigo, let it drop. You have no more son. You have no need of my daughter."

"Master, did you really think *that* was what it was all about? There is always more. Somebody wise told me that. 'Always look deeper,' he told me. Have you looked?"

Junction felt weary. He stood between his daughter and the unicorn. "I've looked. Give yourself to your grief. You can yet have other children. Mordant need not be your last."

Castigo shook his head almost sadly, his cloak hung damply from him like a hatched cocoon. He raised his arms. They swirled. The fire burst, forming in a circle, butterflies of flame licking around him. The younger man said, "Don't you know that the student must always test the teacher—*that's* what this is really about."

"I know," the old man said, "that the death of the teacher is the only way for a student to transform. I would like to remind you that the death is usually symbolic."

"Not this time. Good bye, Junction. We do what we must."

"Don't, Castigo."

The flames whirled into a seething mass, a churning, starving monster, flashing in heat in the clear air. Quickly, Junction's hand flashed silver like a trout, striking, and its movement scribed a strange symbol. Light leapt from somewhere enveloping the magician and his group in a globed, swirling mist. Roaring, the fireball smashed against the glow, shattering, shards clattering across the damp rocks. The molten mass caromed from the protective light and ricocheted back towards Castigo, who stood, watching calmly, his hands at his sides. He was still standing that way as the hungry creature swept, swirling over him, gorging its fill, the heat so intense that, as the flames faded, only ash remained, blowing across the shelf, drifting into crevasses.

The protective globe dissipated.

"Father," Vermillion began " . . . he didn't really have to do that, did he?" She turned her head from the charred spot.

"Perhaps, in a way, he did."

The unicorn nudged Junction and took a few steps back down the mountain.

"Yes, old friend, it's time to go home." He shook his head, thinking of his teaching, thinking of the cave. "I've got to talk to someone." Then he thought of Mara. It was a new thought. He turned to look at his daughter and gestured at the unicorn that trotted at her side. "You know, Verm, you'll never get rid of him now. I do believe he's taken a liking to you."

The unicorn nickered. He seemed to smile.

"You did what?"

"You heard me." He sat on a rock in front of the cave. The rumble from the cloudy mouth seemed indignant with smoke huffing like a straining engine. "I've taught Vermillion some basic magic. Besides, you know it. You knew it when I did it."

"Of course I know. What I'd like to know is why."

The magician slouched, digging his toe into a little earth. This whole thing seemed futile. "Does it make any difference?"

"Why not satisfy my curiosity?" the cave said. "Indulge me—after all, what do you have to lose? It isn't as though you don't have the time."

"Certainly, no—it wouldn't be that. I have all the time in the world."

"Well . . ."

"Well . . . It seemed the only practical answer to a problem."

"A girl."

"My daughter."

"Oh . . . Do I detect a note of indignation," the cave said. "Just because she is *your* daughter?" It belched a smoke ring that wrapped around the old man.

"I'm in no mood for your games," Junction said, waving his arm and dissipating the cloud. "So she's a girl. So what? It was necessary. It was practical. I owed her that much at least."

The old man shifted to his feet and walked over to the small pine tree already grown waist high. Fingering the creamy new green at its tips, he continued, "You have only yourself to blame. I mean, *I* stand the responsibility, but had *you* not given me Agapis, had he not shown me something beyond duty . . ."

"Oh?" the cave seemed interested. "What did he show you beyond duty?"

"He showed me sacrifice."

"Very good. Now, mage, tell me what," the cave asked, "is beyond sacrifice?"

Junction knelt by the pine, breathing its scent. "Beyond sacrifice? Beyond dying for another?"

"Try," the cave said. "You can do it. What is the impetus for such an act?"

"To die for another? . . . Love."

"Ah . . ."

"That's what this is all about? Love?"

"Love," the cave mulled. "Actually, dying for another is relatively *easy. Living* for another is much more difficult and requires even more love. When we pacted, I said that when you learned the ultimate I would give you progeny to whom you would pass your knowledge; then you could stop. Did I ever say it must be a son?"

"You never said that I could teach a daughter." The magician was groping, something was being said but it was tangled.

"I never said you couldn't. You were the one that attached all that importance to a foolish tradition. Besides, it was something you had to come to. One has to *learn* love. It can't be taught. You're a beautiful man, Junction—you've been a fine student and, at last, a good father.

"Junction, you can rest now. Come home."

The magician stood, realizing that his legs were shaky

and cramped. The cave puffed.

"Isn't this what you want?" the cave said. "Have you not pined for release?"

"Yes . . . Only . . ."

"Only . . .?"

The old man looked out over the valley. The purple mountains threw fingers of shadows across the woven tapestry of pines. He looked up at the dead pine where Agapis had perched and he touched the silkiness of the new tree. He said:

"God, it's beautiful."

"It is that. Haven't you noticed it before?"

"Noticed? Yes," replied the mage. "But I've never really *enjoyed* it."

The smoke became a swirl of thoughtfulness. "I thought you wanted out? Humans are so fickle."

Junction's hand came up in protest. "Oh, no, no . . . don't misunderstand. I'm still ready . . . It's just . . . that . . ."

"That . . .?"

"Mara."

"What of your wife?"

"I've not given her much."

"True," the cave said.

Junction walked along the edge of the precipice. A breeze warmed by the lower valley skittered up the cliff face and danced with his robes. "I can give her something now that I didn't know how to give before . . . something I think she has been waiting for. She's never complained. She hasn't many years left here."

"True," the cave said.

"It would be enjoyable to spend that little time with her and Verm . . . to give them both this new thing."

"It would be very enjoyable," the cave said.

"The earth is a beautiful place." The mage began to pick his way down the shifting scree. "Don't go away. I'll be back."

"Take your time, Junction. Enjoy yourself."

The magician paused and turned. He smiled and his eyes sparked with the freshness of new buds. His smile widened into a grin and he laughed. It was a new sound that played, ringing, across the valley.

And the mountain tremored as the cave laughed with him.

The Ern Queen

Jane Newbold

In the court of King Hugh of Kilavarock there were no children nor any kin of the queen. Few were the servants and men-at-arms for the king's wants were simple and the kingdom at peace. In the evening the court gathered for dinner in the great hall and stayed for whatever entertainment found its way to their northern rock.

The hall was dark but for a glow from the hearth. The fire hissed faintly; it would not flame much longer. The people in the shadows stirred, pulling their cloaks closer, settling chins into fur collars, pressing arms to their sides. A lone minstrel sang, plucking minor chords, sighing. It was a long song about the sea and the sky and green leaves and shadows. He was not a famous minstrel but he should have been and he sang with a trace of bitterness and self-mockery. The court waited patiently for him to finish.

A strange noise crept around his song which he had not anticipated. He sang louder; chords crashed, waves thundered, a storm arose, a maiden shrieked, and in the following silence the noise rolled on. The king was snoring amid his dogs. The minstrel put down his lute and bit the inside of his mouth so that he would not glower. The few people murmured and shifted, cleared their throats and sniffed, until the queen stood up and spoke.

"Good friends," she said softly. "The night draws on and it is cold—though your music, Master David, warms our souls. Let us retire to warmer places now." The courtiers rustled and whispered away, and the room was empty save for the sleeping king and his dogs, the queen and the minstrel.

She stood behind the king's chair and her hands rested, white and still, on the roughly carved wood. The minstrel scowled now and moved his foot so that it rested on a dog's tail. "Well, Master David," said the queen sadly and softly, "There is the city."

The minstrel looked up and into her face in the shadows. He thought before he asked, "Do you think I should go there?"

"There is much to your advantage there. More than this court can provide." She did not disparage; she stated a fact. A silence followed. "My brother is there," she said at last. "He could be of help."

Another silence grew until a log collapsed in the fire. "Before the snow comes," she whispered.

He did not answer. She gave him her hand but he did not bow to kiss it; instead he stood holding it in his strong, hard fingers, looking at her. His mouth was bitter but his eyes were not. "We will hear of you," she said.

He shrugged and left her.

She stood a long time looking into the dying fire, feeling the cold creep into her bones. Then she took up a candle, lit it at the fire, and she gazed full at her husband still in his chair. He was a big, broad-shouldered man with a strong brow and a great black beard shot through with grey and silver-white. His dogs were grey and black matted tangles and a spotted young one slept in the chair with him. His big knotted hands curled around the puppy's chest and she knew how strong that grasp could be and how gentle. She listened to the rumble in her husband's nose and chest, and then left him in his chair and went alone through the cold dark halls of stone, up the stairs to her room, her shadow grotesque on the walls beside her.

Cold air flowed over her bare feet as she stepped out of her blue court robe and slippers. She drew near to a window; the icy wind filled her with pleasure. She gazed over rolling hills to where a river glinted in a line pointing toward the sea beyond the edge of the world. Sometimes she imagined she could smell its salt, but tonight she tasted only winter on the wind. The stars glittered around a cold, silver sliver of a moon. She felt her mind spin free among them.

"Yes, but not yet," she cautioned herself, and turned

with a shiver to strip from her fingers the only jewelry she wore. *"Put away our jewels from us,"* she thought and remembered that the minstrel would be gone. She felt very old and heavy as a stone as she crawled into her bed, pulling a woolen cloak over her.

In the morning she found that the minstrel had gone without waiting for a letter of service. She pondered his pride as she set about to write to her brother. "Good Sir," she wrote, "there shall come to your city by the sea a minstrel called Master David of the Moor, who is late of our court. I recommend his songs and his bearing to your hall. He will not be disposed to seek you out, nor should you seek him on my account. But I would deem you a worthy man should you look to his advantage for the sake of his own fine talent and not because of the wish of your fond sister, Elspeth, Queen of Kilavarock." She entrusted the letter to the keeping of a merchant on his way north and gave it no more thought, although she mused often on its subject.

The king and his men stamped in and out, blowing on their fingers, their cheeks and noses growing ruddy and red over their bristling beards. They rode their great shaggy horses over the frozen land and hunted for deer and boar and sometimes loosed their hawks for dove and partridge. There was always enough to eat at the king's table, for if his skill in the wild wood failed, there were acres of wooly muttons throughout his kingdom to feed him and keep him warm.

A mountain of shorn wool, washed and waiting to be carded and spun, fell to the queen and her ladies each winter, for she would not suffer the fur of an animal on her skin unless the warmth of its body still pulsed inside. And so she wore no lynx or ermine collars and wept for seal and otter robes, remembering her wild, silky pets as a sea child. She carded and spun and wove the cloaks and tunics, the hangings and blankets for use in the castle. She no longer embroidered for she found that she could no longer pace her stitches close and even by touch alone in candlelight. "Too long a sight," the king had said when she named a bird to him he could only hear. "Too long looking out to sea after the ships gone a-viking when you could not go."

All winter in the evenings the light from the fire fell over the wooly dogs and the sleeping king; but, instead of minstrel songs of the wind and waves, the sibilant lisps of the priest cautioned the court against the sins of the world and the serpent's desire made flesh. The shadows were deep, the winds wrapped round the castle, cold and keen, and the syllables slipped solemnly as the king snored.

One night the king came to her room and crawled in under her woolen blankets. His dogs followed him and Boris found room on the foot of the bed to curl up behind a bent pair of legs. After they had loved, he told her he must ride to Bragard in the south.

"Is there danger?" she asked.

"Some say," he grumbled into the pillow. She always wanted to talk afterwards when he preferred to drift into sleep.

"But what can they want?" She stared into the dark overhead, stroking idly a dog's ear.

"Port," he said.

"Port? Port wine? Pork?"

"Sea port," he said with great effort and she asked him no more.

"If the Loathians want a sea port, why don't they just ask in trade?" she thought to herself. *"Because they are bloody fools, all temper and push."* She got up from the bed and, wrapping a blanket around her, stood at the window, pulling aside a bit of the curtain. *"If there is to be trouble and Hugh rides into it, perhaps now is the time,"* she thought.

The stars glittered in the night sky and thin, ragged clouds sailed on the wind. *"How can there be trouble* here?" the warm, heavy part of her asked. "Who would fight over sheep pastures?" As far as she could see, the land lay bare and gently rolling.

In the morning her husband left her to ride south with a few of his men—and it was time.

She had to listen to the sermon about flesh wasting from evil ways three more times before she truly knew. And when she took out the book in her room late one night and read over the inscription which her mother had written in the runes her mother had taught her, she knew she had waited longer than she needed. She locked the door and pinned back the curtain at the window. "What if I can't think?" she wondered. "What if I forget what I'm doing and never come back?" A pang touched her heart for only a moment and then she stripped off her cloak and her shift and stood, naked, still slim and small-breasted, shivering in the tower room. She whispered the spell and gave a cry of terror as her feet twisted, wrinkled and sprouted claws, her fingers shot bolts of huge, black feathers, and her breast distended. In a moment where had stood Elspeth, Daughter of Roke, wife of Hugh, Queen of Kilavarock, a huge, black, ungainly eagle rustled and stretched. Its yellow eye was wild and fierce above a beak of ivory and it writhed its neck and extended its wings as though its body did not fit. With a harsh grating cry it leaped to the window and clung, balancing for a moment; then with a scream it fell away from the tower and, awkwardly spreading its wings, soared out under the stars across the cold, sleeping land.

The air on her breast was full of cold needles and her eyes stung. The balance was strange; she hung between her wings, heavy and falling. Her gnarled talons dragged below, opening, stretching at the ground as though to walk through the air; the wind separated the feathers, rattled them, and gave no purchase. She strained and screamed. The runes gave her the form but where came the knowledge to use it? And then the same muscles knew. In her hands when she stretched and tightened, the flight feathers

stiffened into oars. Along her arms the pinions grew taut,
her feet curled up and tucked in and the power to claw
through the air, to glide, to swim, to fly upwards into the
sky came pouring through her form. She rose with great
sweeps of her wings beating down, raising her slowly and
heavily at first, but strong and stronger until she caught a
current of air which lifted her and she could glide and soar
without sinking. Back she looked at the stone tower where
her room lay and she could see the dried vines around her
window ledge. She flowed with the air, a great shadow,
part of the night until she saw the river beneath her and
then, turning, she rowed and swam back to the far side of
the castle to catch the current again.

She flew well enough by the time dawn came. She
found she could count the stones in the walls far below her
and recognize the cottages and lanes. As high as she dared
soar, she could tell below in the moonlight the rabbits
trembling in the withered grass and the pale eyes of the
owls in the trees. She was filled with the joy of it when, tired
and near the end of her endurance, she alighted on the sill
of her window and stepped down into the room in the
shape of a woman. Exhausted and exhilarated, she crept
under the woolen blankets. Her back ached and throbbed;
her breast muscles fluttered from weariness, but she was
happy beyond her expectations.

She flew every night, patiently enduring the supper, the
sermon, the snores of the court, dreaming of the feel of the
wind flowing under her, the horizon curving up and away,
the stars and the moon and the clouds her only companions. *"What a song could be made of this!"* she thought.
She slept late and kept to her room. Her appetite increased
enormously but her woman's body grew taut and thin, her
cheekbones stood out below her eyes and there were blue
shadows at her temples. If her ladies noticed, they did not
speak of it. At night she exalted in the power of her new
form. She flew effortlessly now, gliding for miles, soaring
above the frozen fields and the sheepcotes where the

wooly muttons huddled, steaming, near the thatched cottages. The dogs looked up but did not give alarm. She was too large to be one of the marauders from the coast they guarded against. They slunk into their kennels and whined as she passed over.

Then one evening she avoided the dinner board, saying she felt a cold coming on, and took to her room. She ate lightly there and flew away as the sun was sinking red and wintery in the west. She flew south all night toward Bragard and the king. Morning found her at the top of a tall pine tree near the edge of the town where the roads from the mountain passes converged with the highways from the sea to the north. For most of the morning she scanned the comings and goings of the people. She saw a few Loathians garishly armed, swaggering about, but hardly enough to make a threat or an invading force.

At last she saw one of the king's guard on his shaggy grey ambling through a half-empty square. The sergeant was certainly not on his guard and passed from her sight around the corner of an alley. She risked flapping to another perch to see him dismount at a house painted pink and bang on the door. He was admitted by someone she couldn't see, but a small boy ran around the house, took charge of the horse, and led it to a low barn in the back. She craned her feathered neck and saw Hugh's brown cob munching contentedly under a shed. The pink house contained no kin of Hugh at her last visit to the city, so she flapped up high to look down on the town. She realized the pink house stood half-way down Bawd Street. A pang smote her heart, a twinge of pain and then rage mixed with despair. She veered sharply to the north and sailed back toward the central castle hold.

Winter closed her in, grey and cheerless, snow and sleet blowing straight across the land and sifting about the castle. She drifted about the corridors, wrapped in grey woolen sweaters. Nowhere did she find comfort; listless but restless, she moved from room to room, waiting for the king's return.

"Foolish female," she scolded herself. *"To wait and grieve for what is done. You are old and barren. He cannot seek a wife in such a place. But Oh, there is no pleasure in this place. And the Solstice feast will be grim with no young people here. It may be spring before Hugh returns or word comes from the north."*

She began to dream a lovely song before she woke one morning and, lying half awake, she thought of the minstrel and his fortune in her brother's city. *"I could go there,"* she mused. *"If he is faring well, I would come back with pleasure in that knowledge. If he is poorly or yet unknown, think how great a sight he would make to have a huge, wild thing at his command. They would soon know of Master David and his eagle."* And so she dreamed of how he would not know her in her eagle form but yet be kind and let her share his small room and meager fare, or, if he sought to harm her, how she could forestall his action through her size and strength without revealing who she was. If she found him well, she could tease him with her knowledge of his actions when she as woman saw him next. And from a dream it grew into a plan and preparations so that they would not seek her in her room. With the priest ascowl, she said she would revive the fasting vigil of her people to assure the renewal of the sun's power so that they need not look for her to leave her room until Solstice passed.

On a bright night when the snow sparkled like the stars overhead, she flapped away from the tower and headed north to where the city lay beside the sea. High cliffs there were where she could perch among small cousins of herself, true erns of the coast. She troubled them not but marveled at the grey churning waves and the flaming yellow dawn. She flew about the crags and caves and watched the city on the bright blue day with all the folk astir because of the coming festival. Fires blazed in squares and people hurried back and forth to build the new fires and assemble their feasts. The ships, pulled up on winter moorings, sported evergreens on the tops of masts; and everywhere was hustle and bustle, entertainments, lights and cheer.

From her crag she watched first the streets of inns and sailors haunts, then the merchants' houses and the halls, but nowhere could she see the minstrel. She perched on her brother's house at dusk and listened at the chimney to the merriment and songs but she saw not Master David nor heard his voice. Three days she searched until Solstice Eve and then she waited on the topmost roof and watched.

Out from each house the oldest daughter came with an unlit taper to gather in the square before the priestess and the hearth. She watched, remembering when she had stood on those cold stones until the fire flared, rekindled by the god. Now this fire sparked and through the streets, like spiderwebs of light, slow lines of flickering candles twined, returning a sheltered flame to light their family's hearth. When the sun rose the horns and drums were sounded and all the people shouted at the renewed and growing sun.

She dared not linger longer on the slate and tiles of the roofs but her longing grew to find her minstrel. As she flew up, her anguish cried, *"If he be not abroad, perhaps he lies ill under some dark roof. Perhaps he never came here at all."* There was nothing more she could do. Her ladies would look for her in the morning. She turned inland sadly.

Over a cove she pondered the sea beneath her and dropped down to skim the tops of the icy waves. The shore hung rimed with ice and salt spray flecked her wings, but the heave of the breakers below called back to her the time when she swam with the seals and the sea otters to their rocks. She banked away from the land and skimmed out to sea. There were no seals on the rocks now. She flapped out farther into the grey bank of clouds moiling down from the north.

The winter storm caught her before she was aware, and sleet and wind blew fiercely at her from all directions. An avalanche of wind poured down on her, pressing her down toward the waves, and then caught her up and violently hurled her skyward. She lost her bearings and concentrated only on staying aloft. Buffeted on all sides, ice heavy on her wing feathers, she hardly flew but only fought to stay level in the wind, until a warm fire grew all through her feathered body. A battle it was, as fierce as any berserker's with death as its reward; and she exalted screaming in defiance of the storm wind. She coasted, scattered, ducked, and dived against the wind until the air relented. Triumphant she screamed and spread out her great black wings to fly on the breast of the storm. In the form of a beast she knew the joy of survival. In the surge and power of the storm on her wings, she felt the life of the world. In freedom from human desire she soared, coupled with the storm. All of the power of wind and wave was in her, the curve of the earth could not harm her, the storm embraced her, and she was borne ecstatic, exalted over the land.

Spinning at last in an eddy of falling snow, she found herself over familiar pastures and sailed to her own window at dusk. She dressed carefully, trembling, feeling the power still within her, trying to calm the fierceness in her eyes. Now she knew why her mother's crest had been eagle wings. Now she understood the stories of the great eagles above the viking boats and the battles. The boats were beached now and the plunder divided. But the storm clouds were there. She could wait to fly for them. There she could test her power and strength and fulfill the longings she had never voiced. Perhaps, long hence, she could tell Hugh.

She descended to the hall wearing her best and her jewels. She glowed with radiance as if the rekindled sun had filled her with light. The king had returned and rose to greet her and look wonderingly into her face. She smiled

and wished them all renewed life for the year. They ate.
She listened to their words as though each contained new
wisdom. Transformed by her flight, she spoke little, but
with great kindness and love. At the end of the meal there
was a small stir at the door. A grizzled crofter in a snow
encrusted cloak stood there. He was holding the minstrel's
lute.

As from a great distance she heard and saw all that
happened in the room then, as if she flew far over the
castle. She looked down at the lute, at the nubby, awkward fingers that clutched it and then laid it on the table
before the king, who let it rest. She saw her hands reach
out and take it onto her lap. She smoothed and stroked it
as she heard the halting words of the shepherd who had
found it beside the horse, lamed and staggering, next to
the broken body of the man in the snow. She heard but
could not tell afterward where he was buried. She heard
the man tell over again about the dog barking and the
shape of the horse in the snow. She heard how the man's
head was bloodied and how the leg of the horse had
mended. She looked only on the lute and did not speak.
Finally the crofter handed to her a bundle of parchment
wet from melting snow. "For Elspeth, Queen of
Kilavarock" she read on the top sheaf. She had to stare at it
long to realize it was the song of the winds and the waves.
That was how the crofter knew to come to the court. She
heard his voice from far away, "Perhaps the queen . . .
After all that way . . . On the road and in that terrible
storm . . . with the festival at hand . . ."

There were no words in her head as she drew off her ring
and handed it to the man. He stammered and gasped at
the worth of the reward. She saw how stupid he was, how
fawning. She knew that his dog could have barked at a
horse in the woods or a dying man for days before this
crofter would bestir himself to look. Perhaps his face was
evil enough to strike a blow from behind with a shepherd's
sling, seeking to rifle saddle bags filled only with songs.

Holding the lute and the parchments before her, the

queen left the table and mounted her stairs in the dark. She laid the lute and the songs on her bed and stood, not drained but churning, as though the storm she had partnered was inside her. Was it grief? Did she mourn because she loved him? Was it fear? Did she feel terror at the inscrutable face of death? No, it was fury, wild raging fury at the blindness of the world which had not cherished this man, at the stupidity of people who had wasted the time of his life, at the mindlessness of the storm, the wind and the snow, the trees, the dog, the horse, all around him as he died. When had he died? A month ago? Before she flew? The stupidity of the crofter, his weathered ugly face, blank and broad like his foolish sheep, told her he could have waited a month with his message and all the while she had held, wrapped in the back of her mind, the knowledge he was somewhere in the world to make songs, his happiness her hope. Now he was gone.

He could never see her fly; she could not tell him of the wonder of the storm.

There was a knock at her door. "Elspeth?" her husband called. She opened her door and looked into his face. "Are you all right?" he asked.

"Yes."

"I'm sorry," he said. "I liked him, too."

No. He had snored through the songs. He had been as careless with the gift of music as he was with the gift of love, with his marriage vows.

"Yes," she repeated and closed the door.

Her fury broke inside her, scalding in her throat. Her fingers clenched. She ripped off her gown and flew shrieking back into the night, searching for respite from the violence which tore at her. There were no storm clouds left. The moon shone down on the smooth, white pastures and the clots of huddled sheep. She flapped on almost frantically, heedless of where she flew. A clot of sheep awoke and bolted. From the corner of her eye she saw a ram gallop into a drift and flounder. She descended over him, extending her legs, feeling the soft wool under her talons, and then the warm struggling muscles of the back. She gripped, feeling the writhing beast, hearing his bleats of terror, and carried him easily over the fields to a mound of rocks. When she set her burden down, she found she had broken its back. Her talons clawed out the belly. Her hooked beak ripped strings of wooly flesh from the bones until the ivory dagger was red and reeking and still the madness in her eyes was not extinguished. She left the steaming destruction and flew off to another pasture. It was too easy; there was no slaking of her passion. Six sheep she took that night and left the mangled bodies mixed together on the rocks. Six shepherds found their flocks frantic, the dogs cringing. The dawn found her lying on her bed, breathing deeply, her hands still clenched.

She walked through the castle by day as if asleep and said nothing to those who spoke to her, keeping her eyes cast down. She sat at table like a stone, eating little, drinking less. She spun the wool into long grey ropes beside the king as he drowsed by the fire after dinner. The priest's sermons made her flesh crawl but she spoke not a word. Every night from her window she flew, the spell form on her. She returned at dawn, her feathers stained with blood. The shepherds stood guard with pikes and staves but she carried off the dogs and caught their sticks in mid-air, flying back at their heads. A gigantic eagle, destroying but not eating the sheep at night, was a matter of witchcraft and the people carried crosses to ward her off.

If there had been a storm to buffet her and exhaust her passion, she might have made her peace with the king and her grief; but no storm came, the nights were clear and cold, and her marauding scream floated out under brilliant, blinking stars on the cold wind. The crofters huddled under their roofs and the men muttered and grumbled at spending cold nights in the sheepcotes. Fifty miles round she flew so that no one was safe and everyone feared.

At last they sent a delegation to the king and his bowmen. With the queen beside him he listened to their pleas. She listened to their words and watched them with her wild eyes. The king swept their criticisms and clamor aside with his broad, flat hand and shouted them into silence. He and his men would ride, he promised them, scowling. That night he ate standing in armor and received the priest's blessing. He kissed the queen's cold face and strode from the hall with her blazing eyes on him.

She flew that night low over the snow, seeing him far ahead on the stamping horses. Low she skimmed over the crust until, rising sharply behind the men, she shrieked and banked, soaring out of bow range before they could control their mounts. She led them long across the fields and left them to return far ahead, killing a dog on her way back. Three nights they hunted her. The king grew grim and thoughtful. Sometimes she felt his eyes upon her during the day but he said nothing. The priest talked of storm demons and malevolent souls called forth by pagan fires. She watched the king as he looked to his bow and sighted down his arrows but the wildness in her eyes never waned.

At the end perhaps she grew tired of the waste she caused. Perhaps her anger abated. Perhaps his horse went lame and the king returned ahead of the others. He saw the great ern shape against the moon and the queen's tower window near at hand. Before he thought, the arrow was loosed and he did not see it fall. The eagle shape slipped through the window and he gave a strangled cry as he knew what he had done. Two at a time he took the stairs and burst open the door. As he wrapped her naked form in his cloak, she did not speak but put her hand upon his lips. As she died, his arrow in her heart, the fury had faded from her eyes.

Gwydion's Loss of Llew

When I came to the house
You were gone from the hall.
Your cup and knife-handle were cold to touch.
The leaf-red fire warmed no one's hands.
No harpstring trembled of your passing.
The bowstring was long lax.
No one sang in the house,
And when I set my ears into the wind of the hall,
All I could hear was,
I am cold . . . I am cold . . .
It is October.

In the hills it was the same.
I know you loved them,
The crisp, clear trees,
Each with its own color,
Its own pattern twisted in the branches.
You have not seen them this year;
Though they are each as tall and straight as you,
Their numbers as great as your soul,
Yet you are not among them.

The wind tangles the net of branches
That holds it and cannot hold it;
The wind tangles the web
Of color stroked with black,
Lashing it across the sky.
My feet catch on ground-fruit,
Roots, dropped branches, brittle leaves.
If you are up there among the leaves
I cannot tell
If you have become the many
If you are the one—

Then the wind blows the net open
And all I see is sky.
Oh, Llew, be not gone from me!
I would renounce them,
Wind, leaf, and tree
If I could find you
In a place where nothing grows.

—*Ellen Kushner*

Amigo Heliotropo

Félix Martí-Ibañez

At noon the circus wagons came to a halt. The country-side was not very impressive. The sky was lofty and a radiant blue, but the land was dry and bare except for a few stunted poplars which stood there meekly announcing that, all things considered, this was the best that could be done. A few rocky hills, covered with lime dust, looked like buns sprinkled with sugar in the great oven of the desert. At the foot of the hills there circled a veinlet of faded green water. The huge sun was like a bell hanging from the blue, ringing out light instead of sound. And that was all, that and the houses, white with rust-colored roofs, of the town of Santa Ana, which in the distance looked like a group of small girls playing at Little Red Riding Hood.

The Great Floriani, owner of the circus and magician, raised his muscular arm and cried, "Halt!" and then jumped down from the box of the first wagon.

"Rest!" joyfully shouted Mama Floriani, whose two hundred pounds in weight and half a century in years seemed in no way to impair her tightrope act.

"Lunch!" exclaimed Pipo and Rico, the clowns, who by force of habit always spoke in a duet.

"Nap!" said Samson (according to his billing, the strongest man in the world), who had clandestinely de-voured a loaf of bread and a can of sardines on the road.

And Colombina, the bareback rider, always romantic, opened wide her eyes, the color of forget-me-nots, and sighed, "A river!"

The rest of the caravan—Filipon, juggler *extraordinaire;* the Rossoffs, animal trainers; Cascabel, the snake man; the twin sisters, Dora and Rita; the Condor trio, "human eagles"; the trained dogs, cats, monkeys and birds—said nothing but their thoughts ran along identical lines. The similarity in ideas of a circus troupe at lunch time after a foodless morning is astonishing.

Ten minutes later the four wagons were arranged in a semicircle; the horses—when traveling, beasts of burden, when performing, Arab mounts for Colombina—were grazing on a spare plot of grass; and the animals in their cages were having an extra ration of water to compensate for the shortchanging in food. Mama Floriani and the twin sisters, Dora and Rita, spread a red and white oilcloth on the ground; the Great Floriani made a fire with some dry branches; and the rest of the performers lent a hand here and there in the preparation of the customary meager repast.

After a most unrewarding tour through Honduras, the Great Floriani Circus had arrived, weary yet hopeful, to give their first performance in El Salvador. This was, they had been told, a great country, inhabited by people made bold and brave by their constant struggle with a hostile nature. The art of the Floriani Circus would, no doubt, meet with great critical and box office success. And they needed it badly. Otherwise, in a few weeks even the monkeys would disappear, as had Antonini's trained hens. Poor Antonini! After many years of hard labor he had worked out quite an effective act. Then came lean days for the circus. At each performance Antonini exhibited one hen less. At night he would weep tears of remorse over the smooth bones, ending up by gnawing at them, tears streaming down his cheeks. One day Antonini stepped out on the arena without hens and tried to fill in with a stupendous vocal imitation. But even before he had finished he stepped out again—right out of the circus.

Mama Floriani was losing weight fast, "which is good for your act," commented the Great Floriani; Colombina's horses were so famished that they could hardly lift their hoofs from the ground, much less prance smartly; the snake man was growing so alarmingly thin that he feared that one day he would tie his body into a knot which he would never be able to untie; Samson had to stuff the sleeves of his tights with burlap to compensate for his lost biceps; and the great ferocious bear "brought from the

Russian steppes," supposed to be the *pièce de résistance*
in the animal trainer's act, would lumber over to the children in the audience like a meek beggar as soon as he
detected the odor of bread and sausage. But in the face of
hunger they were all closely united, tightening their individual belts in collective hope.

The scanty meal was soon ready. At the height of noon
the sky was all sun. The thin vein of water had turned into a
shimmering ribbon of silver. The aroma of roast corn
scented the air. The monkeys beatifically picked their fleas
in the sun, and the horses in their lassitude abandoned
their backs to the flies. In the blue distance, the little white
town held out a happy promise, like a white dove.

The Great Floriani wound up the phonograph and soon
the hushed warm air woke to the tender notes of the
melody that for years had been the trade-mark and theme
song of the circus: "In a Little Spanish Town." On the red
and white oilcloth the ears of corn glistened like bars of
baked gold. Mama Floriani artfully decorated a wooden
platter with tomatoes and onions. Samson approached
carrying a head of lettuce in his powerful hands as if it were
a bouquet of gardenias. From the oil bottle there flowed a
shimmering blond liquid. The vinegar drops were ame-
thyst tears in the sun. The salad began to smell heavenly.

It was at that moment that the stranger appeared. No
one saw him come. The Great Floriani was the first to
notice his long shadow and then his tall, emaciated body.

He had a gaunt dark face, and the long hair that tumbled
wildly around his brow was the color of ashes and chest-
nuts. But his smile was as crisp and fresh as the lettuce
leaves in the salad, and his limpid blue eyes were in
keeping with his smile.

"Hello," he greeted them in a sweet liquid voice. And
pointing to the corn, "It looks tender and the salad very
appetizing."

Mama Floriani buried her wooden fork deep in the salad
bowl and a delicious aroma accompanied the spatter of oil
and vinegar.

"Corn," she explained, "should be well roasted outside but tender inside, and nothing could be better than salad in this heat."

"Who are you?" interrupted the Great Floriani, pouring water for the coffee.

The newcomer gallantly relieved Mama Floriani of a pile of wood she had picked up.

"My name is Miguel and I come from Cojutepeque. Where shall I put the wood?"

"There, next to the fire," replied Cascabel, the snake man, approaching with the plates.

The stranger set down his load together with an orange-colored pouch that he had been carrying on his shoulder.

"May I offer the group something?" he asked.

Samson burst into laughter. "A ham," he suggested mordantly, looking at the flaccid pouch and dusty sandals of the stranger.

"And a couple of bottles of red wine," shouted one of the twins who approached with tin cups for the coffee.

The stranger smiled and, without saying a word, disappeared behind the wagons.

"Where did that hobo come from?" Pipo asked gruffly, for hunger always soured his temper.

But the next moment a great clamor from his companions brought him quickly to the side of the Great Floriani, who with eyes wide with amazement was brandishing a huge ham and a jug of wine.

Mama Floriani snatched the ham from her husband and gave it a resounding kiss.

"I won't believe it until I dig my teeth into it," she cried.

They all agreed with her, and a minute later, at a signal from the Great Floriani, the performers were devouring the ham, letting the corn get cold. The stranger, seated in their midst, pecked at the salad like a bird. Suddenly his fork, a piece of tomato on it, stopped midway between the plate and his mouth. From behind the cage, where the "wild" animals shared hunger and fleas, a resounding slap rang out and then Colombina emerged. Not far behind her, one side of his face afire, Filipon, the juggler, tried unsuccessfully to hide the mark from the blow. Neither paid any attention to the visitor as they sat down as far apart as possible. But for the remainder of the feast the stranger could no longer eat. Colombina's face, white and pure as milk, with lips like dark red berries, fascinated him.

When the meal was finished, the Great Floriani examined his happy surfeited troupe through the smoke of his cigar. On the oilcloth there remained some purple wine stains, a few grains of corn, bread crumbs, and, like the skeleton of a prehistoric monster, the polished bone of the ham. From the cage came a mew of protest.

"Give the bones to the animals," said Samson generously. And with a nostalgic sigh, "How fortunate they are to be hungry!"

While the women went to the brook to wash the dishes, the others picked up scattered utensils. The Great Floriani, beaming beatifically at his spouse, turned to the stranger.

"Thanks for your gifts, my friend. I had forgotten what ham tasted like."

The stranger, seated with his legs crossed under him, deprecatingly raised a long pale hand with a wrist so thin that it looked like the ivory back-scratchers used by wealthy Mandarins.

"No thanks are due. I shared your salad."

This was far from true, for his plate lay untouched on the oilcloth and myriads of sun-spangled flies were feasting on it.

Only when she heard his velvety voice did Colombina, languid and detached throughout the entire meal, take note of the stranger's presence.

"You ate nothing," she said to him in a tone of friendly reproach. "Have an almond," she added with the air of one saving a poor hungry soul from starvation.

The stranger took the peeled almond but did not eat it. His radiant eyes sprinkled the round pale face of Colombina with the essence of lilies.

"Where are you going?" she asked him.

"I don't know. Nowhere. Wherever you go."

"We are going to Santa Ana," Mama Floriani explained. "Tomorrow is May first, the Tree Festival in this country, and we shall make our debut in the city."

"I shall go there with you," the stranger said smiling.

"Will you come to see the circus?" Colombina asked, delicately picking the golden crumbs from her white skirt and placing them within reach of the ants.

"I shall go *with* the circus," he corrected, looking at her with dazzled eyes.

"But we have room for no one but the performers," protested the Great Floriani.

"I shall work with you."

Samson looked at him with the contempt of a strong man.

"What can you do?"

"Nothing, I'm afraid," was the sad answer.

"Where did you work before?"

"Nowhere," the stranger declared. "In Cojutepeque I tried to make cigars but I was no good at it. In Llobasco I tried to make pots but they all broke. In Ahuachapán I worked in the mines but I missed the fresh air and I left. I'm afraid I don't know how to do anything," he repeated sadly.

"Only a great man would make such an admission," Colombina remarked, and he thought that all the light of the heavens had gathered on her fair brow.

"We all do something here," said the Great Floriani. "Almost all," he corrected severely, looking at Pipo snoring under a wagon.

"I could learn," the stranger implored.

"Why do you want to join the circus?" asked Mama Floriani, her maternal instinct sharpened by the ham and the wine.

"Because it fascinates me. It's a perpetual holiday. The gaiety . . . the color . . . the music . . . the slow processions on country roads . . . the arrivals in villages at sundown when the cows on the roadway fill the air with golden dust . . . the nights outdoors, watching the stars bathing in the ponds . . ."

"The poor man is mad," Dora whispered to her sister. If the stranger heard her, he paid no attention.

"To sleep in a wagon," he continued, "listening to the crystal drumsticks of the rain on the roof above . . . to watch the sun light up the eyes of every child during the performance . . ."

"He is crazier than I thought," Dora insisted to her sister. But the latter stared at him with languid calf's eyes.

"Either crazy," she granted, "or a poet."

The Great Floriani studied the stranger in perplexity.

"If you were bigger you might fight Samson, if you were skinnier you might work with Cascabel as snake man number two, if you knew sleight of hand you might help me. . . ."

"It would be a great honor," the stranger interrupted him humbly.

"It's very difficult, young man, very difficult. Look!" His hand moved quickly in the air and out of nowhere it suddenly pulled three colored ribbons. "Just this little trick took me three years of practice. To be a magician takes a lifetime."

"I should think so!" the stranger said with admiration.

"Very well. Since you are so eager, you may help me. Pity you have no specialty."

"I never learned anything, except a little trick," said the stranger.

He stepped forward quickly, passed his hand over Colombina's hair and pulled out a sprig of heliotrope.

"¡Qué diablos!" cried the Great Floriani, who forgot his language when he was excited.

"¡Ostras!" echoed his wife, who ran him a close second.

"Magnificent!" said Colombina, standing on tiptoe just as she did when greeting her audience.

"Where did you learn that?" Dora asked, while her sister's mouth formed a capital O.

"It's nothing, really." The stranger's eyes had turned the color of dry leaves. "I learned it when I was a child."

"Do it again. And the flowers are real! Where do you hide them?" the Great Floriani roared.

The stranger's pale hands fluttered like butterfly wings and little sprigs of heliotrope sprouted everywhere—from Mama Floriani's double chin, from Cascabel's mustache, from the wheel of a wagon and even from the tail of Leal, the Rossoffs' dog.

"This must be hypnotism," declared Filipon scornfully, for he was an educated man.

"You're coming with us, my friend," the Great Floriani declared firmly. "This trick—you'll explain it to me when we're alone—can be added to my act. You'll be my assistant. But first we must give you a name."

"Let's call him Amigo Heliotropo," Colombina suggested.

"That will be my name," said the stranger, smiling his sweet smile.

The next night Heliotropo made his debut with the Floriani Circus at the Tree Festival in Santa Ana. In the morning the circus had made a triumphal entrance into the town to the strains of the perennial "In a Little Spanish Town." Santa Ana's narrow streets were blindingly white with lime dust and sun. The washed blue of the sky formed a lofty arch above the red-roofed houses. The children astride the green fences cheered as the cage of wild animals rolled by, and the roosters in the barns provided a counterpoint. Samson, in his burlap-stuffed violet tights, lavished his most ravishing smiles upon the dark-eyed señoritas on the balconies. The air smelled of soap and lavender.

It was indeed a glorious spectacle the circus afforded, its bright red tent unfurled in the public square, its multicolored banners waving gaily in the soft May breeze. It was like a ship with sails ready to soar through the blue.

The show was a great success, such as the troupe had

never witnessed before. The tent was filled for every one of the three performances. Cascabel twisted his body into figures of eight; the Rossoffs drew roars—of boredom, no doubt—from their wild animals; the twin sisters used a chair for everything except what it was intended for; the clowns' wintry jokes sparkled with the freshness of spring. Everyone performed as though burning with the fire of creation.

Heliotropo, dressed in gold tights, looked like a golden stalk of wheat. Indefatigable, he was everywhere, helping everyone. He was usher, groom, maid and announcer. He served as foil for the clowns and he stood up against the board to be outlined by Filipon's knives. He even found time to laugh with the children and, from a distance, to admire Colombina in her white tulle costume and wig of silver braids. Finally, he assisted the Great Floriani.

The old maestro was superb that day. Such feats of magic had never been seen in Santa Ana. He made coins vanish into thin air, guessed cards by the dozens, produced one rabbit after another out of a hat, drew multicolored ribbons from the bald head of a man in the first row, and had Colombina step into a box and sawed her in two. For the finale, he pointed to different places in the audience from which Heliotropo promptly plucked sprigs of heliotrope, which he then presented to the señoritas in the audience.

As they were going to bed that night, Mama Floriani asked the Great Floriani, "How does he do it?"

"Damned if I know!" retorted the great magician, slapping down mosquitoes as noisy as jet planes. "He won't tell me his secret, but he gives me all the credit. That's all that matters. Among magicians secrets are respected."

The days that followed were the fulfillment of a glorious dream for Heliotropo. The whole fascinating country rolled under the slow wheels of the circus wagons. The circus traversed the vast, undulating indigo plantations of La Libertad and unfurled its huge tent overlooking the glittering Bay of Fonseca, where Heliotropo made Colombina a present of a lovely seashell box—one of the port's typical arts—for her combs; and in Santa Tecla, at the foot of the Volcano San Salvador, which made Pipo shut his mouth in sheer amazement; and in the village of San Miguel, where the splendor of the silver lodged in the entrails of the earth was reflected in the sky on moonlit nights; and in Santa Rosa and San Vicente, where Colombina bought herself a hat of gold-colored straw. In Sonsonate, Heliotropo shared with his adored écuyère one of the locality's famous cream cheeses and their faces were anointed with snowy goat's milk.

"To share this cheese between us," whispered Heliotropo, "is to take communion from the same Eucharist." And she, more orthodox, pretended to be frightened by his profanity.

Heliotropo earned no money with the Great Floriani. They offered him no remuneration and he asked for none. With the coins the people tossed him for pulling sprigs of heliotrope out of nowhere he bought little gifts for Colombina, and this was all that mattered to him. She, like the Great Floriani and the others, tired of asking him to explain his trick and finally came to regard it as just another act. Just the same, Colombina, a child who had never quite become a woman or a woman who had never ceased being a child, never stopped being thrilled at her friend's ability to offer her at any hour of the day or night a sprig of the tiny fragrant blue flower.

And soon the emaciated young man with dreamy eyes and the courageous girl with supple ankles began to exchange tender glances above the tiny bouquets. While their traveling companions watched them with wise smiles and friendly whispers and the Florianis dreamed of another bond within the circus family, Filipon raged in silence. Even before Heliotropo's arrival he had sought Colombina's favor in vain. His carefully trimmed mustache, his man of the world manners, his brilliantined hair and his spectacular knife-throwing act, though now he outlined Heliotropo instead of a dummy, had failed completely. His attentions had elicited no more response from Colombina than stones tossed into an empty well. And now the simple, meek Heliotropo was eliciting from her the same exalted response as a great artist achieves with his violin. Things went on in this way while the circus wheels rolled past the shadows of the volcanoes San Miguel and San Vicente, Izalco and Santa Ana, past the trembling mirror of the thousand rivers of the Lempa and the Paz, the painted lakes, the Guija and the Llopango, the plantations of wheat and rice, the woods of Peru balsam and the indigo, the fields of pochote and frijoles, the biblical flocks of sheep and goats. The circus, and with it Colombina and Heliotropo, marched on with the inexorability of an astronomic phenomenon. Until one night they came to a village on the Guatemalan frontier.

It was a hamlet with a few houses huddled together at the foot of a towering green mountain. The wagons stopped at the edge of a lyre-shaped lake with quiet gray waters. In the trees that solemnly watched over the sleeping lake, invisible birds sang as though enchanted. A hawk fluttered in the twilight blue, like an evil omen in a witches' tale. The bells of a white hermitage, which hung like a nest on the side of the mountain, underscored the peace of the evening.

The Great Floriani, feverish from a cold, soon took to his bed, but the others were having a fine dinner, old wine, songs and dancing by a crackling fire. The night slowly reclined upon the treetops, sultry and voluptuous like an amorous odalisque. With the last carmine rays of the setting sun, the underbrush yielded its wild aromas and the crickets burst into their staccato singsong.

When they went to bed—all except Filipon, who devoured by jealousy and mosquitoes lingered on to spy in the shadows—Colombina and Heliotropo were alone by the dying fire. The glowing embers tinted the round little face of the girl rose. The lake, invisible in the darkness, lapped gently against the shore. The moon was hidden but a thousand yellow stars blinked brightly, though not as brightly as the stars that leaped from the fire. It was the languid hour of midnight.

Colombina and Heliotropo, holding hands, silently gazed at each other. From their lips hung a kiss that like a timid little bird dared not assert itself. The romantic message that had grown through long hot days, moonlit nights and hours of work, insomnia and hope, struggled silently to make itself known.

Finally Colombina rose. He followed her silently. She climbed into the wagon where she slept alone among many a prop and bale. From the top step she looked down at him, her lips shimmering with scarlet tremors.

"Come," she said to him, and entering the wagon she closed the door.

Heliotropo did not move. Filipon, who had witnessed the scene from the shadows, went to his own wagon blind with pain and rage. Heliotropo, standing still, was like a statue burnished in silver by a curious moon.

Sleepless, trembling, Colombina waited in vain. Her door never opened again that night.

"In a Little Spanish Town" . . . The melody announced the opening number. The circus was giving a gala performance in the mountain village of Cojutepeque. Colombina, her eyes red and swollen, passed Heliotropo without even glancing at him and went through her act with waxen face and pale lips.

Unfortunately the Great Floriani was too sick to perform. After a feverish night, visited by severe fits of coughing, he lay exhausted on his cot under the hot poultices the inexorable Mama Floriani applied to his vast chest every few minutes. A short consultation had taken place at his bedside. It was agreed that Heliotropo would do all he could to entertain the public, and then as a finale they would put on Filipon's invariably spectacular knife act.

The Great Floriani gave final instructions to a shaking Heliotropo.

"Do all you can," he implored him. "At least make a coin vanish or change the color of a ribbon or two."

The roll of drums, which usually heralded the entrance of the Great Floriani and was now announcing Heliotropo, sounded to him like the prelude to his execution. The dais he had to mount in the center of the ring was the guillotine, the sand reminded him of the cemetery, and the audience was the Roman mob that with a turn of their thumbs brought death upon the victim's head.

He bowed clumsily and became even more flustered when he noticed Colombina staring at him with eyes of steel and a mocking smile. The anxious faces of the children in the first row made his fright mount to new heights. He tried the trick with the coin but it fell to the ground. Just as he was beginning the ribbon trick, the blue banners of the next trick dropped out from under his cape. He tried to draw flame out of a hat and almost started a fire.

Filipon's resounding guffaws mixed with the shouts of protest from the audience. Heliotropo, completely disconcerted, looked around for some means of escape. But something in Colombina's eyes stopped him.

Suddenly, without hesitating, Heliotropo approached a little boy and no sooner did he make him put out his hands than they held a nest of quivering white doves. Then he picked up a handful of sand and tossed it in the air, and instead of sand a cloud of gold spangles drifted down to the ground. The audience began to applaud. Heliotropo, pale but smiling, next changed the rope round the ring into a garland of flowers, the old tired horses into multicolored zebras, and the wrinkled, paper peanut bags into canaries of yellow flight and golden song. Never before had an audience seen such skill. The performers, standing together, stared at Heliotropo in stupefaction. Heliotropo raised a pale hand and there fell from the canvas roof a shower of colored confetti, streamers and balloons. From between the knees of a young man he produced a white pony bedizened in gorgeous velvet and silver mail. In the center of the ring he called forth a fountain of feathers and pearls, and from a paper envelope he drew a twenty-foot-high palm tree with coconuts and monkeys high up in the branches. The audience went completely mad. It was then that Heliotropo, as his finale, signaled to Colombina to lie in the box in which she was sawed in two by the Great Floriani. At that moment, the Great Floriani, who had been kept apprised of the extraordinary happenings by an astonished and stammering Cascabel, uttered a bloodcurdling scream.

"Look!" he cried to Mama Floriani. "There is the painted rubber saw with which I cut Colombina in two, and yet I saw Filipon take out a saw for the act. He must have taken the one used for cutting wood."

He had to say no more. Mama Floriani executed a truly astonishing leap, considering her weight, and darted out of the wagon toward the circus. The Great Floriani, bathed in a cold sweat of terror, at any minute expected Mama Floriani to walk in with a bloody Colombina under her arm. What a monstrous revenge! The jealousy-crazed Filipon had arranged for Heliotropo to cut his beloved in half. The Great Floriani thought he could hear Colombina's screams, which Heliotropo would mistake for the false cries she lavished on the audience every time Floriani pretended to cut her in two with the imitation saw. And this time the legs held up to the public would be real and not artificial ones dripping with red paint.

The wagon door was suddenly pushed open. The Great Floriani clenched his fists. But his wife was alone.

"I can't believe it," she panted, sitting down on a mustard plaster in her confusion. "That boy is the greatest magician in the world. He pulled a giraffe out of a hat and threaded a needle with a rope. And—you'll die, Floriani!—he really *did* saw Colombina in two and then put her together again as good as new. No, I'm not crazy. And you have heard nothing yet. It was not sleight of hand. He did it with a real saw and she thought it was the same old trick. And then he stood up for Filipon to throw his knives at him. I swear he threw them at him to kill! Right at his heart! And Heliotropo, smiling, changed them into golden lilies as they came at him.''

Nobody slept that night, nobody in the town and certainly nobody in the circus. Filipon had fled, his teeth chattering with terror. The Florianis made great plans for the future and dreamed of Heliotropo's becoming the star of their troupe. The other performers waited in a frenzy for morning to come to express their admiration to Heliotropo. Colombina spent the night interrogating the lofty stars with tearful eyes. After the show Heliotropo had left for the hermitage on the mountain, explaining that he wanted to spend the night alone. They had respected his wish.

At dawn, Colombina could wait no longer and knocked at the door of the Florianis' wagon. Mama Floriani, her hair disheveled and her eyes red from a sleepless night, opened the door.

"Mama Floriani," Colombina implored, "you must come with me to find him."

"Where did he go?"

"To the hermitage on the mountain."

They left Floriani snoring under layers of blankets and began their climb to the hermitage. The sky was tinged by the pink of dawn. Birds burst into early song to frighten away the last star. The scent of rosemary perfumed the air. From a pool a single frog stared at them with beady little eyes. Invisible cocks crowed, giving the sun the signal to rise. Colombina, pale and anxious, climbed the path lightly, followed by her hard-breathing companion.

The hermitage was small, white and sad, like the deep sigh of a tearful child. Outside the sun polished the roof with its gold emery board. Inside there were wooden benches, a small altar with a stone saint, the aroma of flowers, and an early-rising friendly hermit. When he saw the two women staring with ecstatic faces at the saint, he approached them with a benevolent gesture.

"Are you admiring the angel San Miguel? Fine manly

figure of a saint. You won't believe it but he was a sinner in
his youth. There is a beautiful legend about him. In his
lifetime God punished him for breaking his vow of chastity
with a girl. His penance was to return to earth time and
again dispossessed of his miraculous powers, which he
had abused once to please a woman. God commanded
him to wander over the earth until he could withstand the
temptation of a woman's love. Only then would he again
recover God's grace and with it his power to perform
miracles. The Lord, however, allowed him in his peniten-
tial wanderings one little miracle: he could make flowers
appear anywhere. But until he could prove that he preferred divine grace to a woman's arms, he would have to
wander through the world, a young man of light head and
yielding heart. This is his statue and these his flowers.
Don't you smell the perfume of the blue heliotrope, the
favorite flowers of the angel San Miguel?''

Once again night and silence have descended upon the
circus. Performers and animals are in deep sleep. A moon
as huge as heaven itself bathes the circus in its chaste light.
The air suddenly stirs with the footsteps of a divine presence. And in the morning Cascabel wakes up in silk tights
embroidered with gold; the horses are harnessed in the
finest wrought silver; the twin sisters find bolts of gold cloth
at their feet; Samson's weights are filled with precious
jewels; the Florianis' wagon is a princely chariot, all precious metals, silk hangings and brocades. And Colombina
opens her eyes and finds in her hand a sprig of heliotrope.

The Golden Goat

Michael de Larrabeiti

One cold night more than a hundred years ago, on a dark hillside in the country of Provence, an old shepherd knelt by a wood fire and shook his sleeping son awake. As the boy opened his eyes the shepherd prodded the fire with his staff and a bright flame leapt upwards, making yellow shapes out of the black trees and revealing crooked twigs which clutched like witches' fingers at the shepherd's silver hair.

"Pacorro," said the shepherd, "three of our sheep have wandered up the valley. I can hear their bells and you must go after them."

The boy rubbed his eyes and stood, pulling his cloak up with him to settle it on his shoulders; then, with only one word of farewell, he left the firelight and stepped into the forest darkness.

Since early childhood Pacorro had run with his father's flock and he was as sure-footed as the nimblest goat alive and never had he slept under a roof or in a bed, for his father owned no pastures but grazed his sheep on the common land by the roadside and on the rocky hills by the sea. So Pacorro the shepherd boy was not afraid of the forest; he passed through the first of the trees, touching their uneven bark with his finger-tips, and followed a narrow valley that led away from the sea and towards the mountains. Above him in the sky was half a moon but it was prowling behind low clouds and gave no light. Every now and then the boy stopped to listen for the sound of sheep-bells but he heard only the trees around him as they scraped their branches together, sounding for all the world like rough voices whispering in the forest.

"May God protect me," said Pacorro, "but there are Saracens abroad in the woods tonight," and he drew his cloak more tightly about his neck and walked on.

For nearly an hour he searched, sometimes hearing the

faint sound of a bell in the distance, sometimes not, but however far he walked the sound came no nearer and he began to despair of ever finding his father's sheep. It was then, almost on the point of giving up his task, that he saw a light shining. It flickered through the trees and out along the sides of a dry river-bed like sunlight on the sea. Pacorro heard a strange noise too, not the ordinary harshness of his own sheep-bells but a clear and simple ringing, like silver touching silver. The shepherd boy quickened his step; this light could only come from a shepherd's fire, he thought, and the ringing would be their sheep-bells. He would talk with them and they would help him to find his missing sheep.

Suddenly the river-bed turned one last turn and Pacorro fell, throwing his arms up in fear, blinded by what seemed to be a golden flame. Never had he seen a light so golden, not the heart of a fire, nor the center of the sun. Pacorro waited, wondering if his sight was truly lost. Minutes went by and when at last the shepherd boy lowered his hands from his face he saw that he could still see.

He had come to a gully whose rocky walls almost touched overhead, a gully made impenetrable by growths of sturdy thorn, strong and matted. It was one of these bushes that gave out the mysterious light and the sound of the silver bell, a pathetic jangling noise as some animal vainly struggled to free itself from the powerful grip of some unseen thing. Against his will Pacorro was drawn forward. He gazed into the light and, deep in the thorn bush, in the center of a cloud of diffused gold, was a graceful and elegant goat, caught by her long ebony horns in a deadly trap. Slowly she turned her face to look at the shepherd boy, contemplating him with eyes of incredible sadness. She was beautiful and Pacorro stared, holding his breath with the wonder of it.

The goat's fleece was long and touched her feet, it was combed and groomed but it was the colour of the coat that made Pacorro gasp. The colour was the light that filled the gully and the light was golden; it gleamed and shone in a

magical way, flaming with a fire that was not a fire and
burning with a flame that could entice men to their deaths.
Fear struck at the boy's heart and he knew that he was in
great danger. He had found the Golden Goat of Abd-al-
Rhaman, trapped by its horns in a hunter's noose. On its
head it wore the Caliph's seven-pointed coronet of gold, a
crown made of metal so soft and pure that a man might
draw his name across it with the slightest touch of his
finger-nail.

Pacorro drew his knife; it was broad-bladed and sharp.
The old legends said that the Golden Goat was evil and
dangerous. He who was unlucky enough to find her
should slay her and seize the crown she wore on her head.
The boy's thoughts went to his father and the fields the old
man dreamt of buying for his flock, and a hut too where the
shepherd might live in comfort when he was too weary to
follow the sheep. Pacorro raised his knife to strike but, to
his astonishment, the Golden Goat turned her lovely head
and spoke to him, speaking in a voice that was as beautiful
as she was and that men found impossible to resist.

"Do not slay me, shepherd," she said. "Cut me free and
I will show you all the treasure of the Caliph, Abd-al-
Rhaman, and you may choose from it three times and take
from it all that you can carry. One ruby alone would make
you and your father rich, and your son and your son's son
rich also."

Pacorro wound his hand into the goat's long hair. It was
spun gold and yet softer to his touch than the wool of a
rainwashed lamb. The goat still looked at him with her
brown eyes and seemed as human as he. Pacorro did not
answer; he stood still and remembered the old story as his
father had told it to him, many times.

Several hundreds of years before Pacorro's birth the
Saracens had appeared over the edge of the sea in their
war-galleys and had conquered Provence and taken it for
their very own. Under the orders of their leader, Abd-al-
Rhaman, they had built a castle on the steepest of the hills
and called it Fraxinetta. For years it had remained im-

pregnable and the Saracens were ready to rule the land for ever, taking whatever they wanted, raiding and killing wherever they wished.

At long last the Princes and Abbotts of Provence decided to win back the country they had lost and so they raised a great army and fought the Saracens in many long and savage wars and after ten years of cruel and bloody fighting they forced the Caliph to take refuge in his castle.

The seige was long and bitter and Abd-al-Rhaman, looking down from his battlements, came to realise that he could not win this last campaign and he begged his enemies to let him go in peace, promising never to return and, rather than see their soldiers slain in war the Abbotts and the Princes granted the Caliph's request, but only on condition that the Saracens did not take their plunder away with them.

But Abd-al-Rhaman was subtle and double-tongued and under cover of darkness he had his slaves carry his treasure into a deep cavern where they threw it down in haste and the entrance to the cave was shut fast by the spell of an Arabian sorcerer, the most powerful wizard that ever lived. The next day the Saracens slipped aboard their galleys and in less than an hour their ships had disappeared over the horizon.

Of course the Caliph's promise had been a false promise. He had secretly sworn to revenge himself on his enemies, to recover his vast riches and in order to prove to his followers that he meant to return the Caliph left behind a priceless possession: his only daughter, the Princess Suhar.

The Princess wept to be left alone but her father was cruel and ignored her tears. He commanded his sorcerer to change Suhar into a superb mountain goat, sure-footed and speedier than the finest horse that ran. She was to guard the treasure and, should searchers ever come near the cavern, she was to entice them to their deaths or bring them to the brink of madness. In return the sorcerer vowed that the Princess should live forever, just as long as she was not captured by hunters. To protect herself, should she be captured, she was given the power of gentle and persuasive speech. On the other hand, if she left the cavern to live the life of an ordinary mortal she would regain her former shape but she would become subject to age and decay as she had been before.

But the Caliph never returned to claim his riches and for centuries men had sought to capture the Golden Goat, believing that under the threat of death she could be forced to reveal the whereabouts of the cave of treasure. The goat had been seen often enough over the years, glimpsed between the dusk and the dawn, but no one had come near her and lived unscathed to tell the tale. Once or twice in a generation a poor witless shepherd had been found, wandering far from his sheep, muttering crazily that he had met and talked with the Princess Suhar and seen her treasure.

Pacorro stirred himself, wound his hand deeper into the goat's long hair and thought of one other thing that his father had told him. The Golden Goat would lie, cheat and deceive, would murder and betray, would do anything to escape from he who found her. He who wished to take her treasure would have to become as cunning and as evil as she. "If you find her, kill her," the old shepherd had said, "before she drives you mad."

Pacorro pushed his knife between the goat's horns and cut the noose that held her.

"There," he said, "you are free."

No sooner did the rope fall from her than the goat leapt twenty paces along the river-bed, clearing bushes and trees in a gigantic bound. Pacorro was wrenched from his feet, dragged through the thorns and his legs were made bloody and his body was bruised, but he did not relax his grip on the goat's long hair. When he regained his feet, angry with pain and surprise, he raised his knife to the goat's neck and pressed the blade close up against the vein that throbbed there and only a thought kept the knife from the blood.

"My father needs a house," said Pacorro, "so show me your treasure as you promised or I will slaughter you as I have slaughtered many other goats, and skinned them too."

"I only leapt for joy," said the goat. "I rejoice that I am free and will see my treasure again." She nuzzled the boy's shoulder and said, "Come, we have far to go."

And so the goat led the shepherd boy across the slanting darkness of the hillsides, hoping to exhaust him, hoping that his grip on her fleece would weaken. As she ran she spoke to him, trying to deceive his senses with her soft voice but Pacorro only tightened his fist in the golden hair and ran pace for pace with the goat and as nimbly, gritting his teeth and thinking of the land he would buy for his father.

At last the goat rested in a deep ravine and Pacorro felt the full weight of her brown eyes upon him as she told of the great battles of the past, how many men the Caliph had tortured and slain for his pleasure. She told of the slaves he had captured too and the shepherd boy shivered as he heard the sounds of death and the clashing of weapons and the cries of the wounded. He saw the ghosts of dead warriors and he felt the touch of their breath on his cheek and fear crept under his skin like a maggot, but he was brave and again tightened his hold on the fleece and said, "I swear I will slay you and steal your crown if you do not keep your promise."

"I tell you stories of the Caliph," said the goat, "so that the road we travel may seem less wearisome," and she led Pacorro into a cleft that was narrow and full of stubborn bushes carrying thorns of sharp iron-wood. As the goat advanced the thorns swayed back from her though they clutched at Pacorro and brought blood to his arms and face. The noise of battle and the screams of the injured were louder here and the boy wanted to turn and run to his father but now he did not dare.

Suddenly the clamour stopped. The Golden Goat halted before a blank rock wall in which there was no fissure or crack. She lowered her head and spoke in Saracen words more than a thousand years old and the granite wall rolled aside and the goat stepped into a cavern whose roof was so high that it could not be seen. Pacorro was drawn in with her and the cavern door closed behind him. He was deep under the hillside, shut in with the Golden Goat of Abd-al-Rhaman.

Now Pacorro released his hold on the fleece and stumbled forward. There was treasure all about him and the light from it dulled even the sheen of the goat's golden coat. Here in the cavern was everything that a man, even in his greatest greed, could desire. Everything that the Saracens had torn from the conquered land, stolen at the price of blood, death and slavery. The floor was ankle deep in precious stones, they overflowed from deep seachests, carelessly filled. There were ivory statues draped with gowns of silk and cloth of gold; there were orbs and sceptres, thrones and crowns, tapestries and gem-woven vestments, still stained with the blood of dying priests. It was all thrown down in disorder and it had lain there for hundreds of years, waiting for the Caliph to return.

The goat stalked proudly into the cavern and Pacorro followed, his eyes unequal to the task of looking at so much splendour. The goat went on and everywhere she walked there was treasure. At last she stopped by a huge throne of gold thickly decorated with diamonds; across its arms rested a great jewelled sword in a scabbard of silver. The goat looked in disdain at the trembling shepherd boy and her eyes blazed up with pride and greed. "What a mighty fellowship," she said, "was the fellowship of my father the Caliph. Stronger than all your Princes, bolder than your kings and more daring than your knights. How they feared us."

She touched the throne with a horn, "This we took from an Archbishop, those tapestries we took from his cathedral . . . those caskets of jewels we had in ransom for your most powerful king, and all you see is mine until my father

returns . . . Then I shall be a princess once more and I
shall live with my own people."

The goat moved on and Pacorro walked with her, his
scarred and filthy feet stepping over rich silks and precious
stones, but the boy did not forget his father and he
thought of the little he had. Once more he showed his
knife. "And where is my reward?" he asked. "Three
choices from amongst your riches you promised me. I
want them; remember that I saved you from the hunter's
noose."

The goat lowered her head and her eyes went dull.
"Shepherd boy," she said, "choose."

Pacorro pointed to the jewelled sword on the magnificent throne. "The sword," he said, thinking that he could
strap it to his body, leaving his arms free to carry something
more.

"Oh choose some other thing," answered the goat, "for
that was the Caliph's favourite sword. I would be disgraced
if he were to return and find it gone."

Pacorro pointed next to a caftan made of gold and silver
thread, heavy with rubies and saphires and opals and
pearls of matching beauty. "That," he thought, "I shall be
able to slip over my shoulder and leave my hands free to
carry something more."

The goat stamped a foot and her voice was angry.
"Fool, you cannot take the caftan of the Caliph; when he
returns he will look for this caftan before any other thing."

Pacorro felt pity for the goat in her trouble and cast his
eyes all round the cavern for another treasure to bear away
with him. "I will have that turban," he said at length,
thinking that he could place it upon his head leaving his
hands free to carry away something more. The turban
bore a rich diamond at its front, a diamond as big as the
boy's clenched fist.

The goat placed her head on Pacorro's shoulder and her
brown eyes filled with tears as she looked at him. "My
father wore this turban on his wedding day, I dare not
let you take it . . . he would punish me sorely if I let
it go."

Still Pacorro had pity and chose again but the goat made yet another excuse and bade him choose elsewhere. But whatever it was that the boy chose the Golden Goat refused and hours went by in this way and Pacorro grew weary and fell silent, realising that the goat would allow nothing to be taken from her hoard, not the smallest diamond nor the meanest silver pin, and he began to fear that he would die amongst all that treasure. He felt a madness beginning to stir in his brain and he forgot about a field in the mountain and a field in the valley with a hut for his father. He longed to be out in the night air but at the same time a wave of pity rose in his heart and he wept, weeping for the Princess Suhar, abandoned, alone, loveless for so long. He knew, as every shepherd knew, that the Caliph and his sorcerer had been dead for hundreds of years and would never return to seek the treasure and to change the Golden Goat back into the form of a young princess.

Pacorro took the goat's lovely head in his arms. "Princess," he said, "leave this horrible place. Better to be a shepherdess in the sun than live a thousand years alone. Come away and you will sleep under the stars and listen to the sheep bells at dawn."

The goat shook her head. "How could I leave my father's treasure? The Caliph might return tomorrow."

"Princess," said Pacorro, "your father will never return. He and his sorcerer are dead."

The goat wandered a step from Pacorro and gazed steadily over all her possessions. "I know," she said, "but the Caliph was not the man to let death defeat him. Besides, how could I leave? I am used to the feel of silk, the sight of gold and the glint of rubies. If I went with you I would become a woman again but I would lose the power of opening the cave. I could never live as you live—poor, dirty, a barefoot shepherd."

Pacorro was angered. "Living as we live is better than living as you live," he cried.

"And dying as you die," said the goat softly, "and how is that?"

"Dying a shepherd is better than living a goat," sobbed Pacorro and the tears ran down his face.

The goat came close to Pacorro and put her soft mouth into the place where his neck met his shoulder. "Your tears are kind," she said, "and you are right, I will come with you but you must help. It will not be easy for me."

"Yes," said Pacorro and he brushed away his tears with the back of his hand. He put an arm round the goat's neck and he half-led, half-dragged her, to the doorway of the cavern and the goat spoke the word and the rock wall opened and Pacorro saw the pale starlight outside. The goat trembled and the shepherd boy held her tightly but, as they were about to cross the threshold, Pacorro thought of all the wealth he was leaving behind and he thought once more of his father and how one pearl only would shelter him from the cold nights of his advancing age. So Pacorro, hoping that the goat would not see him, squeezed the toes of his right foot around a small ruby that lay in his path, meaning to hobble with it into the outside air.

But the goat knew at once what he had done, feeling it in his touch, and she reared from his embrace. "Oh, do not take that ruby," she cried, "my father would search for it in the very moment of his return."

Pacorro allowed the ruby to drop to the floor and went towards the goat, his arms outstretched but the goat re-treated, back into the cavern.

"I cannot go," she said, "I cannot betray my father."

"It is not your father that keeps you here," said Pacorro, "it is the treasure," and he leapt forward, seized the goat by the head and by the horns and he dragged her, stiff-legged, through the doorway.

Suddenly Pacorro fell backwards and rolled into a thicket of briar and bramble; he pulled himself free with bloody hands. The goat had disappeared from his grasp and there in its place stood the slender form of the Princess Suhar, regal and beautiful. Her long dark hair was black and where it was darkest it was blue, like the midnight sky, but her face was somber and sad with centuries of waiting. The gown she wore was the colour of saphires and it was patterned over with the finest diamonds from the Caliph's store, each diamond purer than the last and carrying in its heart a flickering candle flame. Across the princess's forehead glittered the Caliph's coronet of gold with the seven points.

The princess looked about her. She raised her hands and looked closely at them, moving her fingers. She stared at her feet, she touched her face, her arms, her hair, and then she screamed.

"No," she cried, a dreadful moaning in her voice. "How strange I feel, how horrible this shape, this cannot be beautiful. How long would I live in this body? I would grow old like you, die like you, unable to run, forever, sure-footed across the hills." And with these words she stepped back over the threshold of the cave and as the Princess Suhar disappeared the Golden Goat wheeled on its four fine feet in the doorway and spoke the word and the rock door of the cavern began to rumble and roll forward.

Pacorro, his blood still wet on his hands, leapt into the entrance and grabbed the goat's horns and fought with her. But the goat was decided now and she lowered her head and shook it hard and the shepherd boy was flung from the cave and his breath was knocked from him. The door rolled on and shut fast.

In a little while Pacorro recovered and crawled to the door and stood before it. He felt carefully with his hands but no opening could he find. It was dark again. The golden splendour had vanished with the goat and her treasure, only cold dawn light shone above the cleft now and that too weak to reach the ground.

Pacorro began to grope his way along the gully, his eyes uncertain after the sights they had seen. He felt before him and in those first doubtful steps his foot struck something which rang out with an ancient sound as it moved against a stone.

Pacorro knelt and his wounded hands searched in the dust until he touched the thing. He could not see what it was and so he raised it above his head and held it against the stars. It was round and smooth with seven points, it was the golden coronet, fallen from the goat's head during her last struggle with the shepherd boy. Pacorro smiled to himself in the darkness; the dream of his father would come true after all; as much pasture as he wanted now.

As the boy smiled there came a terrible sobbing from the depths of the hillside; the great door began to open and there came the sound of that voice which no man could resist.

"And what will the Caliph say?" it called. "What will the Caliph say when he finds his crown stolen by a shepherd? Return it to me and you may choose what else you will from this treasure . . ."

The great door of rock opened completely now and Pacorro saw the Golden Goat again, shining brighter than the brightness of the treasure behind her. And as the light grew stronger the goat stepped across the threshold once more and took the form of the Princess Suhar, holding out her arms and speaking in tones of great sadness.

"Will you leave me here like this for ever, without my father's crown? Return it to me, shepherd boy, and I will teach you the secret word that opens this cave and you and your father will be as rich as Abd-al-Rhaman once was."

Still clasping the coronet Pacorro raised his hands to his head and tried to close his ears but the voice of the princess was like the voice of reason itself and the light from the cavern burned into his eyes and blinded him and he moved towards the door and felt soft lips whispering to him of wealth and power beyond belief and gentle hands led him back into the cavern to choose what he would and slowly the great rock door closed behind him.

And three days later Pacorro's father found his son lying on his back in a gully whose rocky walls almost touched overhead, a gully made impenetrable by growths of sturdy thorn, strong and matted. The old shepherd cut his way to his son's side and knelt beside him but Pacorro did not recognise his father and the man wept. The boy's mind had gone. He said nothing and stared at the sky out of unseeing golden eyes.

The Island and the Cattle

Because he sent a head of cattle on
Further than they should go, over the dykes,
Driving them with a switch and a dog beside him:

They sank in the quag, and he,
Frightened because of his sin, disappeared,
Never to be noticed again in that country:

Because he told them, in a letter,
That it was not his fault, he had gone mad,
Driven towards the sea by a vision of birds

Who whistled over his head in the wind,
Leading to a quiet island. He found a girl there,
Lay with her in the rushes, her beauty

Like a star being too much for him.
The wind rose, the morning was grey, his vision gone:
There was no girl, there were no cattle, and it was day.

—*Nicholas Moore*

"Wherever we stand, we are within
a hairsbreadth of the fallen country"

The Fallen Country

Somtow Sucharitkul

He had blank, sky-blue eyes and confused blond hair.
He had a wry, dry voice with just a lemon twist of longing in
it. He was small for his age, almost as though he had willed
himself not to grow. As I closed the door behind us, my
hand brushed against his and he flinched away violently in
the split second before willing himself to smile; from this I
pegged him as a victim of child abuse.

"Hi," I said, answering him. "My name is Dora Marx." I
eased him into the brown, wombish chair that faced my
desk. "You may call me—" I sat down myself, with the
stuck-record-in-a-groove smoothness that comes from
seeing a thousand children a year for twenty years,
"—either Dora, or Mrs. Marx. Whichever makes you feel
more comfortable."

"I think I'd prefer Mrs. Marx," he said. "But," he added,
"You can call me Billy." Touché.

He didn't look at me. I went to the window to slam out
the eleven o'clock yelling from the schoolyard. God damn
it, they should never make you work under these condi-
tions . . .

I said, "You're the one who—"

"They found at five in the morning, clinging to the
steeple of Santa Maria's. You read the papers?"

"Sometimes," I said, flicking the clipping out of his file.
BILLY BINDER, AGE 12—

"Where'd you get that scar?"—*like an albino earthworm, wriggling into the sleeve of his teeshirt.*

"Fell off my bike." Sure.

—FOUND HALF-DEAD ON THE LEDGE, HIS ARMS
AROUND THE STEEPLE ON THE SIDE OVERLOOK-
ING ANGEL PLAZA. FATHER EPSTEIN, SUMMER-
TIME PASTOR STANDING IN FOR FATHER SANTINI,
WHILE TRYING TO RING THE BELL—

"It says here," I said, "that you were suffering from severe frostbite."

"Yes. From the snow."

"It doesn't snow in Florida in the middle of August—" No point trying to argue with him yet. My job was to listen, only to listen. I wasn't trained to root out traumas. It wasn't up to me to pronounce the kid an attempted suicide either, or to solve the mystery of how he got to the topmost turret of a locked historical monument, or to elucidate the medical wonder of frostbite in a hundred-degree heatwave. I was only a counsellor in a parochial school too poor and stupid to afford an expert.

I wouldn't get anywhere by questioning his story. Perhaps I should start with something else. "How often do they beat you up?" I said.

"What?" Terror flecked his eyes for a second. Then they went dead. He said, "Almost every day." It was in the same tone of voice.

"Who?"

"Pete, my Mom's boyfriend."

"What?"

He told me about it, never raising his voice. I had been doing this for twenty years. After a while you grow iron railings round your brains. Nothing hurts anymore. I listened, staring at my hands and wishing a ton of Porcelana on them. I knew I would sit there and endure until the catalogue of beltings and poundings had dissolved into incoherence, into tears, into hysteria, and then I would flow into the cracks in the kid's soul like epoxy glue and make him seem whole for a while . . . but he didn't give me a chance. He went on in that same monotone, detail after detail, until it was I who was ready to crack. I held up my hand. He stopped.

"Don't you ever cry?" I said.

"Not any more," he said. "I've promised."

"What do you mean, you promised?"

"The Snow Dragon."

"Tell me about him."

"I knew it!" he cried. Now he was exultant, taunting. I

wasn't prepared for the change in mood; I started most unprofessionally. "You're supposed to be trying to help me or something, but all you want to do is listen to me lie!"

Shifting gears to accommodate his outburst: "Is that why he hits you?"

"Yes! Yes! But I won't stop!"

"It's all right," I said. "You can lie if you want. You can tell all the lies you want in this room. Nothing will ever escape from here . . ."

"Like a confessional? Like a black hole?"

"Yes." Imaginative imagery, at least. This kid was no dummy. "Like a black hole." He looked me in the eye for the first time. His eyes were clear as glass; I could read no deceit in them.

"Good," he said firmly. I waited. I think he had begun to trust me.

"So what were you really doing, then, up there. Straddling the steeple, I mean."

"Rescuing a princess."

That's how he started telling me the stories. The stories! They would have been the envy of any clinical psychiatrist with a pet theory and a deadline and a paper to be churned out in a fury. To me they were only stories. Of course I did not believe them; but my job was to listen, not to judge.

Billy had been adopted by one set of parents after another. He couldn't remember the first few. After the divorcees had played musical chairs for a while he had settled with the third or fourth mother, Joan, and they'd moved to our town, a spiderweb of brash fast food places that circled the Eighteenth Century Spanish church that was the town's one attraction. Billy shed pasts like a snake sloughing its skin or a duck shaking off canal water. The only thing he kept was the name, Billy Binder. He'd always been adamant about his name. He'd always gotten his way about it somehow: throwing tantrums, whining, running away. It was the only part of him he'd ever kept successfully. Days his mother typed accounts in a doctor's office; nights she went to school, dreaming vaguely of a softer future. As I grew to know Billy I would go over and meet her sometimes at the doctor's. She was a dark-haired, tired, cowering, rake-thin woman; I never got much of a feel for her. And somehow I never met Pete. I never went to their house, except once, at the end of my association with Billy; and I shall never return there.

Pete came on a motorcycle and took over their lives. He and Billy exchanged a single glance and understood each other to the core: *enemy.* But Pete was the stronger, physically anyway. He wielded his leather belt like a lion tamer in a circus. Nights, after it was over—and it almost always happened, every night—Billy went to his closet of a room and lay down choked with anger. He never tried to disguise his weals. He flaunted them in school, never offering any explanation for them. And no one dared ask him for one. They saw him shrouded in anger as in a burning forceshield, and they were afraid to touch his loneliness.

A night came when the anger burst at last. It was long past midnight and the pain had died down a little. Billy got out of bed, wriggled into some old cutoffs, pulled on a teeshirt, wincing as it raked against new welts. He tiptoed out of the house. He found his old bike leaning against the front door, and then he biked like a maniac into the burning night. He did not know what drove him. A quick twisty path rounded some shadowy palms and crossed an empty highway and skirted the beach for some miles. It was a night without stars, the heat wringing moisture from the blackness. At first he heard the sea, but the surf-shatter faded quickly. In the distance rose a wall of luxury hotels, distant giants' tombstones. In a while he made a left turn into the town. He was not biking with any particular purpose. It began to snow.

He didn't take it in at first. His anger was everything. But it didn't stop. Fragments of cold were pelting his face, and then great sheets of white, but Billy had never seen snow before, and he was too busy being angry to realize that this was a blizzard. . . .

(*I'll kill him!* he was thinking, forcing the pedals against the ever-piling snow . . .)

And then it thinned. He came to a stop, stuck against a rock or a drift. A dead, sourceless light played over vistas of whiteness. It didn't feel like the world at all. The snow didn't stop. Sometimes it tickled his face. Sometimes it swirled in the sky, its flakes like stars in a nebula. There was no sun or moon. Misty in the horizon, an impossibly far horizon, Billy saw white crenellated castle walls that ran behind a white hill and emerged from the other side of it; they went on as far as he could see, twisting like marble serpents. Billy began walking towards the hill. He did not wonder at where he was. The cold didn't touch him, not like sticking your hand in the freezer. He walked. By a strange foreshortening or trick of perspective he found himself facing the hill—

The hill's wings flapped, eyes flared briefly, fire-brilliant blue. It was a dragon. Again the eyes flared, dulled, flared, dulled . . . Billy gazed at the dragon for a long time. In a rush that sent the wind sighing, the dragon spread its wings, sweeping the snow into fierce sudden flurries. Billy saw that the dragon had no scales but little mozaic-things of interlocking snowflakes; when the dragon's eyes flashed, the flakes caught rainbow fire and sparkled for a few seconds.

The dragon said, "Billy Binder, welcome to the fallen country."

Billy was afraid at last. "Send me home!" he cried. And then he remembered Pete and said nothing.

When the dragon spoke, its voice was piping clear, emotionless, like the voice of a child's ghost. It wasn't a booming, threatening voice at all.

"What are you thinking?" he said. "That I don't sound fierce and threatening the way a dragon should? That I don't roar?" He did roar then, a tinny, buzzing roar like an electric alarm clock.

Billy said, "Who has stolen your roar?" He felt a twinge of pity for the dragon; but then his anger slapped it down.

"This is the fallen country, Billy. Here there is no emotion at all. We cannot love or hate. We cannot utter great thunderous cries of joy or terror . . . the world is muted by perpetual snow. That is why you are here.''

"What do you mean?" Billy was scared and wanted to go back to his bike. He looked behind him and saw it, impossibly far away; it seemed strange that he could have walked this far, through the trudge-thick snowdrifts, in only a few minutes. Perhaps time was different here. He knew that time was different in different countries.

The dragon said, "You are here because you are full of anger, Billy Binder. In the fallen country we need such anger as yours. Anger is strength here . . . if I could feel such anger, such love, such hatred as you can feel, I would die, Billy. . . ."

Wrenching his feet out of the knee-deep coldless snow, Billy forced himself to walk toward the dragon. Even the dread he had been feeling had passed away now. "But who has done this to you? Who has stolen your feelings?"

"You know. You have touched his shadow. His shadow has come pursuing you. The Ringmaster. With his whip of burning cold."

Pete! "You should kill him!" Whiteness burned all around him, making the tears run.

"He cannot be killed. He slips from world to world as easily as you have done." Again the pitiful whinebuzz that passed for a roar. "But we can work against him. Slowly, slowly we can sap him of his strength. Your anger is powerful here. Your anger can build bridges, can burn pathways through the snow. Try it, Billy."

Billy clenched himself, feeling the rage course through him, and when he opened his eyes he saw greenery poking through the snow for a few seconds, but then it was misted over by white again.

"Do you see?" the dragon said. "You are Binder."

"That's my name," said Billy, "but—"

"Your roots are in the fallen country. That is why you have never felt truly at home in your world, why you have been tossed from household to household, taking only the name *Binder* with you."

Thunder shuddered through the cloud-haze. For a moment the sky parted. A whip cracking, halving the sky, retracting into the grayness, a burst of sound that could have been applause or a circus band starting up or a crowd deriding a fallen clown—

"Pete!" he blurted out.

"No," said the dragon, "only the shadow; the Ringmaster has a thousand shadows, and it is only a shadow of his shadow that has followed you all the way to your distant world."

Billy nodded, understanding suddenly.

Then he saw a red weal open on the dragon's neck, blood trickling in slow motion onto the snow, blood that stained the whiteness like a poppy-cluster—"He's hurt you!" he said. They were akin then, he and this alien creature. Both were at the mercy of—"Can't you cry out?" he cried into the howling wind. "Can't you feel anything?"

"No." The dragon's voice did not change. "Here one need feel no pain at all. It's better to feel nothing, isn't it? Come now. Ride me."

He extended a wing; it fanned out into a diamond-speckled staircase. When Billy stepped onto it he realized that he felt no cold at all. He should be freezing to death through his worn sneakers, but he felt only numbness. It was less real than a dream.

"Let's go now. We'll have adventures, rescuing princesses, fighting monsters and such. Isn't that what every child wants to do? A lot of children find their way into the fallen country. And they find a use for themselves here . . . one day we'll have a whole army of them."

"But I want to find the Ringmaster himself! I don't want him to hurt you and me anymore. I want to kill him."

The dragon only laughed, a wretched ghost of a laugh. Billy clambered up the wing.

"Every child who comes here dreams of reaching the Ringmaster. Of shaping his anger into a bridge that will touch the very heart of the Ringmaster and topple the circus where he wields his whip. They learn better, Billy."

"I want to kill him!"

Again a specter of a laugh. Billy settled on the dragon's back; it was ridged with soft dunes of snow. The dragon flapped his wings, not resoundingly, but with a thud like a cellar door slamming shut in a next-door house.

The dragon said, "You'll never need to cry again, Billy. From now on you will have to save your grief, your anger, save it for here where it will be of some use. Listen! I am the Snow Dragon, the last surviving dragon of the fallen country. I survived by purging myself of all that made me dragon: my fire, my rage, my iridescing, sparkle-flashing scales that gleamed silver in the moon and gold in the sun. Now sun and moon are gone. And I have waited for a thousand years, so long that I have lost the capacity to feel any joy at your coming . . . I, the Snow Dragon, tell you to dry your tears for the last time. Promise me."

"I promise." Billy found himself acceding, on impulse, without thinking it out. Already his eyes felt drained. Only the melting snowflakes moistened his cheeks. He felt no motion, but saw the ground fall from the dragon's claws. They were rising.

They flew through snowstorms into landscapes overcast and lightly puffed with snow: here and there the outlines of castles, here and there a spire poking through the whiteness. There were oceans frosted with vanilla icing. There were cities full of silent people, trudging listlessly, never pausing to watch the dragon swooping in the sky, never lifting their glazed-dead eyes from the snow. At times the sky opened, the whip cracked once, twice, thunderclap-swift, raising fresh welts in the dragon's hide. They flew on; and the Snow Dragon never seemed to notice the Ringmaster's capricious punishments.

"Do you still want to kill him?" said the dragon. The air streamed past Billy's face, and yet he felt nothing, as though he carried around him a bubble of utter stillness. "After what you've seen he can do—"

"Yes! Yes!" Billy cried fiercely. Anger pounded inside him. "I see what I have to do now; I see why I was brought here!" And he closed his eyes, thinking of the bridge of anger. And again and again the lightning-whip cracked. Although he didn't feel its wetness he saw he was sitting in a pool of congealing blood. Dragon's blood. Purple, smoking in the chill air.

I pushed myself into a nice, controlled, professional posture. "I liked your story," I said, noting from the silence through the window that the forty-five minutes were over. *How can he sit there and spin such a haunting web of dreams*—I was shivering in my chair. So was Billy, as thought from terrible cold. I thought, *He has plucked, out of the septic tank of the human unconscious, an image of such precision, such startling profundity, an image of the dark country we all carry inside us* . . . I checked myself, knowing I was beginning to sound like a pretentious academic paper. *Get a grip on yourself.*

"Billy," I said, trying to gauge my tone, to show just the right blend of concern and unconcern. His story cried out for involvement, for belief, the way poetry does even when it lies. But my job was not to sit back and revel in the mystery and the beauty of his delusions. It was to help him find reality . . . to shatter the crystal goblet with my sledgehammer of platitudes. "I liked it," I repeated.

"It wasn't a story."

"Of course not."

Pause. "See you next week." I tried a noncommittal half-smile.

"Sure." And suddenly he was gone, leaving me alone to hunt for shadows in the shadowless sunshine.

The following week, Billy said, "I wait until it builds up, until I can't stand it any more. And then it bursts out of me and I'm free to enter the fallen country. And afterwards, I'll find myself in bed or maybe in some strange place, and sometimes I'll be blue with cold and my joints will feel like icicles and I'll be shaking all over . . ."

I found the mother, Joan, at a desk in an office in a huge building, coffined in by expanses of naked glass, always reaching for the phone.

I said, "You know there's at least one way of ending the problem, don't you?"

She said, "Yes." When she looked at me she reminded me of myself, and I was unnerved by this. She was a dark-haired, slight woman, who didn't look like Billy at all—well, that was only to be expected. Unlike her stepson, she did not hide her feelings well. I saw her guilt very clearly.

I said, "Then why don't you get rid of the man?"

She paused to take an appointment. A crisp, mediciny odor wisped by for a moment. Outside, palm-fringed concrete paths criss-crossed a carpet of harsh, brash green. But I was thinking of snow, of cold, numbing snow. Finally she answered me, speaking with difficulty.

"I can't, I can't!" She was crying a little, and I found myself turning away, embarrassed. "What can I do, Mrs. Marx? He's a force, not a person—he's not human. And what about Billy's lies? Will they suddenly end?"

"By imagining that Pete is not human," I said cruelly, "you make it a lot easier on yourself, don't you?" *Mustn't lose control* . . .

Feeling very foolish, I turned around and walked out. I don't know what I was trying to accomplish. All I knew was that I was well past my good years, and that I longed for the snow, for the fallen country that we all keep locked in our hearts. I wanted to be like Billy. I was looking forward to his next appointment, even as I felt guilty, because I had been spying on another's pain.

Then there were the princesses: some were in dungeons, buried neck-deep in the snow; others were chained in the topmost turrets of candycane castles of intertwisting tourmaline and olivine, half-veiled by the clinging whiteness. Billy saved a princess the second or third time he came to the fallen country.

They were swooping down from where the sun should have shone, and Billy saw the castle, a forest of ice-caked spires, mist-shrouded, dull gray in the unchanging cold light of the fallen country.

"Time to rescue a princess!" said the dragon.

They circled the tower, for a minute Billy reveled in the rushing of the wing-made wind. The dragon's flight was a dance that almost seemed like joy. But when Billy asked the dragon, "Are you happy, Snow Dragon? Has my coming done this to you, then?" the dragon's swooping seemed to lose its passion.

The dragon said, "Now, Billy, isn't rescuing princesses one of the oldest compulsions of your world? Isn't it what every earth creature longs to do?"

"I wouldn't know," said Billy, who didn't always do too well in school, and did not know of such things as myths. "Where's the princess?"

"In the castle, of course. And now—" they were skimming the turret's edge, almost, and the windrush had become still—"you must do what you know best how to do."

"I don't know what you mean!"

"Your anger, Billy . . ."

And Billy understood, then, what he was capable of doing. He took the anger inside him, he thought of Pete and of terrible nights lying awake and burning for vengeance, he concentrated all this anger until it took shape, took form . . . a bridge sprang up where the dragon had hovered, clawing the emptiness—a bridge of thin ice, as though someone had sliced up a skating rink and slung it into the sky. The bridge ran all the way to a round window, gaping with serrations like a monster's mouth, at the top of the tower. Billy sprang lightly from the dragon's back. He looked down for a moment, thinking *I should be scared but I'm not, I'm too angry.*

Beneath him the whiteness stretched limitlessly. He could not be scared; you could not gauge the distance of things at all, the ground seemed cushiony-soft, not a death-trap at all. He took a couple of steps on the bridge. It was slippery. He looked at the dark yawning jaws of the window, feeling no fear, fueled instead by his terrible anger, and he began walking.

He leapt gingerly from the bridge into the room; he expected it to be dark but it was lit by the same depressing sourceless light that illuminated the world outside. The princess was chained to the wall. He closed his eyes and shattered the chains with a swift spurt of anger, and the princess came towards him. She was a typical blonde, boyish, unvoluptuous princess like the ones in Disney cartoons, with kohl-darkened eyelashes fluttering over expressionless glittering eyes that seemed almost faceted like an insect's. She did not smile, but walked towards him stiffly and thanked him.

"That's all I get?" he said.

"What did you expect?" said the princess. Her voice was like the dragon's voice: thin, toneless, uninterested.

"But I expected—"

The princess laughed. "Expected what? Something strange and beautiful and romantic? How can that be, with *him* up there, watching, watching? He'll catch me again, don't you fret."

I want to kill him!

"I know you want to kill him," the princess said, seeming to read his mind. "But you won't, you know. He is more real than you will ever be."

And then she stepped out of the window and left him stranded; for the bridge was gone, melted into the air. And it was because he had lain aside his anger for a moment.

"That's how I ended up on top of the church," Billy told me. But how could I believe such a thing? And yet it was so neat, so cleverly paradigmaticized. That the real world and the fantasy should have such interfaces of confluence: the church, the castle. Piety and passion, authority and rebellion, father-shadow and princess-anima, superego and id. An amateur analyst's dream.

I said to Billy, "Let's work together now, you and I. Let's come out of the fallen country into the real world, let's fight this inner grief of yours." The words sounded so false. They *were* false.

"You know what he told me?" said Billy. "The Snow Dragon, I mean."

"What?"

"He told me that I would never have to leave if I didn't want to."

That bastard Pete! But it's people like him who pay my rent. I too am a vampire, feeding myself on children's emotions. Would Billy understand, if I told him, how we all have a piece of Pete inside us?

Billy said, "Our time's up, Mrs. Marx."

"Wait a moment—" I had no business going on longer than the allotted time. "Billy, won't you stop and just let me help?"

He paused at the door. We confronted each other for a moment, an innocent child who daily harrowed hell and a middle-aged, middle-class, middle-grade couosellor jaded with trivialities who must supposedly know all the answers. His face was trusting. He was a pathological liar, a liar of frightening vividness, but all I saw was a frightened kid who yearned for something I did not have to give. He said, "How can I let you help me if you won't even believe me?"

I said—I couldn't lie, even to reassure him—"No, I don't believe you."

"But until you believe me, Mrs. Marx, we'll never get anywhere."

To my surprise I found myself longing to agree with him.

When I looked up he was gone. I saw that carefully, methodically, I had been shredding his file with my fingernails. Hating the sunlight, I found myself walking through the schoolyard, wishing it would snow.

I live in a luxury condominium—there are dozens such in our town—where children cannot come. There the old people hide. There I am protected from the nightmares that I must face every day.

Usually I do not remember any dreams; but that night— the fourth week of Billy's visits with me—I do remember things: dragons' wings, leathery, hung with icicles . . . Did my father ever beat me? I couldn't even remember, damn it!

Waking up. Outside—a hurricane building up? Beating of giant wings?

I sat up on the bed. Through the mosquito netting of the open window I heard night-sounds, insects, the ocean hidden by a dozen Hiltons and Ramada Inns. I thought of calling Pop, whom I hadn't thought about in years, but I knew it was too late to patch up my life now—

There was a knock on the door.

Not the buzzer, not the little loudspeaker I use to force strangers to admit that they came in peace. I did not move. It came again, and then that voice, that heart-wringing voice: "I'm cold, Mrs. Marx."

Children may not enter this domain.

How had he gotten past the security? Unless he had just materialized, like in his stories . . . I pulled on a bathrobe and went, through the dusty little living room, to the door, opened it—

He collapsed into my arms. It was like . . . when I was a kid, hugging a snowman. "For God's sake, Billy."

"I killed a monster today!" His voice frail, defiant. "But now I'm ready for *him!*"

"Don't try to attack Pete, he's too strong for you—"

"Pete? Screw Pete. I mean *him.*"

He's going into fugue. Got to keep him here, got to keep him warm, or God knows what he'll try—

"Look at me, you bitch!" He ripped his teeshirt open. I saw blood. I saw scars. I saw blue bruises. Red, white and blue, like the goddamn American flag. But his eyes were dry. And blazing. "Now try to believe. You're all I have, Mrs. Marx. I'm going back like the Snow Dragon says, maybe forever. Or until I kill the Ringmaster."

"No!" I tried to hold on to him, but he twisted away from me. Somehow he had warmed up, as though the very fever of his anger could melt away the cold. I knew how unbearable the real world was, I knew the cold hard beauty of his imaginary one, but I couldn't let him run away from reality, I couldn't let him hide inside himself, I was conditioned to helping the children face the truth—

"Believe me!" he shouted. "Come with me!"

Grasping at straws, "All right. All right." Quickly I was pulling on an old dress, not caring that he could see my sagging breasts—we had come too close for modesty now—I was shepherding him out of the door, down the steps, into the car, thinking *Hospital, doctor, shrink, anything, just anything . . .*

I am ashamed to admit that I was also afraid that seeing me walking through the condo grounds at midnight would jeopardize my rental agreement, would force me out of my own fallen country.

As we pulled out onto the highway, it began to snow.

I panicked, fumbling for the wipers. Billy watched me solemnly, with a kind of I-told-you-so superiority. The snow grew from powder-fluffy to blizzard sheets; I stomped on the accelerator and slithered, I couldn't see the road at all.

"I knew it," Billy was saying softly, "I knew you had it in you to come with me."

He understands, I thought suddenly. *About my secret fears, about the pain I think I hide so successfully. And all the while I thought I was taking the lead.* We ploughed through the thick whiteness, until—

I stalled out. I pushed hard on the door handle, cursing old clunkers. When I got the door open the snow flew in, whipping my face and flooding the car floor with chalky ice.

"Out of the car now," Billy said.

"We'll freeze!" I didn't want to lose control of the fantasy, didn't want to relinquish myself into the hands of a demented kid.

"No we won't," he said firmly. He scooted over me, a bony breadcrust of a boy, and then he was walking out into the billowing whiteness, was striding, oblivious to the cold, had become a gray shadowghost streaked with white.

I tried to remember the things he'd told me. *Be angry!* I

told myself. *Anger will warm you.*

Why didn't I pinch myself? Why didn't I think I was going mad? I must have known all along, the realness of Billy's fantasy must have touched me all along. . . .

I followed the kid cautiously. Soon I too felt nothing. The wind lashed my face and I could have been in a shopping mall buying shoes. I called out the kid's name but he was too intent to answer. I fell into the fallen country's strange detachment; it lured me, it drugged my pain, I knew that I could live there forever.

The snow whirled around me and I saw nothing but eye-smarting toothpaste commercial dazzlewhite, and then, through the burning white, two pinpoints of blue fire.

The Snow Dragon!

The storm subsided a little. There he hovered. I watched him, believing in him completely. The wings were not leathery—my nightmares had lied to me—but like a thousand layers of crystal-stitched gauze. He landed, shook a snowdrift from his back—whiteness peppering whiteness—and I saw the sky open and the whip crack and I saw the blood trickle down him, and he did not even tense in pain. I called his name, "Snow Dragon."

"You have brought another one?" The dragon spoke only to Billy. I was here only as an observer, then.

"She's been hurt, too, Snow Dragon! Only she doesn't see it; sometimes she hides it too well."

"You are back too soon. Something is wrong with things. The fallen country is all disordered."

"This time I've come to kill him!"

"You cannot kill him." He sounded resigned. "You haven't energy enough."

"I *am* energy enough! She's seen! She can tell you!"

The dragon seemed not to hear. The wing came down, lashing the snow and making it dance for a moment. Without hesitating Billy leapt up. I followed, searching in vain for my fear.

And then we broke through the thick mist, and still there was no sunlight, only a kind of gray clarity in the air. I sat hunched into a ridge on the dragon's spine, my shapeless blotchy dress fluttering a little. I saw the castles blanketed with white; I saw the distant ice-sea, the snow-forts ringing the snow-hills.

"My bridge of anger," Billy said. His voice did not waver. The dragon circled slowly. I felt the kind of unease you feel on a plane in a holding pattern, but only for a second; then I felt nothing again. It was good to feel nothing.

Billy stood. The dragon braked in mid-air, an eerie, weightless feeling. And then Billy began to dream his bridge into being.

At first nothing. Then the whip, cracking in the sky, over and over, the dragon shivering himself into stillness as though concentrating the pain deep inside himself, and I was sitting in fast-hardening purple blood, and the dragon's breath came harder, clouding the chill wind. And as the cloud cleared I saw that a bridge was growing in the air, a suspension bridge with great columns of ice sprouting up from the mistiness below, pathway of living ice, thrusting in a rainbow-curve across the sky, reaching for the crack in the sky where the whip still cracked, from which great thunder-howls of laughter burst forth now, shrieks of a blood-lusty crowd.

The bridge hung there. Girders, rainbow-fringed from the sourceless light, a boy-wide road that thinned in the distance into a point.

"Your anger," the dragon said, "you are exhausting your anger, see, it will soon be gone, Billy Binder."

"Never!" the boy cried resolutely. "Only when he dies, *that'll* kill my anger, only that." He stepped out onto the ice. Again I felt a second's anxiety, and then the fallen country's spell drug-dragged it from me.

"Let me come too!" I yelled after him. Already he was tiny in the distance. Space and time seemed to work differently in this country. An adventuress now, this old woman who had made nothing of her life, I ran after him, my low-heels clicking like castanets on the thin ice. I had to be with him. I was angry too, angry because of all the times I'd listened to the kids and done nothing while they bawled their guts out onto the floor of my little office. I was going to kill one child abuser in my lifetime! I was going to crush this dream-Pete that Billy had created, to throttle him to death with my twenty years of rage! Already I felt my fury fueling the bridge, making it firmer, easier to run on.

I was getting tired fast. But Billy still ran ahead, relentless as a wind. With a burst of anger I caught up with him, we ran neck and neck for a moment, and I saw that he wasn't even tired yet, and I knew I was wrong to think I could help or that I had anger enough in me—I who had never been hurt like that, who experienced the hurt only vicariously. The bridge soared up, steep in the strange foreshortening, and now even Billy was gasping. Then I was lurching forward, seeing the bridge telescope contact between my eyes, seeing the splitting sky.

A circus tent now, walls of flapping canvas painted sun moon stars shivering sheep-cloudlets, floors of mist-steaming packed snow, countless rings where bone-bare children leapt through fire-hoops, their faces tense with terror, frightened seals with planets whirling on their noses, scared to drop them, elephants trampling with earthquake feet, toppling skyscraper building-blocks, trumpeting thunderstorms. . . .

I stood there, panting, exhausted, couldn't take anything in. But Billy . . . he strode through the chaos, single-minded, seeking the center of things. And then I saw him, a little man with a whip, and he was dancing as he waved the whip, his eyes were as cold and expressionless as tundra-snow that has never thawed. And I knew his face. My face, Pete's face, even Billy's face, a template of human faces, always changing. I even saw Pop. I swear it, even Pop . . . Pop whom I couldn't remember beating me, until tonight.

The Ringmaster bowed to the audience. The cacklebuzz that had been a constant background, soft-brush percussion to the raucous band music, died down. He spoke very quietly. I recognized a little of Snow Dragon in his voice, and I was chilled by it.

The Ringmaster stepped out of his ring. He advanced towards Billy; again I saw that I was being ignored, that I was a watcher in another's confrontation, that I might as well have been sitting at the desk in the office listening to the screaming children in the yard.

The Ringmaster cracked his whip. Once. Worlds whirled! Children leapt! Blood spattered the sand! And then, like clockwork winding down, they sank into slow motion.

"You came, Billy Binder," said the Ringmaster. "I've been expecting you."

"You bastard!" Billy cried. "But I'm strong enough to get you!" Laughter echoed from the stands; I spun round to watch, and I saw that they all had his face, his face that was also mine and Billy's and Pop's and everyone else's, and they all laughed in unison, as though animated by a single hand.

"So come and get me!"

Billy reached out with his rage, a fireball burning tracks in the snow. I saw grass for a split second.

"You've got it all wrong!" the Ringmaster said. "You haven't come here to kill me at all! I sent for you. I bred you to be another shadow, another Ringmaster even—that's how you were able to find me. I granted you this gift of anger so you could build a way to me."

"No!" he shrieked.

"A shadow of my shadow," said the Ringmaster, raising his whip but never his voice, "You too are to become a shadow of my shadow, like Pete, like all the others.

"Billy, Billy . . ." the Ringmaster said. "You could be just like me, I have no pain, I only *give* pain now; I've been freed . . . Hate me, Billy. Hate me! Your anger only makes me greater, only binds you more to me! For you are my son, Billy Binder; be free, Billy, be free, like me . . ."

Billy stood, catapulting firedarts of anger, and the Ringmaster absorbed them all and grew tall, and snow-tempests swept around him, blurring him. Once I tried to step in, to add to Billy's store of rage, but I was frozen to the floor of snow.

The Ringmaster went on, "Oh, Billy, how can you turn your back on this? We are alike, you and I. You too can wield the whip and make a thousand universes dance with pain, and never feel the pain yourself."

"I'll never be like you! Never never never—" Billy screamed, and then I saw a final blast of rage explode from him and the canvas wall split open for a moment and I saw for an instant another whip, and another face of another Ringmaster up in the sky above us, and behind him another and another.

Then I looked at Billy, saw him shrunken, spent, the anger burned from him. I looked at the Ringmaster, panicking, thinking: *We're stranded here now, we'll never get back to the real world; we'll stay and rescue princesses and fight monsters and see the princesses get recaptured and the monsters get reborn, for ever and ever.*

I began to yell hysterically at the Ringmaster. He stood for everything I'd ever been angry about. I shouted: "I hate you! There's no reason for you to be; you're senseless, you screw up the whole universe!"

But Billy said, very quietly, "I don't have any anger left." And the Ringmaster's face grew pale, and he said, "But you *must* hate me! I bred you to hate me! I followed you and beat the hatred into you . . ."

Billy turned and spoke to me at last. "Don't you see?" he said. "I could have been like that. He's not the real Ringmaster at all. You glimpsed it, didn't you? I was so angry that I opened up . . . another country, the fallen country behind the fallen country, and I saw that the Ringmaster was only a shadow himself, that he danced to the whip of a higher ringmaster . . . How can I hate him?"

"Don't . . ." the Ringmaster said. I saw anguish cross his face for the first time. Or maybe I was just imagining it. It was only for a second.

Deliberately, quietly, Billy turned his back on him.

I followed the boy like an idiot. The dragon waited by the bridge, the bridge was already dissipating into mist, the dismal, cold light was brightening into sunlight, and—

By the car, patches of green.

Billy said to the dragon, "It's true, isn't it? What he said. That he's my father."

The dragon said nothing. I knew, though, that he did not disagree. And then Billy said, "It's strange, isn't it, how he plants in all his kids a little shred of something . . . that could destroy him, like he was dancing for his Ringmaster and secretly working to sabotage him at the same time."

The dragon said, "I too am part of the shadow, Billy, the part that seeks the shadow's own death, the left hand that does what the right hand dares not know about. You have killed us both: him by your compassion, me by compelling me to feel love for you . . .

"The snow is melting. The fallen country will be closed to you now." He did not speak again, but uttered a roar that rent the sky as sunlight broke the cloud-veils, a cry both of heartache and of joy, and he spread his wings and soared upwards with a heart-stopping whistlerush of wind. And then he was gone, disintegrated like a windgust, like a dream, like a half-stirred memory.

There was the car. I drove like a madwoman, churning up snow, bursting suddenly into the known world of concrete roads and forests of hotels and condominiums bleached lifeless by loneliness—

Police sirens! Lights! "The house!" Billy cried. We rounded a turn, he sprang out and sprinted towards the house, red blur of revolving sirens everywhere, swirling . . . We watched, silently. They brought Joan out, shaking, and then a stretcher, a covered one. I heard the onlookers muttering, looking curiously at Billy, avoiding his eyes, heard them say how Pete had gone crazy and just gone and crashed his motorbike into the house.

"*I* killed him," Billy said softly, for me alone. And I believed him. For he had found the way into Pete's soul, and in understanding it, in giving it peace, had destroyed it. The inner and outer worlds are congruent in a thousand places. Wherever we stand, we are within a hair's breadth of the fallen country.

Billy had understood things which I had never understood, I, whose job was understanding. I'd been so sure of myself, coaxing traumas out of children, beating on their little minds until they danced out their pain for me in my office. But where was *my* peace? My suffering was trivial, and so was my reward—to be beset by little things only, to be a watcher, not one who can compress the shadow-substance of her dreams until they become diamond-hard, like truth.

I moved closer to him, trying irrationally to shield him from the screaming sirens. Quietly, but openly, without shame, he had begun to cry.

If only we could wear our griefs as lightly as the snow wears the sneakerprints of children's dreams.

I went closer to him, almost touching him now, and began to do what I am trained to do. At first no words would come. *Damn it, Dora Marx,* I thought. *Who has stolen your roar?* I groped—

"Sure," I murmured. "Sure." I wondered if he would flinch if I tried to hug him.

Small Dragon

I've found a small dragon in the woodshed.
Think it must have come from deep inside a forest
because it's damp and green and leaves
are still reflecting in its eyes.

I fed it on many things, tried grass,
the roots of stars, hazel-nut and dandelion,
but it stared up at me as if to say, I need
foods you can't provide.

It made a nest among the coal,
not unlike a bird's but larger,
it is out of place here
and is quite silent.

If you believed in it I would come
hurrying to your house to let you share my wonder,
but I want instead to see
if you yourself will pass this way.

—Brian Patten

The Twelve Dancing Princesses

If you danced from midnight
to six A.M. who would understand?

The runaway boy
who chucks it all
to live on the Boston Common
on speed and saltines,
pissing in the duck pond,
rapping with the street priest,
trading talk like blows,
another missing person,
would understand.

The paralytic's wife
who takes her love to town,
sitting on the bar stool,
downing stingers and peanuts,
singing "That ole Ace down in the hole,"
would understand.

The passengers
from Boston to Paris
watching the movie with dawn
coming up like statues of honey,
having partaken of champagne and steak
while the world turned like a toy globe,
those murderers of the nightgown
would understand.

The amnesiac
who tunes into a new neighborhood,
having misplaced the past,
having thrown out someone else's
credit cards and monogrammed watch,
would understand.

The drunken poet
(a genius by daylight)
who places long-distance calls
at three A.M. and then lets you sit
holding the phone while he vomits
(he calls it "The Night of the Long Knives")
getting his kicks out of the death call,
would understand.

The insomniac
listening to his heart
thumping like a June bug,
listening on his transistor
to Long John Nebel arguing from New York,
lying on his bed like a stone table,
would understand.

The night nurse
with her eyes slit like Venetian blinds,
she of the tubes and the plasma,
listening to the heart monitor,
the death cricket bleeping,
she who calls you "we"
and keeps vigil like a ballistic missile,
would understand.

Once
this king had twelve daughters,
each more beautiful than the other.
They slept together, bed by bed
in a kind of girls' dormitory.
At night the king locked and bolted the door
How could they possibly escape?
Yet each morning their shoes
were danced to pieces.
Each was as worn as an old jockstrap.
The king sent out a proclamation
that anyone who could discover
where the princesses did their dancing
could take his pick of the litter.
However there was a catch.
If he failed, he would pay with his life.
Well, so it goes.

Many princes tried,
each sitting outside the dormitory,
the door ajar so he could observe
what enchantment came over the shoes.
But each time the twelve dancing princesses
gave the snoopy man a Mickey Finn
and so he was beheaded.
Poof! Like a basketball.

It so happened that a poor soldier
heard about these strange goings on
and decided to give it a try.
On his way to the castle
he met an old old woman.

Age, for a change, was of some use.
She wasn't stuffed in a nursing home.
She told him not to drink a drop of wine
and gave him a cloak that would make
him invisible when the right time came.
And thus he sat outside the dorm.
The oldest princess brought him some wine
but he fastened a sponge beneath his chin,
looking the opposite of Andy Gump.

The sponge soaked up the wine,
and thus he stayed awake.
He feigned sleep however
and the princesses sprang out of their beds
and fussed around like a Miss America Contest.
Then the eldest went to her bed
and knocked upon it and it sank into the earth.
They descended down the opening
one after the other. The crafty soldier
put on his invisible cloak and followed.
Yikes, said the youngest daughter,
something just stepped on my dress.
But the oldest thought it just a nail.

Next stood an avenue of trees.
each leaf made of sterling silver.
The soldier took a leaf for proof.
The youngest heard the branch break
and said, Oof! Who goes there?
But the oldest said, Those are
the royal trumpets playing triumphantly.
The next trees were made of diamonds.

He took one that flickered like Tinkerbell
and the youngest said: Wait up! He is here!
But the oldest said: Trumpets, my dear.

Next they came to a lake where lay
twelve boats with twelve enchanted princes
waiting to row them to the underground castle.
The soldier sat in the youngest's boat
and the boat was as heavy as if an icebox
had been added but the prince did not suspect.

Next came the ball where the shoes did duty.
The princesses danced like taxi girls at Roseland
as if those tickets would run right out.
They were painted in kisses with their secret hair
and though the soldier drank from their cups
they drank down their youth with nary a thought.

Cruets of champagne and cups full of rubies.
They danced until morning and the sun came up
naked and angry and so they returned
by the same strange route. The soldier
went forward through the dormitory and into
his waiting chair to feign his druggy sleep.
That morning the soldier, his eyes fiery
like blood in a wound, his purpose brutal
as if facing a battle, hurried with his answer
as if to the Sphinx. The shoes! The shoes!
The soldier told. He brought forth
the silver leaf, the diamond the size of a plum.

He had won. The dancing shoes would dance
no more. The princesses were torn from
their night life like a baby from its pacifier.
Because he was old he picked the eldest.
At the wedding the princesses averted their eyes
and sagged like old sweatshirts.
Now the runaways would run no more and never
again would their hair be tangled into diamonds,
never again their shoes worn down to a laugh,
never the bed falling down into purgatory
to let them climb in after
with their Lucifier kicking.

—Anne Sexton

The Courtship of Mr. Lyon

Angela Carter

Outside her kitchen window, the hedgerow glistened as
if the snow possessed a light of its own; when the sky
darkened towards evening, an unearthly, reflected pallor
remained behind upon the winter's landscape, while still
the soft flakes floated down. This lovely girl, whose skin
possesses that same inner light so you would have thought
she, too, was made all of snow, pauses in her chores in the
mean kitchen to look out at the country road. Nothing has
passed that way all day; the road is white and unmarked as
a spilled bolt of bridal satin.

Father said he would be home before nightfall.

The snow brought down all the telephone wires; he
couldn't have called, even with the best of news.

The roads are bad. I hope he'll be safe.

But the old car stuck fast in a rut, wouldn't budge an
inch; the engine whirred, coughed and died and he was far
from home. Ruined once; then ruined again, as he had
learned from his lawyers that very morning; at the conclu-
sion of the lengthy, slow attempt to restore his fortunes, he
had turned out his pockets to find the cash for petrol to take
him home. And not even enough money left over to buy
his Beauty, his girl child, his pet, the one white rose she said
she wanted; the only gift she wanted, no matter how the
case went, how rich he might once again be. She had
asked for so little and he had not been able to give it to her.
He cursed the useless car, the last straw that broke his
spirit; then, nothing for it but to fasten his old sheepskin
coat around him, abandon the heap of metal and set off
down the snow-filled lane to look for help.

Behind wrought-iron gates, a short, snowy drive performed a reticent flourish before a miniature, perfect, Pal-
ladian house that seemed to hide itself shyly behind snow-
laden skirts of an antique cypress. It was almost night; that

house, with its sweet, retiring, melancholy grace, would have seemed deserted but for a light that flickered in an upstairs window, so vague it might have been the reflection of a star, if any stars could have penetrated the snow that whirled yet more thickly. Chilled through, he pressed the latch of the gate and saw, with a pang, how, on the withered ghost of a tangle of thorns, there clung, still, the faded rag of a white rose.

The gate clanged loudly shut behind him; too loudly. For an instant, that reverberating clang seemed final, emphatic, ominous, as if the gate, now closed, barred all within it from the world outside the walled, wintry garden. And, from a distance, though from what distance he could not tell, he heard the most singular sound in the world: a great roaring, as of a beast of prey.

In too much need to allow himself to be intimidated, he squared up to the mahogany door. This door was equipped with a knocker in the shape of a lion's head, with a ring through the nose; as he raised his hand towards it, it came to him this lion's head was not, as he had thought at first, made of brass, but, instead, of solid gold. Before, however, he could announce his presence, the door swung silently inward on well-oiled hinges and he saw a white hall where the candles of a great chandelier cast their benign light upon so many, many flowers in great, freestanding jars of crystal that it seemed the whole of spring drew him into its warmth with a profound intake of perfumed breath. Yet there was no living person in the hall.

The door behind him closed as silently as it had opened, yet, this time, he felt no fear although he knew by the pervasive atmosphere of a suspension of reality that he had entered a place of privilege where all the laws of the world he knew need not necessarily apply, for the very rich are often very eccentric and the house was plainly that of an exceedingly wealthy man. As it was, when nobody came to help him with his coat, he took it off himself. At that, the crystals of the chandelier tinkled a little, as if emitting a pleased chuckle, and the door of a cloakroom opened of its own accord. There were, however, no clothes at all in this cloakroom, not even the statutory country-house garden mackintosh to greet his own squirearchal sheepskin, but when he emerged again into the hall, he found a greeting waiting for him at last—there was, of all things, a liver-and-white King Charles spaniel crouched, with head intelligently cocked, on the Kelim runner. It gave him further, comforting proof of his unseen host's wealth and eccentricity to see the dog wore, in place of a collar, a diamond necklace.

The dog sprang to its feet in welcome and busily shepherded him (how amusing!) to a snug little leather-paneled study on the first floor, where a low table was drawn up to a roaring log fire. On the table, a silver tray; round the neck of the whisky decanter, a silver tag with the legend *Drink me,* while the cover of the silver dish was engraved with the exhortation *Eat me,* in a flowing hand. This dish contained sandwiches of thick-cut roast beef, still bloody. He drank the one with soda and ate the other with some excellent mustard thoughtfully provided in a stoneware pot, and when the spaniel saw to it he had served himself, she trotted off about her own business.

All that remained to make Beauty's father entirely comfortable was to find, in a curtained recess, not only a telephone, but the card of a garage that advertised a twenty-four-hour rescue service; a couple of calls later and he had confirmed, thank God, there was no serious trouble, only the car's age and the cold weather . . . . Could he pick it up from the village in an hour? And directions to the village, but half a mile away, were supplied, in a new tone of deference, as soon as he described the house from where he was calling.

And he was disconcerted but, in his impecunious circumstances, relieved to hear the bill would go on his hospitable if absent host's account; no question, assured the mechanic. It was the master's custom.

Time for another whisky as he tried, unsuccessfully, to call Beauty and tell her he would be late; but the lines were still down, although, miraculously, the storm had cleared as the moon rose and now a glance between the velvet curtains revealed a landscape as of ivory with an inlay of silver. Then the spaniel appeared again, with his hat in her careful mouth, prettily wagging her tail, as if to tell him it was time to be gone, that this magical hospitality was over.

As the door swung to behind him, he saw the lion's eyes were made of agate.

Great wreaths of snow now precariously curded the rose trees, and when he brushed against a stem on his way to the gate, a chill armful softly thudded to the ground to reveal, as if miraculously preserved beneath it, one last, single, perfect rose that might have been the last rose left living in all the white winter, and of so intense and yet delicate a fragrance it seemed to ring like a dulcimer on the frozen air.

How could his host, so mysterious, so kind, deny Beauty her present?

Not now distant but close at hand, close as that mahogany front door, rose a mighty, furious roaring; the garden seemed to hold its breath in apprehension. But still, because he loved his daughter, Beauty's father stole the rose.

At that, every window of the house blazed with furious light and a fugal baying, as of a pride of lions, introduced his host.

There is always a dignity about great bulk, an assertiveness, a quality of being more *there* than most of us are. The being who now confronted Beauty's father seemed to him, in his confusion, vaster than the house he owned, ponderous yet swift, and the moonlight glittered on his great, mazy head of hair, on the eyes green as agate, on the golden hairs of the great paws that grasped his shoulders so that their claws pierced the sheepskin as he shook him like an angry child shakes a doll.

This leonine apparition shook Beauty's father until his teeth rattled and then dropped him sprawling on his knees while the spaniel, darting from the open door, danced round them, yapping distractedly, like a lady at whose dinner party blows have been exchanged.

"My good fellow—" stammered Beauty's father; but the only response was a renewed roar.

"Good fellow? I am no good fellow! I am the Beast, and you must call me Beast, while I call you Thief!"

"Forgive me for robbing your garden, Beast!"

Head of a lion; mane and mighty paws of a lion; he reared on his hind legs like an angry lion yet wore a smoking jacket of dull red brocade and was the owner of that lovely house and the low hills that cupped it.

"It was for my daughter," said Beauty's father. "All she wanted, in the whole world, was one white, perfect rose."

The Beast rudely snatched the photograph her father drew from his wallet and inspected it, first brusquely, then with a strange kind of wonder, almost the dawning of surmise. The camera had captured a certain look she had, sometimes, of absolute sweetness and absolute gravity, as if her eyes might pierce appearances and see your soul. When he handed the picture back, the Beast took good care not to scratch the surface with his claws.

"Take her her rose, then, but bring her to dinner," he growled; and what else was there to be done?

Although her father had told her of the nature of the one who waited for her, she could not control an instinctual shudder of fear when she saw him, for a lion is a lion and a man is a man, and though lions are more beautiful by far than we are, yet they belong to a different order of beauty and, besides, they have no respect for us; why should they? Yet wild things have a far more rational fear of us than is ours of them, and some kind of sadness in his agate eyes, that looked almost blind, as if sick of sight, moved her heart.

He sat, impassive as a figurehead, at the top of the table; the dining room was Queen Anne, tapestried, a gem. Apart from an aromatic soup kept hot over a spirit lamp, the food, though exquisite, was cold—a cold bird, a cold soufflé, cheese. He asked her father to serve them from a buffet and, himself, ate nothing. He grudgingly admitted what she had already guessed, that he disliked the presence of servants because, she thought, a constant human presence would remind him too bitterly of his otherness, but the spaniel sat at his feet throughout the meal, jumping up from time to time to see that everything was in order.

How strange he was. She found his bewildering difference from herself almost intolerable; its presence choked her. There seemed a heavy, soundless pressure upon her in his house, as if it lay under water, and when she saw the great paws lying on the arm of his chair, she thought: They are the death of any tender herbivore. And such a one she felt herself to be, Miss Lamb, spotless, sacrificial.

Yet she stayed, and smiled, because her father wanted her to do so; and when the Beast told her how he would aid her father's appeal against the judgment, she smiled with both her mouth and her eyes. But when, as they sipped their brandy, the Beast, in the diffuse, rumbling purr with which he conversed, suggested, with a hint of shyness, of fear of refusal, that she should stay here, with him, in comfort, while her father returned to London to take up the legal cudgels again, she forced a smile. For she knew with a pang of dread, as soon as he spoke, that it would be so and her visit to the Beast must be, on some magically reciprocal scale, the price of her father's good fortune.

Do not think she had no will of her own; only, she was possessed by a sense of obligation to an unusual degree and, besides, she would gladly have gone to the ends of the earth for her father, whom she loved dearly.

Her bedroom contained a marvelous glass bed; she had a bathroom, with towels thick as fleece and vials of suave unguents; and a little parlor of her own, the walls of which were covered with an antique paper of birds of paradise and Chinamen, where there were precious books and pictures and the flowers grown by invisible gardeners in the Beast's hothouses. Next morning, her father kissed her and drove away with a renewed hope about him that made her glad, but all the same, she longed for the shabby home of their poverty. The unaccustomed luxury about her she found poignant, because it gave no pleasure to its possessor, and himself she did not see all day as if, curious reversal, she frightened him, although the spaniel came and sat with her, to keep her company. Today the spaniel wore a neat choker of turquoises.

Who prepared her meals? Loneliness of the Beast; all the time she stayed there, she saw no evidence of another human presence but the trays of food that arrived on a dumbwaiter inside a mahogany cupboard in her parlor. Dinner was eggs Benedict and grilled veal; she ate it as she browsed in a book she had found in the rosewood revolving bookcase, a collection of courtly and elegant French fairy tales about white cats who were transformed princesses and fairies who were birds. Then she pulled a sprig of muscat grapes from a fat bunch for her dessert and found herself yawning; she discovered she was bored. At that, the spaniel took hold of her skirt with its velvet mouth and gave it a firm but gentle tug. She allowed the dog to trot before her to the study in which her father had been entertained and there, to her well-disguised dismay, she found her host, seated beside the fire with a tray of coffee at his elbow from which she must pour.

The voice that seemed to issue from a cave full of echoes, his dark, soft rumbling growl—after her day of pastel-colored idleness, how could she converse with the possessor of a voice that seemed an instrument created to inspire the terror that the chords of great organs bring? Fascinated, almost awed, she watched the firelight play on the gold fringes of his mane; he was irradiated, as if with a kind of halo, and she thought of the first great beast of the Apocalypse, the winged lion with his paw upon the Gospel, Saint Mark. Small talk turned to dust in her mouth; small talk had never, at the best of times, been Beauty's forte, and she had little practice at it.

But he, hesitantly, as if he himself were in awe of a young girl who looked as though she had been carved out of a single pearl, asked after her father's law case; and her dead mother; and how they, who had been so rich, had come to be so poor. He forced himself to master his shyness, which was that of a wild creature, and so she contrived to master her own—to such effect that soon she was chattering away to him as if she had known him all her life. When the little cupid in the gilt clock on the mantelpiece struck its miniature tambourine, she was astonished to discover it did so twelve times.

"So late! You will want to sleep," he said.

At that, they both fell silent, as if these strange companions were suddenly overcome with embarrassment to find themselves together, alone, in that room in the depths of the winter's night. As she was about to rise, he flung himself at her feet and buried his head in her lap. She stayed stock-still, transfixed; she felt his hot breath on her fingers, the stiff bristles of his muzzle grazing her skin, the rough lapping of his tongue, and then, with a flood of compassion, understood: All he is doing is kissing my hands.

He drew back his head and gazed at her with his green, inscrutable eyes, in which she saw her face repeated twice, as small as if it were in bud. Then, without another word, he sprang from the room and she saw, with an indescribable shock, he went on all fours.

Next day, all day, the hills on which the snow still settled echoed with the Beast's rumbling roar. Has master gone a-hunting? Beauty asked the spaniel. But the spaniel growled, almost bad-temperedly, as if to say that she would not have answered, even if she could have.

Beauty would pass the day in her suite reading or, perhaps, doing a little embroidery; a box of colored silks and a frame had been provided for her. Or, well wrapped up, she wandered in the walled garden, among the leafless roses, with the spaniel at her heels, and did a little raking and rearranging. An idle, restful time; a holiday. The enchantment of that bright, sad, pretty place enveloped her and she found that, against all her expectations, she was happy there. She no longer felt the slightest apprehension at her nightly interviews with the Beast. All the natural laws of the world were held in suspension here, where an army of invisibles tenderly waited on her, and she would talk with the lion, under the patient chaperonage of the brown-eyed dog, on the nature of the moon and its borrowed light, about the stars and the substances of which they were made, about the variable transformations of the weather. Yet still his strangeness made her shiver; and when he helplessly fell before her to kiss her hands, as he did every night when they parted, she would retreat nervously into her skin, flinching at his touch.

The telephone shrilled; for her. Her father. Such news!

The Beast sunk his great head on his paws. You will come back to me? It will be lonely here, without you.

She was moved almost to tears that he should care for her so. It was in her heart to drop a kiss upon his shaggy mane, but though she stretched out her hand towards him, she could not bring herself to touch him of her own free will, he was so different from herself. But, yes, she said; I will come back. Soon, before the winter is over. Then the taxi came and took her away.

You are never at the mercy of the elements in London, where the huddled warmth of humanity melts the snow before it has time to settle; and her father was as good as rich again, since his hirsute friend's lawyers had the business so well in hand that his credit brought them nothing but the best. A resplendent hotel; the opera, theaters; a whole new wardrobe for his darling, so she could step out on his arm to parties, to receptions, to restaurants, and life was as she had never known it, for her father had ruined himself before her birth killed her mother.

Although the Beast was the source of the new-found

prosperity and they talked of him often, now that they were so far away from the timeless spell of his house it seemed to possess the radiant and finite quality of dream and the Beast himself, so monstrous, so benign, some kind of spirit of good fortune who had smiled on them and let them go. She sent him flowers, white roses in return for the ones he had given her; and when she left the florist, she experienced a sudden sense of perfect freedom, as if she had just escaped from an unknown danger, had been grazed by the possibility of some change but, finally, left intact. Yet, with this exhilaration, a desolating emptiness. But her father was waiting for her at the hotel; they had planned a delicious expedition to buy her furs and she was as eager for the treat as any girl might be.

Since the flowers in the shop were the same all the year round, nothing in the window could tell her that winter had almost gone.

Returning late from supper after the theater, she took off her earrings in front of the mirror: Beauty. She smiled at herself with satisfaction. She was learning, at the end of her adolescence, how to be a spoiled child and that pearly skin of hers was plumping out, a little, with high living and compliments. A certain inwardness was beginning to transform the lines around her mouth, those signatures of the personality, and her sweetness and her gravity could sometimes turn a mite petulant when things went not quite as she wanted them to go. You could not have said that her freshness was fading, but she smiled at herself in mirrors a little too often these days, and the face that smiled back was not quite the one she had seen contained in the Beast's agate eyes. Her face was acquiring, instead of beauty, a lacquer of the invincible prettiness that characterizes certain pampered, exquisite, expensive cats.

The soft wind of spring breathed in from the nearby park through the open windows; she did not know why it made her want to cry.

There was a sudden, urgent, scrabbling sound, as of claws, at her door.

Her trance before the mirror broke; all at once, she remembered everything perfectly. Spring was here and she had broken her promise. Now the Beast himself had come in pursuit of her! First, she was frightened of his anger; then, mysteriously joyful, she ran to open the door. But it was his liver-and-white spotted spaniel who hurled herself into the girl's arms in a flurry of little barks and gruff murmurings, of whimpering and relief.

Yet where was the well-brushed, jeweled dog who had sat beside her embroidery frame in the parlor with birds of paradise nodding on the walls? This one's fringed ears were matted with mud, her coat was dusty and snarled, she was thin as a dog that has walked a long way, and if she had not been a dog, she would have been in tears.

After that first, rapturous greeting, she did not wait for Beauty to order her food and water; she seized the chiffon hem of her evening dress, whimpered and tugged. Threw back her head, howled, then tugged and whimpered again.

There was a slow, late train that would take her to the station where she had left for London three months ago. Beauty scribbled a note for her father, threw a coat round her shoulders. Quickly, quickly, urged the spaniel soundlessly; and Beauty knew the Beast was dying.

In the thick dark before dawn, the stationmaster roused a sleepy driver for her. Fast as you can.

It seemed December still possessed his garden. The ground was hard as iron, the skirts of the dark cypress moved on the chill wind with a mournful rustle and there were no green shoots on the roses, as if, this year, they would not bloom. And not one light in any of the windows, only, in the topmost attic, the faintest smear of radiance on a pane, the thin ghost of a light on the verge of extinction.

The spaniel had slept a little, in her arms, for the poor

thing was exhausted. But now her grieving agitation fed Beauty's urgency, and as the girl pushed open the front door, she saw, with a thrust of conscience, how the golden door knocker was thickly muffled in black crepe.

The door did not open silently, as before, but with a doleful groaning of the hinges and, this time, onto perfect darkness. Beauty clicked her gold cigarette lighter; the tapers in the chandelier had drowned in their own wax and the prisms were wreathed with drifting arabesques of cobwebs. The flowers in the glass jars were dead, as if nobody had had the heart to replace them after she was gone. Dust, everywhere; and it was cold. There was an air of exhaustion, of despair, in the house and, worse, a kind of physical disillusion, as if its glamour had been sustained by a cheap conjuring trick and now the conjurer, having failed to pull the crowds, had departed to try his luck elsewhere.

Beauty found a candle to light her way and followed the faithful spaniel up the staircase, past the study, past her suite, through a house echoing with desertion up a little back staircase dedicated to mice and spiders, stumbling, ripping the hem of her dress in her haste.

What a modest bedroom! An attic, with a sloping roof, they might have given the chambermaid if the Beast had employed staff. A night light on the mantelpiece, no curtains at the windows, no carpet on the floor and a narrow, iron bedstead on which he lay, sadly diminished, his bulk scarcely disturbing the faded patchwork quilt, his mane a grayish rat's nest and his eyes closed. On the stick-backed chair where his clothes had been thrown, the roses she had sent him were thrust into the jug from the washstand, but they were all dead.

The spaniel jumped up on the bed and burrowed her way under the scanty covers, softly keening.

"Oh, Beast," said Beauty. "I have come home."

His eyelids flickered. How was it she had never noticed before that his agate eyes were equipped with lids, like those of a man? Was it because she had only looked at her own face, reflected there?

"I'm dying, Beauty," he said in a cracked whisper of his former purr. "Since you left me, I have been sick. I could not go hunting. I found I had not the stomach to kill the gentle beasts, I could not eat. I am sick and I must die; but I shall die happy because you have come to say goodbye to me."

She flung herself upon him, so that the iron bedstead groaned, and covered his poor paws with her kisses.

"Don't die, Beast! If you'll have me, I'll never leave you."

When her lips touched the meat-hook claws, they drew back into their pads and she saw how he had always kept his fists clenched but now, painfully, tentatively, at last began to stretch his fingers. Her tears fell on his face like snow and, under their soft transformation, the bones showed through the pelt, the flesh through the wide, tawny brow. And then it was no longer a lion in her arms but a man, a man with an unkempt mane of hair and, how strange, a broken nose, such as the noses of retired boxers, that gave him a distant, heroic resemblance to the handsomest of all the beasts.

"Do you know," said Mr. Lyon, "I think I might be able to manage a little breakfast today. Beauty, if you would eat something with me."

Mr. and Mrs. Lyon walk in the garden; the old spaniel drowses on the grass, in a drift of fallen petals.

Lord of the Reedy River

She fell in love with a swan
Her eyes were filled with feathers
He filled her with song
in the reedy river

She in her boat long hours
He in his royal plumage
She threw him some flowers
in the reedy river

Black was the night and starry
She loosened up her garments
and let fall her hair
in the reedy river

Sadly they mourn and sigh
whilst in the evening twilight
two swans glide and fly
o'er the reedy river

—Donovan Leitch

In the Hall of Grief

Jane Yolen

I was thirteen summers, the last turning of childhood, when great-grandmother became ill. She was exiled upstairs to the windowless room under the thatch to practice lying in darkness. So it is with the very old whose lives are spent in dusk, just as newborns must learn to live in the dawn.

It was not great grandmother's illness that made me eligible to enter the Hall of Grief, but my own signs of adulthood: the small breasts just beginning to bud, the fine curlings of hair in the cave places of my body, the rush of fresh blood from the untested nest of my womb.

I was ready. Had I not spent many childhood hours playing at the Hall game? My sisters and brothers and I had built our own Halls of willow branch and alder snappings. We had decked the tables, made signs, drawn pictures. Always, always my table was best, though I was the youngest of us all. It had more than just an innocent beauty, decked in ribbons and bordered by wildflowers: red trillium for life, blue-black elderberry for death, and the twinings of green boughs for the passage between. No, my tables had a character that was both mine and the grieven one's. It had substance and imagination and daring, even from the time I was quite young. Everyone remarked on it. The other children sensed it. But the elders who came and watched us at our play, they knew for sure. I heard one say, overheard really, "She has a gift for grief, that one. Mark her well."

But even before that, I had known. As a child I had started crafting my own grief poems. The first aped the dirges and threnodies I had been taught, but always with a little twist of my own. One in particular I remember, for my parents shared it with the elders as a sign of my gift. It began:

> *I sail out on my dark ship*
> *Towards the unmarked shore*
> *With only the grievings*
> *Of my family to guide me.*
> *The ship breasts the waves . . .*

The dark ship, the unmarked shore, they were but copies of the usual metaphors of grief. But the wording of the fifth line, the *penta,* that foreshadowed the central image—that of a carved figurehead of a nude woman, something of which I should have had no knowledge for we were a people of the Middle Lands—convinced them all. I was a prodigy. I basked in their praises for weeks and tried hard to repeat my success. But that time I could not. It was years before I realized that, truly, I grieved best when trying for no effect at all, though the critics and the public did not always know the difference. But the craftswoman knows.

And then the day came when I was old enough to enter the Hall of Grief. I rose early and spent many minutes in front of the glass, the only one in the house not covered with the grey mourning cloth. I drew dark circles under my eyes and deep shades on my lids. Of course I overdid it. What new griever does not? I had yet to learn that true grief makes its own hollows in the face, a better sculptor of the body's contours than all our paints and pencils. Artifice should only heighten. But I was young, as I have said. And even great-grandmother in her dusky room was not enough to teach me then.

That first day I tried something daring. Even that first day my gift for invention showed. I painted my nails the color of my eyelids and, on the left hand, on the thumb, I took a penknife and scraped the paint on the thumbnail into a cross, to signify the bisecting of life and death. Yes, I see you understand. It was the beginning of the carvings I would later do on all my nails, the carvings that would become such a passion among young grievers and would be given my name. I never do it myself anymore. It seemed such a little thing then: some extra paint, an extra dab of darkness onto light. An instinctual gesture that others took, mistook, for genius. That is, after all, what genius is: a label for instinct.

I plaited my long dark hair with trillium and elderberry, too. And that was much less successful. As I recall, the trillium died before the morning was over, and the berries left my braids sticky with juice. But at the moment of leavetaking, when I went upstairs to give great-grandmother the respect I owed her, I felt the proper griever. And she turned in her bed, the one with the carvings of wreaths on the posters, the one in which all the women of our house have died. Then she looked at me with her luminous, half-dead eyes.

"You will make them remember me?" she asked.

"Great-grandmother, I will," I replied.

"May your lines of grieving be long," she said.

"May your time of dying be short," I answered. And the ritual was complete. I left, for I was far more interested in the Hall of Grief and my part in it then her actual moment of death, when the breath leaps from the mouth in a great upward sigh. That is a private moment, after all, though grieving is all done in public. Still, I know now that all our mourning, all our grieving, all the outward signs of our rituals are nothing compared to that one quick moment of release. Do I startle you with my heresy? It is an old woman's right.

I did not look back, but ran down the stairs and into the light. My mother and her mother walked with me to the Hall of Grief. And though we marched to the slow metronome of the funerary drums, my heart skipped before.

The Hall was even larger inside than I had dreamed. Great massive pillars with fluted columns and carved capitols held up the roof. I had seen the building from afar—for who had not—but had never been close enough to distinguish the carvings. They were appropriate to the Hall, weeping women with their long hair caught up in fanciful waterfalls. You laugh. Only in the countryside

could such banal motifs still be seen. It was a very minor
Hall to be sure. But to my eyes then it was magnificent,
each marble weeper a monument to grief. I drank it all in,
eager to be a part.

Inside the clans had already set up their tables, and
mother and grandmother threaded their way through the
chaos with an ease born of long experience to our usual
stand. Under the banner proclaiming our colors—we had
always been the Queen's own, even in our little
backwater—was a kidney-shaped table. It was littered with
the memoria of our dying ones. We had three that year, a
small number, counting great-grandmother in our attic. I
can still recite the birth lines of the other two: Cassania, of
Cassapina, of Cassuella, of Cassamerra was the one.
Peripia of Perrifona, of Persivalia, of Perdonia was the
other. And of course, in my own direct line, I can still go
back the twenty-one requisite names. We have no gap in
the line, of which I am still, though it sometimes makes me
laugh at myself, inordinately proud. I am the last, as you
know. No one grieves for me, no sister of the family, no
blood griever, and sometimes it still bothers me that this is
so, my own sisters having gone before when I was too
young to grieve for them.

The daughters of Cassania and Peripia were already
there, having no attic grievers of their own and no new
grievers to prepare for their first Hall. They had born only
boys. And my own three sisters had gone in the winter
sickness, leaving me the only hope of our clan. Our table
was piled high with pictographs, for this was before we had
learned to capture life-impressions with the photo-box of
the strangers. Changes come too quickly now that even
boys are taught to grieve.

Since Cassania's daughters were known for their fine
hand, there were many ornately-lettered lamentation
plaques on the table. But the table, for all its wealth of
memoria, was disordered, and that disturbed me greatly.

I spoke in an undertone to my mother. "May I be
allowed to arrange great-grandmother's part?"

She did not understand my distress at the disorder, taking my request as a display of eagerness. But I was still too young to do more than look. I had yet to apprentice to a griever, to one of my older cousins. I had only a meager background, the pretendings of a child with children, and brothers at that.

So I was sent away while the older women worked, sent off to look at the other tables in the Hall, to discover for myself the many stages and presentations of Grief.

The other tables were as disordered as our own for, as I have said, we were only a Minor Hall, and the grievers there unsophisticated in their arrangements. One or two had a rough feeling that I have since tried to replicate in my own work. Touching that old country grief has, I think, often given me my greatest successes.

To think of it, walking in a Hall before the days of the strangers for the first time. The sound of the mourners lining up in the galleries, waiting for the doors to open. Some of them actually wailed their distress, though in the Major Halls that rarely happens anymore. Except on great occasions of State: an exiled priestess, the assassination of a princess, a fallen Queen.

Inside the Hall, the grievers moved silently, setting up their tables and stalls. I remember one old woman lovingly polishing a spear, the symbol of the warrior her dying grand uncle had been. And another placing a harp with a broken string beneath the lamentation: *One last song, one final touch.* I have always liked the simplicity of that line, though the broken string was a bit overdone.

And then the doors were flung open, and the mourners came in. In the first crush, I lost sight of our own table, and was flung up against the wall. But soon the crowds sorted themselves, and I could see how the lines made a kind of pattern. There were long lines by the tables that gave away garlands and crying towels, though the longest by far was in front of the harper's stall where a live singer recalled in song all that had been great in the harper's life.

I learned two things that day, before ever apprenticing:

that to please the crowd and draw a line is easy, but to keep the lines coming back again and again and again is not. Once the garlands were gone and the towels all given away, once the singer stopped for a draught of wine, the line of mourners broke apart and formed again somewhere else. And none of the mourners remembered the grieven one's name for longer than that day, though some remembered the names of the grievers. There is no immortality in that.

By noon I had toured the entire Hall, carrying with me a wilted garland and three towels embroidered with names of grieven ones whose deeds I no longer recalled. And I came back again to the place I had begun, the stall of my own clan, piled high with memoria.

"Let me take a turn while you eat. It will be a slow time, now, while the funeral meats are set out," I told my aunts and my mother, my grandmother having gone home to get her mother's last meal. And because they thought I could do no harm then, they left me by myself at the table.

I busied myself at once, re-arranging the overwrought items in a new way so that the whole picture was one of restraint. And then I sat down and composed a threnody, the first of the ones recognizable in my so-called "Gray Wanderer" period because for the first time the figure of the cloaked soul-traveler appeared. I wrote quickly, much faster than I was to work in later years, the words tumbling over themselves. I have always had a facility which, at times, betrays me.

You know the poem, of course: *"The lines of her worn and gray cloak. . . ."* which scholars insist refer to the lines of mourning. I did not mean that, just that the cloak fell from her shoulders in comfortable, familiar folds. But never mind. The scholars seem to know more about such things than we grievers do. You smile. You have heard me say all this before. Do I, in my age, repeat myself endlessly? Well, what else is there to do, lying in darkness, but retrace the steps of light? Here I throw no shadows, but once my

shadow, the shadow of the Gray Wanderer, covered the
entire land.

I had just finished the writing of the threnody and was
tracing out the words onto a tablet, and it was slow going. I
had not the grace of my aunts' hands and each letter was
painstakingly drawn. You have such grace, and that is one
of the reasons why I kept you past your training. No, do not
blush, child, you know it is true. Do not confuse humility
with self-denial. You have an old hand grafted onto a
young arm. Not for you are the easy strangers' ways, the
machines that multiply machine-drawn letters. Hold to it.
Pass it on.

Yes, I drew the words slowly, and my hand faltered on a
phrase. Oh, the phrase was fine, but the lettering was
traitor to its truth. I was casting around for a scraper, when I
realized that someone was standing over me. I looked up
and it was a youth just past that blush of boyhood, when
the skin still has a lambent glow yet is covered with soft
down that has not yet coarsened into beard.

"I would have liked them," he said, nodding at the
memoria to my great-grandmother and great-great aunts.

It is the ritual opening, of course, the mildest approach to
an unknown grieven one. But somehow I sensed it was
sincerely meant, and though I answered with the words
that have been spoken already a million million times by
grievers, he knew my own sincerity in them.

"They would have grown by your friendship."

I scraped the linen free of the ink and finished the
threnody while he watched. Then I pulled it free of its
stretcher. The linen curled up at the edges just a bit, which
was what I had hoped. It meant that a reader had to flatten
it by hand and that way actually participate in the reading.

He took the time to read it, not once but several times.
And then he read it aloud. His voice had already changed,
and it was low and musical. He was in training for Queen's
Consort, you see. And in his mouth the words took on an
even more palpable sense of grief. A Singer can make a

song, you know.

Soon we were surrounded by the other table watchers.
He knew how to project his voice, and they had caught
phrases that had beckoned them, drawn them in.

And that was how my mother and my great-aunts found
us when they returned, with a long line of mourners standing by the table and all the other stalls empty, even of the
watchers. The mourners were saying with him, as he repeated the threnody yet one more time, the chorus which
is now so famous:

> Weep for the night that is coming,
> Weep for the day that is past.

Yes, it is simple. Every child knows it now, in the time of the
strangers. But I wrote it in a fever that day, when the
strangers were not even a dream, and I wove my great-
grandmother's name into the body of the poem that she
would not be forgotten. Her lines were long indeed. I was
glad to have done it that day, for she was dead when we
returned home, and already her husk had been set out on
the pyre and pylons for the birds of prey.

The next seven days we mourned upon the stage of the
Hall for our grieven one's passage to the world of everlast-
ing light. How my great-grandmother must have smiled at
her lines of mourning, for they lit her way through the dark
cave of death. Never had there been such lines in our
Minor Hall, except when General Verina died who had
been born in the town next but one to ours and whose
relatives numbered in the hundreds in the countryside.
And of course, I was told, the last Queen. I wrote three
more Gray Wanderer threnodies and one 32-verse dirge
which the harper set to a modal tune. The Hall throbbed
with it for days, though one can hear it only occasionally
now. It takes too long in the singing, and the strangers
brought with them a taste for short songs. But great-

grandmother has not been forgotten and I still have pride in it for I made it so.

After the seven days, it was incumbent upon my mother to find me a Master Griever among our clan though, by tradition, I should have had a year between my first entrance into a Hall and my formal apprenticeship. But even the elders had come to her as soon as the Seven was over and begged her to forgo that year. They even suggested seeking out some long connection in one of the coast towns, where gold flowed along the seashore. But we did not have the means to do such a thing.

That very day there came a knock at the door. I see you are ahead of me. Have I told this before? It was the singer, the one from the Hall. He had left after the first day, gone I had assumed to finish his young man's pilgrimage from Hall to Hall. It is part of the training, you know, singing in front of different mourners, learning *all* the ways of the land. But he had not gone on along his route. Instead he had doubled back and told the Queen herself what had happened in the Hall. It had taken him three days to get an audience with her, and a day for her to make up her mind. But at last she had said to him, "Bring me this Gray Wanderer, that I may see her for myself." And that, of course, was how I was named.

So I was brought before her, the Queen, from whose own body would spring the next rulers. Only she was girl-barren. Her many men plowed her, but there was no harvest. She had no girl children to grieve for her, only boys. And she did not know then that her bearing days were over and that her sister's girls would rule after her, to the great tragedy of our world. For those Queens invited in the strangers who brought with them the rule of men. But we did not know all that then, and she asked to see me out of curiosity.

I dressed, as was appropriate to my age and clan, in a simple long gray gown pricked through with red and black and green embroidery. I had done it myself, the trillium twined around the boughs with a sprinkling of elderberries along the hem. And my hair was plaited and pinned up on my head, a crown as simple as the Queen's was ornate. I was never any great beauty, but pride in bearing can make the difference. I held my head high.

She saw me and smiled. I was so young, she told me later, and so serious, she could not help it.

"Come, child," she said, leaning forward and holding out her hand.

I did not know any better and took her hand, oblivious to the mutterings around me. Then I leaned forward and whispered so that she alone could hear it. "Do not fear the dark, my lady, for I am sent to light your way."

It was not the speech I had practiced with my mother, nor yet the one I had made up along the way. But when I saw her, with the grief of all those girl-barren years sitting above her eyes, I knew why I had come. So I spoke those words, not for the applause of the court but for her alone. And because I did it that way, she knew I was speaking the truth.

She bade me sit by her feet. I was never to leave.

She asked to see my grief poems and I took the first of the Gray Wanderer ones from the carry-basket. They are in the museum now where only the scholars can read them but once they had been set out for anyone to see.

She read them with growing interest and called the Priestess to her.

"A child can lead the way," the Priestess said, cryptically. They always speak thus, I have found, leaving a leader many paths to choose from. Grievers and priestesses have this in common, I think, though they would claim True Knowledge and Infallibility while I can only speak in symbols what I feel here, here in the heart.

The Queen nodded and turned to me. "And can you make me another threnody? Now. Now, while I watch so that I can see that you made these without the promptings of your elders?"

"I have no one to grieve for, my Queen," I said.

She smiled.

In those days, remember, I was young and from a small village and a Minor Hall. I thought it was a pitying smile. I know better now. It was a smile of power.

Three days later word came that my grandmother had died. I had much to grieve for then. And though I was not allowed to go home to do my grieving, the Queen herself set me up at table in a Major Hall and on that stage, surrounded by sophisicated mourners, I began my public life. I wrote thirteen threnodies in the seven days and composed a master lament. My grief was fed by home-sickness; and I had those hardened mourners weeping within a day. The Queen herself had to take to bed out of grief for my grandmother.

The Queen called the best grievers in the land to teach me in relays after the Seven was up. And within the year I knew as much as they of the history of mourning, the structure of threnodies, and the composition of the dirge. I learned the Queen's birth lines to twice the twenty-one names, and the lines of her sisters as well. And once I had a prince as a lover, though I never bore a babe.

But there is a question in your eyes, child. Do not be afraid to ask. Wait, let me ask it for you. Did I regret the years of service to my queen when I learned she had had my grandmother slain? Child, you have lived too long under the influence of the strangers. One does not ques-tion a Queen. And my grandmother's lines were long, and full of royal mourners; her dying was short and without pain. Would that we could all start our journey that way.

It was proclaimed, then, that a Master Griever of the Queen's own choosing, not a birthrite griever, could mourn her and hers. It was the first change in a time full of change. Thus it was that I served the Queen and her sisters' children after, both the girls and now these weak, puling boy kings. It does not matter to the griever. We have always mourned for men and women alike, for do not we all have to take those final steps into the dark cave? But, oh the land mourns and has become as barren as my first

Queen. For who can tell which man is father when all men sow the same? Yet a woman in her time of ripening is each as different as a skilfully wrought dirge.

I know not if the land dies because of the kings or because of the strangers. They would have us wound the earth with our dead, and many follow them. But what does the earth want with our husks? And why set them down into a dark cave forever? Rather we must put them out above the earth, turning the dead eyes up towards the light.

Things change too quickly, my child. But remember, you promised me that you would set my husk out on the pyre and pylons we built together, hand on hand. Outside this cave, far from the strangers and their bright, short ways.

Here, I have set down a threnody of my own. The first Gray Wanderer I have composed in many years, and the last. I want you to start my mourning today with it. I know, I know. Such was never done before, that a griever should grieve for herself. But I have no child of my womb, no girl to call the lines, and even though you are my own chosen one, it is not the same. Besides, was the Gray Wanderer ever the same? Even in my own dying I must be different.

Bring me the last meal now, and the cup of sleep, for the pain is great today and my head swirls with darkness. It is time. And you will make them remember me, will you not?

Say it. Say it. Do not cry. Crying does not become a griever.

And may your lines of grieving be long.

Now, paint your eyelids, but lightly. Draw a cross on the darkened thumbnails. Pinch your cheeks. Good. And may your time of dying be short, too. Now go.

Magic Strings

The Witch pours her libation,
    and clouds gather in the sky;
In the jade brazier, flaming coals
    and fumes of incense throb.
Sea-gods and mountain nymphs
    all come to take up their seats.
Votive papers crackle, turn to ash,
    and dance in the whirlwind's howl.
She holds an inlaid lute of passionwood
    adorned with a gold dancing phoenix;
Knitting her brow to each muttered phrase,
    She plucks the strings.
She summons stars and demons:
    Come, enjoy the feast.
When goblins feed,
    mankind shudders.
The sun sinks behind the Chung-nan Mountains
And the gods are here, visible yet invisible,
    present between somewhere and nowhere.
Spasms on the Witch's face reflect
    their anger or their pleasure.
Then the gods, in myriad chariots, depart
    to go back to the blue mountains.

                —Li Ho
                    (arr. M. Arnold from
                    various translations.)

A
Tale
for
Children

The Handsomest Drowned Man in the World

Gabriel García Márquez

Translated by Gregory Rabassa

The first children who saw the dark and slimy bulge approaching through the sea let themselves think it was an enemy ship. Then they saw it had no flags or masts and they thought it was a whale. But when it washed up on the beach, they removed the clumps of seaweed, the jellyfish tentacles, and the remains of fish and floatsam, and only then did they see that it was a drowned man.

They had been playing with him all afternoon, burying him in the sand and digging him up again, when someone chanced to see them and spread the alarm in the village. The men who carried him to the nearest house noticed that he weighed more than any dead man they had ever known, almost as much as a horse, and they said to each other that maybe he'd been floating too long and the water had got into his bones. When they laid him on the floor they said he'd been taller than all other men because there was barely enough room for him in the house, but they thought that maybe the ability to keep on growing after death was part of the nature of certain drowned men. He had the smell of the sea about him and only his shape gave one to suppose that it was the corpse of a human being, because the skin was covered with a crust of mud and scales.

They did not even have to clean off his face to know that the dead man was a stranger. The village was made up of only twenty-odd wooden houses that had stone courtyards with no flowers and which were spread about on the end of a desertlike cape. There was so little land that mothers always went about with the fear that the wind would carry off their children and the few dead that the years had caused among them had to be thrown off the cliffs. But the sea was calm and bountiful and all the men fit into seven boats. So when they found the drowned man they simply had to look at one another to see that they were all there.

That night they did not go out to work at sea. While the men went to find out if anyone was missing in neighboring villages, the women stayed behind to care for the drowned man. They took the mud off with grass swabs, they removed the underwater stones entangled in his hair, and they scraped the crust off with tools used for scaling fish. As they were doing that they noticed that the vegetation on him came from faraway oceans and deep water and that his clothes were in tatters, as if he had sailed through labyrinths of coral. They noticed too that he bore his death with pride, for he did not have the lonely look of other drowned men who came out of the sea or that haggard, needy look of men who drowned in rivers. But only when they finished cleaning him off did they become aware of the kind of man he was and it left them breathless. Not only was he the tallest, strongest, most virile, and best built man they had ever seen, but even though they were looking at him there was no room for him in their imagination.

They could not find a bed in the village large enough to lay him on nor was there a table solid enough to use for his wake. The tallest men's holiday pants would not fit him, nor the fattest ones' Sunday shirts, nor the shoes of the one with the biggest feet. Fascinated by his huge size and his beauty, the women then decided to make him some pants from a large piece of sail and a shirt from some bridal brabant linen so that he could continue through his death with dignity. As they sewed, sitting in a circle and gazing at the corpse between stitches, it seemed to them that the wind had never been so steady nor the sea so restless as on that night and they supposed that the change had something to do with the dead man. They thought that if that magnificent man had lived in the village, his house would have had the widest doors, the highest ceiling, and the strongest floor, his bedstead would have been made from a midship frame held together by iron bolts, and his wife would have been the happiest woman. They thought that he would have had so much authority that he could have drawn fish out of the sea simply by calling their names and that he would have put so much work into his land that springs would have burst forth from among the rocks so that he would have been able to plant flowers on the cliffs. They secretly compared him to their own men, thinking that for all their lives theirs were incapable of doing what he could do in one night, and they ended up dismissing them deep in their hearts as the weakest, meanest, and most useless creatures on earth. They were wandering through that maze of fantasy when the oldest woman, who as the oldest had looked upon the drowned man with more compassion than passion, sighed:

"He has the face of someone called Esteban."

It was true. Most of them had only to take another look at him to see that he could not have any other name. The more stubborn among them, who were the youngest, still lived for a few hours with the illusion that when they put his clothes on and he lay among the flowers in patent leather shoes his name might be Lautaro. But it was a vain illusion. There had not been enough canvas, the poorly cut and worse sewn pants were too tight, and the hidden strength of his heart popped the buttons on his shirt. After midnight the whistling of the wind died down and the sea fell into its Wednesday drowsiness. The silence put an end to any last doubts: he was Esteban. The women who had dressed him, who had combed his hair, had cut his nails and shaved him were unable to hold back a shudder of pity when they had to resign themselves to his being dragged along the ground. It was then that they understood how unhappy he must have been with that huge body since it bothered him even after death. They could see him in life, condemned to going through doors sideways, cracking his head on crossbeams, remaining on his feet during visits, not knowing what to do with this soft, pink, sea lion hands while the lady of the house looked for her most resistant chair and begged him, frightened to death, sit here, Esteban, please, and he, leaning against the wall, smiling, don't bother, ma'am, I'm fine where I am, his heels raw and his back roasted from having done the same thing so many times whenever he paid a visit, don't bother, ma'am, I'm fine where I am, just to avoid the embarrassment of breaking up the chair, and never knowing perhaps that the ones who said don't go, Esteban, at least wait till the coffee's ready, were the ones who later on would whisper the big boob finally left, how nice, the handsome fool has gone. That was what the women were thinking beside the body a little before dawn. Later, when they covered his face with a handkerchief so that the light would not bother him, he looked so forever dead, so defenseless, so much like their men that the first furrows of tears opened in their hearts. It was one of the younger ones who began the weeping. The others, coming to, went from sighs to wails, and the more they sobbed the more they felt like weeping, because the drowned man was becoming all the more Esteban for them, and so they wept so much, for he was the most destitute, most peaceful, and most obliging man on earth, poor Esteban. So when the men returned with the news that the drowned man was not from the neighboring villages either, the women felt an opening of jubilation in the midst of their tears.

"Praise the Lord," they sighed, "he's ours!"

The men thought the fuss was only womanish frivolity. Fatigued because of the difficult nighttime inquiries, all they wanted was to get rid of the bother of the newcomer once and for all before the sun grew strong on that arid, windless day. They improvised a litter with the remains of foremasts and gaffs, tying it together with rigging so that it would bear the weight of the body until they reached the cliffs. They wanted to tie the anchor from a cargo ship to him so that he would sink easily into the deepest waves, where fish are blind and divers die of nostalgia, and bad currents would not bring him back to shore, as had happened with other bodies. But the more they hurried, the more the women thought of ways to waste time. They walked about like startled hens, pecking with the sea charms on their breasts, some interfering on one side to put a scapular of the good wind on the drowned man, some on the other side to put a wrist compass on him, and after a great deal of *get away from there, woman, stay out of the way, look, you almost made me fall on top of the dead man,* the men began to feel mistrust in their lives and started grumbling about why so many main-altar decorations for a stranger, because no matter how many nails and holywater jars he had on him, the sharks would chew him all the same, but the women kept piling on their junk relics, running back and forth, stumbling, while they released in sighs what they did not in tears, so that the men finally exploded with *since when has there ever been such a fuss over a drifting corpse, a drowned nobody, a piece of cold Wednesday meat.* One of the women, mortified by so much lack of care, then removed the handkerchief from the dead man's face and the men were left breathless too.

He was Esteban. It was not necessary to repeat it for them to recognize him. If they had been told Sir Walter Raleigh, even they might have been impressed with his gringo accent, the macaw on his shoulder, his cannibal-killing blunderbuss, but there could be only one Esteban in the world and there he was, stretched out like a sperm whale, shoeless, wearing the pants of an undersized child, and with those stony nails that had to be cut with a knife. They had only to take the handkerchief off his face to see that he was ashamed, that it was not his fault that he was so big or so heavy or so handsome, and if he had known that this was going to happen, he would have looked for a more discreet place to drown in, seriously, I even would have tied the anchor off a galleon around my neck and staggered off a cliff like someone who doesn't like things in order not to be upsetting people now with this Wednesday dead body, as you people say, in order not to be bothering anyone with this filthy piece of cold meat that doesn't have anything to do with me. There was so much truth in his manner that even the most mistrustful men, the ones who felt the bitterness of endless nights at sea fearing that their women would tire of dreaming about them and begin to dream of drowned men, even they and others who were harder still shuddered in the marrow of their bones at Esteban's sincerity.

That was how they came to hold the most splendid funeral they could conceive of for an abandoned drowned man. Some women who had gone to get flowers in the neighboring villages returned with other women who could not believe what they had been told, and those women went back for more flowers when they saw the dead man, and they brought more and more until there were so many flowers and so many people that it was hard to walk about. At the final moment it pained them to return him to the waters as an orphan and they chose a father and mother from among the best people, and aunts and uncles and cousins, so that through him all the inhabitants of the village became kinsmen. Some sailors who heard the weeping from a distance went off course and people heard of one who had himself tied to the mainmast, remembering ancient fables about sirens. While they fought for the privilege of carrying him on their shoulders along the steep escarpment by the cliffs, men and women became aware for the first time of the desolation of their streets, the dryness of their courtyards, the narrowness of their dreams as they faced the splendor and beauty of their drowned man. They let him go without an anchor so that he could come back if he wished and whenever he wished, and they all held their breath for the fraction of centuries the body took to fall into the abyss. They did not need to look at one another to realize that they were no longer all present, that they would never be. But they also knew that everything would be different from then on, that their houses would have wider doors, higher ceilings, and stronger floors so that Esteban's memory could go everywhere without bumping into beams and so that no one in the future would dare whisper the big boob finally died, too bad, the handsome fool has finally died, because they were going to paint their house fronts gay colors to make Esteban's memory eternal and they were going to break their backs digging for springs among the stones and planting flowers on the cliffs so that in future years at dawn the passengers on great liners would awaken, suffocated by the smell of gardens on the high seas, and the captain would have to come down from the bridge in his dress uniform, with his astrolabe, his pole star, and his row of war medals and, pointing to the promontory of roses on the horizon, he would say in fourteen languages, look there, where the wind is so peaceful now that it's gone to sleep beneath the beds, over there, where the sun's so bright that the sunflowers don't know which way to turn, yes, over there, that's Esteban's village.

Windling

Haunted

Through the imponderable twilight tumbles
    A fuzzy mass, uncertain at the edges.
This, so they tell me, is the ghost that grumbles,
    The spectre that goes backwards through the hedges,

The goblin garrulous but rarely witty,
    The harmless phantom and the wraith endearing,
That hops around and sings a tuneless ditty
    And interrupts himself with bursts of cheering:

A spirit fairly lovable and decent,
    Some say he is the shade of Charles the Martyr;
Others incline to a demise more recent,
    Claiming he is a Mr. Eustace Carter,

A man who flourished here in eighteen-fifty
    And fell into a pond while trapping rabbits.
At all events, although a trifle shifty,
    The spectre has few irritating habits,

Never comes after dark, but in the twilight,
    And rarely frightens people, or not badly,
But sits in summer evenings on the skylight,
    Scratching himself, and singing, rather sadly.

—*R. P. Lister*

Visitors to a Castle

Sylvia Townsend Warner

Mynnydd Prescelly is the westernmost mountain in Wales. It is of only moderate height but its sweeping contours, rising from a gentle countryside, dominate the skyline. Sometimes it is there, sometimes not. Giraldus Cambrensis, who wrote the "Itinerarium Kambriae," must often have looked inquiringly toward it from his birthplace, Manorbier Castle. In the "Itinerary," however, all he has to say of Prescelly is that a man dwelling on its northern slope dreamed that if he put his hand into a certain spring he would find a rock and beneath it a golden torque; and being covetous, did so, was bitten by a viper, and died. It may be that Giraldus wrote more fully about Prescelly in a lost chapter of the "Itinerary"; otherwise, this is another instance of his credulity distracting him from more serious matters.

Since time out of mind, there has been a small Elfin Kingdom of Castle Ash Grove, which lies in a valley of Mynnydd Prescelly. Its name harks back to a time when its inhabitants did not care to build and had not developed a social hierarchy of flying servants, strolling gentry. At nightfall, regardless of class distinctions, they flew up into the boughs of an ash grove and slept there.

They were still sleeping in trees when a mortal came among them, a civil old man in a single garment, very coarse and verminous, who had voyaged from Ireland into St. Brides Bay on a slab of granite. This he told them, while they hospitably combed the lice from his single garment. True hospitality includes receiving travellers tales, and they asked him how he had made the granite slab seaworthy. He replied, "By Faith." The word was new to them. He preached them a sermon on the nature of Faith, and how its apartness from knowledge, its irreconcilability with all human experience, proved that it was a spark of the heavenly mind. "Faith can remove mountains!" he exclaimed. But Faith was not for them. Being Elfins, they had no souls. Without souls, they could not enjoy the advantages of Faith, not so much as to say to a pebble, "Be thou removed."

Till now, they had listened politely. But at this last statement their Welsh pride put up its hackle. They did not contradict him to his face, but when he had limped on to convert the heathen in Carmarthenshire they exploded with resentment and set themselves to disprove it, each and all saying to his chosen pebble, "Be thou removed!" Not a pebble stirred. They decided that pebbles were too small to be worth removing anyway, and that it would be simpler to work on Mynnydd Prescelly. Prescelly did not comply; their Welsh pride would not yield. Matters were at a deadlock when the Court Poet's nephew said that if they seriously wished to remove Mynnydd Prescelly they must sing. There is nothing so powerful as singing. Everyone who sings knows this with an inward certainty.

He was a stout young fairy with a light tenor voice. Previously, no one had paid much attention to him. Now he assumed command. When they proposed to sing immediately, he quelled their impatience: they must give their voices, hoarse and ravelled from shouting at pebbles, a chance to recover. Not a note till sundown tomorrow; meanwhile, a light supper and early to bed after a gargle of blackberry juice and honey. For his part, he would compose a special Removal Song, to be sung without accompaniment, and of narrow compass so that all could join in it.

At sundown precisely, they met to sing. Not a cough was heard among them. The Poet's nephew mounted a stool and took them through the Removal Song till they had it by heart. The tune, as he had promised, was one they all could join in. It was in a three-beat measure and within the compass of a sixth. The words "Mynnydd Prescelly, Be thou removed" they knew already, and after a few niceties had been attended to he signalled them to a pause and said, "Now, all together. One, two, three?"

They began with their gathered breaths. At first, they sang in unison. Then they sang in thirds. As the power of song took hold of them, they threw in some spontaneous descants. When they realized that the song could be sung in canon, like Three Blind Mice and Tallis's Evening Hymn, their joy knew no bounds. They sang. They sang. The Poet's nephew, singing himself and conducting with both hands, led them from an ample *forte* to a rich *fortissimo* and tapered them down to a *pianissimo espressivo* and roused them again and again calmed them. Each sang, putting his whole heart into it as though everything depended on him, and at the same time felt the anonymous ardour of those singing with him. They sang so intently that they did not hear the ash trees rustle as though a solemn gale blew over them. When the Poet's nephew had brought them back to a unison and slowed them to a close, they looked round on each other as though on well-met strangers. Glorified and exhausted by a total experience, they ate an enormous supper, climbed into their ash trees, and slept till well past sunrise.

It was as though they had woken in a new country. Rubbing their eyes, they stared at an unfamiliar aspect of day. The mountain was gone. When they flew up to see what had happened to it, they saw the distant coastline and the mysterious pallor of the sea.

A dandelion clock could not have vanished more peacefully. There was no sign of uprooting; the hare tracks printed their established pattern but on level ground, the brook ran in its same bed, but unhurrying. Wherever the mountain had gone to, it had gone without ill will.

Three nights later it came back, unobserved, and was settled in its old place before day.

Its return was more sobering than its departure had been. It had gone because they had willed it to do so. It came back of its own will. The Court Poet in his Welcoming Ode compared it to bees, cats, pigeons, and other animals with homing instincts, but it was felt that he was using too much poetic licence. There were stories from the

Kingdom of Thule of individualistic underground springs which burst into towering activity and deluged everybody with hot water and cinders. Though nothing of that sort had ever happened in Wales, neither had a disappearing and reappearing mountain. But Mynnydd Prescelly embraced its inhabitants as quietly as ever, and sheltered them as reliably from the north wind, and bumblebees hummed up and down its slopes, and harebells grew where they always did. Presently the more light-minded and scientific fairies began to experiment in removal by Faith—not the mountain, of course, but rocks and stones which nobody needed—and when there was a small landslide, nothing would content them but another singing assembly. Again the mountain disappeared—this time in a heavy sea fog; and again it came back, looking, as one might say, unmoved. Before five centuries had passed, moving the mountain had become a regular ceremonial, carried out because the mountain would expect it. By then, research had established what happened. Mynnydd Prescelly rose up in the shape of a cloud, and travelled to Plynlimon. There it descended as a heavy rain, and after it had rained on Plynlimon for the inside of a week, the cloudy Mynnydd Prescelly would travel back, fall as rain, solidify as mountain. And human beings who had noticed its absence from the skyline would say, "There's Mynnydd Prescelly again, so we'll start harvesting."

Whether one sleeps in an ash tree cradle or under the thatch of a modest castle, a moist mountainy air is a better soporific than any good conscience. The Elfins of Castle Ash Grove prided themselves on being good sleepers, and had remarkably inoffensive consciences. Music was their preoccupation. They brewed an incomparable mead. They also prided themselves on being good neighbours: if a peasant's cow strayed into their park, they allowed it to graze; if a peasant's horde of children wandered into their valley, they sat in trees and watched them with benevolence. This did not happen very often, however; it was a poor countryside and thinly populated. As the martyred

Irishman's teaching spread among the descendants of his hearers, being an Elfin good neighbour became less easy: women pestered them with offerings, tied dirty rags on their trees, and dipped scrofulous babies in their brook; men threw stones at them, aiming in the direction of their voices. But the music and the mead continued, and the link with Plynlimon, and the satisfaction of knowing that they were instrumental in swelling the baby Severn into a real river. For though it rains copiously on Plynlimon, the contributions of their own Mynnydd Prescelly must surely count for something: if they had not all sung so powerfully to confute the Irishman and for the honour of Wales, the mountain—extraordinary thought!—might never have removed.

Perhaps it aided time to slip away so peacefully that all their queens were called Morgan. There was the notorious Morgan le Fay. There was Morgan Philosophy, whose long scholarly amour with Taliesin taught him to be a salmon and acquainted him with Alexander the Great. There was Morgan Breastknot of Music, whose page, grown old, wept on his death bed because all living memory of her singing would perish with him. The reign of her successor, Morgan Spider (so titled because of her exquisite fine spinning), saw a new manifestation of Castle Ash Grove's devotion to music. Ignoring the traditional Elfin aloofness from mankind, a party of music lovers democratically disguised themselves as mortals and went to Worcester Cathedral, masked and in riding mantles, to hear Thomas Tomkins play on the organ; and later, wearing bonnets and top hats, attended a performance of the Messiah at the Three Choirs' Festival.

By now we are within sight of the twentieth century.

It was a fine autumn evening in 1893. The mountain had just come back from Plynlimon. Morgan Spider and some of her court were strolling in the park, saying how pleasant it was to feel sheltered from the outer world again, when they heard an astonishing assortment of noises—a frantic ting-a-ling, a metallic crash, loud mortal bewailings and cries for help. They moved cautiously toward the cries. Where their valley curved under the slope of a steep hill-side they saw a massive young woman in a dark-blue uniform sprawled on the grass, weeping convulsively and draped in what seemed to be a tattered metal cage—and was, in fact, a bicycle.

In order not to alarm her, they made themselves visible, as they had made themselves visible at Worcester and the Three Choirs' Festival in order not to be sat on.

"I am afraid you're in some trouble," said Morgan Spider.

"I should think I am in some trouble," replied the young woman. "My brake wouldn't hold and my bike's smashed and my knee's cut to the bone. And I'd like to know what's been going on here," she continued, glaring at them. "It wasn't like this last week."

Consulting among themselves, they agreed that this was not the moment in which to explain about the mountain.

The young woman launched into a resentful narrative of a road which went on going uphill, so she knew it must be the wrong one, of the track she had turned into which led to a bog, of other tracks leading nowhere, of exhaustion, desolation, bulls, gnats, distant cottages which turned out to be sheepfolds, birds that got up behind her with a noise like a gun, vipers that threatened her with their stings, and never a sign of life and always uphill. "And if that wasn't enough—" She broke off and exclaimed, "Where's my bag?"

A large black bag lay nearby. Morgan Spider's page picked it up and handed it to her.

When she opened it, they all started back in horror at the appalling smell that came out. She pulled up her skirts, rolled down a black stocking, and displayed a bloodied knee. She unstoppered a small bottle. The appalling smell was redoubled. Dame Bronwen fainted. The mortal poured a well-known disinfectant on a wad of cotton wool, laid the wad (with howls) on her knee, and tied on a white bandage very deftly. Looking up, she saw them ministering to Dame Bronwen. "One of those who can't stand the sight of blood," she remarked. "My job wouldn't suit her."

A mortal who delighted in the sight of blood was not the guest they would have chosen. But hospitality is a sacred duty among Elfins. Trying not to inhale her, they supported the young woman to the castle, sat her down in the parlour, and gave her a glass of mead. There was a rather long silence. Morgan Spider looked out of the window and saw Dame Bronwen approaching, and the page doing his best with the bicycle and the bicycle retaliating. And she looked at the tranquil darkening sky, and then at the massive, reddening young woman, who was twirling her glass.

But hospitality requires more than refilling a glass. Morgan Spider mentioned that the mead was homemade, and the young woman commented that they were quite old-fashioned, weren't they.

"And where do you come from? Is it far away?"

"Nottingum."

A beautified simper spread over the young woman's face, and she dwelt on the word as though it were a jujube. "Nottingum," she repeated, and held out her glass dreamily. "Born there. Educated there. And look at me now. All my qualifications, and they've sent me to this back-of-beyond district. And that Mrs. Jones I saw last week sends a message to say she's taken unexpected and would I come soon as I could. And if I lose her, I suppose they'll blame me. Slave driving, I call it."

"Where does this Mrs. Jones live?" demanded Morgan Spider. The young woman started. She groped in her pocket and handed over a screw of paper. "It's in Welsh. Even if I could say it, it wouldn't get me there. It's my poor bike I'm worrying about."

While she wept, Morgan Spider told the page to fetch her muff—for it would be a cold night to fly in.

"Madam, Madam! Your Majesty's surely not going to fly?"

"The woman's in labour. Do you expect me to go in a

procession?'' She snatched the muff and ran out. They
saw her flicker down the valley like a bat. The uppermost
thought in every heart was envy.

When Morgan Spider returned, rosy with triumph and
night air, she heard singing. As she entered, it broke off.
Her whole court was assembled round the District Nurse,
who lay on the floor dead drunk, with her right hand
clenched on a pair of scissors.

After her departure, they explained, the mortal talked
about lockjaw and said she must renew the dressing on her
knee. The bandage was peeled off and rerolled with exac-
titude. The bottle was unstoppered, the wad soaked and
reapplied. As before, she howled, but now a great deal
louder. Brandishing a pair of scissors, she staggered round
the room trying to get at the page in order to cut the grin off
his face, tripped over the Keeper of the Archives—a slow
mover—and subsided on the floor. There she had lain
ever since. All felt she should be removed. None was
willing to approach her, in case she might come to. The
Keeper of the Archives, with a quotation from Vergil, said
that in special difficulties one should turn to tradition. For a
great many centuries the mountain had been removing
itself unprompted, but he supposed the Removal Song
would be as effective as ever. After a few false starts, they
remembered the tune. Altering the words so that there
should be no misunderstanding, they began singing, and
had been singing for an hour and three-quarters:

              "Nottingum, Nottingum,
                Be thou removed.''

Morgan Spider said they must put more life into it. It was
a fine old tune, and would stand up to a little impiety.
Joined by their Queen, the singers did better; some almost
believed they saw the dark-blue mass rise a few inches
from the floor.

Morgan Spider clapped her hands. "Stop! I see what's

wrong. We're barking up the wrong tree. 'Nottingum, Nottingum, Be thou removed' means nothing to her.''

They objected that the mortal had said "Nottingum."

"She said she was born there. Wherever it is, it's just a place."

One of the younger ladies said, with a giggle, "Suppose it's working there?"

"That's no affair of ours. It isn't working here. But if we can't remove her, we can remove ourselves. So we'll have a quick supper and then fly to Plynlimon."

She spoke to be obeyed. On the morrow, glittering in the rays of the newly risen sun, they descended like a swarm of fireflies on the vast, green, featherbed expanse of Plynlimon.

When they had recovered from the fatigue of the journey, they found themselves delighted to be there. Even Elfins are susceptible to the Zeitgeist. The Zeitgeist of the day was to resort to the Simple Life—nature, nuts, sleeping out-of-doors, an escape from convention and formality. Plynlimon afforded exactly that. Doing nothing, they were never at a loss for something to do. They snared rabbits and roasted them over a wood fire they had rekindled from the ashes of a fire abandoned by travelling gipsies. Collecting enough fuel to keep the fire going was a labour of love, eating rabbit with their fingers was a feat. When the Keeper of the Archives found a thrown-away iron cauldron in a ditch, they cooked gipsy stews, flavouring the rabbit with chanterelle mushrooms and wild garlic, and supping the broth from snail shells. All these things called for much time and invention and were achievements—unless they went wrong, when they were things to laugh about. The more active went for immense walks. Others picked watercress and wild strawberries or sat talking on large subjects. At night, they admired the stars. Their feet were usually wet and they were all in perfect health.

Morgan Spider, but for whom they would not have come to Plynlimon, disclaimed any particular hand in it. It was a mass rising, she said; she had chanced to speak first, but the thought was in every mind. The voice of Nature had said, "Be thou removed," as it spoke to swallows and cuckoos and ice-cream vendors and nightingales; and the happy migrants obeyed. When the voice of Nature directed, they would fly back to Castle Ash Grove, and settle down for a comfortable winter, telling stories and brewing more mead. Every trace of the visitor would have been broomed and aired out of the castle. It had been left in the care of reliable changelings, who had detested Nottingum as only blood relations can.

One thing only slightly troubled her—Dame Bronwen's incapacity to delight in what everyone else found so delightful. At the announcement that they would remove to Plynlimon, Bronwen had welcomed the idea, so impatiently that she wanted to start at once. On their first day there, she was the earliest to be up and about, as excited as a child by the change of air, the change of scene, the prospect of an entirely new way of life. By midday, the bright morning clouded over. Politely admiring, politely enjoying, she remained aloof. Though Morgan Spider had for the time shaken off the responsibilities of a queen, she still felt the obligations of a hostess. It occurred to her that Bronwen was sulking because she felt in some way slighted.

A little favouritism might put this right. Noticing the tufts of wool which brambles and thistles had plucked off passing sheep, she had idly planned to take home the best of them to card and spin during the winter. She invited Dame Bronwen to come woolgathering. Sometimes they wandered together, sometimes apart. The air was perfectly still. There were a great many flies about, which they beat off with bracken whisks. Morgan Spider fell behind to pull some particularly fine tufts from a thorn brake. Beyond the thorn brake, she came on Dame Bronwen, who was standing motionless in a cloud of flies. She whisked her bracken frond. Dame Bronwen started violently; it was as if she had been found out in some atrocious fault.

"A penny for your thoughts, Bronwen."

It was the wrong thing to say. Dame Bronwen locked up her face, and after a pause remarked on the flies, saying that they were the only drawback to Plynlimon; adding politely that they were only a nuisance on windless days.

They walked on together, Morgan Spider making experimental conversation and getting nothing but a Yes or No for her pains. There was a crooked sloe bush ahead of them, and she said to herself, "Before we reach the sloe bush I'll get it out of her." But they were level with the bush before she said, "Bronwen, what ails you?"

Bronwen said, "A bad smell." She pressed a branch of the sloe to her bosom as though its thorns would help her to speak. "Do you remember the smell that came out of the bottle?"

"And was so appalling that it made you faint? Of course I remember it. But by the time we go back, Castle Ash Grove will have been cleaned and aired. I shall send the page ahead of us to make certain; we won't start till he tells us the smell is gone."

"It will never be gone."

Dame Bronwen pressed the branch so hard to her bosom that a sloe burst and its juice spurted out.

"When I fainted it was because of what was shown me. I saw trees blighted and grass burned brown and birds falling out of the sky. I saw the end of our world, Morgan— the end of Elfin. I saw the last fairy dying like a scorched insect."

She was mad. But she spoke with such intensity it was impossible not to believe her.

A Tourist Camped on a Donegal Field

Oh, good evening. Yes sir; a lovely night indeed and—
Gotcha! Beg your pardon? Well
Of course I knew; the shamrock in your tam.
You're caught, my good man: I can grasp your little legs and arms
All in one hand, so there's no help for it.
Give us your name.
Oh good lord. I can't speak even modern Gaelic. Eh?
Ah right, the great escape:
Yes; turn, turn, a lion a snake a bear a goat
and "Look! Yer shoe's untied!" Do what you must.
Yield? Land's sakes—you're panting. Calm down.
Here—want a bottle of Guiness?
For sure . . . I mean, you're welcome.
Now we talk.
About your ransom price.
No good to cuss. Yeah, I allow as how we mortals *are* all the
    same,
But frankly, I don't want your gold.
I want safe conduct.
I want to meet your kin.
I want to listen, I want to watch.
Barmy? Yeah. It is. I probably am. But
The bards are dead,
Long dead is the thing,
While a terrible thirst for their songs is growing;
And a Sunday tea in your barrow,
A few nights of jigs and blarney,
A few good rounds and tots of whisky
Are more seductive than the promised thighs of the elf queen;
For thus I'll learn to turn *my* leaves to gold.
I'll even bring the chips and ale.
Cheap won for you, my friend, a bargain indeed.
But dear to me. My price.
Deal?

—*Bellamy Bach*

Gran and the Roaring Boys

Jenny Sullivan

In some circles, it might be considered a social disadvantage to have a witch for a grandmother.

But not in Aberllyn. My Gran was nobility in Aberllyn. Gran was an asset at any village teaparty and Gran, as often as the local GP, was consulted in times of crisis. Mostly, of course, it was just sick cows, or injured birds brought to the back doorstep, or a love potion. Very good on warts, too, was Gran, a bit of spit, a rub with a potato cut in two, six lines of the Old Language, and Tuesday week—no wart!

Possibly Gran was so popular because she didn't look like a witch. The only apparent familiars she had were Sws and me, and us part time, being summer visitors only. Gran was five feet nothing, and round as a cottage loaf above and below the ties of her apron. Her skin was the colour of the milk left in the churn when the butter's taken off, with a spot of colour added on each cheek from the little pot she kept hidden down the side of her armchair. There was nothing witchy about the house, either. Clean as a washboard, bright with check curtains, wood tables scrubbed until the surface had faded to cream and the grain rubbed soft as flannel on the palm of the hand; willow china in quantity, and a fire glowing in the belly of the squat, blackleaded range summer and winter. Back door never locked and flung wide all summer to the pungent scents of the herb garden loud with bees and fluttering distracted with cabbage whites and clean washing.

Not everybody, of course, believed that Gran was a witch. Good with herbs, they said, and a quaint old character, but witches, they said, don't exist. But that didn't stop Mrs. Gomer Jones Very Holy sneaking into Gran's kitchen with her rheumaticky knees, nor the Chapel ladies ducking into curtsies when Gran sailed into Evans Grocer.

Gran had a Reputation, and them as was wise didn't cross her. There were two that did, and they—well, better start in the morning, like Gran says, and finish at sunset.

It all happened the summer Sws turned sixteen. Nine years older than me, and up until that year all scratches and slaps, except when Gran was there. "Brothers and sisters, cats and dogs, fighters all" our Gran used to say. "But do it here and I will string the pair of you like runner beans." Meant it, too, although she never actually lifted a finger to either of us. Mostly Gran was twinkles, hot scones and hugs, but cross her and it was black looks and hide if you knew what was good for you!

Anyway, Sws was sixteen and me seven, and that summer we decided we liked each other. Sws was coming very mysterious and lumpy in the front with bosoms, but for all that she would still race me up Bryn Glassllyn and duck me in the lake. But that year there was another, dark side to Sws, very quiet, and thinking a lot, and looking under her lashes at the Roaring Boys. Troubled me, this side of Sws, for it shut me out; some days she wasn't interested in the lithe sewin barring the river inches from our fishing lines, or the frogs leaping frantic in the side pools avoiding our swarming fingers, or even the crabs scuttling sideways over our bare feet in the beach pools, Sws being too busy thinking deep and chewing hair. But even thinking Sws was pretty to turn heads.

The village biddies, even, who wouldn't have had a good word for St. Peter unless he turned Chapel, looked at her with softness in their button eyes when she bobbed her head and wished them "bore da." Sws had a dark, intense Welshness, the Celtic look of her softened by the high rose tints of my mother's Hereford English, and white teeth like the little fragments of shell we found on the beach, in a mouth that could sulk and pout, being female, but mostly smiled. But her eyes were eyes to startle, being green as Glasllyn in spring, and with Gran's way of looking into one's face as if eyes were windows and the soul on show without curtains. Only no wrinkles, of course, round Sws' eyes, since Gran had plenty for both!

The Roaring Boys set eyes on Sws that year, and the

village girls sulked and poked their noses in the air and bustled a lot with "I don't cares," made a point of ignoring the Roaring Boys, who didn't notice.

Twenty years each, had the Roaring Boys, being twins, and count their length in yards. Llew and Choss, fishermen's faces tanned into spider web lines round the eyes; handsome, strong, and both paid on Friday, more was the pity, since every Friday night saw them together in the Aberllyn Arms, money that should have been in their pockets swishing in their bellies with froth on top, and coming out loud in the way they bickered, and bellowed, and shouted. A roaring, quarrelsome pair, these, and they quarrelled loudest over Sws. Sws laughed with me and rationed them to a smile a day, although I could tell she was a little bit pleased at all the fuss.

Gran, being Gran, missed nothing, and anyway, the Roaring Boys made no secret of it, mooning under Sws' window night after night. They came to blows under it, too, one Friday, and I scurried down to Sws' room to crouch nosy behind the curtain and peer down on the struggling pair below. Sws looked at me, once, and in her eyes was wonder at the madness that was in them. Madness it seemed to me, too, since Sws was all right as sisters go, but nothing, as far as I could tell, to fight over.

But suddenly Gran was out there, buckets full sloshing over the pair of them, plaits bristling over her nightdress with indignation, chasing them into their cottage and the bucket slung after for good measure.

Round to apologize next morning, both of them, and return the bucket, puffed eyes, cut lips and all, gawking on the doorstep for a glimpse of Sws, daft as sheep, and Gran warned them off, five foot nothing seeing to two at six and a half, and them listening, since Grans, in our part of the world, were people to listen to, and mine in particular for reasons already mentioned.

"You leave her, you hear?" she ordered, eyes sparkling, wagging finger chopping the air. "Sws is only sixteen, and too young for you." Gran folded her arms across the starched armament of her pinna and put her head back to see up at the loft of them, squinting her eyes against the morning sun. "You know what people call me," she said. "Some laugh, but I warn you. Lay a finger on Sws and the devil himself won't know where to hide you."

The Roaring Boys shuffled their feet, scratched their heads, smirked at each other, handed over the bucket and trooped down the path.

But Gran came very tightlipped that day, and baked two lots of scones without slipping us even one, hot from the oven. We sat and sniffed at the fragrant steam in anguish, since Gran with a Misery was not to be pestered and them what asked didn't get.

The Roaring Boys stole Sws on Monday night. Out at seven with a jar of embrocation for Mrs. Gomer Jones Very Holy's creaky knees, delivered the medicine and disappeared.

When our Carmarthen grandfer clock chimed ten and still Sws' nose hadn't come round the back door, Gran skewered her pancake hat to her bun, wrapped her shawl round her shoulders, and went looking. Back came Gran in half an hour, chin trembling to scare me stiff, but no Sws. She whisked me from my nightshirt and into my trews, and tugged me flying behind down the road for Meirion Police.

Policemen came very scarce round Aberllyn in those days, there being only Meirion in a twenty mile radius, and him not averse to a sly salmon taken from the Teifi below the Castle when the moon was ducking into cloud and the gamekeeper firing off snores instead of two barrels.

But we found Meirion Police eventually, by a process of elimination, shamefaced with his boots off in the front parlour of Mrs. Waldo Rhys Atlantic Sailor where, Gran told him sharp, he had no right to be, and better poach for salmon than honest men's wives, especially with crime all over the place while his back was turned.

Gran bustled Meirion Police off to look for Sws, tugged me home, fed me milk and, preoccupied, sent me to bed. Twice she sent me, and three times I crept down, peering through the bannisters lonely for Sws. I sat on the knotted rag rug at the top of the stairs and watched Gran unlock the big corner cupboard and fetch stone pots and glass bottles; mix, burn, tie and strew, the Old Language wafting around the rafters like steam and with a bit of special Gran swearing for good measure. The flames of the fire leapt blue in the grate with the handfuls of herbs crackling pungent on it.

And suddenly in the firelight was Cat: erect, black and motionless to be hardly there, wreathed in smoke like a left-over dream. Then the triangular mask opened in a cavernous, high-barred yawn, green eyes slitting, pink tongue curved and cupped delicate behind the needle teeth.

Yawns being contagious, I yawned with him, blinked once, and Cat was gone.

Deeply regretful I felt for the Roaring Boys.

Meirion Police brought back our Sws at four in the morning. Gran said "diolch" shut the door in his curious face, and bustled us to bed. I crept in with Sws for comfort and company, and we lay spooned together for what remained of the night.

Nobody ever saw the Roaring Boys again, although Meirion Police sleuthed all over Aberllyn, very serious, with licked pencil and a new notebook.

I never saw Cat again, either, but he came back just once after the house slept, because Tuesday morning there were two dead rats on Gran's Blaenau slate back doorstep, big black ones, side by side, all nice and tidy, with inches of scaly tails and long yellow teeth poking from half-open mouths. I wanted to keep them, being partial to a bit of nature study on a dull morning, but Gran clipped my ear, said "Ach-y-fi" and buried them under the blackcurrant bush by the ty-bach.

Homecoming

My seven sons came back from Indonesia.
Each had ruled an atoll twenty years alone.
Twenty years of loneliness, twenty years of craziness,
Of hell's and Eden's silence on an exiled coral throne.
My six grunting sons had forgotten what a language is;
My seventh was a warlock, chanting every language known.

My seven sunburnt sons arrived at the airport.
The airport had a banner up. Its words were "WELCOME
    HOME."
The mayor made a speech, and the virgins rainbowed over them
The many-tongued hooray of confetti's polychrome.
But, though seven new Rolls-Royces sped them richly to my
    parlor,
They only filed their long sharp teeth; the warlock's were afoam.

The day before my seven sons returned from atoll-loneliness,
The butler starched his livery to welcome them in style;
"*Thé dansant* for the young masters?" gushed the housemaid,
    strewing doilies;
I bought my sons a set of Proust to titilate their guile.
My seven Dresden China cups were waiting, hot with tea;
And all was ready as my sons tramped in. They didn't smile.

"You homesick boys from far-off Indonesia,
Relax and romp," I said, "and know you're loved.
It's true that twenty years alone with coral
Is not God's hand at its most velvet-gloved.
But let's test your sense of humor; don't be morbid;
I'll get tantrums if my welcome is rebuffed."

Did they listen? No, they only watched the seventh . . .
Till he made a kind of signal. Then they roared and went amok.
Two swung from chandeliers and pounced on the butler.
Two held the maid down, and clawed off her smock.
Two ate the Proust set. "Be careful, kids," I wheedled;
"Romp all you like but spare my teacups any shock.

"I can buy you chubby housemaids by the dozen.
You can eat a butler, even eat a book.
But whoever chips—no matter who—my china,
He'll get magicked back to nature's loneliest nook."
"No matter who?" the warlock asked—and tripped me
Right across my magic teacups. I awoke

On this hellish, Eden-beautied reef of coral
In a perfect climate full of perfect food,
Where my sense of humor's tested by the silence
And I've nothing else to do but fish and brood.
"Sons, come back and get me out of Indonesia!"
But, of course, they couldn't hear me. No one could.

—*Peter Viereck*

The Little Dirty Girl

Joanna Russ

Dear _____,

Do you like cats? I never asked you. There are all sorts of cats: elegant, sinuous cats, clunky, heavy-breathing cats, skinny, desperate cats, meatloaf-shaped cats, waddling, dumb cats, big slobs of cats who step heavily and groan whenever they try to fit themselves (and they never do fit) under something or in between something or past something.

I'm allergic to all of them. You'd think they'd know it. But as I take my therapeutic walks around the neighborhood (still aching and effortful after ten months, though when questioned, my doctor replies, with the blank, baffled innocence of those Martian children so abstractedly brilliant they've never learned to communicate about merely human matters with anyone, *that my back will get better*) cats venture from alleyways, slip out from under parked cars, bound up cellar steps, prick up their ears and flash out of gardens, all lifting up their little faces, wreathing themselves around my feet, crying *Dependency! Dependency!* and showing their elegantly needly little teeth, which they never use save in yearning appeal to my goodness. They have perfect confidence in me. If I try to startle them by hissing, making loud noises, or clapping my hands sharply, they merely stare in interested fashion and scratch themselves with their hind legs: how nice. I've perfected a method of lifting kitties on the toe of my shoe and giving them a short ride through the air (this is supposed to be alarming); they merely come running back for more.

And the children! I don't dislike children. Yes I do. No I don't, but I feel horribly awkward with them. So of course I keep meeting them on my walks this summer: alabaster little boys with angelic fair hair and sky-colored eyes (this section of Seattle is Scandinavian and the Northwest gets very little sun) come up to me and volunteer such compelling information as:

"*I'm* going to my friend's house."

"I'm going to the store."

· "My name is Markie."

"I wasn't really scared of that big dog; I was just *startled.*"

"People leave a lot of broken glass around here."

The littler ones confide; the bigger ones warn of the world's dangers: dogs, cuts, blackberry bushes that might've been sprayed. One came up to me once—what do they see in a tall, shuffling, professional, intellectual woman of forty?— and said, after a moment's thought:

"Do you like frogs?"

What could I do? I said yes, so a shirt-pocket that jumped and said *rivit* was opened to disclose Mervyn, an exquisite little being the color of wet, mottled sea-sand, all webbed feet and amber eyes, who was then transferred to my palm where he sat and blinked. Mervyn was a toad, actually; he's barely an inch long and can be found all over Seattle, usually upside down under a rock. I'm sure he (or she) is the Beloved Toad and Todkins and Todlekrancz Virginia Woolf used in her letters to Emma Vaughan.

And the girls? O they don't approach tall, middle-aged women. Little girls are told not to talk to strangers. And the little girls of Seattle (at least in my neighborhood) are as obedient and feminine as any in the world; to the jeans and tee-shirts of Liberation they (or more likely their parents) add hair-ribbons, baby-sized pocketbooks, fancy pins, pink shoes, even toe polish.

The liveliest of them I ever saw was a little person of five, coasting downhill in a red wagon, her cheeks pink with excitement, one pony-tail of yellow hair undone, her white tee-shirt askew, who gave a decorous little squeak of joy at the sheer speed of it. I saw and smiled; pink-cheeks saw and shrieked again, more loudly and confidently this time, then looked away, embarrassed, jumped quickly out of her wagon, and hauled it energetically up the hill.

Except for the very littlest, how neat, how clean, how carefully dressed they are! with long, straight hair that the older ones (I know this) still iron under waxed paper.

The little, dirty girl was different.

She came up to me in the supermarket. I've hired someone to do most of my shopping, as I can't carry much, but I'd gone in for some little thing, as I often do. It's a relief to get off the hard bed and away from the standing desk or the abbreviated kitchen stools I've scattered around the house (one foot up and one foot down); in fact it's simply such a relief—

Well, the little, dirty girl *was* dirty; she was the dirtiest eight-year-old I've ever seen. Her black hair was a long tangle. Her shoes were down-at-heel, the laces broken, her white (or rather grey) socks belling limply out over her ankles. Her nose was running. Her pink dress, so ancient that it showed her knees, was limp and wrinkled and the knees themselves had been recently skinned. She looked as if she had slid halfway down Volunteer Park's steepest, dirtiest hill on her panties and then rolled end-over-end the rest of the way. Besides all this, there were snot-and-tear-marks on her face (which was reddened and sallow and looked as if she'd been crying) and she looked—well, what can I say? *Neglected.* Not poor, though someone had dressed her rather eccentrically, not physically unhealthy or underfed, but messy, left alone, ignored, kicked out, bedraggled, like a cat caught in a thunderstorm.

She looked (as I said) tear-stained, and yet came up to my shopping cart with perfect composure and kept me calm company for a minute or so. Then she pointed to a box of Milky Way candy bars on a shelf above my head, saying "I like those," in a deep, gravelly voice that suggested a bad cold.

I ignored the hint. No, that's wrong; it wasn't a hint; it was merely a social, adult remark, self-contained and perfectly emotionless, as if she had long ago given up expecting that telling anyone she wanted something would result in getting it. Since my illness I have developed a fascination with the sheer, elastic wealth of children's bodies, the exhaustless, energetic health they don't know they have and which I so acutely and utterly miss, but I wasn't for an instant tempted to feel this way about the Little Dirty Girl. She had been through too much. She had Resources. If she showed no fear of me, it wasn't because she trusted me but because she trusted nothing. She had no expectations and no hopes. Nonetheless she attached herself to me and my shopping cart and accompanied me down two more aisles, and there seemed to be hope in that. So I made the opening, social, adult remark:

"What's your name?"

"A. R." Those are the initials on my handbag. I looked at her sharply but she stared levelly back, unembarrassed, self-contained, unexpressive.

"I don't believe that," I said finally.

"I could tell you lots of things you wouldn't believe," said the Little Dirty Girl.

She followed me up to the cashier and as I was putting out my small packages one by one by one, I saw her lay out on the counter a Milky Way bar and a nickel, the latter fetched from somewhere in that short-skirted, cap-sleeved dress. The cashier, a middle-aged woman, looked at me and I back at her; I laid out two dimes next to the nickel. She really did want it! As I was going into the logistics of How Many Short Trips From The Cart To The Car And How Many Long Ones From The Car To The Kitchen, the Little Dirty Girl spoke: "I can carry that." (Gravelly and solemn.)

She added hoarsely, "I bet I live near you."

"Well, *I* bet you don't," I said.

She didn't answer, but followed me to the parking lot, one proprietary hand on the cart, and when I unlocked my car door, she darted past me and started carrying packages from the cart to the front seat. I can't move fast enough to escape these children. She sat there calmly as I got in. Then she said, wiping her nose on the back of her hand:

"I'll help you take your stuff out when you get home."

Now I know that sort of needy offer and I don't like it. Here was the Little Dirty Girl offering to help me, and smelling in close quarters as if she hadn't changed her underwear for days: demandingness, neediness, more annoyance. Then she said in her flat, crow's voice: "I'll do it and go away. I won't bother you."

Well, what can you do? My heart misgave me. I started the car and we drove the five minutes to my house in silence, whereupon she grabbed all the packages at once (to be useful) and some slipped back on the car seat; I think this embarrassed her. But she got my things up the stairs to the porch in only two trips and put them on the unpainted porch rocker, from where I could pick them up one by one, and there we stood.

Why speechless? Was it honesty? I wanted to thank her, to act decent, to make that sallow face smile. I wanted to tell her to go away, that I wouldn't let her in, that I'd lock the door. But all I could think of to say was, "What's your name, really?" and the wild thing said stubbornly, "A. R." and when I said, "No, really," she cried *"A. R.!"* and facing me with her eyes screwed up, shouted something unintelligible, passionate and resentful, and was off up the street. I saw her small figure turning down one of the cross-streets that meets mine at the top of the hill. Seattle is grey and against the massed storm clouds to the north her pink dress stood out vividly. She was going to get rained on. Of course.

I turned to unlock my front door and a chunky, slow, old cat, a black-and-white Tom called Williamson who lives two houses down, came stiffly out from behind an azalea bush, looked slit-eyed (bored) about him, noticed me (his pupils dilated with instant interest) and bounded across the parking strip to my feet. Williamson is a banker-cat, not really portly or dignified but simply too lazy and unwieldy to bother about anything much. Either something scares him and he huffs under the nearest car or he scrounges. Like all kitties he bumbled around my ankles, making steam-engine noises. I never feed him. I don't pet him or talk to him. I even try not to look at him. I shoved him aside with one foot and opened the front door; Williamson backed off, raised his fat, jowled face and began the old cry: *Mrawr! Mrawr!* I booted him ungently off the porch before he could trot into my house with me, and as he slowly prepared to attack the steps (he never quite makes it) locked myself in. And the Little Dirty Girl's last words came suddenly clear:

I'll be back.

Another cat. There are too many in this story but I can't help it. The Little Dirty Girl was trying to coax the neighbor's superbly elegant half-Siamese out from under my car a few days later, an animal tiger-marked on paws and tail and as haughty-and-mysterious-looking as all cats are supposed to be, though it's really only the long Siamese body and small head. Ma'amselle (her name) still occasionally leaps on to my dining room windowsill and stares in (the people who lived here before me used to feed her). I was coming back from a walk, the Little Dirty Girl was on her knees, and Ma'amselle was under the car; when the Little Dirty Girl saw me she stood up, and Ma'amselle flashed Egyptianly through the laurel hedge and was gone. Someone had washed the Little Dirty Girl's pink dress (though a few days back, I'm afraid) and made a half-hearted attempt to braid her hair: there were barrettes and elastic somewhere in the tangle. Her cold seemed better. When it rains in August our summer can change very suddenly to early fall, and this was a chilly day; the Little Dirty Girl had nothing but her mud-puddle-marked dress between her thin skin and the Seattle air. Her cold seemed better, though, and her cheeks were pink with stooping. She said, in the voice of a little girl this time and not a raven, "She had *blue* eyes."

"She's Siamese," I said. "What's your name?"

"A. R."

"Now look, I don't —"

"*It's A. R.!*" She was getting loud and stolid again. She

stood there with her skinny, scabbed knees showing from under her dress and shivered in the unconscious way kinds do who are used to it; I've seen children do it on the Lower East Side in New York because they had no winter coat (in January). I said, "You come in." She followed me up the steps—warily, I think—but when we got inside her expression changed, it changed utterly; she clasped her hands and said with radiant joy, "Oh, they're *beautiful!*"

These were my astronomical photographs. I gave her my book of microphotographs (cells, crystals, hailstones) and went into the kitchen to put up water for tea; when I got back she'd dropped the book on my old brown-leather couch and was walking about with her hands clasped in front of her and that same look of radiant joy on her face. I live in an ordinary, shabby frame house that has four rooms and a finished attic; the only unusual thing about it is the number of books and pictures crammed in every which way among the (mostly second-hand) furniture. There are Woolworth frames for the pictures and cement-block bookcases for the books; nonetheless the Little Dirty Girl was as awed as if she'd found Aladdin's Cave.

She said, "It's so . . . sophisticated!"

Well, there's no withstanding that. Even if you think: what do kids know? She followed me into the kitchen where I gave her a glass of milk and a peach (she sipped and nibbled). She thought the few straggling rose bushes she could see in the back garden were wonderful. She loved my old brown refrigerator; she said, "It's so big! And such a color!" Then she said anxiously, "Can I see the upstairs?" and got excited over the attic eaves which were also "so big" (wallboard and dirty pink paint) to the point that she had to run and stand under one side and then run across the attic and stand under the other. She liked the "view" from the bedroom (the neighbor's laurel hedge and a glimpse of someone else's roof) but my study (books, a desk, a glimpse of the water) moved her so deeply and painfully that she only stood still in the center of the room, struggling with emotion, her hands again clasped in front of her. Finally she burst out, "It's so . . . *swanky!*" Here my kettle screamed and when I got back she had gotten bold enough to touch the electric typewriter (she jumped when it turned itself on) and then walked about slowly, touching the books with the tips of her fingers. She was brave and pushed the tabs on the desk lamp (though not hard enough to turn it on) and boldly picked up my little mailing scale. As she did so, I saw that there were buttons missing from the back of her dress; I said, "A. R., come here."

She dropped the scale with a crash. "I didn't mean it!" Sulky again.

"It's not that, it's your buttons," I said, and hauled her to the study closet where I keep a Band-Aid box full of extras; two were a reasonable match: little, flat-topped, pearlized, pink things you can hardly find any more. I sewed them on to her, not that it helped much, and the tangles of her hair kept falling back and catching. What a forest of lost barrettes and snarls of old rubber bands! I lifted it all a little grimly, remembering the pain of combing out. She sat flatly, all adoration gone:

"You can't comb my hair against my will; you're too weak."

"I wasn't going to," I said.

"That's what *you* say," the L.D.G. pointed out.

"If I try, you can stop me," I said. After a moment she turned around, flopped down on my typing chair, and bent her head. So I fetched my old hairbrush (which I haven't used for years) and did what I could with the upper layers, managing even to smooth out some of the lower ones, though there were places near her neck nearly as matted and tangled as felt; I finally had to cut some pieces out with my nail scissors.

L.D.G. didn't shriek (as I used to, insisting my cries were far more artistic than those of the opera singers on the radio on Sundays) but finally asked for the comb herself and winced silently until she was decently braided, with rubber bands on the ends. We put the rescued barrettes in her shirt pocket. Without that cloud of hair her sallow face and pitch-ball eyes looked bigger, and oddly enough, younger; she was no more a wandering Fury with the voice of a Northwest-coast raven but a reasonably human (though draggly) little girl.

I said, "You look nice."

She got up, went into the bathroom, and looked at herself in the mirror. Then she said calmly, "No, I don't. I look conventional."

"Conventional?" said I. She came out of the bathroom, flipping back her new braids.

"Yes, I must go."

And as I was wondering at her tact (for anything after this would have been an anti-climax):

"But I shall return."

"That's fine," I said, "but I want to have grown-up manners with you, A. R. Don't ever come before ten in the morning or if my car isn't here or if you can hear my typewriter going. In fact, I think you had better call me on the telephone first, the way other people do."

She shook her head sweetly. She was at the front door before I could follow her, peering out. It was raining again. I saw that she was about to step out into it and cried "Wait, A. R.!" hurrying as fast as I could down the cellar steps to the garage, from where I could get easily to my car. I got from the back seat the green plastic poncho I always keep there and she didn't protest when I dumped it over her and put the hood over her head, though the poncho was much too big and even dragged on the ground in the front and back. She said only, "Oh, it's swanky. Is it from the Army?" So I had the satisfaction of seeing her move up the hill as a small, green tent instead of a wet, pink draggle. Though with her tea-party manners she hadn't really eaten anything; the milk and peach were untouched. Was it wariness? Or did she just not like milk and peaches? Re-membering our first encounter, I wrote on the pad by the

telephone, which is my shopping list:
Milky Way Bars
And then:
1 doz.

She came back. She never did telephone in advance. It
was all right, though; she had the happy faculty of somehow turning up when I wasn't working and wasn't busy
and was thinking of her. But how often is an invalid busy or
working? We went on walks or stayed home and on these
occasions the business about the Milky Ways turned out to
be a brilliant guess, for never have I met a child with such a
passion for junk food. A. R.'s formal, disciplined politeness
in front of milk or fruit was like a cat's in front of the
mass-produced stuff; faced with jam, honey, or mar-
malade, the very ends of her braids crisped and she attacked like a cat flinging itself on a fish; I finally had to hide
my own supplies in self-defense. Then on relatively good
days it was ice cream or Sara Lee cake, and on bad ones
Twinkies or Mallo-bars, Hostess cupcakes, Three Mus-
keteers bars, marshmallow cream, maraschino chocolates,
Turkish taffy, saltwater taffy, or—somewhat less horribly—Doritos, reconstituted potato chips, corn chips,
pretzels (fat or thin), barbecued corn chips, or onion-
flavored corn chips, anything like that. She refused nuts
and hated peanut butter. She also talked continuously
while eating, largely in polysyllables, which made me
nervous as I perpetually expected her to choke, but she
never did. She got no fatter. To get her out of the house
and so away from food, I took her to an old-fashioned
five-and-ten nearby and bought her shoelaces. Then I
took her down to watch the local ship-canal bridge open
up (to let a sailboat through) and we cheered. I took her to
a department store (just to look; "I know consumerism is
against your principles," she said with priggish and mystify-
ing accuracy) and bought her a pin shaped like a ladybug.
She refused to go to the zoo ("An animal jail!") but allowed as the rose gardens ("A plant *hotel*,") were both

pleasant and educational. A ride on the zoo merry-go-round excited her to the point of screaming and running around dizzily in circles for half an hour afterwards, which embarrassed me—but then no one paid the slightest attention; I suppose shrieky little girls had happened there before, though the feminine youth of Seattle, in its Mary Jane shoes and pink pocketbooks, rather pointedly ignored her. The waterfall in the downtown park, on the contrary, sobered her up; this is a park built right on top of a crossing over one of the city's highways and is usually full of office-workers; a walkway leads not only up to but actually behind the waterfall. A. R. wandered among the beds of bright flowers and passed, stooping, behind the water, trying to stick her hand in the falls; she came out saying:

"It looks like an old man's beard," (pointing to one of the ragged Skid Row men who was sleeping on the grass in the rare, Northern sunlight). Then she said, "No, it looks like a lady's dress without any seams."

Once, feeling we had become friends enough for it, I ran her a bath and put her clothes through the basement washer-dryer; her splashings and yellings in the bathroom were terrific and afterwards she flashed nude about the house, hanging out of windows, embellishing her strange, raucous shouts with violent jerkings and boundings-about that I think were meant for dancing. She even ran out the back door naked and had circled the house before I—voiceless with calling, "*A. R., come back here!*"—had presence of mind enough to lock both the front and back doors after she had dashed in and before she could get out again to make the entire *tour de Seattle* in her jaybird suit. Then I had to get her back into that tired pink dress, which (when I ironed it) had finally given up completely, despite the dryer, and sagged into two sizes too big for her.

Unless A. R. was youthifying.

I got her into her too-large pink dress, her baggy underwear, her too-large shoes, her new pink socks (which I had bought for her) and said:

"A. R., where do you live?"

Crisp and shining, the Little Clean Girl replied, "My dear, you always ask me that."

"And you never answer," said I.

"O yes I do," said the Little Clean Girl. "I live up the hill and under the hill and over the hill and behind the hill."

"That's no answer," said I.

"Wupf merble," said she (through a Mars Bar) and then, more intelligibly, "If you knew, you wouldn't want me."

"I would so!" I said.

L.D.G.—now L.C.G.—regarded me thoughtfully. She scratched her ear, getting, I noticed, cholocate in her hair. (She was a fast worker.) She said, "You want to know. You think you ought to know. You think you have a right. When I leave you'll wait until I'm out of sight and then you'll follow me in the car. You'll sneak by the curb way behind me so I won't notice you. You'll wait until I climb the steps of a house—like that big yellow house with the fuchsias in the yard where you think I live and you'll watch me go in. And then you'll ring the bell and when the lady comes to the door you'll say, 'Your little daughter and I have become friends,' but the lady will say, 'I haven't got any little daughter,' and then you'll know I fooled you. And you'll get scared. So don't try."

Well, she had me dead to rights. Something very like that had been in my head. Her face was preternaturally grave. She said, "You think I'm too small. I'm not.

"You think I'll get sick if I keep on eating like this. I won't.

"You think if you bought a whole department store for me, it would be enough. It wouldn't."

"I won't—well, I can't get a whole department store for you," I said. She said, "I know." Then she got up and tucked the box of Mars Bars under one arm, throwing over the other my green plastic poncho, which she always carried about with her now.

"I'll get you anything you want," I said; "No, not what you want, A. R., but anything you really, truly need."

"You can't," said the Little Dirty Girl.

"I'll try."

She crossed the living room to the front door, dragging the poncho across the rug, not paying the slightest attention to the astronomical photographs that had so enchanted her before. Too young now, I suppose. I said, "A. R., I'll try. Truly I will." She seemed to consider it a moment, her small head to one side. Then she said briskly, "I'll be back," and was out the front door.

And I did not—would not—could not—did not dare to follow her.

Was this the moment I decided I was dealing with a ghost? No, long before. Little by little, I suppose. Her clothes were a dead giveaway, for one thing: always the same and the kind no child had worn since the end of the Second World War. Then there was the book I had given her on her first visit, which had somehow closed and straightened itself on the coffee table, another I had lent her later (the poems of Edna Millay) which had mysteriously been there a day afterwards, the eerie invisibility of a naked little girl hanging out of my windows and yelling; the inconspicuousness of a little twirling girl nobody noticed spinning round and shrieking outside the merry-go-round, a dozen half-conscious glimpses I'd had, every time I'd got in or out of my car, of the poncho lying on the back seat where I always keep it, folded as always, the very dust on it undisturbed. And her unchildlike cleverness in never revealing either her name or where she lived. And as surely as A.R. had been a biggish eight when we had met, weeks ago, just as surely she was now a smallish, very unmistakable, unnaturally knowledgeable five.

But she was such a *nice* little ghost. And so solid! Ghosts don't run up your grocery bills, do they? Or trample Cheez Doodles into your carpet or leave gum under your kitchen chair, large smears of chocolate on the surface of the table (A. R. had) and an exceptionally dirty ring around the inside of the bathtub? Along with three (count 'em, three)

large, dirty, sopping-wet bath towels on the bathroom
floor? If A. R's social and intellectual life had a tendency to
become intangible when looked at carefully, everything
connected with her digestive system and her bodily dirt
stuck around amazingly; there was the state of the bathroom, the dishes in the sink (many more than mine), and
the ironing board still up in the study for the ironing of
A.R.'s dress (with the spray starch container still set up on
one end and the scorch mark where she'd decided to play
with the iron). If she was a ghost, she was a good one and I
liked her and wanted her back. Whatever help she needed
from me in resolving her ancient Seattle tragedy (ancient
ever since nineteen-forty-two) she could have. I wondered
for a moment if she were connected with the house, but
the people before me—the original owners—hadn't had
children. And the house itself hadn't even been built until
the mid-fifties; nothing in the neighborhood had. Unless
both they and I were being haunted by the children we
hadn't had; could I write them a psychotherapeutic letter
about it? ("Dear Mrs. X, How is your inner space?") I went
into the bathroom and discovered that A. R. had relieved
herself interestingly in the toilet and had then not flushed it,
hardly what I would call poetical behavior on the part of
somebody's unconscious. So I flushed it. I picked up the
towels one by one and dragged them to the laundry basket
in the bedroom. If the Little Dirty Girl was a ghost, she was
obviously a bodily-dirt-and-needs ghost traumatized in
life by never having been given a proper bath or allowed to
eat marshmallows until she got sick. Maybe this was it and
now she could rest (scrubbed and full of Mars Bars) in
peace. But I hoped not. I was nervous; I had made a
promise ("I'll give you what you need") that few of us can
make to anyone, a frightening promise to make to anyone.
Still, I hoped. And she was a businesslike little ghost. She
would come back.

For she, too, had promised.

Autumn came. I didn't see the Little Dirty Girl. School

started and I spent days trying to teach freshmen and freshwomen not to write like Rod McKuen (neither of us really knowing why they shouldn't, actually) while advanced students pursued me down the halls with thousand-page trilogies, demands for independent study, and other unspeakables. As a friend of ours said once, everyone will continue to pile responsibility on a woman and everything and everyone must be served except oneself; I've been a flogged horse professionally long enough to know that and meanwhile the dishes stay in the sink and the kindly wife-elves do *not* come out of the woodwork at night and do them. I was exercising two hours a day and sleeping ten; the Little Dirty Girl seemed to have vanished with the summer.

Then one day there was a freak spell of summer weather and that evening a thunderstorm. This is a very rare thing in Seattle. The storm didn't last, of course, but it seemed to bring right after it the first of the winter rains: cold, drenching, ominous. I was grading papers that evening when someone knocked at my door; I thought I'd left the garage light on and my neighbor'd come out to tell me, so I yelled "Just a minute, please!", dropped my pen, wondered whether I should pick it up, decided the hell with it, and went (exasperated) to the door.

It was the Little Dirty Girl. She was as wet as I've ever seen a human being be and had a bad cough (my poncho must've gone heaven knows where) and water squelching in her shoes. She was shivering violently and her fingers were blue—it could not have been more than fifty degrees out—and her long, baggy dress clung to her with water running off it; there was a puddle already forming around her feet on the rug. Her teeth were chattering. She stood there shivering and glowering miserably at me, from time to time emitting that deep, painful chest cough you sometimes hear in adults who smoke too much. I thought of hot baths, towels, electric blankets, aspirin—can ghosts get pneumonia? "For God's sake, get your clothes off!" I said, but A. R. stepped back against the door, shivering, and wrapped her starved arms in her long, wet skirt.

"No!" she said, in a deep voice more like a crow's than ever. "Like this!"

"Like what?" said I helplessly, thinking of my back and how incapable I was of dragging a resistant five-year-old anywhere.

"You hate me!" croaked A. R. venomously; "You starve me! You do! You won't let me eat anything!"

Then she edged past me, still coughing, her dark eyes ringed with blue, her skin mottled with bruises, and her whole body shaking with cold and anger, like a little mask of Medusa. She screamed:

"You want to clean me up because you don't like me!

"You like me clean because you don't like me dirty!

"You hate me so you won't give me what I need!

"You won't give me what I need and I'm dying!

"I'm dying! I'm dying!

"I'M DYING!"

She was interrupted by coughing. I said "A. R.—" and she screamed again, her whole body bending convulsively, the cords in her neck standing out. Her scream was choked by phlegm and she beat herself with her fists, then wrapping her arms in her wet skirt through another bout of coughing, she said in gasps:

"I couldn't get into your house to use the bathroom, so I had to shit in my pants.

"I had to stay out in the rain; I got cold.

"All I can get is from you and you won't give it."

"Then tell me what you need!" I said, and A. R. raised her horrid little face to mine, a picture of venomous, uncontrolled misery, of sheer, demanding starvation.

"You," she whispered.

So that was it. I thought of the pleading cats, whose open mouths (*Dependency! Dependency!*) reveal needle teeth which can rip off your thumb; I imagined the Little Dirty Girl sinking her teeth into my chest if I so much as touched her. Not touched for bathing or combing or putting on shoelaces, you understand, but for touching only. I

saw—I don't know what; her skin ash-grey, the bones of
her little skull coming through her skin worse and worse
every moment—and I knew she would kill me if she didn't
get what she wanted, though she was suffering far worse
than I was and was more innocent—a demon child is still a
child, with a child's needs, after all. I got down on one knee,
so as to be nearer her size, and saying only, "My back—be
careful of my back," held out my arms so that the terror of
the ages could walk into them. She was truly grey now, her
bones very prominent. She was starving to death. She was
dying. She gave the cough of a cadaver breathing its last, a
phlegmy wheeze with a dreadful rattle in it, and then the
Little Dirty Girl walked right into my arms.

And began to cry. I felt her crying right up from her belly.
She was cold and stinky and extremely dirty and afflicted
with the most surprising hiccough. I rocked her back and
forth and mumbled I don't know what, but what I meant
was that I thought she was fine, that all of her was fine: her
shit, her piss, her sweat, her tears, her scabby knees, the
snot on her face, her cough, her dirty panties, her bruises,
her desperation, her anger, her whims—all of her was
wonderful, I loved all of her, and I would do my best to take
good care of her, all of her, forever and forever and then a
day.

She bawled. She howled. She pinched me hard. She
yelled, "Why did it take you so long!" She fussed violently
over her panties and said she had been humiliated, though
it turned out, when I got her to the bathroom, that she was
making an awfully big fuss over a very little brown stain. I
put the panties to soak in the kitchen sink and the Little
Dirty Girl likewise in a hot tub with vast mounds of rose-
scented bubble bath which turned up from somewhere,
though I knew perfectly well I hadn't bought any in years.
We had a shrieky, tickly, soapy, toe-grabby sort of a bath, a
very wet one during which I got soaked. (I told her about
my back and she was careful.) We sang to the loofah. We
threw water at the bathroom tiles. We lost the soap. We
came out warm in a huge towel (I'd swear mine aren't that

big) and screamed gaily again, to exercise our lungs, from which the last bit of cough had disappeared. We said, "Oh, floof! there goes the soap." We speculated loudly (and at length) on the possible subjective emotional life of the porcelain sink, American variety, and (rather to my surprise) sang snatches of *The Messiah* as follows:

> *Every malted*
> *Shall be exalted!*

and:

> *Behold and see*
> *Behold and see*
> *If there were e'er pajama*
> *Like to this pajama!*

and so on.

My last memory of the evening is of tucking the Little Dirty Girl into one side of my bed (in my pajamas, which had to be rolled up and pinned even to stay on her) and then climbing into the other side myself. The bed was wider than usual, I suppose. She said sleepily, "Can I stay?" and I (also sleepily) "Forever."

But in the morning she was gone.

Her clothes lasted a little longer, which worried me, as I had visions of A. R. committing flashery around and about the neighborhood, but in a few days they too had faded into mist or the elemental particles of time or whatever ghosts and ghost-clothes are made of. The last thing I saw of hers was a shoe with a new heel (oh yes, I had gotten them fixed) which rolled out from under the couch and lasted a whole day before it became—I forget what, the shadow of one of the ornamental tea-cups on the mantel, I think.

And so there was no more five-year-old A. R. beating on the door and demanding to be let in on rainy nights. But that's not the end of the story.

As you know, I've never gotten along with my mother. I've always supposed that neither of us knew why. In my childhood she had vague, long-drawn-out symptoms which I associated with early menopause (I was a late baby); then she put me through school, which was a strain on her librarian's budget and a strain on my sense of independence and my sense of guilt, and always there was her timidity, her fears of everything under the sun, her terrified, preoccupied air of always being somewhere else, and what I can only call her furtiveness, the feeling I've always had of some secret life going on in her which I could never ask about or share. Add to this my father's death somewhere in pre-history (I was two) and then that ghastly behavior psychologists call The Game of Happy Families—I mean the perpetual, absolute insistence on How Happy We All Were that even aunts, uncles, and cousins rushed to heap on my already bitter and most unhappy shoulders, and you'll have some idea of what's been going on for the last I-don't-know-how-many years.

Well, this is the woman who came to visit a few weeks later. I wanted to dodge her. I had been dodging academic committees and students and proper bedtimes; why couldn't I dodge my mother? So I decided that *this time I would be openly angry* (I'd been doing that in school, too).

Only there was nothing to be angry about, this time.

Maybe it was the weather. It was one of those clear, still times we sometimes have in October: warm, the leaves not down yet, that in-and-out sunshine coming through the clouds, and the northern sun so low that the masses of orange pyracantha berries on people's brick walls and the walls themselves, or anything that color, flame indescribably. My mother got in from the airport in a taxi (I still can't drive far) and we walked about a bit, and then I took her to Kent and Hallby's downtown, that expensive, old-fashioned place that's all mirrors and sawdust floors and old-fashioned white tablecloths and waiters (also waitresses now) with floor-length aprons. It was very self-indulgent of me. But she had been so much better—or I had been—it doesn't matter. She was seventy and if she wanted to be fussy and furtive and act like a thin, old guinea-hen with secret despatches from the C.I.A. (I've called her worse things) I felt she had the right. Besides, that was no worse than my flogging myself through five women's work and endless depressions, beating the old plough horse day after day for weeks and months and years—no, for decades—until her back broke and she foundered and went down and all I could do was curse at her helplessly and beat her the more.

All this came to me in Kent and Hallby's. Luckily my mother squeaked as we sat down. There's a reason; if you sit at a corner table in Kent and Hallby's and see your face where the mirrored walls come together—well, it's complicated, but briefly, you can see yourself (for the only time in your life) as you look to other people. An ordinary mirror reverses the right and left sides of your face but this odd arrangement re-reflects them so they're back in place. People are shocked when they see themselves; I had planned to warn her.

She said, bewildered, "What's that?" But rather intrigued too, I think. Picture a small, thin, white-haired, extremely prim ex-librarian, worn to her fine bones but still ready to take alarm and run away at a moment's notice; that's my mother. I explained about the mirrors and then I said:

"People don't really know what they look like. It's only an idea people have that you'd recognize yourself if you saw yourself across the room. Any more than we can hear our own voices; you know, it's because longer frequencies travel so much better through the bones of your head than they can through the air; that's why a tape recording of your voice sounds higher than—"

I stopped. Something was going to happen. A hurricane was going to smash Kent and Hallby's flat. I had spent almost a whole day with my mother, walking around my neighborhood, showing her the University, showing her my house, and nothing in particular had happened; why should anything happen now?

She said, looking me straight in the eye, "You've changed."

I waited.

She said, "I'm afraid that we—like you and I were not—are not—a happy family."

I said nothing. I would have, a year ago. It occurred to me that I might, for years, have confused my mother's primness with my mother's self-control. She went on. She said:

"When you were five, I had cancer."

I said, *"What? You had what?"*

"Cancer," said my mother calmly, in a voice still as low and decorous as if she had been discussing her new beige handbag or Kent and Hallby's long, fancy menu (which lay open on the table between us). "I kept it from you. I didn't want to burden you."

Burden.

"I've often wondered—" she went on, a little flustered; "they say now—but of course no one thought that way then." She went on, more formally, "It takes years to know if it has spread or will come back, even now, and the doctors knew very little then. I was all right eventually, of course, but by that time you were almost grown up and had become a very capable and self-sufficient little girl. And then later on you were so successful."

She added, "You didn't seem to want me."

Want her! Of course not. What would you feel about a mother who disappeared like that? Would you trust her? Would you accept anything from her? All those years of terror and secrecy; maybe she'd thought she was being punished by having cancer. Maybe she'd thought she was going to die. Too scared to give anything and everyone being loudly secretive and then being faced with a daughter who wouldn't be questioned, wouldn't be kissed, wouldn't be touched, who kept her room immaculate, who didn't want her mother and made no bones about it, and who kept her fury and betrayal and her misery to herself, and her schoolwork excellent. I could say only the silliest thing, right out of the movies:

"Why are you telling me all this?"

She said simply, "Why not?"

I wish I could go on to describe a scene of intense and affectionate reconciliation between my mother and myself, but that did not happen—quite. She put her hand on the table and I took it, feeling I don't know what; for a moment she squeezed my hand and smiled. I got up then and she stood too, and we embraced, not at all as I had embraced the Little Dirty Girl, though with the same pain at heart, but awkwardly and only for a moment, as such things really happen. I said to myself: *Not yet. Not so fast. Not right now,* wondering if we looked—in Kent and Hallby's mirrors—the way we really were. We were both embarrassed, I think, but that too was all right. We sat down: *Soon. Sometime. Not quite yet.*

The dinner was nice. The next day I took her for breakfast to the restaurant that goes around and gives you a view of the whole city and then to the public market and then on a ferry. We had a pleasant, affectionate quiet two days and then she went back East.

We've been writing each other lately—for the first time in years more than the obligatory birthday and holiday cards and a few remarks about the weather—and she sent me old family photographs, talked about being a widow, and being misdiagnosed for years (that's what it seems now) and about all sorts of old things: my father, my being in the school play in second grade, going to summer camp, getting moths to sit on her finger, all sorts of things.

And the Little Dirty Girl? Enclosed is her photograph. We were passing a photographer's studio near the University the other day and she was seized with a passionate fancy to have her picture taken (I suspect the Tarot cards and the live owl in the window had something to do with it), so in we went. She clamors for a lot lately and I try to provide it: flattens her nose against a bakery window and we argue about whether she'll settle for a currant bun instead of a do-nut, wants to stay up late and read and sing to herself so we do, screams for parties so we find them, and *at* parties impels me towards people I would probably not have noticed or (if I had) liked a year ago. She's a surprisingly generous and good little soul and I'd be lost without her, so it's turned out all right in the end. Besides, one ignores her at one's peril. I try not to.

Mind you, she has taken some odd, good things out of my life. Little boys seldom walk with me now. And I've perfected—though regretfully—a more emphatic method of kitty-booting which they seem to understand; at least one of them turned to me yesterday with a look of disgust that said clearer than words: "Good Heavens, how you've degenerated! Don't you know there's nothing in life more important than taking care of Me?"

About the picture: you may think it odd. You may even think it's not her. (You're wrong.) The pitch-ball eyes and thin face are there, all right, but what about the bags under her eyes, the deep, downward lines about her mouth, the strange color of her short-cut hair (it's grey)? What about her astonishing air of being so much older, so much more intellectual, so much more professional, so much more —well, competent—than any Little Dirty Girl could possibly be?

Well, faces change when forty-odd years fall into the developing fluid.

And you have always said that you wanted, that you must have, that you commanded, that you begged, and so on and so on in your interminable, circumlocutory style, that the one thing you desired most in the world was a photograph, a photograph, your kingdom for a photograph—of me.

A Young Man, Gleaming, White

João Guimarães Rosa

**Translated By
Barbara Shelby**

On the night of November 11, 1872, in the district of Serro Frio in Minas Gerais, there occurred eerie phenomena which were referred to in contemporary newspapers and registered in the astronomical tables. According to these accounts, a glowing missile hurtled out of space, accompanied by booming blasts. The earth rocked in a quake that shook the mountain heights, made rubble of houses, and caused the valleys to tremble. Countless people were killed. The torrential rainstorm that followed caused greater floods than any ever seen before; the water in the streams and rivers rose sixty feet above its normal level. After this cataclysm the features of the country for a league around were entirely changed; all that was left were the wrecks of hills, caves newly blasted open, creeks shifted from their courses, forests uprooted, new mountains and cliffs upthrust, farms swallowed up without a trace—strewn rocks covering what had been fields. Even some distance away from the monstrous happenings, many men and animals perished by being buried alive or drowned. Others wandered at random, going wherever it pleased God to send them, in their confusion at no longer finding the old roads they knew.

A week later, on the day of St. Felix the Confessor, one of these poor fugitives, who had doubtless been driven from his home by hunger or shock, appeared in the courtyard of Hilário Cordeiro's Casco Ranch. Suddenly he was there, a youth with the appearance of a gentleman but in a pitiable state. Without even rags to cover his nakedness, he had wrapped himself in a thick cloth like a horse blanket, which he had found God knows where. Bashfully, he showed himself there in the early morning light and then disappeared behind the fence of the cow pasture. He was of an amazing whiteness, not at all sickly or wan, but of a

fine paleness, semi-gilded with light, which caused him to
gleam as if he had a source of brightness inside his body.
He seemed to be a foreigner of some kind never met with
before in those parts, almost as if he constituted a new race
all by himself. They talk about him to this day, though with
a good deal of confusion and uncertainty because it was so
long ago. The story is told by the children and grandchildren of men who were adolescents, or perhaps even children, when they were fortunate enough to know him.

Because Hilário Cordeiro, a good, God-fearing man,
was generous to the poor, more especially in those first
days after the catastrophe in which his own relatives had
died or suffered total ruin, he unhesitatingly offered the
youth hospitality and thoughtfully provided him with clothing and food. The stranger was in dire need of such help,
for, as a result of the extraordinary misfortunes and terrors
that he had suffered, he had completely lost his memory
and even his use of speech. In his condition perhaps the
future was indistinguishable from the past; since he had
lost all sense of time and could understand nothing, he
answered neither yea nor nay. His was a truly pitiful state.
He seemed not even to try to understand gestures, or at
any rate often interpreted them to mean the opposite of
what was intended. Since he was bound to have a given
name already, he could not just be given some made-up
one; but no one had any idea what his Christian name was
any more than the surname he must have inherited from
his unknown progenitors. He seemed to be the Son of No
Man.

For days after his arrival the neighbors came to inspect
him. Stupid they certainly did not find him, but he was
subject to a kind of dreamy disinvolvement, tinged by
sadness. They were surprised, though, at how unobtru-
sively observant he could be—noting every little charac-
teristic of people and of things. This odd combination of
careful scrutiny and misinterpretation only began to be
understood later on. Nevertheless, they all liked him. And

the person who was perhaps most attached to him was the Negro José Kakende, who was a bit odd himself. This former slave of a half-witted musician had been touched in the head ever since a shock he had suffered during the calamities in the county, so that he began to wander from place to place, shouting warnings to the people and crying out wild lunatic tales about a portentous apparition that he swore he had seen on the banks of the Rio de Peixe just before the cataclysm. Only one person had a grudge against the youth from the beginning, and that was a certain Duarte Dias, the father of a beautiful girl named Viviana. He swore the youth was a rascal, a secret criminal, who, in better times, would have been banished to Africa or put in irons and thrown into the king's dungeon. But because he was known to be a hot-tempered, overbearing man, and malignant and unjust besides, with a heart of pure adamant, nobody paid much attention to him.

One particular day they took the youth to mass, and though he gave no sign of being a believer or an unbeliever, he did nothing untoward. He listened to the singing and the choral music, seriously and with considerable feeling. He was not sad exactly, but it seemed as if he felt a greater nostalgia than other people, a deeper yearning. Perhaps because he understood nothing of the service, his feeling was refined into a purer ecstasy—the heart of a dog who hears his master. His smile, which was more a matter of the lips than of the eyes and which was never broad enough to reveal his teeth, sometimes lingered on his face for long periods, as if he were thinking of some other place, some other time. After mass, when Father Bayáo gave a kindly talk to the youth, he prefaced it by unexpectedly making the sign of the cross over him but found that the young man was not made at all uneasy by the holy gesture. It seemed to the priest that he floated a little above the earth, held there by some inner buoyancy denied to the earthbound. "Compared to him, all of us ordinary mortals have hard expressions and an ugly look of habitual weariness." These lines were written by the priest in a letter which he signed and sealed as a witness coming of the exquisitely strange wanderer and sent to Canon Lessa Cadaval of the Mariana See. In this letter he also mentioned the Negro José Kakende, who had approached him on the same occasion with loud and extravagant accounts of the vision he had had at the riverside: ". . . the dragging wind and majesty of the cloud full of splendor, and in it, swirled round by fire, a dark-yellow moving object, a flying vehicle, flat, with rounded edges, and surmounted by a glass bell of a bluish color. When it landed, there descended from it archangels, amidst wheels, flaring flames, and the pealing of trumpets." Along with the excited José Kakende came Hilário Cordeiro to take the youth home with him again, as tenderly as if he were his real father.

At the door of the church was a blind beggar, Nicolau. When the youth caught sight of him he gazed at him deeply and with his whole attention (they say his eyes were the color of a rose!) and then he walked straight up to the beggar and hastily handed him a bit of something out of his pocket. No Christian soul could see that blind man, sweating in the sun, without noting the irony of his having to bear the heat of that burning orb and at the same time be denied the ability to rejoice in the beauty of the sun or the moon. The blind man fingered the gift in his hand and then, instead of wondering what outlandish manner of money it could be and then realizing it was no money at all, brought it up to his mouth at once, only to have the child who was his guide warn him that it was not something to eat but only a seed from some kind of tree pod. The blind man angrily put the seed away and only planted it months later, long after the events soon to be related had already taken place. From the seed sprouted a rare and unexpected bluish flower, several contraposed flowers in one, all commingled impossibly in lovely confusion. The tints were of a kind not seen in our times; no two people could even agree on precisely what the colors were. But soon it wilted and withered away, producing no seeds nor shoots; even the insects had not had the time to learn to seek it out.

Just after the scene with the blind man, though, Duarte Dias appeared in the churchyard with some of his friends and servants, ready to make trouble and astonishing everyone by demanding that the youth go with him, on the grounds that because of the whiteness of his skin and his aristocratic ways, he must be one of the Resendes, Duarte Dias's rich relatives who had been lost in the earthquake; and that therefore, unless some definite news was received that the youth was no Resende, it was his responsibility to hold him in his custody. This proposal was promptly contested by Hilário Cordeiro, and the argument might easily have become a real altercation because of Dias's loud insistence, if he had not finally given in to the persuasion of Quincas Mendanha, a political notable from the capital, who was also purveyor for the Brotherhood.

Soon it became clear that Hilário Cordeiro was righter than he knew when he protected the youth so zealously. He began to be lucky in everything: all in his household were healthy and lived in harmony, and his business prospered. It was not that the youth gave him much overt help; he could hardly have been expected to do rough farm labor with his dainty, uncallused hands, as white and smooth as a courtier's. In fact, he spent most of his time dreamily wandering about here and there at will, exercising an airy freedom and a taste for solitude. People said he must be under some magic spell. Magic and delicate hands to the contrary notwithstanding, the youth did take an extremely important part in everything to do with the machinery and the tools used on the place. He was extraordinarily good at mechanics, inventing and repairing in the cleverest, most careful way. At those times he was wide-awake enough. He was also an astronomer, but one with the odd habit of continually watching the sky by day as well as by night. Another amusement of his was to light fires, and everyone noticed how eagerly he took part in lighting the traditional bonfires on St. John's Eve.

It was on that very St. John's Eve that the incident with the girl Viviana occurred, a story which has never been told accurately before. What happened was that when the youth, accompanied by the Negro José Kakende, came up and saw that the girl, though so pretty, was not amusing herself like the others, he went up close to her and gently, but startlingly, laid the palm of his hand delicately on her breast. And since Viviana was the loveliest of all the girls, the wonder was that the beauty of his deed in no way altered his vague melancholy. But her father, Duarte Dias, who had been watching, bawled out, over and over: "They've got to be married! Now they have to get married!" He declared that since the stranger, who was unmarried, had shamed his daughter, he would have to take her to wife, will-nilly. Though the young man listened pleasantly to all this and made no objection, Duarte Dias never stopped bellowing until Father Bayao and some of the older men remonstrated with him for his nonsensical anger. Young Viviana soothed him, too, by her radiant smiles; from the moment of the youth's touch there was awakened in her an unending joy, a pure gift which she enjoyed for the rest of her life. Incomprehensibly, Duarte Dias later added to the general amazement, as we shall see.

He came to Casco Ranch on August 5, the day of the mass of Our Lady of the Snows and Eve of the Transfiguration, and asked to speak to Hilário Cordeiro. The youth was present, too, so otherworldly and graceful that he made one think of moonlight. And Duarte Dias begged them to let him take the young man home with him, not out of ambition or because he wanted to pretend to a rank he didn't have, nor out of any petty self-interest, but because he really wanted and needed to have with him one for whom his contrition and remorse had led him to conceive the strongest esteem and affection. He was so moved that he could scarcely speak, and copious tears flowed from his eyes. Those who heard him could not understand such a change in a man who had never been able to express any emotion at all except in some violent, impetuous way. However, the youth, bright as the eye of the sun, simply took him by the hand and, accompanied by the Negro José Kakende, led him off through the fields to a place on Duarte's land where there was an abandoned brick kiln. There he made signs for the men to dig, and they found a diamond deposit—or maybe a big pot of gold, as another story has it. Naturally, Duarte Dias thought he would become a very rich man after this, and he changed from that day on into a good, upright man, so his awestruck contemporaries claimed.

But on the Venerable St. Bridget's Day something more was heard of the imperturbable youth. It was said that the night before he had made one of his customary disappearances, but this time by way of the sky, at a time of dry thunder. All José Kakende would say was that he had secretly helped light nine bonfires in a pattern. Aside from that, he only repeated his old wild descriptions of a cloud, flames, noises, round things, wheels, a contraption of some sort, and archangels. With the first sunlight, the youth had gone off on wings.

Each one, in his own way, mourned his life long whenever he thought of the youth. They doubted the air they breathed, the mountains, the very solidity of the earth—but remembered him. Duarte Dias actually died of sorrow, though his daughter, the maiden Viviana, never lost her joy. José Kakende had long talks with the blind man. Hilário Cordeiro, like many others, said he felt he was half in his grave whenever he thought of the youth. His gleam remained when he was gone. That's all there is to tell.

Cerridwen and the Quern of Time

Paul Hazel

Cerridwen was old, so old she did not remember the days of her youth—or even if ever she had had them. Year followed year. Winter and summer, keeping the same deep rhythm, Cerridwen turned the whirling nights toward morning. The little hut where she worked the quern trembled with the growl of the stone. The rough planking jolted under her feet. Cerridwen did not stop to listen.

Beyond the thin door the seas broke on the coast of Tywy, the women's holding. Summer and winter the slate beaches crumbled. Cold nights spilled over her, black nights frosted with stars. The old woman scarcely noticed.

There were fogs in autumn. In April journeying birds alighted moment to moment on the rooftrees. Then in the hall the mortal women were filled with loud cheerfulness. Cerridwen seldom went among them. In the hall there was grieving. Birth came there and, in equal measure, death came. To her it was much the same. The shadows blackened on the wall of her hut. Without puzzling, she pushed the worn shaft of the wheel, dragging the darkness back into morning.

Above the alders, over the roofs and the sea, the wide, hollow sky was dark then light again, endlessly.

When they gave a thought to it, the women imagined that time was a river, its true current bearing them steadily westward, with never a fault. But Cerridwen had stayed in one place. The river went by her. Nightly, her shoulder pressed against the shaft, she had come to feel the smallest shifts in the cogs, the fitful laggings, the sudden unaccountable leaping of the stone. Once, angered, she had merely watched from her cot as the shadows climbed the wall of her hut. Then in its lodging under the sea the cooled sun had lingered: the tall alders stiffened and the barley had blackened in the fields. And once, though there were none now alive who remembered it, she had kept the stone wildly turning when morning came. The sun had crossed and recrossed the hills. In the hall a woman was bedded and had given birth between what should have been midnight and morning. But an age had come and gone since she had done that. Now when she went out on the shore the little girls laughed at her hobbling walk and at the rime of barley dust that coated her arms. She had a cast in one eye. The staring children wondered whether this left her half blinded.

"Watch where you step, old one," a pretty red-haired girl called across the bog to her, "or you will walk into the sea. Then, if you're drowned, the seallords will not marry you."

"I'll not marry," the old woman said.

Though the girl blushed at being taken seriously, her high spirits soon got the better of her. "And why not, Cerridwen?" The girl's eyes were black as currants and sparkled. At first Cerridwen could not think of a word to say to her. Things went on as before. When the girl was an old woman herself and had been laid in the ground, Cerridwen limped over the mossed stones to her grave and stood over it. But although she had thought on the matter a good while longer, still she did not have an answer.

There were men in the holding, bandy-legged and small. Their little hands could not go around the waist of a woman. Their only talk was of the silver herring they chased in all weathers over the sea. The holding lay on the furthest edge of land. Beyond it, in the far icy waves, it was said, the sealmen lived in their palaces under the sea. But no one was certain of that and the women took husbands from the men they knew. Yet when they woke in the night, it was the wet black hair and broad shoulders of the seallords they remembered.

The surf flung its spray under the stars. The women moved restlessly onto the porches. The voices of the water carried up to them. This, at least, was more than women's talk. Once in the cold and the starlight a man had come walking across the black bedded stones. No one could say out of what place he had come. Yet the brine still dripped from his beard. A woman had gone away with him. Little needed to be said of it. Daughters saw the certainty in their mothers' eyes. Now and again a copper-haired girl would go out into the falling darkness, her slender back stiffening to the fires of the holding. Desperately she waited as mile on mile, from the earth's end, the flame-killing ocean flooded the shoals.

Before Cerridwen quite awoke there was knocking. The doorlatch rattled. She crouched further down under the rag of her blanket. The knocking pursued her, unmercifully as children's laughter. Cerridwen pulled herself up on her elbows.

"Go away from me," she grumbled.

"Come quickly," an excited voice cried through the doorlatch.

"It is no small thing I do," Cerridwen said. "I am weary." A streak of sunlight fell across the foot of her cot. Indeed, it is a great thing, Cerridwen thought raising her face to the sun and judging it.

"You must come," the voice went on eagerly.

Cerridwen sat up straighter and rubbed her dry forehead. "Only the Mughain may order me," she said.

"Old one, I have come from her."

"For what cause?"

The voice on the other side of the door laughed joyously. "There is a god on the shore!"

When Cerridwen hobbled out into the morning, the holding lay still in the sunlight. The one cart-rutted street, the yards, even the great hall itself were each deserted. For a time she wandered aimlessly. But when she had turned the corner by the wellshed, she saw the hill where the women were gathered, crowded up on the rim of dune. Now she could hear the close withdrawing roar of the ocean. The women were quiet.

Cerridwen frowned. They were not her sisters; they were not her remotest kin; for a short time only they shared with her this little neck of stone jutting into the sea. The Mughain was merely the latest of the many queens who had gone before, the numberless others who must surely come after. Seeing the heaving curve of the young queen's breasts, Cerridwen gave a deep, angry sigh. With short, painful steps she mounted the hill and, after a great effort, stood side by side with the women staring over the shore.

"I am here, Mughain," she said, "though I have no part in this."

"I have summoned each of you," the queen said. Her mind was elsewhere.

The god paced the beach below. He was a heavy man with brown shoulders. A tangle of seahair hid his face. The little men rushed at him. When the tide fell back, it was crimson. Little heads, surprised to be without their necks and seeking company, knocked together in the foam. "He will murder us as well as our husbands," a woman said.

The god looked up. His rage had not abated.

Out of her proud eyes the young queen saw the huge man striding over the stones. Since her mother's time the beaches had been empty. Her head bent pondering, she saw the same emptiness running ahead, as it had run backwards, toward the final emptiness of her death.

"He must see we are women," she said fiercely. The women looked at her in horror. But presently a woman smiled. Quickly she fingered the strings of her gown. Long folds of cloth came over her head. Three others, looking at nothing, joined her until finally, one after another, all stood as women were made. Only Cerridwen had not moved a finger to her laces.

"How are you different?" The queen's voice was harsh.

Cerridwen's well-worked hands gripped the stick that held her upright. She had no answer. They were not alike, any more than one night, though the same stars are blazing, resembles the next. The resemblance was less when at the queen's word the women stripped her. Trembling, she tried to hide her breasts with her arms. Her breasts were without roundness or beauty, their dried flesh the color of mud. Alone, she stood in their company, like a wren among doves.

At the crest of the hill the god was still running. With each imposing stride he covered three yards of ground. Up close he was taller than they had imagined, far taller than any of the men of the holding, with a long, wild, comely face and shining black eyes. There was blood on his thick arms, blood matted between his webbed fingers.

"Lord, I welcome you," the young queen said.

Before the bold nakedness of the women the god's face seemed suddenly awkward. He was no longer running but his strange, bewildered eyes went on staring. Cerridwen saw clearly how those troubled eyes traveled over them. For the first time in her memory she realized that a man had looked on her and not seen her.

A darkness was sending its roots into the meadow; the grove of alders becoming a broad gray wall. At the foot of the hall pillar Cerridwen waited. Nine bands of gold she had wrapped on her arms. On the left side of her head, where the hair was wildest, she had thrust a comb. She stood a moment longer, not daring to go in. On the beach the men were burning the corpses. The smoke was nearly invisible in the dusk. Because of the smell the men hung back from the fires. In the hall the women gathered close to the hearthwall by the great bench and twittered like starlings.

The god pulled at his beard. Often their husbands had done the same and yet the hair of his beard was as black as a raven's coat and as green as malachite. He pinched a tiny crab that remained tangled under his chin.

"I had been killing kraken close to the shore," the god said. "There was a terrible rage in me because of the killing. The sea itself was full of tumult. So I did not notice the kraken had finished its screams and went on killing whatever came to hand." His voice was husky with exhaustion. "Truly," he said, "you have my apologies."

The young queen had scoured the crusted blood from his arms until her own arms ached. Beads of sweat trickled down the back of her gown. She had taken care that no other would touch him.

"It must be cold in the sea," she said tentatively.

His face was like a child's face wanting sleep. "Very cold it is, lady," he said and though he was weary, he looked at her deeply, as if he wished her to see how bitter the cold was there. "And dark," he said quietly, "and without comfort."

The women were hovering but the queen spoke to them sternly. From her corner Cerridwen watched them going away. She stood unnoticed and unmoving. There was a pain under her breasts. Baffled, she laid her hands flat against them, feeling the dry weightlessness of her flesh. "Oh," she said feebly. But the only sounds the young queen heard were the groans of her quickening breath.

The darkness lasted three days. The blank walls of heaven were pocked with the same dim stars. The same moon, like a smouldering lamp, hung part way up the sky. The night air smelled of half-burned oil. On the second night the women came to Cerridwen's hut. They banged on the door but she would not open it.

"Old one," they cried to her.

"Go away," she hissed and turned over on her cot.

On the third night the queen came herself. Her proud eyes were tense with sleeplessness. She had come away quickly and had not bothered to cover herself with her cloak. There were bites on her shoulders. Her hair fell straggling to either side of her neck. She did not push it back.

"Cerridwen," she called almost inaudibly.

But the old woman knew her. "Why have you not gone with him into the sea?" she asked from back in the hut.

The queen examined the doorlatch. "I expect he means to stay," she said softly.

It was cold, a cold that neither shifted nor changed.

Cerridwen put her lame feet on the floor. Beside the quern, when she had wrapped her rough hands around the wheelshaft, the old woman burst into tears. The water ran down her cheeks, running steadily, without a fault. With you and me, Cerridwen thought, it is much the same. Then with only one thing different, she set again to her work.

Soon afterwards the young queen climbed to the top of the dune, to the trampled place where she could watch the sweep of the ocean. Already the waves were taking color from the rising brightness. In the west, larger than it ever was at dawn, the red sun lifted its splendid head. With all the strength she could muster the young queen, growing younger, gazed seaward at the first light of evening.

The Ship from Away

Evangeline Walton

Young Devlin told me this story; told it with the shame-faced, frightened reluctance of the materialist—reared in speaking of the unbelievable, and with the eagerness, the excitability of one anxious to unbosom a preying obsession.

We were in a little Forty-second Street tea room, managed by one of those Eastern-influenced cults. Quiet, soft-voiced men and women going in and out; walls symbolically painted with sun and moon zigzagging lightning: it was perhaps the fittest setting that New York could provide for a tale like this. The boy sat across from me, his dark eyes burning, his lowered voice vibrant as the fever of narration mounted within him.

"It happened last year. My people had taken a castle on the Scots shore for the shooting season. Tourists often do. I don't shoot. I never could bear to kill things, and the others laughed at me for that. So I spent a good deal of time in the curragh, drifting or rowing in that little arm of the sea between Scotland and Ireland, usually with a book by Yeats or O'Grady along, or something else that brought me close to the wild barbarity, the fairy mysticism of the ancient Celts.

"It was on an evening that the thing happened, a peculiarly calm, placid evening. I had been lying on my back in the curragh not really thinking or feeling, but watching the gray cloud banks that were like phantom mountains against the horizon. The sea itself was already dark, an immense purplish mass, undulating softly as if at the stir of some hidden life beneath.

"It was then that, quite suddenly, I saw the ship. The unaccountable suddenness of its appearance startled me. I sat up, rubbing my eyes. How could it have come so close without my knowing? And then, as I looked, I saw the peculiarities of its structure, of the tall prow and wing-like sails. It was utterly unlike any boat or schooner I had seen in those waters or in any others. More like an ancient picture . . .

"It was coming closer. I was, I suppose, too surprised, too puzzled, to notice that the oars made no sound, that water did not part before the bow. These details, subconsciously seen, came back to me later. Though the deck was in deep shadow, I could make out figures on it: men in bright-coloured cloaks, and women with light glancing off metal ornaments in their braided hair.

"I stared, dumbfounded, every wheel in my brain locking in the frantic effort to understand. And then I noticed something which I must have subconsciously seen and been vexed by, all along, something which only now leaped sharp and clear into my consciousness. The waves about the ship and beyond it, were clear and shining. *It cast no shadow.*

"I am sure every hair on me stood upright, then; my spine was stiff. I felt an indescribable shrinking horror, like the repugnance we feel for physical contact with certain people, except that this was not disgust, but a deep, icy chill.

"I didn't wait, in that first moment of panic, for another look; I turned about and rowed like mad in the opposite direction, keeping my eyes on the bottom of the boat, telling myself that I was mad. And yet, when an irresistible fascination made me look over my shoulder, there was nothing there."

He paused, gripping my arm convulsively, his sensitive face twisted, his dark eyes wide. Except for his very obvious emotion, I might have set it down to the wild fantasies brilliant, precocious youngsters like him will indulge in. There was always a strain of over-imagination in him, a sort of aloofness foreign to our hustling mechanical twentieth century. He seemed to shrink from realities.

"I can't blame you if you don't believe me. I didn't dare to tell anyone when I went home. They'd have thought me mad. I wondered if I weren't myself. The ship, the people in ancient dress, their inexplicable disappearance, were impossible. I couldn't stop thinking of it. There was a curious, obsessing fascination about it—a rather regretful fascination. Not many could see a thing like that, and I had run away.

"It's easier to think such things up there. The people, whether on the Scotch or the Irish side of the water, are much the same—Gaelic, a queer, ancient people, full of old tales. Banshees, mysterious lights on the water, and the like, and once an old man told me of a fisherman in the Aran Isles who had been followed for miles by the *Gan Ceann*, the headless one, until he threw it a gold ring. They take the incredible for granted you see.

"The more superstitious still believe in a shadow-race, older than the earth, who carry away mortals they take a fancy to, and these tales began to get a hold on me. Was it these shadows I had seen, or ancient ghosts? I was losing all hold on normality, perhaps, but the thing that had happened to me was unbalancing and the need for secrecy always fosters such a growth.

"I got into the habit of going out in the curragh at twilight, never admitting to myself that I had any real purpose, always telling myself there was nothing to fear. Hopeful and magnetized, yet afraid. And then one evening, when I had given up hope and was thinking of something else, I saw it suddenly, the ship's dark silhouette against the sky. For an instant I didn't recognize it, then, setting my teeth, I paddled towards it. The superstitious revulsion of the flesh was not going to cheat me a second time, though I could feel its return. An immaterial thing could not harm me.

"And the ship seemed to favor my design; it was coming towards me much faster than I could go to it. I could see those aboard clearly now; men and women with many-coloured garments and long, flowing hair. Their faces were beautiful, but their eyes were oddly, unhumanly luminous. Their unnatural radiance, at once welcoming and *claiming,* sent a thrill of the old horror through me, but after a moment I saw that it was beautiful. They were smiling at me, welcoming me as one long-lost and now returned. Their meaning flooded through me without words, and as I looked, a queer delusion overcome me. Those shadow-faces seemed, all at once, familiar, dearer and far more intimate than any I have ever known.

"I can't explain it," he paused a moment. "It was a little like one of those strange feelings we have in childhood, the feeling that one's whole life, one's ties and home, are a dream, like those in the night, from which we shall awaken presently—to what? What sort of life, of home, of—world? A dizzy, tremendous thought.

"Well, it was a little like such an awakening. All my life *did* seem like a half-hour's trivial, shallow dream, and those people on the ship were my own, inexpressibly nearer, closer, than any others had ever seemed before or have again. I flung out my arms, half rising in the curragh to go to them, and at the movement the physical impossibility of stepping onto that immaterial deck occurred to me. The uncanniness of it all swept over me in a wave, and I dropped to the bottom of the curragh in a cold sweat, hiding my face. When I dared to look up there was nothing there."

He seemed to slump. The excitement had gone out of him. "I never dared to go out in the curragh again. I was glad when we left Scotland not long after, for soon I might have had to go. Something was drawing me to the ship, irresistibly, like steel to a magnet. Would I have been *taken,* like Thomas the Rhymer, carried off to be one of them, no longer human, if I had? It's incredible. You know his vision of the Three Worlds: Heaven, Hell, and the other that we moderns inaccurately call Fairyland. It must be dangerous for a human soul to be taken like that, away from its work, in to a world that has stopped, where there has been no change, and will be none till the end of time. The promise of rest, happiness, companionship far more intimate than any on earth, but a change terrible, complete as death . . ."

Did he guess then, I wonder? He must have known that within the month his family was leaving again for Scotland. Was it the strain of that knowledge which drove him to speak, to tell of the thing that was at once his heart's desire and his greatest dread? For that his fear was as great as his desire I cannot doubt. Though escape from reality may be the deepest need of a romanticist, there are few who would buy it at the cost of their humanity.

Thus I was surprised when I heard he had returned to Scotland with his family. I was not surprised at the news that came later. Afterward, his mother told me that when the body was washed ashore the half-obliterated features still wore a strange and startling smile, as if of joyous anticipation, greeting.

The Day the World Died

On the afternoon of the day the world died, many women unbraided their hair. The wind no longer felt a compulsion to move. Sweet fragrance seemed, to the flowers, a rather pointless affair.

The world died in many ways. It died in its sleep while everyone was breathing softly. It died a lingering death that only birds and small animals noticed and mourned. It died violently as the oceans drowned themselves and the mountains choked under their own weight. It died without leaving an obit that wrapped things up.

Many people knew the world had died. They walked into the streets and stood, and more came and still more, until the streets were filled with people standing. This was a kind of memorial for the world that no longer was, so no one would forget it.

In the evening of the day the world died, the sun set as it had set uncounted billions of times before. The sunset was a spray of red and orange like blood on the sky. Many people cried, remembering the world. And then the sun set, dragging its blood along with it.

The night of the day the world died was dark and starless and filled with the shiverings of forest creatures. Chill winds whistled at the windows.

—Thomas Wiloch

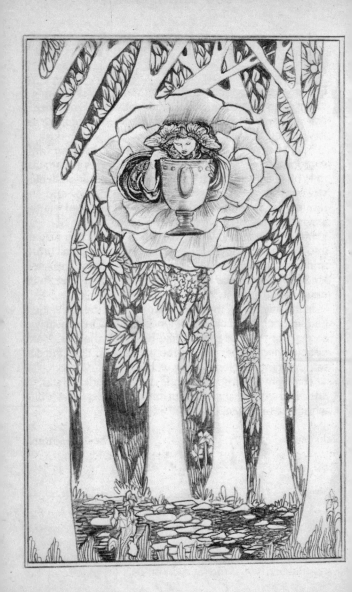

Blood and Dreams

Richard Monaco

The rain had stopped and the summer air was steamy. I was trying not to think, just riding home again. The sun on my bare head and armor was getting worse. No one ever got used to sitting in a steel suit. Especially in August.

When I was seventeen I killed a man and took his gear. I learned chivalry. A blond boy full of dreams. Everyone agreed that I was like a giant nine-year-old. My mother had hated the world and kept me locked away from it as long as she could. Now, almost twenty years later, I wished she'd done an even better job. And I'm still sorry I killed that first knight.

Always sorry for something; sorry to be going home because my family was there, wife, son and daughter. It's hard, when you don't like one another. I've always let them down, going when I shouldn't and coming when I wouldn't; a poor husband and father and sorry for that, too.

Going home again after another bloody bit of work for Arthur. I was sick of it. The older the king got the worse it became. He was afraid of everybody now. Trusted no one. He'd taught me ambition. My God.

When I was seventeen it had all been a dream. With bright, shifting scenes where everything made sense because I wasn't trying too hard and wasn't looking too closely at details. My youth always haunted me with promises unkept . . . yes . . . and simple peace and glory . . . lost.

I stopped to water my charger and myself. We'd been going since dawn and now the sun was slanting down the west. I glanced over my shoulder but really didn't expect anyone to be following.

"No one leaves my service against my will!" Arthur had shouted across the dim and drafty hall. I'd paused in the

doorway. Most of the knights had been uneasy. Worried he'd sic them on me.

"That's a silly attitude, my lord," I'd answered. The morning sun had been splashing all around the door. "I'm weary. I want no more."

"You'll get more than you bargained for!" he'd promised as I'd gone out into the dazzle of morning.

I stooped to cup a palmful from the pool; ripple reflections flashed like scattered coins. Noticed myself in the water: hair still mainly gold; face long; and still not fat. Then I saw a woman's face: pale; smoothly shaped; flamehaired.

I stood up, I licked the water from my lips, I bowed slightly. She was smallboned, softly melted together with dull blue, secret eyes. I always react the wrong way to women. I should just run away at once.

"You have a soft step, my lady," I told her.

Watching me, she did subtle things with her mouth.

"Am I?" she asked.

"Pardon?"

"Your lady."

I smiled—my second mistake. The first was not running away. I was tired. Nine hours riding; a saddle isn't a silk bed.

"I'm too far from fortune's graces," I replied, falling into courtly manner and hating myself for it, "to hope so high." I looked around but there was no horse or entourage visible. The damp, hot summer woods were lush and silent. The light was fire in her hair. I managed not to say so. She was watchful: was that fear, or calculation?

"You don't look to be," she told me, lightly brushing my cheek with her fingertips. "Are you in disfavor with your lord?"

"I don't know which is worse," I said. "Favor or disfavor." I liked looking at her milky, delicate face.

"Well said. I see you have served the great."

"The great are the lesser standing on others' backs."

"Better and better. Providence led you to me."

I thought I knew what was coming. When I was seventeen, at least I had an excuse for stupidity. I was sophisticated twenty years later, not wise.

"I war not with providence," I said, stroking the flank of my slaked mount. She climbed slightly up and sat sideways, relaxed, behind the highbacked sadde. Smiled with her vaguely troubled eyes. She kept looking about, then back to me.

"I lost what I rode," she told me. "I need you to bear me home." That was close to what I expected. She was watching me. "I think . . . I hope . . . I may trust you."

"To steer my horse?" I climbed up in front and her hands reached around my iron lap—pity it wasn't solid iron. She was silent. We rode away. She pointed out a trail and I followed it. Why not?

The sunbeams slanted through the full trees. The air smelled green and seemed to sparkle. The sketchy path cut and curved back on itself a dozen times in half a mile. We always appeared to be going a different way. When I was seventeen I'd hunted the Holy Grail—my father-in-law had convinced me not to sleep with his daughter until I found it. It took a long time for me to really get the hint. "Follow the sun," dear father had advised, and so I'd aimed myself east at morning, gradually south all day and finally west come evening. I'd looped across the country. Nothing had ever suited me better, I thought.

"You needn't tell me anything," I said. "I enjoy riding in circles. Makes me feel young again."

She seemed to come back from far thoughts.

"Are you so old, sir?"

"I don't keep count," I lied. Her flesh, where she held me, was soft as fluff.

"I won't deceive you," she said. Her breath was a thrill along my neck. "I am Lady Morgana."

That was a surprise, if true. The red hair was right. I'd never seen Arthur's famous sister or half-sister or whatever part thing she was. Incest in great families was like fleas on a dog. The witch, she was called. So young, too. Well, that might be witchcraft.

"Glad to hear it," I said. We took a violent twist through the trees and the setting sun was suddenly in my face, shattering through the dense leaves. "I haven't been deceived in days. I want to keep my record unblemished."

"My God," she murmured, "are you truly so bitter?" Her voice melted with soft, young hopefulness.

"You haven't tasted me yet," I said, then relented. "I've been too long at court."

"Ah, I see," she murmured with sweet compassion, "you're a great lord yourself."

"Great? Maybe across the shoulders."

"Will you name yourself?"

"My mother did that once," I said, and shrugged. We came out of the forest. Across a blue-green rush of field an immense castle towered. The sun was going down behind it and the crenelated shadow reached towards us like an immense road of darkness.

"I need help," she said. "Desperately."

"Naturally. Chivalry binds me to your service. Without chivalry," I said, "the world would no longer be perfect."

"You may even be too cynical for court life."

"I've retired."

"Halt the steed here."

"We reined up. The charger began to browse the dimming ground. I twisted around in the saddle. The twilight had deepened; her substance was just hinted.

"Yes?" I waited.

"My life is in danger. I was fleeing when you found me. And yet my welfare is of less importance than the mission I have undertaken."

I was interested. The famous witch, Morgana. Amusing.

"You didn't seem out of breath," I said, "from fleeing."

"Nothwithstanding. I fled. Death was close."

"When isn't it?" The twilight gradually melted us together.

Her face came nearer. I could feel her scented breath.

"You've heard of the Holy Grail, I trust?" she asked. I snorted. Didn't quite chuckle. "As what knight has not."

"A child's tale," I suggested, waiting.

"Things hidden are not things false. Since the Grail was brought to this land a chosen few have guarded it through generations. The Grail is power. Many seek it. Always."

There was a time when people believed I'd found the damned thing. And followed me, tortured me, ruined whatever of my life I'd left unspoiled hounding me out of the country . . . *Farewell, lady,* I almost said. I wish I had.

"What kind of power? A strong smell?"

"Jest not," she said, with an edge now. She was used to commanding and I was getting used to not obeying. "These are deep matters."

"I once worried about deep matters. And magic and mystery." I shrugged. "What happened to your vassals?" I peered around into the glimmering that was dying into night. The castle was a depthless shape against the sky.

"We were ambushed. My loyal servants died for the Holy mission." She found my bare hands and firmly held them. Her voice was vibrant and I heard the tears I couldn't see. She seemed so young, determined and strong, yet softly vulnerable. I was touched. Her hands felt good. I felt myself starting to drift. "So now I cast myself upon your honor. You have a cynic's voice but I read grace in your heart."

"Alright," I said. Her touch was a promise in the dreaming dusk. "I've taken the bait. Draw me in at your pleasure, Lady Morgana."

Scented breath, and then a kiss so light and soft I thought of a butterfly flicker.

"Thank you, sir," she said. "Sir whom? Is your name covered over by a vow?"

"A vow of good sense, which I've just broken, my lady." I hoped she'd try for another kiss. She didn't. "My name is Parsival."

Most would have known me by the ruby red armor.

"Ah, and you pretend to know nothing of the Grail?

You, of all knights?" Her voice seemed older, now.

"That was all moonspinning. I was a boy then."

Suddenly shadows leaped and jingled, already far too close: the kiss had distracted me. I drew and slashed too late, aware I'd already let her down, wondering how many had been hiding in the brush here. Had they expected her or me? My head burst in white fire and I was gone.

Then images spilled over me like surf: I floated in deep darkness, greenish dimness, the blinding surface far, far above . . . drifted and was held, tangled somehow . . . gleaming eyes watched . . . and then a pale fire swam over me, graceful, and long hands felt me . . . sharp teeth nibbled softly as underwater wind, hurting and soothing in luminescent dreaming . . . tender sharpness stirred deep into my body and I couldn't tell myself from the wash of hungry need that pulsed and probed into me, mercilessly sweet . . .

When I woke up I assumed, obscurely, that I was dead. I was naked; the world was colorless and muffled in the gray light of limbo. Everything was too soft and cloying.

I kept blinking and when I shifted my head (surprised to find it on my shoulders) the pain told me I was still in the thick of things. Daylight filtered down from slit apertures high in the buttressed ceiling. The floors were deeply cushioned by rugs and I seemed to be laid out on silk cushions. Very comfortable except for my skull.

When I tried to touch the wound I discovered the next hair in the egg: my wrists were chained above my head. I sighed and groaned faintly. Nothing was ever easy. Every time I kissed somebody, trouble followed a breath later. When I was seventeen the first woman had a husband who tracked me for years; the second one I had to marry; the third hurt my feelings and the fourth wept . . . and somebody always wanted to kill me . . .

The underwater dream came back to me. Was it all dream? How long had I been lying here and what had gone on? Maybe I'd missed something good, at that.

"Now what?" I wondered aloud.

"What, indeed," a foreign accent sounded behind me. I peered back and saw an upside-down, massive man in mail armor.

"Where's the lady?"

"Where, indeed."

"Don't strain yourself trying to answer." I was irate. Pain kept flashing across my forehead.

"I like your spirit," the massive man returned, obliquely. "Yes indeed. Men with spirit and imagination are needed. That's the trouble in your country, sir. Lack of real imagination. Imagination, plus the will to rise high and achieve much, there's completeness. A man like yourself, I think, might—"

"What do you know about me?" I cut him off. Everyone cut him off, it turned out. He never seemed to mind. "Besides the fact that I'm easy to hit on the head."

"Yes, yes, you should have been more circumspect."

The place was so muffled, so soft, I had to resist sleep. The air was comfortable. There wasn't too much pain unless I moved.

"Did the king send you after me?" I wanted to know.

"What? Nonsense, nonsense. Set your mind at rest on that point, Sir Parsival. A chance meeting. A happenstance crossing of paths, sir. Yes, shall we say?"

"Shall we?"

"By all means."

"Get me out of this ridiculous position. I'm a knight and we're all full of pride and so forth."

"Young men are so, so hasty." He seemed deeply grieved and pained by my impatience. "Let's talk awhile. Let's see what sort of men we both are, eh? Surely you're not uncomfortable?"

"Neither am I young, you fat slob." My head hurt.

"Now, now, civility, sir, civility sweetens the intercourse of noble men."

Intercourse? Well, I was undressed and bound to a bed; and that dream, there was no telling what had gone on. A new voice joined us, from deeper back in the dim grayness. A reedy, nervous voice. I didn't like it.

"So," it piped. "So. What's this?" A little runt in runt armor sort of staggered closer. I thought he was drunk, but it was a severe limp. "Why don't we teach him gentility, Howtlande?" he wondered.

"There's time for that," Lord Civility reproved. "I have a proposition to put, first. If you're a man of sense you'll see the wisdom of my words. If—"

"If I have unusual lusts you'll satisfy them?" For some reason they didn't worry me. Maybe I just didn't care.

"We know your reputation," fat Howtlande ignored me. "Yes indeed. We're in an enterprise here where a stout sword arm would not go unrewarded. Yes, indeed."

"To use my arm you'll have to put a blade in my hand."

"Assuredly, ah yes . . . most certainly. We simply need your word, Sir Parsival of the Round Table, to serve us faithfully."

"Round Table," scoffed the runt. "Round as a chamberpot."

"I'm not a paid assassin," I pointed out. Except that's just what I'd become. I wore the hat but refused the name. I frowned and stared into the depths of the long chamber. Where was this place?

"Great rewards can be yours, sir," Howtlande went on. "We ask only your aid against attack. No more."

The reedy-voiced little cripple swayed above me. His features were puckered to one side and his eyes shifted and rolled constantly as if tracking movement all around the walls. He'd drawn his sword. When he pointed the tip at me, I liked him less and less. His steel was ill-kept: rusty and gritty. "Howtlande," he squeakily gloated, "let's just cut his throat. I don't trust him."

They weren't in charge, I decided. Parsival was starting to get clever. "There's nothing to trust me with," I pointed out. "I haven't said yes."

Howtlande leaned over me. His gray mail and silks billowed like sails. His nose was a harsh, sharp hook in the putty of his face. "Yes would be a wise word to use, just now," he said. It was hard to disagree.

"Very well," I said, "whom do you serve?"

"What?" He didn't like that. I grinned. Why not? I could play these games all day or evening or whatever.

"Don't trouble yourself over these things," the runt recommended. "Be grateful to keep your head."

"It does me little good," I replied. "It fills with worries and makes a tempting target." I really disliked him.

"Well, he's with us, Gobble," Howtlande said optimistically. "Dread not, Sir Parsival, you'll learn more as the days proceed in their inevitable round of bright and dark and—"

I shook my chains at him. "Why don't we trade places and I'll give *you* dull platitudes?" I suggested.

"Bear with it a moment," he told me, and left. There was more to it, more to come. Somebody obviously had to be asked for the key. I consoled myself, thinking at least this was more interesting than going home. I didn't wish to wait for whoever it was to say yes, no or maybe; but I needed motivation. Always did.

"Cripple," I called out, "your face looks like rat shit!" The wild eyes tracked around. For all I knew he'd feel complimented. But he didn't like me either. He couldn't resist twisting over and waving the sword at me.

"You carrion—" he began, but since I could fill in the rest myself I hooked his bent leg out from under him. He bounced almost noiselessly on the padded floor. As he rose, he whipped the blade down hard enough to split me.

I rolled aside, violently jerked the chains and they hummed and snapped with a brittle, bright *ping!* As I expected. Mother always said, "Your strength is a curse from your father who perished of his own." Mother was like that.

Gobble really popped his eyes this time, and scuttled backwards as I stood up, sour, rubbing my lacerated wrists. The manacles were thin and both had given way. I grinned at Runty. He chopped a desperate cut and I caught his forearm and took away his sword. His eyes were spinning with hate and dread. "Where's the lady?" I asked, testing the rusty edge with my thumb.

"Here, Sir Parsival," her voice lilted behind me. She and the fat man had emerged from the massed, muffled hangings. I debated holding a pillow across my naked loins but decided that would be worse. She didn't seem to mind.

"I think I can serve you better now," I told her, flicking the sword in an easy arc. Howtlande's expression was alert and thoughtful in the background. "Shall I start?"

She was almost smiling. "These gentlemen and I," she said, "have come to an understanding. I won't deceive you. The real danger still lies ahead."

"I'll face it better in my armor."

"Naturally, naturally," Howtlande said. "However—always best to not be too hasty, sir. With patience, determination, and imagination we all reach our respective goals." Nodded. "Ambition, drive, how rare these qualities are becoming in our time."

What a windbag. I was getting restless. "Somebody better make sense soon. Where in hell are we? Why was I trussed up like this?"

"We were, well," said Howtlande, "unsure of your ultimate position in this affair."

"What affair?"

"Anyway," Morgana put in, moving closer to me, something faintly like disappointment showing, "the fact is we're all in it together now."

"In what?" I was exasperated.

"We all, if I may say so," interjected Howtlande, "now share a common ground and purpose." He looked like his neck was sweaty though he didn't mop it. "Circumstances can lead men on to greatness and, in the end, form deeper bonds than mere ties of affection and—"

"We're in the castle of the Grail," she broke in as the bloat was warming to his subject. "The very place you found as a boy."

"I was seventeen, to be exact," I said. A year that haunts me. "I never saw the Grail—you're all a bit old for this, don't you think?"

"Imagination, vision—" Howtlande began. Gobble cut him off this time.

"We know you never understood anything, Parsival. That's no secret." Looked at the others. "He's useless. We don't need him for the rest of it. My master says—"

"Never mind your master," she snapped and he lunged to his feet and snarled his way to her.

"You want to steal it for yourself," he hissed, furious and uncoordinated. "You'll pay for that bit of treachery, my sweet lady! The master—" She cut him off by spitting in his face. He clutched at her with raking nails, so I tapped him, not too hard, atop his narrow head. The twisted leg flipped out from under him and he flopped to the deep carpet. Then he snaked his skinny neck about and chomped his teeth into my bare foot. I hopped and yelled and nearly sliced his head off; he wriggled aside, still chewing, my blood running from the corners of his long mouth. The needle pain blinding me, I finally stood on his strange skull and kicked myself loose. He rolled away over the cushions and carpets.

"Stop it," she demanded. Across the room, he crouched, his restless stare shifting past me. He snarled, and my blood dribbled down his cheeks and neck.

I dabbed at my foot with a pillow, staining the fluffy lace. "I ought to cut yours off," I muttered at my twisted friend. I'd be limping for days, if nothing worse. He'd ripped into the sole and heel, half a tooth deep.

"Parsival," Morgana went on, touching me while I tore some silk coverlets into long, wide strips and knotted them around my loins like a diaper. Appropriate. "Ignore this pettiness. We must work together or perish together."

"Where were you?" I asked her.

"When?"

"Until you came in here."

"Begging them not to be fools and kill you." Her dark blue look said nothing. "We need one another. We've been followed here by assassins."

I grunted. Gobble was back on his twisted feet. Howtlande was hovering, tentative, anxious. "What happened
to the rest of them?" There'd been a half dozen, at least,
milling around me in the dusk before the blade smacked
my skull sidewise.

"You slew two and the rest fled," she declared. "You
were very terrible."

"Where did these two gems come from?"

"They followed after."

"I love a good joke," I said.

"It's true," Howtlande put in (now that he had the story,
I supposed), "which is why we left you chained. Natural
caution is understandable. Why, such a warrior as you,
I've never seen such power. And I at once thought: here's
the very fellow to round out our determined numbers
and—"

"You liar," Runty snarled, "you wanted to cut his throat
while he lay there and—"

"Peace, enough!" she commanded. "We were fleeing
the men you cut down. There were worse things chasing
me than these two."

"We're all in it, for now," the runt declared. "Together."

I just shook my head at them. What a crew!

So we followed her through endless, padded corridors
and muffled chambers. I limped and cursed the gimpy little
Gobble, who always managed to be just out of reach. Well,
unless his teeth were poisoned like an asp's, my foot would
heal. Grayish light gloomed in the high slit windows. We
went on . . . and then the corridor reached a triple
branching and Morgana stopped, perplexed and nervous.
Paced back and forth.

"Well," Howtlande said, "never fear, never fear. You'll
recall the way, eh? Confidence is the soul of all human
endeavor—"

"I've never been here before, you ass," she snapped. I

grinned and adjusted my diapers, glad this place was so inexplicably padded and deserted. Warm, for a castle. They claimed my armor was missing when they went back for it.

"Do you hear a voice," I wondered, "that guides you? I wish I did."

"This isn't funny," she informed me. "I had directions from an old druid. But he knew only the way to the chamber of three directions." She gestured at the corridors.

"She tortured the old bastard," Gobble hissed, "and he died when he came to this part." He grinned with malice, his small teeth a shark flash in halflight.

Morgana flicked a glance at me. "He always lies." Flicked one over him. "You twisted little thing."

He poked his tongue between his teeth. But before he could speak she held up her hand for silence, and listened, alert. I made out a faint click-clack back behind us. Howtlande looked more uneasy. "Pursued," he muttered. "Alas, how all human precautions sink beneath human misjudgement—"

"Shut up!" she snarled, secret eyes flaming now like a bright dagger's edge. Howtlande suddenly lunged for Gobble and nearly caught him. He had surprising speed, too. The ferret-faced cripple had to resort to his floor writhing tactics to escape.

"You little wretch!" the fat man cried, stomping his iron shod feet at the other's frail but repulsively supple limbs. "You betrayed us! You betrayed us"

God, what a crew!

"Morgana," I demanded, "you'd better choose." I could hear muffled footsteps and weapons banging, and her two henchmen were going at it with a passion.

"Only one way leads to the Grail," she said, searching my face as if the answer lay there. "The others lead to certain destruction."

"So, it would seem, does staying here." I glanced at the

burly knight, who was towering over the cringing cripple. "He betrayed us to black Clinschor!" he insisted. "His foul dwarves are at our heels!"

"Someone's always at my heels," I commented. "Come on." I strode down the central corridor as if I knew where I was going. Each step hurt. "Anyway," I said over my shoulder, "they'll have two ways to go wrong when they reach this spot."

She was right behind me. Howtlande talked steadily. I think he was disputing with Gobble. Even here, the walls and floor were padded. What a vast deserted place. What a waste of time.

"I hear them!" Howtlande said. "A single misjudgement is a keystone pulled from an arch! All must fall!"

"Aaaah, you bloated coward!" his companion whined. "I tell you, the master's men will aid us."

Master Clinschor, I thought, what nonsense. Everybody claimed he was alive and in hiding here or there. For twenty years men rumored him to life. Amazing ghost he must be to still claim followers.

"They're hard upon us!" Howtlande cried. He was right. Pounding feet and plinking chainmail. There were lots of feet.

"Well, great champion," she said, "I hope you're equal to the tales they tell of you."

I sighed. "I'd prefer a better shield than reputation, at the moment." My foot hurt. I saw Gobble lurching near me. I slammed the flat of my blade across his rear end just where the armor spread a little and was rewarded by a yelp and a snarl. I felt better.

"Just greasing my joints," I explained.

"You bastard," said Gobble, adding some other memorable things. I felt refreshed. Then he was yelling into the shadows behind us, "Hear me! I am Lord Gobble of the Inner Circle! I expect to be obeyed!"

I wondered if he'd also expected the ax that grazed his shoulder and seemed to drag a huge, panting warrior after it.

"Worm!" Gobble shrieked, sticking his dagger into the fellow's foot right between the iron plates. He seemed bent on making everyone like himself. The knight howled inside his faceplate and hopped from wall to wall. Howtlande laid him low, two-handed in a blur to my left as I met the next two big, clanking gentlemen. I spun flat into the wall hangings so they missed me, and then hit the nearest. Oh, I was good at this work! I was good. They'd sent this many because everyone knew it: these had to be Arthur's hirelings. Arthur thought being a ruler meant never giving anything up. He hadn't always been that way. We were all ducking, dodging, hacking shadows. Howtlande held his own, not talking for once, and little Gobble slunk and stabbed and squeaked and hit the floor when pressed, wriggled and writhed away and stabbed at feet and calves. My sword broke, in someone's skull, I think.

Morgana plucked at me, softly.

"Come," she said. "Now."

She tugged me along the tapestries as the rest banged on in milling confusion. I groped into what had suddenly (as if in a dream) become a slanting tunnel with damp, bare, cobbled walls and floor.

"Interesting," I remarked. "What next?"

She stopped and turned to me. We were suddenly kissing. The soft, soft hands flowed sweetly over me. I held her with my empty hand. I was getting dim flashes of intelligence now.

"You knew they were waiting for me, didn't you?" I asked her. She was rubbing into me, ever so slightly, as if I tried to hold a perfumed cloud. Very heady. She was designed for my special faults.

"Lord God," she sighed, moving her amazing mouth across my chest and belly, "you rend my soul . . ."

"I'm just standing here," I just managed to say.

"Poor Parsival."

"Come on," I said, lifting her. It was now or never. "Tell me more stories."

"Don't you trust me?"

"Dung and daydreams. What do you really want with me?"

"You," she whispered. I felt her trembling a little.

"What do you want?" I kept my mind away from how she'd felt. "Stop trying to fool me."

"I think I want to kill you," she said, breathing hard.

That worried me: maybe I'd murdered some relative or lover. You never know, once you start slaying people, who's going to object.

"Are you really Morgana?" I asked.

"Yes. I'm not that old and I don't age much."

"Why would you—"

"Because I love you," she cut me off. "You bastard."

"Are you—"

"Yes," she snapped. "You bastard."

"But—"

"Yes. I want the Grail, too. I never meant to love you." I felt her shrug. We started walking again. In silence and blackness. I groped with the broken sword. This way had to be wrong. All ways had to be wrong.

"Alright," I finally said. "What do you want from me?"

"Hm," she replied, unhelpfully.

"What should I do?"

"About what?"

"The Grail . . . anything?" The benefit of the doubt. Another weakness of mine.

"That's up to you, isn't it?"

"You expect me to solve your puzzle?"

She sighed again. She seemed numb. "It's like an enchantment," she said. "I'm . . . I keep wanting you . . . Still, I must have the Grail."

"That's nice."

"I'll share the power with you." She seemed pained to say these things. "I'll find a way . . . you could be King . . ."

I raised both eyebrows in the darkness. "This is like a minstrel's tale," I said. "An old one, at that."

"I'll find a way . . ." I felt her grip my arm. "You swear you don't remember seeing the Grail?" It seemed so important to her. Her voice held me by the shoulders. "It would be so much better . . ."

"Don't you mean easier?"

She sighed. "I confess. I was using you. I didn't mean for this to happen to me. But it's happened and I don't want it or like it much, sir, yet I can do nothing to stem it."

"That sounds right," I said.

"And there's more." She was whispering again. "I am not good to love nor be loved by. Not good."

"Is that a warning? A curse?" And then the blade sparked as I walked into a wall. I felt the cool stones. It seemed a dead end. Appropriate.

A mass of stone crashed down, blocking the way back. I hardly had to crack my sore skull again to prove it.

"Christ's molars!" I raged. I'd hit the wound. What felt like hot oil filled my head. My breath sobbed. I knew she was on the other side. I yelled; my voice was too loud and yet dead in the stone space. I leaned there for a few minutes, I suppose. As soon as the pain was merely unbearable I groped around the small, utterly unlit space.

I was ready to start worrying.

"Damn it!" I yelled. "Stop this crap!" Maybe those were magic words. I heard a rumble, a scrape and felt a draught. The wall had obviously opened.

I didn't know whether I was going back or forwards, but hefted the sword stub and hoped for someone to hit with it. Suddenly the darkness opened onto a wider, echoing space. And there was a rich, golden brilliance across a tremendous, empty hall. I thought it was the sun, a door out. I ran for it. I really wanted to be outside. I made some vows about going straight home, reforming myself, and so on . . . about five paces away I realised it was a door shaped, faceted mirror of beaten gold set with oil lamps under a tall painting of a mounted knight wrestling with a

formless, scaly, tufted spectral beast. Three steps and the
floor was gone; I treaded air; the light flew up and vanished. Too bad I hadn't made out what the man was
fighting. Even falling into nothingness I knew a message
when I saw one.

Like so much else, the bottom was cushioned. I never
learned by what. I groped to my feet among damp, soft
heaps which might have been furry bodies or mildewed
hides. . . . I tried the magic words again.

"Damn it! Stop this crap!" My voice fell flat. I twisted
myself around, hoping I'd heard an answer or even an
echo, then saw it: a luminescent, slender woman's shape
across the cavernous room. Strained and strange from the
darkness, I accepted that she was made of light and wondered how such flesh would feel.

I staggered to her, and found myself leaning on what
turned out to be daylight spraying through loosely set
planks: a door cut out to trace a female form. The portal
that wasn't a woman swung outward and I winced into a
flood of sunshine. I wandered forward, weeping and blinking . . .

. . . into a walled garden where massed flowers broke
in billows and fountaining gushes higher than my head:
rippling roses; spurts of lily; foaming daffodils growing the
afternoon in slow luxury as the sun pressed sweet upon my
naked body. Even the walls ran blossoms like a waterfall.
The air seemed thick with color. I sighed and let tension
flow from me; it was as if I'd stepped through time and was
seventeen again, wandering in unending wonder.

"Knight, knight," a weird, nasal, high pitched voice
cried out from behind the blurs of a six foot cresting pink
bloom. As I blinked and adjusted, the fuzziness flashed and
sharpened. A new joke. How would a stranger know that a
practically nude man dangling a shattered weapon was a
knight?

"Knight, knight," I echoed, waiting for more.

"I beseech you."

"You too?" I peered through the flowers where cool

shadows were fractured by bright sunshafts. A long, floppy gown and knee-length tresses were visible through the leaf netting.

"For shame, knight, to mock a poor woman. Know you not this be sacred ground?"

"Have saints made water on it?"

"This is the garden of the Holy Grail!"

"How wonderful. And you're the deadly keeper."

"Jest not, foolish man." Her voice kept cracking.

"Wouldn't dream of it," I said across the web of light, stem and thistle. I was working my way through the dense brush. Not easy, naked.

The lady backed into a mass of sunflowers so that by the time I emerged into the lane of lush billows she was gone.

"Beseech me some more. I love it."

"The Grail is held in vile thrall," said the voice from the bushes. "The evil keeper stifles its virtues and holds the world dark."

"Ah ha."

"Find the Grail and protect it! This is God's will, Parsival!" A crashing crunch behind me. The keeper of the Grail, I thought and then saw it was the keeper of the bulk and the wind: Howtlande himself puffing through a field of blue and white that flowed across his bright silver suit like water. His helm was on, but open, and he kept winking at me, immediately talking—no, still talking.

". . . a man of sense and imagination, like yourself, not to mention real sensitivity, must appreciate the situation, sir. Those people. That witch, all degenerates, sir. All. I threw my lot in with them purely from necessity." He stopped and stood, gleaming and winking. "There's a peerless treasure here, and that crippled, fanatical little bastard wants it all for his poisonous master. But," he lifted a steel-gloved hand in a pointless gesture, "you and I, sir, are men of sense and sensibility. Morgana merely wants to destroy her brother. But you and I—" he gestured with vacant intimacy.

"Never mind that. Where is she?"

"A scheming, treacherous head, my dear Parsival."

"Spare the opinions," I snapped, pointing my broken sword at him. "I want to find her."

"Go carefully," he solemnly advised, shaking his round head. "There is more here than you guess."

"That's nothing new. How did you get here?"

"We fought free." He shrugged. "I think they were the same men we battled last night, when you were struck down."

I was thinking. She was behind my saddle as I fought. Could she have . . . I stopped the idea short.

"We went back the other way, Gobble and I, and he said we'd have to try the garden." He shrugged.

"Why?"

"Morgana hoped you'd know the tunnel route. The short way. She says there's an entrance here," gestured wide, "but the dread keeper," and looked behind with a trace of unease, "haunts these lovely paths. Morgana has tried before, remember. But we can beat the pair of them, Parsival." His eye couldn't help itself; it winked again.

"How exciting," I said. I wondered if even he really knew what he believed and meant. What were they trying to do with me? I was angry and nervous. I wanted to see her for one too many reasons, the worst one foremost.

"She followed you from Camelot. That was no chance meeting, sir. Gobble tracked her, and I came behind the pair of them." That was about what I'd expect from them, I thought. He seemed well pleased with himself now. "They think the Grail will show itself to you here. By means of magic. Morgana has searched many times and so she sent . . . er, rather, came herself. Neither of them can be trusted." Nodded heavily, squinted. I frowned at nothing in particular. "I speak true." I worked the frown some more to see what else might emerge. He had to be sweating under his iron shell. "They mean to use magic on you again."

"Again?"

"They've already tried."

"I'm too old to shock." After all these years people still followed me around looking for the fulfillment of hopeless dreams. Incredible. "What's *your* big idea? Don't be afraid to speak up now, I pray you." Sarcasm had become my sole balm.

"I've studied this thing," he explained, forgetting even to wink in his intensity and sincerity. He was really afraid of me. Men were, while women laughed. "The Grail is power, yes. The disciples of Our Lord Jesus Christ," he crossed himself with hypocritcal fluidity, "needed to secure some of the wealth they were garnering and conceal it from the Romans." His eyes shrank to dark slits. The sun was getting uncomfortable on my shoulders as it slanted down. "They were enterprising men in those times, men with scope and—"

"*Say* something!"

"What? The Grail, you see," he said, pointing a stubby finger like an ironclad doctor of philosophy, "the Grail is a cup of the most precious jewels of the ancient world! Daughters of kings gave all that they had to follow Him! His own advice, sir." He grinned. No improvement. "The rarest pearls and emeralds and rubies of that sumptuous Herodic age, sir." Bobbed his head with satisfaction. "You and I, eh? I have plans, you see, sir," gestured, "great plans—"

"What do you think I'll remember?" I suddenly just wanted to leave. I'd been snatched up on the road by a demented crew. They were all mad, but no madder than the kings and lords and every other crackpot I'd met and yes, no madder than me, if it came to that. "Where's my gear?"

"I don't know, Parsival. She took it somewhere."

Something moved in the crest of gold and green where the strange woman had vanished. "Who was that repulsive lady?" I wondered.

"Which?"

"With the dreadful voice."

"Where?" He had no idea.

"She's still creeping around, I think." The bushes moved. "Excuse me," I said, reaching and swishing out his sword and handing him the broken one. I wondered if he'd take it. He did.

I limped toward the movement, cursing the twisted Gobble and his ragged teeth. The foot wound was sore and swelling.

"Are you with me?" Howtlande asked my back.

"Of course!" I exclaimed with wasted irony. "Christ, I'm with everybody!"

"I'll wait here, in case they come this way. Once we find the Grail we'll elude them both. Morgana swears it's hidden somewhere under this garden. The old man they tortured mentioned it, I suppose."

I took a narrow path between mountainous waves of flowers, dazzling in the stippled sun. In a few steps I was lost in a perfumed silence. I felt clean and strangely young; if a way had opened I would have just gone on without concern for all absurd plots and obsessions. I was hungry too, and a little lightheaded.

The odd lady blocked the trail, standing in a billow of gray gown that flapped as if hung out to dry under the listless, drooping, lifeless hair. She was covered with face-paint; in the shreds of sunlight it seemed a disease of the flesh; caked, runny, and cracked hot pinks, dark reds, mud, pale packings—a death mask clinging to the narrow head. She reached, and rested one skinny hand on my chest. Clammy. I could feel the little bones. I resisted shoving her away; that's called chivalrous training.

"Just ahead," said the odd, mocking, cracking voice, "the keeper waits. Find the Grail and flee with me now!"

"With you, nightmare?" I didn't feel polite.

"The keeper waits."

"Fine. Where's Morgana?" She leaned up and kissed me on the mouth. Her teeth touched me and felt slimy. My soul didn't melt and sag my knees with need. The makeup clung to my face.

"Sweet young man," she said as I wiped at the stains.

She smiled. Her teeth were too small and numerous and something flashed; this face, tiny teeth . . . "Forget her." The voice went too deep, then bounced up an octave. "You may have me."

"I get so many offers," I said, "I can't keep up."

The eyes shifted too much and the body canted steeply inside the flopped clothing when she moved and I was sure now. I clutched and caught the long, dried hair and, of course, it came away in my hand.

The limping little transvestite laughed and veered into the banked flowers as if a wave of green and white had sucked him under.

"Come back," I suggested, calmly enough. "I've got something for you, Gobble. Something nice." I tossed the limp wig aside and probed through the wash of blossoms and honeyed sunbeams. Mock me, would they? What bent lusts . . .

And then the skewed path ended in a long field where the overgrown wall had crumbled to floral rubble. Yellow flowers, solid as a carpet, covered the ground. Solid pine trees closed off the far end. There was movement there, branches shaking, and scraping noise like metal bones and scales. For an instant I felt a child's fear and nearly bolted in the face of lost tales crashing into reality: a scintillant dragon, golden plated, head high above mine, eyes shattering the angled light, clumped and creaked toward me.

"Is this supposed to remind me of the Grail?" I wondered, then turned to look at two knights who'd emerged from the flower mass behind me. Their faceplates were open and I knew them both. "So," I remarked, "this is getting to be social." I didn't believe in the dragon for one minute. "Galahad and Sir Bors. Well, well. Planning to slay me—" I gestured across the field, "—or that thing first? And just the two of you?" Likely as bees in winter. Galahad looked perturbed.

"Ahh, ah," he demurred, "why not just come back to court with me?"

"Sick of being a paid head-chopper, too?" He should

have been. His eyes showed it: strained and drained empty. They were focussed on my chest.

"Strange dress, Parsival," Bors chimed in.

"It's fashion here." We never liked each other. Never.

"Ha! Saxons and Irishmen have more modesty!" Bors had really small eyes. His graying beard had food fragments caught in it. He always seemed to spit when he talked. Galahad, on the other hand, had excellent personal hygiene.

"The dragon doesn't worry you either?" I asked. It was flashing and advancing, obviously mechanical, Like a seige machine.

"It's nonsense," Galahad said. "We know what's going on here." He nodded as if that proved it.

"That's sooth," Bors muttered. He was a brooding butcher. But Galahad made you feel he'd been driven to murder against his will and wanted, if possible, pity from his victim. A sighing slayer.

"Come back," he said sincerely, "and all's well again."

"So it was you and your lads on the road," I realised. "You've just been waiting for your best moment or more men." Galahad's style was fearless at ten to one odds.

The dragon clanked and thudded closer; it sounded like a drawbridge going up. Was I supposed to imagine the Grail was inside? Was I supposed to care?

Actually, it was coming faster than I had thought: suddenly the bronze claws, jerky but quick, hooked at Sir Bors, who was standing nearest. He cursed and chopped his sword at the metal and leather sides, closing with the giant toy. Blossoms splashed as he hacked unintelligently at the inanimate eyes. *Clang! Clang!* Then he was knocked down and flipped into the brilliant flowers in a sparkle of steel.

Armed men and knights sprouted everywhere. Galahad was yelling, "Attack! Destroy that thing!" Then, aside to me, "We'll share the treasure if you throw in with us."

I gaped at him. "You too? Who next? The pope? Beowulf of the Danes? I gawked at the inane battle: the machine clanked and flailed with awkward swiftness, missing everyone except when they were packed so thick that not scoring would have taken great skill. "Going to share the Grail with Arthur, too?" The flowers were getting the worst of it. I backed carefully away from this peculiar melée.

"What do you say?" Galahad wanted to confirm, keeping pace with my retreat.

I smiled brightly.

"I'm with everyone," I told him. God, what a crew!

"Good," he said. Bors was up again, and back in the nonsensical fray. Part of the beast was torn; iron studded leather flapped about a broken wooden bone. Someone had actually thought this festival puppet would drive fighting men off. Amazing. I could hear voices fuming inside. One clawed leg had jammed, the gears were grinding. I realized it truly *was* the keeper, comic as it seemed. Perhaps there was something to keep, after all . . .

Galahad's men had swarmed all around the dragon's rump and were levering it over, rocking in unison. Bors still pounded at the senseless head. He had the stiff claw-strokes pretty well timed now.

And then we were flooded with dwarves, lots of dwarves, dwarves wearing jet armor that brought a shudder of recognition: ebony steel with silver, grotesque facemasks. When I was seventeen, Clinschor's deadly minions wore the same suits in larger sizes. They seemed to be charging to the dragon's rescue.

And there was Gobble, limping in their midst, probably happy to be taller than someone. He still wore the silly gray gown, but brandished a sword. His makeup had been badly rubbed off.

This was entertainment no acting troupe could match.

The dragon crashed on its side just as waves of poisonous mites broke into the full-sized knights. Black steel gleamed like beetle carapaces as the midgets sank head deep in the gushed flowers and then sprang out slicing vicious ax and sword thrusts, hewing legs like trees. Gobble was nearly dancing with delight. All he needed was a maypole.

The keeper fell apart, and wild-bearded druid priests tumbled out. Druids? Why not? Only Christians insisted the Grail was Christ's alemug. There they were, in any case, druids, yelling, ducking and scattering. Maybe a dozen. I could see the wheels and ropes that worked the dragon. Then a few dwarves got close enough to distract me. They fought well, but I'd been bopped on the skull enough. A knight in shining diapers, I probably looked easy. Well, I battered and batted them towards safer game.

Galahad was happy. He must have figured these were a perfect size for him because he was spinning and smashing everything in reach . . . I glimpsed Howtlande bobbing stealthily through the lush greenery where two or three of the priests seemed to be getting away.

I backed into the sweet bushes. Not my fight. I felt sorry for the priests but it was too late to help. Too many people had followed too many others for one toy dragon to discourage.

I thought about softness and scent and red hair. Where was she? Maybe Howtlande knew. I headed for where I'd seen him last. Glanced back and saw dear little Gobble pointing me out. His dwarves (he'd clearly planned best of the lot) were actually bouncing, popping in and out of the deep washes of flower and brush, like deadly stinkbugs, avoiding most strokes, stabbing and slashing at knees and shins.

Gobble was suddenly trapped between two furious knights and I saw him resort to snake tactics again, vanishing in the foamy gold—then his sword lashed up from the dense bush right into one man's eyeslit.

The deadly steel beetles were suddenly chopping the fronds all around me. A sword flicked a wavy trace across my torso. I slapped a stroke back, and hit stems.

I wasn't dressed for this. I ducked and ran through a hedge of roses. I wasn't dressed for that either. By the other side I was netted with rips and criss-crossed blood.

There was a little space and the first three dwarves coming after me regretted it. They couldn't duck and pop: I hit them so hard I saw stars from the impacts. That was that. For a few breaths, anyway.

A few yards later I blundered across a crushed wake wide enough to be either the dragon's or Howtlande's. Then I saw him, face down. Butterflies flitted about his head. His helmet was missing and a bloody lump had closed one eye. Life went on here in the garden. I could hear bees. I moved cautiously, straining to see into the shifting light and shade . . . the fighting gradually drifted and thinned into a meaningless drone . . . I was tired and really hungry now . . . found it hard to concentrate on anything . . . wanted to sit, inhale the rich air, stretch out . . . this garden was like a world in itself: human absurdity and natural beauty all mixed with blood and dreams . . .

Behind me Howtlande strained and struggled to one knee, holding his hurt head and sucking wind.

"Ah God . . ." he whispered. "Ah . . ." I waited. ". . . a foul blow . . . treacherous . . ." He finally noticed me. "Parsival . . . Parsival . . . she means to have it all herself . . . the foul bitch . . ."

"All the great nothing for herself?"

"When I saw that dread machine," he gently fingertipped his wound, "of fell magic . . ." shook his round head, "rending over those sweet fields . . ."

"The dread machine is overthrown," I told him, running my thumbnail along my lower lip. "Gobble's midgets won the day."

The eyes went wide. "He has the Grail?" he hissed. "Does he? The worm, the—"

"Maybe. I don't know."

The eyes went small and hard again. His senses, such as they were, had returned. He tried to gesture me into his insanity again.

"But can't you remember where it's hid?" he pleaded, jowls joggling.

"Ask the druids."

"What?"

"They were inside the dread machine."

"Druids," he muttered, patting his wound again.

"Exactly what went on while I was unconscious and chained?" I laid the flat of the blade along his bruised and puffy cheek. "Hmm?" The late sunlight beaded and broke along the steel.

"There may still be time, sir, for the two of us to get our share." He was afraid but more impatient than anything. "Where are the—"

"What did you do to me?" I asked quietly, holding the edge still. He was sweating. With reason.

"They questioned you, hoping to learn—"

"What else?" My eyes were cold and bleak, I'm sure. That's how I felt. I could hear bees humming in the syrupy air where flowers swayed and leaves rattled.

"Well . . . It was a rite . . ."

"More like a wrong. Go on."

"A ritual magic. She, ah . . . used . . . you. You know . . ." He shrugged and tried to subtly lift his cheek away from the blade. "For magic, to find the Grail . . ."

"What did your little friend do? Hmm?"

He was really sweating now.

"He did . . . things . . ."

The eyes told me enough. I gritted my teeth. "A rite," I muttered.

"I had nothing to say about that, sir." My eyes must have been very bleak now.

"Used me for magic, did they?" Soft skin . . . and red hair . . . and twisted, naked cripples . . . and blood . . . and prodding me with himself undersea, bony, shark-mouthed, prodding me with his bent, outsized self . . . the two of them . . . "Magic."

Howtlande made a squeaking: my blade had pressed against his neck, and blood creased his jowls. "Please," he begged. "Please, sir. I—"

"Is there more?"

"The . . . the rite was not finished but I swear I don't

know how the rest goes . . . spare me, Parsival, we'll work hand in hand. I'm a loyal man, sir. A loyal man . . ." Everyone's so loyal when you're armed.

"I can't tell you how much that means to me, Howtlande," I saw flowers move against the wind.

"If she has not found what she seeks—" The eyes went sly briefly; blood beaded from the slight slash I'd made, "—as I think now, she hasn't . . . then she'll try more ritual . . . I overheard her telling him the Grail is wedded to your soul, Parsival . . . and will reveal itself to her witch vision when . . ." I could see he wanted to husband and trickle information now that the tension had lifted a little. It was too late for that.

"When?"

"When you die."

He stopped here, or perhaps I wasn't listening. Gobble, in his tattered gown, and several armored beetles seemed to float towards me.

And . . . "Well, well," I said. "A happy meeting." My blood red ruby armor had just arrived, stalking me, blank helmet shut tight. The sword looked keen. When I was seventeen I'd punched a spearpoint through the previous owner's neck and was baptized into knighthood by the drizzling blood. My first work for King Arthur.

"I don't suppose," I said, "you'll just take it off?"

My steel didn't reply.

Gobble grinned, rolled his bugeyes up into his forehead and began to spin in a circle and mumble a chant while the jolly killer insects spread out, bobbing through the garden like the iron offspring of some strange machine. The mad cripple went faster and faster, a child's spinning toy. I assumed he was having a fit. Howtlande was crossing himself rapidly in what seemed spiritual excess.

"He's doing magic," he informed me breathlessly.

My armor charged, sword cocked, just as a pair of dwarves ducked out long enough to loop ax cuts at my bare legs. That set me hopping. Nasty little nits. I hadn't noticed Howtlande leaping loyally in yet, on any side.

My armor aimed one for my face. I blocked, then spun aside as a fang faced midget scuttled by, hacking, petals flying like sweet summer snow. I tried a stab but the shield was up fast and two little killers surfaced at my back. They were all silent; perhaps they were mutes. One nicked my side but I got off a good backhand and the little arm flickered off and vanished into the shimmering, sunlaced colors with a scream of steel but no other: just a muffled sputter and puff in the little helmet . . . almost caught a strong downchop from my armor . . .

The shield folded and the armor sagged backwards as I got in a good two-handed bang. My specialty. I tried to follow through but the rest of the tiny knights sprang and I batted one in mid-air; four others clutched my legs and nearly chopped me down before I could toss them away. The red armor went to its knees. Gobble danced on sliced flowers until the air stormed with petals. What was supposed to happen? Would I drop dead from a curse? Since I really didn't want to damage the armor overmuch, I carefully bashed the red helmet with my hilt. Whoever was inside said, "Ohhhh . . ." Howtlande was gone, the remaining dwarves were fleeing or hiding or creeping under the foliage.

Gobble veered at me like a demented top, screaming in circles, "Smite him, O Powers!!"

The powers were late. I smacked his whizzing sword away and hobbled aside and he fell and went on spinning, rolling through the blossoms. He seemed unable to stop. Plands crackled and whipped and shattered in his path. I watched, fascinated, as he kept rolling away, yelling for Morgana, the Devil, and his master to help him. He spasmed along. Flowers shook further on . . . then he broke into sight, slamming down the grass . . . then was gone again, fifty yards off . . . still yelling . . . I was amazed. Amazed. Rolled on . . .

I stood too long in swordreach of the red knight and I yelped in shock as I took one in the rear ribs. It felt like a burning torch. I went to my knees, gasping. And there was something else: I felt it, the rest of the magic spell, as if all the rich, bright world was instantly flat and thin as a parchment painting; the dream was pushing through, trying to gather me into it, holding me, soft and strange, tugging me into its dark tide, down into subaqueous landscapes where *she* waited, phosphorescent, gigantic, commanding, her weird substance dominating in dark currents . . . When I blinked the two worlds flashed together, overlapped.

I got my feet under me. Felt the bleeding pulsate. Reversed my sword like a dagger, with both hands. I struggled in the amber of the dream and the towering, naked goddess moved her ineffable and awesome limbs, her hypnotic eyes radiating compassionless love, her voice a soft roar like vertigo: "For love of thee, mortal, I slay thee but I will keep thee forever in my sleep, thy soul shalt not pass from me and we will walk in glowing fields of eternal splendor in the tender twilight that swells, like the unending sea, in forever's grandeur."

Very pretty. Nicely put, and so was the blade that dipped for my heart.

I threw myself backwards so violently I sailed into a crest of yellow roses. My pathetic, bloodsoaked loincloth was ripped away. The dream goddess ripped at me too. From my knees, weeping with pain, I slashed free in time to meet my armor face to face but dreamless now. I must have looked like that saint full of arrows you see in every church. I surely felt like him.

"You son of a bitch," I managed to snarl.

The incongruous, impossible voice, tinny, muffled, pitched too high—wrong as the twisted runt in the woman's gown, wrong as the brass dragon—cried out, "Wait, Parsival, wait! I—"

My full stroke smashed solid on the red steel chest. As hard as I could hit and no one hits harder. A hot mist of blood puffed out from the rent, like scarlet steam. And I understood and wasn't sorry until after she'd crashed to earth and the thin wail echoed inside the faceless metal head.

Blood was like dew here on the white and golden flowers. I knelt, and carefully twisted the helmet off.

Whatever the plot, whatever the lies, tricks, false traps and real pain, whatever anything . . . magic and dream had stunned and drowned me already and I had to accept it, watching pink froth bubble from the corners of her lips to stain the soft, secret-eyed face, the coppery hair that caught the sun like slow coals in an old fire . . . Morgana.

"My God," I think I said. "My God."

It was suddenly so still. I crouched, dressed only in blood, on my knees in the broken garden. Her mouth struggled with words.

"No," came from my own mouth, "don't tell me anything, Morgana."

"I . . . I'm . . . not . . ."

"Oh Lord Jesus," I said into the darkness of my burning eyes.

"Not her . . . not Morgana . . . sister . . . sister . . ."

"She's your sister. I see. Alright."

"Magic . . . failed . . . Love you . . ."

"Please . . ." I looked at the eyes like secret blue coves where the sun was dying. It was a little late for lies.

"Failed . . . love you . . . Parsival . . . I like to say it . . . even now . . ."

Nothing mattered, not absurdity, madness, stabbing, paths to blank walls or murky pits or the dark gates of hell . . . none of it mattered . . . "Love," I whispered. *"Love."*

"Sister sent me . . . to find you . . . said you . . . wouldn't die . . . not . . . not die . . . magic . . . when I struck you . . . protect . . . magic failed . . . magic . . ." Then all the words were blood. Time passed. I didn't look up. She didn't think I'd die.

"We should have met another way," I told the eyes that

saw no more. Mine burned with weeping as I stood up. "At a better time."

The sun dropped behind the blossom covered wall like a stone in a pond. Two silly, hopeless, armored shadows stood behind me and I ignored them. She'd tried to warn me, once or twice; and tried to kill me, too, but all in the dream, that is, the dream where no one really lived or died.

Galahad and Bors; one cleared his throat. Survivors blending together in twilight's first flowing, noiseless grays.

"Ran out of dwarves?" I asked, not looking at anybody.

"They drew back," Galahad said with a shrug in his voice. "Maybe they lost interest." Sucked his lips. "Who is she?"

"A dead lady."

"In your armor," said Bors. "Unheard of. Did she wrest it from you, Parsival?" I'm sure he was grinning malice.

I undressed her, as gently as I could. Twice now for the same steel. Twenty years later and a woman this time.

"By the time I have this gear on," I said quietly, "you'd do well to be gone."

"What of our bargain?" Galahad fretted.

"We came to kill this arrogant bastard!" Bors yelled. He had a big forehead and scant locks; I wondered what swelled his skull—not brains. "Not to strike bargains with him!" He was excitable.

"Maybe the dwarves already have what they came here for," I suggested. Galahad didn't like that.

"Then we'll take it back from them."

I'd heard that one enough. I had the leg pieces on and was struggling with the mail coat. I kept the sword stuck in the earth, half a reach away. Fumbled with the buckles, straps, plates. No one was going to bother me now. The blood was drying, wounds starting to stiffen. Nothing major. I wrapped the most recent in a shred of something. Decided to wait and bury her. And go home . . . Then I realised I didn't know her name. I wondered if Howtlande knew, or Gobble? It didn't matter. She'd followed me, they'd followed her, then others, dwarves, knights, priests, everybody following everybody in a bloody vicious circle, then everybody met and she was dead and nameless to me.

"Why don't you go fight some more? It's nice and stupid." I was dressed. "Alright, I know where the Grail is. And no one can tell you how to find it but me." The flowers were all one color now.

It got to Galahad.

"Do I hear right?" he asked.

"You do." I pointed to the bloodstained sunset. "Follow the sun. Wherever it goes. Start at once."

He must have been frowning. Bors was still trying to work it out.

"But the sun is set, Parsival," Bors said.

"All the better," I told him, sheathing my sword.

"Parsival—" Galahad began.

"No. Don't ask me anything." I slammed the helmet on my head, kept the face plate open. The bang rang through my poor skull. "Kiss Arthur for me."

I started walking. The next thing was to find a horse. I passed the fallen dragon, a ripped, empty shape full of shadows. Saw the glint of fallen knights and armored dwarves on the field. Nearly stepped on a druid, the just rising moon filling his void stare. I heard a sound that might have been a horse. An archway opened into a courtyard. A likely place. I entered quietly. There were three shapes near what had to be a well. The rest of the yard was empty.

"Is this the spot, priest?" Gobble's unmistakable mistake of a voice demanded. Now I knew the source of the sound. The druid could barely speak. He was kneeling, propped against the well, but not to pray. The final outline was immense, and I didn't have to hear the rambling monologue to know what a sweet reunion this would be.

The priest groaned. That didn't satisfy the Grail hunters. "Plain speech, plain speech," my loyal comrade advised. "It's true wisdom to ease your sufferings, sir. A few words are a slight price to pay for an end to pain. How few men

realise, during their brief turbulent span on earth, the value
of—"

"You dog!" Gobble raged, lashing out at his victim. The
young man screamed wetly, and Gobble tossed something aside. Probably a piece of druid. I felt my teeth grate.
But I'd not managed to do much to Gobble yet, so I'd have
to bide my time. In the dark he'd elude me again, writhe
off. He kicked the helpless man; thud, gasp, groan. He
wasn't wearing his dress anymore. "Is this the place?" he
hissed. "You brought us here. Is this the place?"

"Where? Where?" Howtlande was almost hysterical
with greed. "Point! Point! Point to the place!"

"Bah, he's dying, the pig."

"No, no, he'll be fine and right as rain. Just show us the
exact spot, and we'll tend your wounds, and—"

"Stick his ear back on and his eye back in? I'll chew the
other loose, I swear, if you keep silent." Gobble wanted
results, but he was bargaining himself out of goods. I stared
at the well a long moment, and had an idea as the muti-
lated priest gargled his own blood. A deep and satisfying
idea.

Howtlande saw me. The priest mouthed last words,
". . . never . . . never . . . never . . ."

Tortured, dying, saying never. So much suffering for a
puff of dreams. Gobble ripped the hooked dagger across
the druid's neck, whinnying with insane hate. "Never,
then!"

"Lady?" Howtlande asked, cautiously watching me,
straining to see details. My back was to the moon so the
open helm would have been a blot of darkness.

"So you finally stopped rolling," I said, without anything in my voice.

"Sir Parsival," gasped Howtlande. "Thank God you
prevailed against that cursed witch! I feared—"

"With reason," I said.

"Hah," Gobble snorted, "it was all for nothing." He
spat on the dying man at his warped feet. "Well, there's no

quarrel among us now."

"When will you roll again. I liked that."

He sort of shrugged. "Her magic failed."

"Let bygones be?" I suggested.

"Exactly. I always cut my losses."

"So I saw." Irony missed him.

"Exactly. I serve my master, but this game's ended. We all failed. You too."

"How true," sighed the disappointed fat man. Well, I'd raise his spirits.

"You're both wrong," I told them.

"What's this?" Howtlande was alert.

"I didn't fail."

"Eh?" Gobble came in, slowly.

"The priest didn't lie," I said. "He just repented at the last." I went and peered down the well. It smelled musty and damp. Loosened a pebble from the edge and let it drop. Waited a satisfying time before the distant splash of impact.

"Oh?" Gobble jerked himself alongside of me. "Meaning what, Parsival?" He wasn't the least afraid of me.

"It will take two for the job," I said thoughtfully, still peering down into the utter black beyond the edge of the moon gleam. Howtlande was close on my other side. "I'll need at least one of you."

"Two?" Howtlande murmured, not saying too much for once.

"You both could fight to the death," I suggested, "or we can share the prize three ways." My voice sharpened. "There's more than sufficient."

"Ah," breathed Gobble, and his breath was no delight. "Is this a change of heart, Parsival?"

"I remembered. And I came here, but found you'd come first." Gestured with my head. "It's down there. I remembered. Whoever goes down the rope will need to be hauled up once he has the Grail."

"Ahha," said Howtlande, excited, "Of course, of course! How obvious, once you see a thing. We do the work, good comrades and fast, before Morgana—"

"Morgana, indeed?" I said.

"Or whatever and who. What matters a stray name, eh? When the witch—"

"She's dead, in any case." I stared down the lightless hole into nothing.

"Ah. Pity . . . but, then, sirs, it's ours altogether and without tedious dispute of right?"

"What about his nasty little men?" I felt Gobble weighing and watching. Of all of them, he was the one worth fearing.

"Most fled," he snarled. "Those cowards will regret much once I come before the master again. We used to get fighters who could fight. Now . . ." He was disgusted. He sniffed. "What of your friends?"

"Friends?"

"The great knights from Camelot." He was amused.

"Most of them died," Howtlande mentioned.

"And they came here to kill me," I pointed out.

"That's true," Howtlande confirmed. "The lady knew that. We're all comrades at the last, then." Insects hummed and skreaked outside the walls. "So let's to business, eh? Down the well here, you say?" He peered dubiously. It was a fairly wide opening.

"There's a ledge not far below," I explained.

"Go on, then," Gobble urged. "I trust you to go down alone."

"It has to be somebody small," I said. Silence. "I'm not getting out of this armor again." I waited.

"Ah, yes," said Howtlande. Suited him. There was more silence, maybe a little sweating. But everybody was hooked. What would master say if his pet cripple passed up the chance?

"After you succeed," I said, "you can afford a thousand ladies' gowns." I could feel him stare, feel him thinking, round and round, but there was no way for him to leave and come back. He couldn't possibly risk it.

"Why should I—" he began.

"I'd go," the massive knight declared in his ambiguously over-the-water accent, "but I'm not so nimble as another."

"Even," stated Gobble, "if that other be an elephant." God. What a crew.

I didn't have to say anything. Just wait. He leapt up on the well, still trying to read my face, probing the way a man who's already bought a horse still tries to reassure his judgment. "Why did you suddenly remember?" he asked.

I smiled.

"Strange thing. When the lady in my armor stabbed me in the side, I fell and it all came back in a flash. Like magic." He was sweating, but what could he do? It was his own story. "A strange marvel, don't you think?"

He snarled in parting, and gripped the rope like a spider.

"At last, at last," breathed Howtlande. The rope held, swayed, marked his descent. We watched him drop, a worm on a line, past the level of indirect moonlight. As if he climbed into the nothing before creation. Howtlande, at my elbow, kept murmuring to himself. After many minutes the rope jerked and we heard a muffled, hollow shouting, too far for the words to separate into sense—if there was any.

"He wants to come up," I said. "He's found it."

Howtlande's eyes shone in the puffy darkness of his features. He was almost too excited to speak. But he managed. "Do you think so? I couldn't make out . . . there it is, again." He harked, bent to the next indecipherable volley. I could smell him perspire.

"It's clear enough," I said confidently.

"The three of us . . . or two . . . as you like. We'll raise a kingdom, eh? But if through, er, misguided loyalty, Gobble insists on serving the perverse witchcraft of his master, why, you and I, you and I, Parsival, can—"

"You'd better pull him up."

"Ah . . ." He drew in breath. Looked at me the same way the other had. I thought about the man mangled at my feet and the woman I shouldn't have had to murder. I helped him clamber up onto the narrow well. He steadied himself with the taut and shaking rope.

"Pull," I said. "Go on. You want the Grail, don't you?" Down in the black shaft, Gobble was still hollering. I could just imagine what.

There was no winch for the bucket so Howtlande pulled, strained and cracked his wide back. I watched for a while. His eyes goggled when I drew and sawed my swordedge through the tensed rope. It parted. Howtlande reeled upright, wobbled on the brink, tried to make himself fall back to the ground as I leaned over and listened for the splash.

I never heard anything because Howtlande fell toward the hole, twisting and puffing desperately, pleading at me, his steelshod feet slipping, dancing, sparking on the stones.

"Help!" he screamed. "Please . . . help . . ."

There was a good chance he'd plug it up. I didn't care or want to know. I turned and limped away. My feet rang unevenly on the smooth stones, echoed as I aimed across the castle yard for the archway out. I took a full breath of scented air. I listened to the insects raging and raving all around. I heard a clattering crash—for all I know, he made it.

I was incredibly incurious. I had something to bury and then I'd go home.

Memory is like the earth; and dreams flow like water and like blood.

I'd find a horse. Eat and drink. Blink at tomorrow. Bury whatever I could.

The Trash Dragon of Shensi

There was an ancient worm
on the hills of Shensi
which had six spines upon its back
that flowed red when it flew
at the Spring moon,
ballooning and unballooning its awful wings
in the brick-hearted sun.

Now it has been caught.
They climbed the rootless cliffs
beyond Sian
(they were very brave and very determined)
and someone flung the silken ropes
while he was sleeping,
(dreaming of water and cloud spouts)
over the spiny angles of his rough heads
steaming like fire hydrants.

They damped him with fog,
and a promise of the disklike moon
for his own on Mondays.
They led him with milk.
And now he toils.
He is the eater of garbage for a whole prefecture.
He is known to every corner
as the Trash Dragon of Shensi.
And he is too full of old watermelon rinds
and millet straw to pay any attention
to his wings.

Only in sleep,
vibrating his spiny reptilian pinions,
does a little steam nicker about his nozzle,
does he buzz a little, throb a little like a train.
He is thinking of red searchlights
in a fishlike moony sky,
and the mountains looking like
great flopped-over turtles below
weaving their legs and heads.

But he no longer believes in flight.
He has accepted his silken attachments.
He has even come—almost—
to believe in the ultimate dignity
of the transmutation
of fish bones and broken squash pods.

—*Andrew Glazer*

The Vanishing Trolls

Gaird Wallig

Outside, from the winter dressed slopes of Glittertind's peaks, a growing storm moaned down on Lillehammer, Norway. Inside, Grandfather Tuppa Hilsen stood by the wide red stone hearth with two fingers in the pockets of his waistcoat.

It was yuletide, the eve. The house's air was heavy with holiday. And soon the family, all of them this year, would gather to celebrate. There would be a feast rich with treats like the quartered suckling pigs he had lately dispatched, and joyous laughter and chatterings to rush through the quiet house and his memories for many an evening thereafter. At last, the family would cluster around the glowing fire as tales of other eves, other days, were retold. Yes . . . it would be a good yule.

Already he had donned his yule finery—the black dress suit with the pearly gray lining—but he had yet to put on his shoes. No, there was no hurry. Only his granddaughter, Misa Stivot, and her little girl, Haide, were there. "To help Grandmother Tresse with the decorating and the baking of julekage and things," Misa had mentioned vaguely that early morn.

Yes, Grandfather Tuppa mused, she was a vague-minded girl, that Misa, always had been, but loving for all that. Haide reflected both traits.

Grandfather's dreaming gaze moved from his slippered feet, past the cheery blaze, to the new silver platter. It was the family's gift to Tresse and himself. A precious thing, etched with scaled fish and flowers. On its arrival earlier that day, he himself had placed it on the mantle for all to enjoy, right beside the little wooden figures of his Norway's trolls.

Trolls were ancient evil, yet once said to have ruled the land with all sweetness, even before the Hidden Folk, the

Faëries, had come. Long before the day of Man. But, if any were left, even on Glittertind's highest peak, they were few and far between.

Fat and ugly, squat of form and demeanor, and bald of tail and head, those intricately carved trolls were nonetheless beautiful in Grandfather Tuppa's eyes; they, too, had been a gift one yule.

In the new treasure's mirror-like oval center, he noted little Haide still in the next room. She had stolen into the forbidden front parlor and sat upon the russet carpet. Blond braids gone a bit wispy swung gently over a new picture book. Quiet as she was, the six-year-old seemed the picture of grace, a dainty lady smiling charmingly over a yule gift.

Grandfather Tuppa watched carefully a moment . . . Yes, to be sure, the child was slyly tearing corners from the pages of her new book and placing the bits into her mouth, spitting them out as sopping wads onto the gleaming, newly waxed floor beyond her.

Grandfather bowed his head to the blaze. How should he put an end to such a thing? Shouting at the child did nothing more than make her resentful, more inclined to misbehave; reasoning with her, pointing out that she didn't need to be destructive and unloving, only caused tears— tears that brought the house's atmosphere to gloom. The old man sighed; she had already shed tears through three other incidents this day.

Grandfather Tuppa watched in the platter as Misa came into the parlor and smiled uncertainly at her daughter, eyeing the disorder upon the floor. Then a satisfied secret smile grew upon Haide's plump cheeks as Misa undid her apron, swabbed up the untidiness with it, and murmured, "Come, Child. It is time to change into yule finery." Without another look at her Misa simply took the child by the hand and led her away.

Grandfather Tuppa frowned; he would have wished to see some word spent against what would be the inevitable

next such occasion. He stared at the small wooden trolls.
The child's continuous mischief seemed near to a trollish
meanness, and he knew the family's joy in their gathering
was sure to be disrupted one way or another.

With a sudden shrug, Grandfather Tuppa quietly made
his way out of the room, and out of the house—the butchering shed, a nasty walk in the storm, his objective.

The table before them had been filled to capacity. Now,
all but the remains of the quartered and fruited piglets were
cleared to make way for the coffee, tea, and chocolate, the
parade of sweetmeats, the pies of raisin and apple, the
cakes so rich with butter, cream and sugar-fruit which
would again mask the carved trolls atop their pile of greenery. The trolls had become, long since, the traditional
centerpiece of yule feasts.

Grandfather Tuppa examined each lively face at the
table. From his and Tresse's love for one another had
come seven beautiful sons and daughters, to beget all
told fifteen sons and daughters of Norway of his own
blood. It was true that the sixteenth, little Haide, was a
foundling child—Misa and Nils, her husband, had found
themselves barren—but even Haide had ever been
deemed as true a family member as any other.

Grandfather Tuppa smiled over the child. She had been
perfect of manner the whole supper through, and was
giggling and teasing with the other children, adding her
brightest side to the general mingling of enjoyment.

And then to his eyes flew unhappy circumstance: little
Haide's hands upon the sugar bowl, which she shook, as if
to free a contents gone damp from a dipped spoon. She
shook it too carefully for a child of six. He sought the cause
of this, but nothing else appeared peculiar.

Then he spied the now empty saltceller a little way from
the child's place. It was a large celler, the size of a cup, with
a tiny spoon for sprinkling. The sugar bowl was Tresse's
old and beautiful crystal rose with its leaf lid. It held two

cups of sugar; but another glance at it confirmed his suspicions: it was fuller than it should have been, with the coffee already poured.

He peered into his mug. He had been the last to dip his spoon into Tresse's rose. He tasted the brew. No, it was fine. She must have just accomplished her *little joke,* as she often called her mischief.

Grandfather Tuppa expelled his breath in a small sigh, then stood up and reached for the sugar as was his custom, rather than distract anyone.

Haide's glittering eyes looked at him, but only in passing as she turned, renewing her whispering to her cousin Hildy.

Even on an old man, thought her grandfather. *She would even play off her meanness on me! So . . .* He nodded slowly to himself. *She has decided it for herself.*

He sat down again, and with a sudden seeming carelessness, he let the salted sugar bowl overturn. The contents spilled through his fingers to land in the coffee mug and spill dampness over saucer, table cloth and his knee. At his grunt of mischance, and hasty clasp of Tresse's precious rose, exclamations of concern and commiseration followed from all sides. Their loving tones were soured only by the flash of disappointment hurriedly hidden beneath the innocence on Haide's face.

The course of sweets was done, and the table party was breaking up to move into the parlors when Grandfather Tuppa took a last look at the trolls, then beckoned a gentle finger at little Haide.

As she reached him, still the biddable, sweet innocent, he put his hand atop her soft hair, then leaned down and whispered, "Haide mine, before the grand tale telling begins, I have a special story I would like to share with just you. Shall we go into my workden a moment, so no one else will hear?"

The child nodded instantly, a delighted conspirator, and took the old man's hand.

Once the workden's door was latched and he'd lit the prepared hearth's fire, Grandfather Tuppa took the little girl onto his lap before the wide workdesk. He removed a small, black, leather-and-brass bound chest from the desk's locked top drawer.

Tapping the casket's ornate brass lock, he smiled solemnly down at the child. "This is a very special box," he told her. "Do you know what is kept in here, why this is always locked, and the whole locked into this desk?"

The blue-green eyes grew round with desire to know as she shook her head.

"Well," said the Grandfather, "do you remember that day last summer when you went out alone into the wild country and we all worried about you?"

Haide nodded, then chattingly confided, "But I wasn't lost as everyone thought. I was only hiding because Papa had scolded me for pulling the hen's tailfeathers out—my feelings were hurt."

"And so were the hen's, I would think," replied the old man in a mild tone. "But the story isn't about that.

"Once upon a time—just close to seven years ago now—I was walking in the mountains one gray afternoon . . . and I found myself lost."

"You did?" The child forgot her fidgeting, eyes rapt in surprise.

"I did," confirmed the Grandfather. "And worse, it suddenly started to storm. The storms of our mountains are dangerous things to be caught in, you know, Haide—so very cold. But looking for shelter, I at last found what looked like a cleft in a huge pile of stones, so into it I crept. The cleft turned out to be more: a cave, deep and dark. After I had finished congratulating myself on my luck, I looked about me. A few old windfall sticks were here and there on the dirt, perfect for a cozy fire. When it was burning brightly, I took up a stick and dared to explore deeper in. I was afraid the cave might also hold a sleeping bear or other creature as some are known to do. Luck was still with me; there was no bear nor creature, yet, toward the back where the ceiling was highest and the floor smoothest, there before my searching eyes I saw a most interesting thing."

Haide squirmed, "What Granfather? What?"

"It was a bundle, child, a swaddled bundle of rags. As I watched it, it moved, just a tiny bit. Then one small pink fist curled over the rags' end."

"A pink fist? A baby, Granfather? Was it a baby? In a cave?"

Grandfather Tuppa nodded. "The sweetest-faced infant one could ever hope to see, Haide. I picked it up, peering this way and that for some sign of its mother, but there was nothing. I took my blazing stick and walked all around each and every lump of rock in that cave. Just in case, you understand, that the mother might have laid down to rest, or that there might be a second opening to the cave I might have missed, through which the mother might have stepped out for a moment."

"Did you find her, Granfather?" The child was totally absorbed in the story.

"No, Haide; the walls were as solid as could be and smooth nigh up to the cavern's ceiling, and no sleeping person at all did I find. By and by, and as the hours passed, I decided no one would even come to reclaim the child. No living mother would ever leave such a perfect babe so long unattended. The mother might have been lost in the storm.

"Finally, not too long after my fire burned out, the noise of the storm wind seemed lessened, so I peeped out into the night. The storm had indeed passed, the winds ceased, and the clouds were breaking up. Then I saw the bright star of sailor's reckoning was high in the sky, and I was no longer lost. I gathered up the babe and started for home.

"Once there, I found that Grandmother Tresse, worried about my long absense, had summoned your father and mother and that they were about to set out looking for me. All three fell on my neck, weeping in joy. When they discovered what I carried, the women quickly took the child to feed and wash her. Oh, yes," the old man nodded at the child's squeak, "it was a little girl, Haide. But then Grandmother Tresse called to me from the bedroom. Her voice had fallen very sad, Haide—very very sad and distressed."

"But why, Granfather? Was the baby sick?"

"No, Child, she wasn't sick. In every way she was a perfect, normal babe, except," Grandfather Tuppa had to clear his throat, hard, of a growing, dry tightness, "when her coverings were removed, child, it was discovered she had a tail."

"A tail?"

"A tail . . . and with a neat, red bow upon it . . . the small, curled, hairless tail of a child born of human mother but fathered by a crook-tailed troll."

He watched horror sweep across his great-grandchild's eyes, noted it whitening in her face. He waited, patiently.

"But . . . trolls are bad, Granfather," Haide whispered at last. "Granmother Tresse said so. They do horrible things for fun . . ." The young voice dropped into an unconscious mimic of her elder. "They steal the last bite of bread from winter-starved farmers, they pluck the eyes from birds. They would have their way with any woman they find, they kill and roast poor men along the road who can't fight them off nor give them gold to be free. And they steal babies, then if they cry too much, they eat them too." The little girl looked up seriously at her grandfather. "If I ever found an ugly old baby troll, Granfather, right away I would kill it!"

"Yes, most people would do just that, Haide," the old man murmured. "They would kill any troll in a minute; but you, my child, mustn't ever be so hasty . . . There is more, you see, to this tale." He gazed guilelessly into the upturned face.

"This tiny troll babe was beautiful, you must remember, beautiful beyond reason, and with a smile as spring sunshine itself. Your Grandmother Tresse, your mother and father, even I, couldn't bear to put a pillow over the tiny nose and soft lips. And you know, Haide? Your mama felt particularly that way. Grandmother Tresse, upon finding out the baby was unclaimed, said that an old woman was too nervous, too unfit by her years to care for so young a child, even though her old husband had brought it home to her. She further said that your mama should take it home to raise as her own.''

He patted his hand on the little girl's head. ''Up to that point in your mama's life, Haide, no baby at all had ever nestled in her arms. As we all stood looking at the naked babe, your mama cried and cried every time the small, pink tail wriggled. Finally, after a goodly time of this, with none of us any the happier, your papa gave your mama a hug, then looked at me.

'' 'Grandfather,' he said, in a voice that sounded like he'd swallowed a toad, 'would you do me the honor of fetching your sharpest carving knife from the butchering shed?' ''

Grandfather Tuppa stroked Haide's hair. ''Your mama didn't want me to do it, of course. She made a little noise in her throat and clutched your papa's arm. But after seeing his mind was made up, there was nothing she could do but say, 'If you kill it, I will go from you forever!' hiding her face in her hands.

''When your papa had the knife in his fist, he walked over to the bed and stood over the tiny troll child. I went to stand beside him, to help him do it quickly, while the women held one another. And then, Haide . . . .'' Grandfather Tuppa took the still child's face in both hands and smiled a sad smile down at her, ''your papa put the squalling baby in your mama's arms. She hugged it to her, never to give it up.''

''Oh, that's a good story, Granfather!'' said Haide; yet then, in a moment puzzled, she added: ''But Granfather, it can't be a true tale. Mama has no little girl child but me.''

''Yes, Haide that is true. Nevertheless, it is a true tale.''

''Well . . . what happened then to the baby troll?''

Grandfather Tuppa leaned over and placed a gentle kiss

upon the child's forehead. "She sits here on my lap, Haide mine," he whispered. "The little girl who I so often worry over for her naughty ways like mixing salt with sugar."

"No! No, Granfather," little Haide whimpered. "Say it is not so! I'm not a troll. I don't want to be an ugly troll, and have to live in a cave . . ."

"But I am afraid it is so, my child. Look . . . look into this little chest here," he said softly while unlocking it. "See what I have kept safe all these years."

With horror ripe on her face, the little girl peeped in, and the old man's hands on the box's lid shook in spite of himself.

There, for her to see, rested a tiny pink, still fresh-looking tail, curled. With a bit of a red ribbon tied neatly around.

After the child finished vomiting into the wastebarrel beside the desk, Grandfather Tuppa cuddled her close. He nestled his old soft chin against her sweaty hair and rocked her to and fro, crooning softly, gently, telling her of the worth of family, of loved ones, of the great love of each and every member of any family for the other, no matter what had gone before.

When she quieted, he held her a little way from himself to gaze directly into her tear-blurred eyes.

"Haide mine," he said after a moment, "do you understand at all why it was time I had to tell you that story?"

The child averted her eyes and wretchedly shook her head.

"I'll tell you what. Come—your hands are cold and so are mine. Come over to the fire with me. We will warm ourselves." He set her down, took her hand in one of his, and picked up the box with the other. She gazed at it grievingly as he snapped shut the lid. He walked her over to the bright hearth.

"Haide, now that you have heard the story and have seen this little box's contents . . . I have kept it all these years for only one reason. Your life with us here has made you the child of a human mother, able to run and play in

the bright light of day without taking hurt from it as would
be normal for trolls. You are to all eyes and minds as
human a daughter of Norway as any other. But, Haide
mine, to continue to be a human being, you cannot ever let
the troll side of your nature come to the fore. It will take
over your soul, child, and you will be a troll evermore. You
must remember that. Never for an instant must you forget
what people are—they are kindness and goodness to
others; they are help, not hindrance; they are wishing well
to those who need; they are withholding their own will
when another's will is more important to a moment; and
they are love, in whatever capacity they have, if they are
only allowed to give it. Do you forget this, you allow
yourself instead to be a troll child. Not human."

They stood before the blaze. Grandfather Tuppa
abruptly tossed the little box into the flames.

He watched his great-granddaughter's pinched face as
the fire reduced the casket to ashes and bits of brass
appointments. The instant of shock caused by his act
slowly changed to a look of almost disbelieving hope upon
the dainty, plumping cheeks. Yes; the child might understand.

"Why did you do that, Granfather?" she asked. Her
voice was tiny, hushed.

"Because from now on what you are is up to you,
child," he answered. "The evidence is gone forever, and
unless you tell someone, or decide you don't care to be
human anymore by continuing to play sadly trollish tricks,
no one but you and I can ever say that evidence existed.
You are merely Misa and Nils Stivot's beloved Haide. You
can grow up without fear, marry, and bless me with great-
great-grandchildren to love. And, you know, child," he
added as the little girl buried her face in his coat, hugging
him with all her strength, "by that generation of yours—
with you firmly human-thinking this next decade or so—
your children will be human born, cleansed of all trollish
signs . . . from your determination to be."

Haide looked up in wonder. "Do you mean it, Granfather? Are you sure?"

He gazed silently down at her for the space of several heartbeats, then bent and scooped her up to hold her tightly in his arms. "I have seen it before, child," he told her, rocking them both just a little. He laid his cheek upon her hair and added: "It was thus with my own grandmother; she bore a daughter perfectly human, my mother. And so, in her turn, she bore me."

The Magic Wood

The wood is full of shining eyes,
The wood is full of creeping feet,
The wood is full of tiny cries:
You must not go to the wood at night!

I met a man with eyes of glass
And a finger as curled as the wriggling worm,
And hair all red with rotting leaves,
And a stick that hissed like a summer snake.

The wood is full of shining eyes,
The wood is full of creeping feet,
The wood is full of tiny cries:
You must not go to the wood at night!

He sang me a song in backwards words,
And drew me a dragon in the air.
I saw his teeth through the back of his head,
And a rat's eyes winking from his hair.

The wood is full of shining eyes,
The wood is full of creeping feet,
The wood is full of tiny cries:
You must not go to the wood at night!

He made me a penny out of a stone,
And showed me the way to catch a lark
With a straw and a nut and a whispered word
And a penn'orth of ginger wrapped up in a leaf.

The wood is full of shining eyes,
The wood is full of creeping feet,
The wood is full of tiny cries:
You must not go to the wood at night!

He asked me my name, and where I lived;
I told him a name from my Book of Tales;
He asked me to come with him into the wood
And dance with the Kings from under the hills.

The wood is full of shining eyes,
The wood is full of creeping feet,
The wood is full of tiny cries:
You must not go to the wood at night!

But I saw that his eyes were turning to fire;
I watched the nails grow on his wriggling hand;
And I said my prayers, all out in a rush,
And found myself safe on my father's land.

Oh, the wood is full of shining eyes,
The wood is full of creeping feet,
The wood is full of tiny cries:
You must not go to the wood at night!

—**Henry Treece**

The Healer

Robin McKinley

The child was born just as the first faint rays of dawn made their way through the cracks between the shutters. The lantern-wick burned low. The new father bowed his head over his wife's hand as the midwife smiled at the mite of humanity in her arms. Black curls framed the tiny face; the child gave a gasp of shock, then filled its lungs for its first cry in this world; but when the little mouth opened, no sound came out. The midwife tightened her hands on the warm wet skin as the baby gave a sudden writhe, and closed its mouth as if it knew that it had failed at something expected of it. Then the eyes stared up into the midwife's own, black, and clearer than a newborn's should be, and deep in them such a look of sorrow that tears rose in the midwife's own eyes.

"The child does not cry," the mother whispered in terror, and the father's head snapped up to look at the midwife and the baby cradled in her arms.

The midwife could not fear the sadness in this baby's eyes; and she said shakily, "No, the baby does not cry, but she is a fine girl nonetheless;" and the baby blinked, and the look was gone. The midwife washed her quickly, and gave her into her mother's eager, anxious arms, and saw the damp-curled, black-haired head of the young wife bend over the tiny curly head of the daughter. Her smile reminded the midwife of the smiles of many other new mothers, and the midwife smiled herself, and opened a shutter long enough to take a few deep breaths of the new morning air. She closed it again firmly, and chased the father out of the room so that mother and child might be bathed properly, and the bedclothes changed.

They named her Lily. She almost never cried; it was as though she did not want to call attention to what she lacked, and so at most her little face would screw itself into a tiny red knot, and a few tears would creep down her cheeks, but she did not open her mouth. She was her parents' first child, and her mother hovered over her, and she suffered no neglect for her inability to draw attention to herself.

When Lily was three years old, her mother bore a second child, another daughter; when she was six and a half, a son was born. Both these children came into the world howling mightily. Lily seemed to find their wordless crying more fascinating than the grownups' speech; and when she could she loved to sit beside the new baby and play with it gently, and make it chuckle at her.

By the time her little brother was taking his first wobbly steps it had become apparent that Lily had been granted the healer's gift. A young cow or skittish mare would foal more quietly with her head in Lily's lap; children with fever did not toss and turn in their beds if Lily sat beside them; and it was usually in Lily's presence that the fevers broke, and the way back to health began.

When she was twelve she was apprenticed to the mid-wife who had birthed her.

Jolin by then was a strong handsome woman of forty-five or so. Her husband had died when they had had only two years together, and no children; and she had decided that she preferred to live alone as a healer after that. But it was as the midwife she was best known, for her village was a healthy one; hardly anyone ever fell from a horse and broke a leg or caught a fever that her odd-smelling draughts could not bring down. "I'll tell you, young one," she said to Lily, "I'll teach you everything I know, but if you stay here you won't be needing it; you'll spend the time you're not birthing babies sewing little sacks of herbs for the women to hang in the wardrobes and tuck among the linens. Can you sew properly?" Lily nodded, smiling; but Jolin looked into her black eyes and saw the same sorrow there that she had first seen twelve years ago. She said abruptly: "I've heard you whistling. You can whistle more like the birds than the birds do. There's no reason you can't talk with those calls: we'll put meanings to the different ones, and we'll both learn 'em. Will you do that with me?''

Lily nodded eagerly, but her smile broke, and Jolin looked away.

Five years passed; Jolin had bought her apprentice a horse the year before, because Lily's fame had begun to spread to neighboring towns, and she often rode a long way to tend the sick. Jolin still birthed babies, but she was happy not to have to tend stomach-aches at midnight anymore, and Lily was nearly a woman grown, and had surpassed her old teacher in almost all Jolin had to offer her. Jolin was glad of it, for it still worried her that the sadness stayed deep in Lily's eyes and would not be lost or buried. The work meant much to each of them; for Jolin it had eased the loss of a husband she loved, and had had for so little time she could not quite let go of his memory; and for Lily, now, she thought it meant that which she had never had.

Of the two of them, Jolin thought, Lily was the more to be pitied. Their village was one of a number of small villages, going about their small concerns, uninterested in anything but the weather and the crops, marriages, births and deaths. There was no one within three days' ride who could read or write, for Jolin knew everyone; and the birdcall-speech that she and her apprentice had made was enough for crops and weather, births and deaths, but Jolin saw other things passing swiftly over Lily's clear face, and wished there was a way to let them free.

At first Jolin had always accompanied Lily on her rounds, but as Lily grew surer of her craft somehow she also grew able to draw what she needed to know or to borrow from whomever she tended; and Jolin could sit at home and sew her little sacks of herbs and prepare the infusions Lily would need, and tend the several cats that always lived with them, and the goats in the shed and the few chickens in the coop that survived the local foxes.

When Lily was seventeen, Jolin said: "You should be

thinking of marrying." She knew at least two lads who
followed Lily with their eyes and were clumsy at their work
when she was near, though Lily seemed unaware of them.

Lily frowned and shook her head.

"Why not?" Jolin said. "You can be a healer as well. I
was. It takes a certain kind of man—" she sighed "—but
there are a few. What about young Armar? He's a quiet,
even-handed sort, who'd be proud to have a wife that was
needed by half the countryside. I've seen him watching
you." She chuckled. "And I have my heart set on birthing
your first baby."

Lily shook her head more violently, and raised her
hands to her throat.

"You can learn to whistle at him as you have me," Jolin
said gently, for she saw how the girl's hands shook. "Truly,
child, it's not that great a matter; five villages love you and
not a person in 'em cares you can't talk."

Lily stood up, her eyes full of the bitter fire in her heart,
and struck herself on the breast with her fist, and Jolin
winced at the weight of the blow; she did not need to hear
the words to know that Lily was shouting at her: *I do!*

Lily reached her twentieth year unmarried, although she
had had three offers, Armar among them. The crop of
children in her parents' home had reached seven since she
had left them eight years ago; and all her little brothers and
sisters whistled birdcalls at her when she whistled to them.
Her mother called her children her flock of starlings; but
the birds themselves would come and perch on Lily's
outstretched fingers, but on no one else's.

Lily was riding home from a sprained ankle in a neighboring village, thinking about supper, and wondering if
Karla had had her kittens yet when she realized she was
overtaking another traveller on the road. She did not
recognize the horse, and reined back her own, for she
dreaded any contact with strangers; but the rider had
already heard her approach and was waiting for her. Re-

luctantly she rode forward. The rider threw back the hood
of his cloak as she approached and smiled at her. She had
never seen him before; he had a long narrow face, made
longer by lines of sorrow around his mouth. His long hair
was blond and grey mixed, and he sat his horse as if he had
been sitting on horseback for more years past than he
would wish to remember. His eyes were pale, but in the
fading twilight she could not see if they were blue or grey.

"Pardon me, lady," he greeted her, "but I fear I have
come wrong somewhere. Would you have the goodness
to tell me where I am?"

She shook her head, looking down at the long quiet
hands holding his horse's reins, then forced herself to look
up, meeting his eyes. She watched his face for comprehension as she shook her head again, and touched two
fingers to her mouth and her throat; and said sadly to
herself, *I cannot tell you anything, stranger. I cannot talk.*

The stranger's expression changed indeed, but the
comprehension she expected was mixed with something
else she could not name. Then she heard his words clearly
in her mind, although he did not move his lips. *Indeed, but
I can hear you, lady.*

Lily reached out, not knowing that she did so, and her
fingers closed on a fold of the man's cloak. He did not
flinch from her touch, and her horse stood patiently still,
wanting his warm stall and his oats, but too polite to
protest. *Who—who are you?* she thought frantically; *what
are you doing to me?*

Be easy, lady. I am—here there was an odd flicker—*a
mage, of sorts; or once I was one. I retain a few powers.
I*—and his thought went suddenly blank with an emptiness
that was much more awful than that of a voice fallen
silent—*I can mindspeak. You have not met any of—us—
before?*

She shook her head.

There are not many. He looked down into the white face
that looked up at him and felt an odd creaky sensation
where once he might have had a heart.

Where are you going? she said at last.

He looked away; she thought he stared at the horizon as if he expected to see something he could hastily describe as his goal.

I do not mean to question you, she said; *forgive me, I am not accustomed to—speech—and I forget my manners.*

He smiled at her, but the sad lines around his mouth did not change. *There is no lack of courtesy,* he replied; *only that I am a wanderer, and I cannot tell you where I am going.* He looked up again, but there was no urgency in his gaze this time. *I have not travelled here before, however, and even a—wanderer—has his pride; and so I asked you the name of this place.*

She blushed that she had forgotten his question, and replied quickly, the words leaping into her mind, *the village where I live lies just there, over the little hill. Its name is Rhungill. That way*—she turned in her saddle—*is Teskip, where I am returning from; this highway misses it, it lay to your right, beyond the little forest as you rode this way.*

He nodded gravely. *You have always lived in Rhungill?*

She nodded; the gesture felt familiar, but a bubble of joy beat in her throat that she need not halt with the nod. *I am the apprentice of our healer.*

He was not expecting to hear himself say: *Is there an inn in your village, where a wanderer might rest for the night?* In the private part of his mind he said to himself: there are three hours till sunset; there is no reason to stop here now. If there are no more villages, I have lain by a fire under a tree more often than I have lain in a bed under a roof for many years past.

Lily frowned a moment and said, *No-o, we have no inn; Rhungill is very small. But there is a spare room—it is Jolin's house, but I live there too—we often put people up, who are passing through and need a place to stay. The villagers often send us folk.* And because she was not accustomed to mindspeech, he heard her say to herself what she did not mean for him to hear: *let him stay a little longer.*

And so he was less surprised when he heard himself answer: *I would be pleased to spend the night at your healer's house.*

A smile, such as had never before been there, bloomed on Lily's face; her thoughts tumbled over each other and politely, he did not listen, nor let her know that he might have. She let her patient horse go on again, and the stranger's horse walked beside.

They did not speak. Lily found that there were so many things she would like to say, to ask, that they overwhelmed her; and then a terrible shyness closed over her, for fear that she would offend the stranger with her eagerness, with the rush of pent-up longing for the particulars of conversation. He held his silence as well, but his reasons stretched back over many wandering years; although once or twice he did look in secret at the bright young face beside him, and again there was the odd, uncomfortable spasm beneath his breastbone.

They rode over the hill and took a narrow, well-worn way off the highway. It wound into a deep cutting, and golden grasses waved above their heads at either side. Then the way rose, or the sides fell away, and the stranger looked around him at pastureland with sheep and cows grazing earnestly and solemnly across it; and then at empty meadows; and then there was a small stand of birch and ash and willow, and a small thatched house with a strictly-tended herb garden around it, laid out in a maze of squares and circles and borders and low hedges. Lily swung off her small gelding at the edge of the garden and whistled: a high thin cry that told Jolin she had brought a visitor.

Jolin emerged from the house smiling. Her hair, mostly grey now, with lights of chestnut brown, was in a braid; and tucked into the first twist of the hair at the nape of her neck was a spray of yellow and white flowers. They were almost a halo, nearly a collar.

"Lady," said the stranger, and dismounted.

This is Jolin, Lily said to him. *And you—*she stopped, confused, shy again.

"Jolin," said the stranger, but Jolin did not think it odd that he knew her name, for often the villagers sent visitors on with Lily when they saw her riding by, having supplied both their names first. "I am called Sahath."

Lily moved restlessly; there was no birdcall available to her for this eventuality. She began the one for "talk," and broke off. Jolin glanced at her, aware that something was troubling her.

Sahath, said Lily, *tell Jolin*—and her thought paused, because she could not decide, even to herself, what the proper words for it were.

But Jolin was looking at their guest more closely, and a tiny frown appeared between her eyes.

Sahath said silently to Lily: *she guesses.*

Lily looked up at him: standing side by side he was nearly a head taller than she. *She—?*

Jolin had spent several years travelling in her youth, travelling far from her native village and even far from her own country; and on her travels she had learned more of the world than most of the other inhabitants of Rhungill, for they were born and bred to live their lives on their small land-plots, and any sign of wanderlust was firmly suppressed. Jolin, as a healer and so a little unusual, was permitted wider leeway than any of the rest of Rhungill's daughters; but her worldly knowledge was something she rarely admitted and still more rarely demonstrated. But one of the things she had learned as she and her mother drifted from town to town, dosing children and heifers, binding the broken limbs of men and pet cats, was to read the mage-mark.

"Sir," she said now, "what is one such as you doing in our quiet and insignificant part of the world?" Her voice was polite but not cordial; for mages, while necessary for some work beyond the reach of ordinary mortals, often brought with them trouble as well; and an unbidden mage was almost certainly trouble. This too she had learned when she was young.

Sahath smiled sadly. "I carry the mark, lady, it is true,

but no mage am I." Jolin, staring at him, holding her worldly knowledge just behind her eyes where everything he said must be reflected through it, read truth in his eyes. "I was one once, but no longer."

Jolin relaxed, and if she need not fear this man she could pity him: for to have once been a mage and to have lost that more than mortal strength must be as heavy a blow as any man might receive and yet live; and she saw the lines of sorrow in his face.

Lily stood staring at the man with the sad face, for she knew no more of mages than a child knows of fairy tales: she would as easily have believed in the existence of tigers or of dragons, of chimeras or of elephants; and yet Jolin's face and voice were serious. A mage. This man was a mage—or had been one—and he could speak to her. It was more wonderful than elephants.

Sahath said: "Some broken pieces of my mage-truth remain to me, and one of these Lily wishes me to tell you: that I can speak to her—mind to mind."

Lily nodded eagerly, and seized her old friend and mentor's hands in hers. She smiled, pulled her lips together to whistle "it is true" and her lips drew back immediately again to the smile. Jolin tried to smile back into the bright young face before her: there was a glow there which had never been there before, and Jolin's loving heart turned with jealousy and—fear reawakened. For this man, with his unreasonable skills, even if he were no proper mage, might be anyone in his own heart. Jolin loved Lily as much as any person may love another. What, she asked herself in fear, might this man do to her, in her innocence, her pleasure in the opening of a door so long closed to her, and open now only to this stranger? Mages were not to be trusted on a human scale of right and wrong, reason and unreason. Mages were sworn to other things. Jolin understood that they were sworn to— goodness, to rightness; but often that goodness was of a high, far sort that looked very much like misery to the smaller folk who had to live near it.

As she thought these things, and held her dearer-than-daughter's hands in hers, she looked again at Sahath. "What do you read in my mind, mage?" she said, and her voice was harsher than she meant to permit it, for Lily's sake.

Sahath dropped his eyes to his own hands; he spread the long fingers as if remembering what once they had been capable of. "Distrust and fear," he said after a moment; and Jolin was the more alarmed that she had had no sense of his scrutiny. No mage-skill she had, but as a healer she heard and felt much that common folk had no ken of.

Lily's eyes widened, and she clutched Jolin's hands. Sahath felt her mind buck and shudder like a frightened horse, for the old loyalty was very strong. It was terrible to her that she might have to give up this wonderful, impossible thing even sooner than the brief span of an overnight guest's visit that she had promised herself—or at least freely hoped for. Even his mage's wisdom was awed by her strength of will, and the strength of her love for the aging, steady-eyed woman who watched him. He felt the girl withdrawing from him, and he did not follow her, though he might have; but he did not want to know what she was thinking. He stood where he was, the two women only a step or two distant from him; and he felt alone, as alone as he had felt once before, on a mountain, looking at a dying army, knowing his mage-strength was dying with them.

"I—" he said, groping, and the same part of his mind that had protested his halting so long before sundown protested again, saying, why do you defend yourself to an old village woman who shambles among her shrubs and bitter herbs, mouthing superstitions? But the part of his mind that had been moved by Lily's strength and humility answered: because she is right to question me.

"I am no threat to you in any way I control," he said to Jolin's steady gaze, and she thought: still he talks like a mage, with the mage logic, to specify that which he controls. Yet perhaps it is not so bad a thing, some other part of her mind said calmly, that any human being, even a mage, should know how little he may control.

"It—it is through no dishonor that I lost the—the rest of my mage-strength." The last words were pulled out of him, like the last secret drops of the heart's blood of a dragon, and Jolin heard the pain and pride in his voice, and saw the blankness in his eyes; yet she did not know that he was standing again on a mountain, feeling all that had meant anything to him draining away from him into the earth, drawn by the ebbing life-force of the army he had opposed. One of the man's long-fingered hands had stretched toward the two women as he spoke; but as he said *mage-strength* the hand went to his forehead. When it dropped to his side again there were white marks that stood a moment against the skin, where the fingertips had pressed too hard.

Jolin put one arm around Lily's shoulders and reached her other hand out delicately, to touch Sahath's sleeve. He looked up again at the touch of her fingers. "You are welcome to stay with us, Sahath."

Lily after all spoke to him very little that evening; as if, he thought, she did not trust herself; although she listened eagerly to the harmless stories he told them of other lands and peoples he had visited; and she not infrequently interrupted him to ask for unimportant details. He was careful to answer everything she asked as precisely as he could; once or twice she laughed at his replies, although there was nothing overtly amusing about them.

In the morning when he awoke, only a little past dawn, Lily was already gone. Jolin gave him breakfast and said without looking at him, "Lily has gone gathering wild herbs; dawn is best for some of those she seeks." Sahath saw in her mind that Lily had gone by her own decision; Jolin had not sent her, nor tried to suggest the errand to her.

He felt strangely bereft, and he sat, crumbling a piece of sweet brown bread with his fingers and staring into his cup of herb tea. He recognized the infusion: chintanth for calm, morrar for clear-mindedness. He drank what was in the cup and poured himself more. Jolin moved around the kitchen, putting plates and cups back into the cupboard.

He said abruptly: "Is there any work a simple man's strength might do for you?"

There was a rush of things through Jolin's mind: her and Lily's self-sufficiency, and their pleasure in it; another surge of mistrust for mage-cunning—suddenly and ashamedly put down—this surprised him, as he stared into his honey-clouded tea, and it gave him hope. Hope? he thought. He had not known hope since he lost his mage-strength; he had nearly forgotten its name. Jolin stood gazing into the depths of the cupboard, tracing the painted borders of vines and leaves and flowers with her eye; and now her thoughts were of things that it would be good to have done, that she and Lily always meant to see to, and never quite had time for.

When Lily came home in the late morning, a basket over her arm, Sahath was working his slow way with a spade down the square of field that Jolin had long had in her mind as an extension of her herb garden. Lily halted at the edge of the freshly turned earth, and breathed deep of the damp sweet smell of it. Sahath stopped to lean on his spade, and wiped his forehead on one long dark sleeve. *It is near dinnertime,* said Lily hesitantly, fearful of asking him why he was digging Jolin's garden; but her heart was beating faster than her swift walking could explain.

He ate with them, a silent meal, for none of the three wished to acknowledge or discuss the new balance that was already growing among them. Then he went back to his spade.

He did a careful, thorough job of the new garden plot; two days it took him. When he finished it he widened the kitchen garden. Then he built a large new paddock for Lily's horse—and his own: the two horses had made friends at once, and stood head to tail in the shade at the edge of the tiny turn-out that flanked the small barn. When

they were first introduced to their new field, they ran like
furies around it, squealing and plunging at one another.
Jolin came out of the house to see what the uproar was
about. Sahath and Lily were leaning side by side on the top
rail of the sturdy new fence; Jolin wondered what they
might be saying to each other. The horses had enough of
being mad things, and ambled quietly over to ask their
riders for handouts. Jolin turned and reentered the house.

On the third day after his arrival Jolin gave Sahath a shirt
and trousers, lengthened for their new owner: the shirt-tail
and cuffs were a wide red band sewn neatly on to the
original yellow cloth; the trousers were green, and each leg
bore a new darker green hem. No mage had ever worn
such garb. He put them on. At the end of the week Lily
gave him a black and green—the same coarse green of the
trouser-hems—jacket. He said, *thank you, lady,* and she
blushed and turned away. Jolin watched them, and wondered if she had done the right thing, not to send him away
when she might have; wondered if he knew that Lily was in
love with him. She wondered if a mage might know anything of love, anything of a woman's love for a man.

He propped up the sagging cow shed where the two
goats lived, and made the chicken-coop decently fox-
proof. He built bird houses and feeders for the many birds
that were Lily's friends; and he watched her when he
thought she did not notice, when they came to visit, perch-
ing on her hands and shoulders and rubbing their small
heads against her face. He listened to their conversations,
and knew no more of what passed than Jolin did of his and
Lily's.

He had never been a carpenter, any more than he had
been a gardener; but he knew his work was good, and he
did not care where the skill came from. He knew he could
look at the things he wished to do here and understand
how best to do them, and that was enough. He slept the
nights through peacefully and dreamlessly.

A few days after the gift of the jacket Jolin said to him,
"The leather worker of our village is a good man and

clever. He owes us for his wife's illness last winter; it would please—us—if you would let him make you a pair of boots." His old boots, accustomed to nothing more arduous than the chafing of stirrup and stirrup-leather, had never, even in their young days, been intended for the sort of work he was lately requiring of them. He looked at them ruefully, stretched out toward the fire's flickering light, the dark green cuffs winking above them, and Karla's long furry red tail curling and uncurling above the cuffs.

He went into the village the next day. He understood, from the careful but polite greetings he received that the knowledge of Jolin's new hired man had gone before him; and he also understood that no more than his skill with spade and hammer had gone into the tale. There was no one he met who had the skill to recognize a mage-mark, nor was there any suspicion, besides the wary observation of a stranger expected to prove himself one way or another, that he was anything more or less than an itinerant laborer. The boot-maker quietly took his measurements and asked him to return in a week.

Another week, he thought, and was both glad and afraid. It was during that week that he finished the paddock for the horses. He wanted to build a larger shed to store hay; for there was hay enough in the meadowland around Jolin's house to keep all the livestock—even a second horse, he thought distantly—all the winter, if there were more room for it than the low loft over the small barn.

In a week he went back to fetch his boots: they were heavy, hard things, a farmer's boots, and for a moment they appalled him, till he saw the beauty of them. He thanked their maker gravely, and did not know the man was surprised by his tone: farmers, hired men, took their footgear for granted; he had long since learned to be proud of his craft for its own sake. And so he was the first of the villagers to wonder if perhaps there was more to Jolin's hired man—other than the fact, well mulled over all through Rhungill, that Jolin had never before in over twenty years been moved to hire anyone for more than a day's specific job—than met the eye. But he had no guess of the truth.

Sahath asked the boot-maker if there was someone who sold dry planking, for he had all but used Lily and Jolin's small store of it, till now used only for patching up after storms and hard winter weather. There were several such men, and because the leather-worker was pleased at the compliment Sahath paid him, he recommended one man over the others. Sahath, unknowing, went to that man, who had much fine wood of just the sort Sahath wanted; but when he asked a price the man looked at him a long moment and said, "No charge, as you do good work for them; you may have as much as you need as you go on for them. There are those of us know what we owe them." The man's name was Armar.

Sahath went in his heavy boots to the house he had begun in secret to call home. He let no hint of the cost to his pride his workman's hire of sturdy boots had commanded; but still Jolin's quick eyes caught him staring at the calluses on his long-fingered hands, and guessed something of what he was thinking.

A week after he brought his boots home he began the hay shed. He also began to teach Lily and Jolin their letters. He had pen and paper in his saddlebags, and a wax tablet that had once been important in a mage's work. When he first took it out of its satchel he had stood long with it in his hands; but it was silent, inert, a tool like a hammer was a tool and nothing more. He brought it downstairs, and whittled three styluses from bits of firewood.

"If you learn to write," he said, humbly, to Jolin, "Lily may speak to you as well as she may speak to any wandering—mage." It was all the explanation he gave, laying the pale smooth tablet down on the shining golden wood of the table; and Jolin realized, when he smiled uncertainly at her and then turned to look wistfully at Lily, that he did love her dearer-than-daughter, but that nothing of that love had passed between them. Jolin had grown fond of the quiet, weary man who was proving such a good landsman, fond enough of him that it no longer hurt her to see him wearing her husband's old clothes which she herself had patched for his longer frame; and so she thought, why does he not tell her? She looked at them as they looked at each other, and knew why, for the hopelessness was as bright in their eyes as the love. Jolin looked away unhappily, for she understood too that there was no advice she could give them that they would listen to. But she could whisper charms that they permit themselves to see what was, and not blind themselves with blame for what they lacked. Her lips moved.

Each evening after that the two women sat on either side of him and did their lessons as carefully as the students of his mage-master had ever done theirs, although they had been learning words to crack the world and set fire to the seas. Sahath copied the letters of the alphabet out plainly and boldly, onto a piece of stiff parchment, and Jolin pinned it to the front of the cupboard, where his two students might look at it often during the day.

Spring turned to summer, and Sahath's boots were no longer new, and he had three more shirts and another pair of trousers. The last shirt and trousers were made for him, not merely made over; and the first shirt had to be patched at the elbows. The goats produced two pair of kids, which would be sold at the fall auction in Teskip. Summer began to wane, and Sahath began to wander around the house at twilight, after work and before supper, staring at the bottles of herbs, the basket of scraps from which Jolin made her sachets; and outside in the garden, staring at the fading sun and the lengthening shadows.

Jolin thought, with a new fear at her heart, he will be leaving us soon. What of Lily? And even without thought of Lily she felt sorrow.

Lily too watched him pacing, but she said nothing at all; and what her thoughts were neither Jolin nor Sahath wished to guess.

One evening when Lily was gone to attend a sick baby,

Sahath said, with the uneasy abruptness Jolin had not heard since he had asked one morning months ago if there was any work for a simple man's strength: "It is possible that I know someone who could give Lily her voice. Would you let her travel away with me, on my word that I would protect her dearer than my own life?"

Jolin shivered, and laid her sewing down in her lap. "What is this you speak of?"

Sahath was silent a moment, stroking grey tabby Annabelle. "My old master. I have not seen him since I first began—my travels; even now I dread going back . . ." So much he could say after several months of farmer's labor and the companionship of two women. "He is a mage almost beyond the knowing of the rest of us, even his best pupils." He swallowed, for he had been one of these. "But he knows many things. I—I know Lily, I think, well enough to guess that her voice is something my master should be able to give her."

Jolin stared unblinking into the fire till the heat of it drew tears. "It is not my decision. We will put it to Lily. If she wishes to go with you, then she shall go."

Lily did not return till the next morning, and she found her two best friends as tired and sleepless-looking as she felt herself, and she looked at them with surprise. "Sahath said something last night that you need to hear," said Jolin; but Sahath did not raise his heavy eyes from his tea-cup.

"His—mage-master—may be able to give you your voice. Will you go with him, to seek this wizard?"

Lily's hands were shaking as she set her basket on the table. She pursed her lips, but no sound emerged. She licked her lips nervously and whistled: "I will go."

They set out two days later. It was a quiet two days; Lily did not even answer the birds when they spoke to her. They left when dawn was still grey over the trees. Jolin and Lily embraced for a long time before the older woman put the younger one away from her and said, "You go on now. Just don't forget to come back."

Lily nodded, then shook her head, then nodded again and smiled tremulously.

"I'll tell your parents you've gone away for a bit, never fear."

Lily nodded once more, slowly, then turned away to mount her little bay horse. Sahath was astride already, standing a little away from the two women, staring at the yellow fingers of light pushing the grey away; he looked down startled when Jolin touched his knee. She swallowed, tried to speak, but no words came, and her fingers dug into his leg. He covered her hand with his and squeezed; when she looked up at him he smiled, and finally she smiled back; then turned away and left them. Lily watched the house door close behind her dearest friend, and sat immobile, staring at the place where Jolin had disappeared, till Sahath sent his horse forward. Lily awoke from her reverie, and sent the little bay after the tall black horse. Sahath heard the gentle hoofbeats behind him, and turned to smile encouragement; and Lily, looking into his face, realized that he had not been sure, even until this moment, if she would follow him or not. She smiled in return, a smile of reassurance. Words, loose and filmy as smoke, drifted into Sahath's mind: *I keep my promises.* But he did not know what she had read in his face, and he shook his head to clear it of the words that were not meant for him.

No villager would have mistaken Sahath for a workman now, in the dark tunic and cloak he had worn when he first met Lily, riding his tall black horse; the horse alone was too fine a creature for anyone but a man of rank. For all its obvious age, for the bones of its face showed starkly through the skin, it held its crest and tail high, and set its feet down as softly as if its master were made of eggshells. Lily, looking at the man beside her on his fine horse, and looking back to the pricked ears of her sturdy, reliable mount, was almost afraid of her companion, as she had been afraid when he first spoke in her mind, and as she had not been afraid again for many weeks.

Please, Sahath said now. *Do not fear me: I am the man*

who hammered his fingers till they were blue and black, and cursed himself for clumsiness till the birds fled the noise; and stuck his spade into his own foot and yelped with pain. You know me too well to fear me.

Lily laughed, and the silent chime of her laughter rang in his mind as she tipped her chin back and grinned at the sky. *And I am the girl who cannot spell.*

You do very well.

Not half so well as Jolin.

Jolin is special.

Yes. And their minds fell away from each other, and each disappeared into private thoughts.

They rode south and west. Occasionally they stopped in a town for supplies, but they slept always under the stars, for Lily's dread of strangers and Sahath's uneasiness that any suspicion rest on her for travelling thus alone with him: and he a man past his prime and she a beauty. Their pace was set by Lily's horse, who was willing enough, but unaccustomed to long days of travelling; though it was young and Sahath's horse was old. But it quickly grew hard, and when they reached the great western mountains both horses strode up the slopes without trouble.

It grew cold near the peaks, but Sahath had bought them fur cloaks at the last town; no one lived in the mountains. Lily looked at hers uncertainly, and wished to ask how it was Sahath always had money for what he wished to buy. But she did not quite ask, and while he heard the question anyway, he chose not to answer.

They wandered among the mountain crests, and Lily became totally confused, for sometimes they rode west and south and sometimes east and north; and then there was a day of fog, and the earth seemed to spin around her, and even her stolid practical horse had trouble finding its footing. Sahath said, *There is only a little more of this until we are clear,* and Lily thought he meant something more than the words simply said; but again she did not ask. They dismounted and led the horses, and Lily timidly reached for a fold of Sahath's sleeve, for the way was wide enough

that they might walk abreast. When he felt her fingers he
seized her hand in his, and briefly he raised it to his lips and
kissed it, and then they walked on hand in hand.

That night there was no sunset, but when they woke in
the morning the sky was blue and cloudless, and they lay in
a hollow at the edge of a sandy shore that led to a vast lake;
and the mountains were behind them.

They followed the shore around the lake, and Lily whistled to the birds she saw, and a few of them dropped out of
the sky to sit on Lily's head and shoulders and chirp at her.

What do the birds say to you? said Sahath, a little
jealously.

Oh—small things, replied Lily, a little at a loss; she had
never tried to translate one friend for another before. *It is
not easy to say. They say this is a good place, but—*she
groped for a way to explain—*different.*

Sahath smiled. *I am glad of the good and I know of the
different, for we are almost to the place we seek.*

They turned away from the lake at last, onto a narrow
track; but they had not gone far when a meadow opened
before them. There were cows and horses in the meadow;
they raised their heads to eye the strangers as they passed.
Lily noticed there was no fence to enclose the beasts,
although there was an open stable at the far edge of the
field; this they rode past. A little way farther and they came
to an immense stone hall with great trees closed around it,
except for a beaten space at its front doors. This space was
set round with pillars, unlit torches bound to their tops. A
man sat alone on one of the stone steps leading to the hall
doors; he was staring idly into nothing, but Lily was certain
that he knew of their approach—and had known since
long before he had seen or heard them—and was awaiting
their arrival.

Greetings, said Sahath, as his horse's feet touched the
bare ground.

The man brought his eyes down from the motes of air he
had been watching and looked at Sahath and smiled.
Greetings, he replied, and his mindspeech sounded in

Lily's head as well as Sahath's. Lily clung to Sahath's shadow and said nothing, for the man's one word *greetings* had echoed into immeasurable distances, and she was dizzy with them.

This is my master, Sahath said awkwardly, and Lily ducked her head once and glanced at the man. He caught her reluctant eye and smiled, and Lily freed her mind enough to respond: *Greetings.*

That's better, said the man. His eyes were blue, and his hair was blond and curly; if it were not for the aura of power about him that hung shivering like a cloak from his head and shoulders he would have been an unlikely figure for a mage-master.

What did you expect, came his thought, amused, *an ancient with a snowy beard and piercing eyes—in a flowing black shroud and pointed cap?*

Lily smiled in spite of herself. *Something like that.*

The man laughed: it was the first vocal sound any of the three had yet made. He stood up. He was tall and narrow, and he wore a short blue tunic over snug brown trousers and tall boots. Sahath had dismounted, and Lily looked at the two of them standing side by side. For all the grey in Sahath's hair, and the heavy lines in his face, she could see the other man was much the elder. Sahath was several inches shorter than his master, and he looked worn and ragged from travel, and Lily's heart went out in a rush to him. The blond man turned to her at once: *You do not have to defend him from me;* and Sahath looked between them puzzled. And Lily, looking into their faces, recognized at last the mage-mark, and knew that she would know it again if she ever saw it in another face. And she was surprised that she had not recognized it as such long since in Sahath's face, and she wondered why; and the blond man flicked another glance at her, and with the glance came a little gust of amusement, but she could not hear any words in it.

After a pause Sahath said, *You will know why we have come.*

*I know. Come; you can turn your horses out with the
others; they will not stray. Then we will talk.*

The hall was empty but for a few heavy wooden chairs
and a tall narrow table at the far end, set around a fireplace.
Lily looked around her, tipping her head back till her neck
creaked in protest, lagging behind the two men as they
went purposefully toward the chairs. She stepped as softly
as she might, and her soft-soled boots made no more noise
than a cat's paws; yet as she approached the center of the
great hall she stopped and shivered, for the silence pressed
in on her as if it were a guardian. *What are you doing here?
Why have you come to this place?* She wrapped her arms
around her body, and the silence seized her the more
strongly: *How dare you walk the hall of the mage-master?*

Her head hurt; she turned blindly back toward the open
door and daylight, and the blue sky. Almost sobbing, she
said to the silence: *I came for vanity, for vanity, I should
not be here, I have no right to walk in the hall of the
mage-master.*

But as she stretched out her hands toward the high
doors, a bird flew through them: a little brown bird that
flew in swoops, his wings closing briefly against his sides
after every beat; and he perched on one of her out-flung
hands. He opened his beak, and three notes fell out; and
the guardian silence withdrew slightly, and Lily could
breathe again. He jumped from Lily's one hand to the
other and she, awed, cupped her hands around him. He
cocked his head and stared at her with one onyx-chip eye
and then the other. The top of his head was rust-colored,
and there were short streaks of cinnamon at the corner of
each black eye. He offered her the same three notes, and
this time she pursed her lips and gently gave them back to
him. She had bent her body over her cupped hands, and
now she straightened up, and after a pause of one breath,
threw her head back, almost as if she expected it to strike
against something; but whatever had been there had fled
entirely. The bird hopped up her wrist to her arm, to her
shoulder; and then he flew up, straight up, without swoop-

ing, till he perched on the sill of one of the high windows, and he tossed his three notes back down to her again. Then two more small brown birds flew through the doors, and passed Lily so closely that her hair stirred with the wind of their tiny wings; and they joined their fellow on the window sill. There were five birds after them, and eight after that; till the narrow sills of the tall windows were full of them and of their quick sharp song. And Lily turned away from the day-filled doorway, back to the dark chairs at the farther end of the hall, where the men awaited her.

The blond man looked long at her as she came up to him; but it was not an unkind look. She smiled timidly at him, and he put out a hand and touched her black hair. *There have been those who were invited into my hall who could not pass the door.*

Sahath's face was pale. *I did not know that I brought her—*

Into danger? finished the mage-master. *Then you have forgotten much that you should have remembered.*

Sahath's face had been pale, but at the master's words it went white, corpse-white, haggard with memory. *I have forgotten everything.*

The mage-master made a restless gesture. *That is not true; it has never been true; and if you wish to indulge in self-pity you must do it somewhere other than here.*

Sahath turned away from the other two, slowly, as if he were an old, old man; and if Lily had had any voice she would have cried out. But when she stepped forward to go to him, the master's hand fell on her shoulder, and she stopped where she stood, although she ached with stillness.

Sahath, the master went on more gently, *you were among the finest of any of my pupils. There was a light about you that few of the others could even see from their dulness, though those I chose to teach were the very best. Among them you shone like a star.*

Lily, the master's hand still on her shoulder, began to see as he spoke a brightness form about Sahath's hands, a shiningness, an almost-mist about his feet, that crept up his legs, as if the master's words lay around him, built themselves into a wall or a ladder to reach him, for the master's wisdom to climb, and to creep into his ear.

Sahath flung out a hand and brightness flickered and flaked away from it, and a mote or two drifted to Lily's feet. She stooped, and touched the tips of two fingers to them, the mage-master's hand dropping away from her shoulder as she knelt. She raised her hand, and the tips of her first and third fingers glimmered.

I was the best of your pupils once, Sahath said bitterly, and the bitterness rasped at the minds that heard him. *But I did not learn what I needed most to learn: my own limits. And I betrayed myself, and your teaching, my master, and I have wandered many years since then, doing little, for little there is that I am able to do. With my mage-strength gone, my learning is of no use, for all that I know is the use of mage-strength.* He spread his hands, straightening the fingers violently as though he hated them; and then he made them into fists and shook them as if he held his enemy's life within them.

And more flakes of light fell from him and scattered, and Lily crept, on hands and knees, nearer him, and picked them up on the tips of her fingers, till all ten fingers glowed; and the knees of her riding dress shone, and when she noticed this she lay her hands flat on the stone floor, till the palms and the finger-joints gleamed. As she huddled, bent down, her coil of hair escaped its last pins and the long braid of it fell down, and its tip skittered against the stones, and when she raised her head again the black braid-tip was star-flecked.

The mage-master's eyes were on the girl as he said: *You betrayed nothing, but your own sorrow robbed you by the terrible choice you had to make, standing alone on that mountain. You were too young to have had to make that choice; I would have been there had I known, but I was too far away, and I saw what would happen too late. You saw what had to be done, and you had the strength to do it—that was your curse. And when you had done it, you left your mage-strength where you stood, for the choice had been too hard a one, and you were sickened with it. And you left, and I—I could not find you, for long and long. . . .* there was a weight of sorrow as bitter as Sahath's in his thought, and Lily sat where she was, cupping her shining hands in her lap and looking up at him, while his eyes still watched her. She thought, but it was a very small thought: *The silence was right—I should not be here.*

It was a thought not meant to be overheard, but the blond man's brows snapped together and he shook his head once, fiercely; and she dropped her eyes to her starry palms, and yet she was comforted.

I did not leave my mage-strength, said Sahath, still facing away from his master, and the girl sitting at his feet; but as his arms dropped to his sides, the star-flakes fell down her back and across her spreading skirts.

I am your master still, the blond man said, and his thought was mild and gentle again, *And I say to you that you turned your back on it and me and left us. Think you that you could elude me—me?—for so long had you not the wisdon I taught you—and the strength to make yourself invisible to my far-seeing? I have not known what came to you since you left that mountain with the armies dying at its feet, till you spoke of me to two women in a small bright kitchen far from here. In those long years I have known nothing of you but that you lived, for your death you could not have prevented me from seeing.*

In the silence nothing moved but the tiny wings of birds.

Sahath turned slowly around.

Think you so little of the art of carpentry that you believe any man who holds a hammer in his hand for the first time may build a shed that does not fall down, however earnest his intentions—and however often he bangs his thumb and curses?

Lily saw Sahath's feet moving toward her from the corner of her eye, and lifted her face to look at him, and he

looked down at her, dazed. *Lily*—he said, and stooped,
but the mage-master was there before him, and took Lily's
hands, and drew her to her feet. Sahath touched the
star-flakes on her shoulders, and then looked at his hands,
and the floor around them where the star-flakes lay like
fine sand. "I—" he said, and his voice broke.

The mage-master held Lily's hands still, and now he
drew them up and placed them, star-palms in, against her
own throat; and curled her fingers around her neck, and
held them there with his own long-fingered hands. She
stared up at him, and his eyes reminded her of the doors of
his hall, filled with daylight; and she felt her own pulse
beating in her throat against her hands. Then the master
drew his hands and hers away, and she saw that the
star-glitter was gone from her palms. He dropped her
hands, smiling faintly, and stepped back.

The air whistled strangely as she sucked it into her lungs
and blew it out again. She opened her mouth and closed it;
raised one hand to touch her neck with her fingers, yet she
could find nothing wrong. She swallowed, and it made her
throat tickle; and then she coughed. As she coughed she
looked down at the dark hem of her riding dress; the
star-flakes were gone from it too, and the dust of them had
blown away or sunk into the floor. She coughed again, and
the force of it shook her whole body, and hurt her throat
and lungs; but then she opened her mouth again when the
spasm was past and said, "Sahath." It was more a croak,
or a bird's chirp, than a word; but she looked up, and
turned toward him, and said "Sahath" again, and it was a
word this time. But as her eyes found him she saw the tears
running down his face.

He came to her, and she raised her arms to him; and the
mage-master turned his back on them and busied himself
at the small high table before the empty hearth. Lily heard
the chink of cups as she stood encircled by Sahath's arms,
her dark head on his dark-cloaked shoulder, and the taste
of his tears on her lips. She turned at the sound, and
looked over her shoulder; the master held a steaming

kettle in his hands, and she could smell the heat of it, although the hearth was as black as before. Sahath looked up at his old teacher when Lily stirred; and the mage-master turned toward them again, a cup in each hand. Sahath laughed.

The mage-master grinned and inclined his head. "School-boy stuff, I know," but he held the cups out toward them nonetheless. Lily reached out her left hand and Sahath his right, so that their other two hands might remain clasped together.

Whatever the steaming stuff was it cleared their heads and smoothed their faces, and Lily said, "Thank you," and smiled joyfully. Sahath looked at her and said nothing, and the blond man looked at them both, and then down into his cup. "You know this place," the mage-master said presently, raising his eyes again to Sahath's shining face; "You are as free in it now as you were years ago, when you lived here as my pupil." And he left them, setting his cup down on the small table and striding away down the hall, out into the sunlight. His figure was silhouetted a moment, framed by the stone doorsill; and then he was gone. The small brown birds sang farewell.

It was three days before Lily and Sahath saw him again. For those three days they wandered together through the deep woods around the master's hall, feeling the kindly shade curling around them; or lifting their faces to the sun when they walked along the shores of the lake. Lily learned to sing and to shout. She loved to stand at the edge of the lake, her hands cupped around her mouth, that her words might fly as far as they could across the listening water; but though she waited till the last far whisper had gone, she never had an answer. Sahath also taught her to skip small flat stones across the silver surface; she had never seen water wider than a river before, and the rivers of her acquaintance moved on about their business much too swiftly for any such game. She became a champion rock-skipper, anything less than eight skittering steps across the water before the small missile sank, and she would shout and stamp with annoyance, and Sahath would laugh at her. His stones always fled lightly and far across the lake.

"You're *helping* them," she accused him.

"And what if I am?" he teased her, grinning.

"It's not *fair*."

The grin faded, and he looked at her thoughtfully. He picked up another small flat stone and balanced it in his hand. "You want to lift it as you throw it—lift it up again each time it strikes the water. . . ." He threw, and the rock spun and bounded far out toward the center of the lake; they did not see where it finally disappeared.

Sahath looked at Lily. "You try."

"I—" But whatever she thought of saying, she changed her mind, found a stone to her liking, tossed it once or twice up and down in her hand, and then flicked it out over the water. They did not notice the green-crested black bird flying low over the lake, for they were counting the stone's skips; but on the fourteenth skip the bird seized the small spinning stone in its talons, rose high above the water, and set out to cross the lake.

At last the bird's green crest disappeared, and they could not make out one black speck from the haze that seemed always to muffle the farther shore.

The nights they spent in each other's arms, sleeping in one of the long low rooms that opened off each side of the mage-master's hall, where there were beds and blankets as if he had occasion to play host to many guests. But they saw no one but themselves.

The fourth morning they awoke and smelled cooking; instead of the cold food and kindling they had found awaiting their hunger on previous days, the mage-master was there, bent over a tiny red fire glittering fiercely out of the darkness of the enormous hearth at the far end of the great hall. He was toasting three thick slices of bread on two long slender sticks. When they approached him he gravely handed the stick with two slices on it to Lily. They had stewed fruit with their toast, and milk from one of the master's cows, with the cream floating in thick whorls on top.

"It is time to decide your future," said the mage-master, and Lily sighed.

"Is it true that Sahath might have cured me—himself—at any time—without our having come here at all?" Her voice was still low and husky as if with disuse, but the slightly anxious tone of the query removed any rudeness it might have otherwise held.

The blond man smiled. "Yes and no. I think I may claim some credit as an—er—catalyst."

Sahath stirred in his chair, for they were sitting around the small fire, which snapped and hissed and sent a determined thread of smoke up the vast chimney.

"Sahath always was pig-headed," the master continued. "It was something of his strength and much of his weakness."

Sahath said, "And what comes to your pig-headed student now?"

"What does he wish to come to him?" his old teacher responded, and both men's eyes turned to Lily.

"Jolin is waiting for—us," Lily said. The *us* had almost been a *me*: both men had seen it quivering on her lips, and both noticed how her voice dropped away to nothing when she said *us* instead.

The mage-master leaned forward and poked the fire thoughtfully with his toasting stick; it snarled and threw a handful of sparks at him. "There is much I could teach you," he said tentatively. Lily looked up at him, but his eyes were on the fire, which was grumbling to itself; then she looked at Sahath by her side. "No," said the master. "Not just Sahath: both of you. There is much strength in you, Lily; too much perhaps for the small frame of a baby to hold, and so your voice was left behind. You've grown into it since; I can read it in your face.

"And Sahath," he said, and raised his eyes from the

sulky fire to his old pupil's face. "You have lost nothing but pride and sorrow—and perhaps a little of the obstinacy. I—there is much use for one such as you. There is much use for the two of you." He looked at them both, and Lily saw the blue eyes again full of daylight; and when they were turned full on her she blinked.

"I told Jolin I would not forget to come back," she said, and her voice was barely above a whisper. "I am a healer; there is much use for me at my home."

"I am a healer too," said the mage-master, and his eyes held her, till she broke from him by standing up and running from the hall; her feet made no more noise than a bird's.

Sahath said: "I have become a farmer and a carpenter, and it suits me; I am become a lover, and would have a wife. I have no home but hers, but I have taken hers and want no other. Jolin waits for us: for both of us; and I would we return to her together." Sahath stood up slowly; the master sat, the stick still in his hands, and watched him till he turned away and slowly followed Lily.

I hold no one against his will, the master said to his retreating back; *but your lover does not know what she is refusing, and you to know. You might—some day—tell her why it is possible to make rocks fly.*

On the next morning Lily and Sahath departed from the stone hall and the mist-obscured lake. The mage-master saw them off. He and Sahath embraced; and Lily thought, watching, that Sahath looked younger and the master older than either had five days before. The master turned to her, and held out his hands, but uncertainly. She thought he expected her not to touch them, and she stepped forward and seized them strongly, and he smiled down at her, the morning sun blazing in his yellow hair. "I would like to meet your Jolin," he said; and Lily said impulsively, "Then you must visit us."

The master blinked; his eyes were as dark as evening,

and Lily realized that she had surprised him. "Thank you," he said.

"You will be welcome in our home," she replied; and the daylight seeped slowly into his eyes again. "What is your name?" she asked, before her courage failed her.

"Luthe," he said.

Sahath had mounted already; Lily turned from the mage-master and mounted her horse, who sighed when her light weight settled in the saddle; it had had a pleasant vacation, knee-deep in sweet grass at the banks of the lake. Lily and Sahath both looked down at the man they had come so far to see; he raised a hand in farewell. Silently he said to them: *I am glad to have seen you again, Sahath, and glad to have met you, Lily.*

Lily said silently back: *We shall meet again perhaps.*

The mage-master made no immediate answer, and they turned away, and their horses walked down the path that bordered the clearing before the hill; and just as they stepped into the shade of the trees his words took shape in their minds: *I think it very likely.* Lily, riding second, turned to look back before the trees held him from view; his face was unreadable below the burning yellow hair.

They had an easy journey back; no rain fell upon them and no wind chilled them, and the mountain fog seemed friendly and familiar, with nothing they need fear hidden within it; and the birds still came to Lily when she whistled to them.

They were rested and well, and anxious to be home, and they travelled quickly. It was less than a fortnight after Lily had seen the mage-master standing before his hall to bid them farewell that they turned off the main road from the village of Rhungill into a deep cutting that led into the fields above Jolin's house. As Lily's head rose above the tall golden grasses she could see the speck of color that was Jolin's red skirt and blue apron, standing quietly on the doorstep of the house, with the white birches at one side, and her herb garden spread out at her feet.

Lily's horse, pleased to be home at last, responded eagerly to a request for speed, and Sahath's horse cantered readily at its heels. They drew up at the edge of the garden, where Jolin had run to meet them. Lily dismounted hastily and hugged her.

"You see, we remembered to come back," she said.

The Harrowing of the Dragon of Hoarsbreath

Patricia A. McKillip

Once, on the top of a world, there existed the ring of an island named Hoarsbreath, made out of gold and snow. It was all mountain, a grim, briny, yellowing ice-world covered with winter twelve months out of thirteen. For one month, when the twin suns crossed each other at the world's cap, the snow melted from the peak of Hoarsbreath. The hardy trees shrugged the snow off their boughs, and sucked in light and mellow air, pulling themselves toward the suns. Snow and icicles melted off the roofs of the miners' village; the snow-tunnels they had dug from house to tavern to storage barn to mineshaft sagged to the ground; the dead-white river flowing down from the mountain to the sea turned blue and began to move again. Then the miners gathered the gold they had dug by firelight out of the chill, harsh darkness of the deep mountain, and took it downriver, across the sea to the mainland, to trade for food and furs, tools and a liquid fire called wormspoor, because it was gold and bitter, like the leavings of dragons. After three swallows of it, in a busy city with a harbor frozen only part of the year, with people who wore rich furs, kept horses and sleds to ride in during winter, and who knew the patterns of the winter stars since they weren't buried alive by the snow, the miners swore they would never return to Hoarsbreath. But the gold waiting in the dark, secret places of the mountain-island drew at them in their dreaming, lured them back.

For two hundred years after the naming of Hoarsbreath, winter followed winter, and the miners lived their rich, isolated, precarious lives on the pinnacle of ice and granite, cursing the cold and loving it, for it kept lesser folk away. They mined, drank, spun tales, raised children who were sent to the mainland when they were half-grown, to re-

ceive their education, and find easier, respectable lives.
But always a few children found their way back, born with
a gnawing in their hearts for fire, ice, stone, and the solitary
pursuit of gold in the dark.

Then, two miners' children came back from the great
world and destroyed the island.

They had no intention of doing that. The younger of
them was Peka Krao. After spending five years on the
mainland, boring herself with schooling, she came back to
Hoarsbreath to mine. At seventeen, she was good-natured
and sturdy, with dark eyes, and dark, braided hair. She
loved every part of Hoarsbreath, even its chill, damp shafts
at midwinter and the bone-jarring work of hewing
through darkness and stone to unbury its gold. Her instincts for gold were uncanny: she seemed to sense it
through her fingertips touching bare rock. The miners
called her their good luck. She could make wormspoor,
too, one of the few useful things she had learned on the
mainland. It lost its bitterness, somehow, when she made
it: it aged into a rich, smokey gold that made the miners
forget their sore muscles, and inspired marvellous tales out
of them that whittled away at the endless winter.

She met the Dragon-Harrower one evening at a cross-
section of tunnel between her mother's house and the
tavern. She knew all the things to fear in her world: a
rumble in the mountain, a guttering torch in the mines, a
crevice in the snow, a crack of ice underfoot. There was
little else she couldn't handle with a soft word or her own
right arm. She when he loomed out of the darkness unexpectedly into her taper-light, she wasn't afraid. But he
made her stop instinctively, like an animal might stop,
faced with something that puzzled its senses.

His hair was dead-white, with strands bright as wormspoor running through it; his eyes were the light, hard blue
of dawn during suns-crossing. Rich colors flashed out of
him everywhere in her light: from a gold knife-hilt and a
brass pack buckle; from the red ties of his cloak that were

weighted with ivory, and the blue and silver threads in his gloves. His heavy fur cloak was closed, but she felt that if he shifted, other colors would escape from it into the cold, dark air. At first she thought he must be ancient: the taper-fire showed her a face that was shadowed and scarred, remote with strange experience, but no more than a dozen years older than hers.

"Who are you?" she breathed. Nothing on Hoarsbreath glittered like that in midwinter; its colors were few and simple: snow, damp fur and leather, fire, gold.

"I can't find my father," he said. "Lule Yarrow."

She stared at him, amazed that his colors had their beginnings on Hoarsbreath. "He's dead." His eyes widened slightly, losing some of their hardness. "He fell in a crevice. They chipped him out of the ice at suns-crossing, and buried him six years ago."

He looked away from her a moment, down at the icy ridges of tramped snow. "Winter." He broke the word in two, like an icicle. Then he shifted his pack, sighing. "Do they still have wormspoor on this ice-tooth?"

"Of course. Who are you?"

"Ryd Yarrow. Who are you?"

"Peka Krao."

"Peka. I remember. You were squalling in somebody's arms when I left."

"You look a hundred years older than that," she commented, still puzzling, holding him in her light, though she was beginning to feel the cold. "Seventeen years you've been gone. How could you stand it, being away from Hoarsbreath so long? I couldn't stand five years of it. There are so many people whose names you don't know, trying to tell you about things that don't matter, and the flat earth and the blank sky are everywhere. Did you come back to mine?"

He glanced up at the grey-white ceiling of the snow-tunnel, barely an inch above his head. "The sky is full of stars, and the gold wake of dragon-flights," he said softly.

"I am a Dragon-Harrower. I am trained and hired to trouble dragons out of their lairs. That's why I came back here."

"Here. There are no dragons on Hoarsbreath."

His smile touched his eyes like a reflection of fire across ice. "Hoarsbreath is a dragon's heart."

She shifted, her own heart suddenly chilled. She said tolerantly. "That sounds like a marvellous tale to me."

"It's no tale. I know. I followed this dragon through centuries, through ancient writings, through legends, through rumors of terror and deaths. It is here, sleeping, coiled around the treasures of Hoarsbreath. If you on Hoarsbreath rouse it, you are dead. If I rouse it, I will end your endless winter."

"I like winter." Her protest sounded very small, muted within the thick snow-walls, but he heard it. He lifted his hand, held it lightly against the low ceiling above his head.

"You might like the sky beyond this. At night it is a mine of lights and hidden knowledge."

She shook her head. "I like close places, full of fire and darkness. And faces I know. And tales spun out of wormspoor. If you come with me to the tavern, they'll tell you where your father is buried, and give you lodgings, and then you can leave."

"I'll come to the tavern. With a tale."

Her taper was nearly burned down, and she was beginning to shiver. "A dragon." She turned away from him. "No one will believe you anyway."

"You do."

She listened to him silently, warming herself with wormspoor, as he spoke to the circle of rough, fire-washed faces in the tavern. Even in the light, he bore little resemblance to his father, except for his broad cheekbones and the threads of gold in his hair. Under his bulky cloak, he was dressed as plainly as any miner, but stray bits of color still glinted from him, suggesting wealth and distant places.

"A dragon," he told them, "is creating your winter. Have you ever asked yourselves why winter on this island is nearly twice as long as winter on the mainland twenty miles away? You live in dragon's breath, in the icy mist of its bowels, hoar-frost cold, that grips your land in winter the way another dragon's breath might burn it to flinders. One month out of the year, in the warmth of suns-crossing, it looses its ring-grip on your island, slides into the sea, and goes to mate. Its ice-kingdom begins to melt. It returns, loops its length around its mountain of ice and gold. Its breath freezes the air once more, locks the river into its bed, you into your houses, the gold into its mountain, and you curse the cold and drink until the next dragon-mating." He paused. There was not a sound around him. "I've been to strange places in this world, places even colder than this, where the suns never cross, and I have seen such monsters. They are ancient as rock, white as old ice, and their skin is like iron. They breed winter and they cannot be killed. But they can be driven away, into far corners of the world where they are dangerous to no one. I'm trained for this. I can rid you of your winter. Harrowing is dangerous work, and usually I am highly paid. But I've been looking for this ice-dragon for many years, through its spoor of legend and destruction. I tracked it here, one of the oldest of its kind, to the place where I was born. All I ask from you is a guide."

He stopped, waiting. Peka, her hands frozen around her glass, heard someone swallow. A voice rose and faded from the tavern-kitchen; sap hissed in the fire. A couple of the miners were smiling; the others looked satisfied and vaguely expectant, wanting the tale to continue. When it didn't, Kor Flynt, who had mined Hoarsbreath for fifty years, spat wormspoor into the fire. The flame turned a baleful gold, and then subsided. "Suns-crossing," he said politely, reminding a scholar of a scrap of knowledge children acquired with their first set of teeth, "causes the seasons."

"Not here," Ryd said. "Not on Hoarsbreath. I've seen. I know."

Peka's mother Ambris leaned forward. "Why," she

asked curiously, "would a miner's son become a dragon-harrower?" She had a pleasant, craggy face; her dark hair and her slow, musing voice were like Peka's. Peka saw the Dragon-Harrower ride between two answers in his mind. Meeting Ambris' eyes, he made a choice, and his own eyes strayed to the fire.

"I left Hoarsbreath when I was twelve. When I was fifteen, I saw a dragon in the mountains east of the city. Until then, I had intended to come back and mine. I began to learn about dragons. The first one I saw burned red and gold under the suns' fire; it swallowed small hills with its shadow. I wanted to call it, like a hawk. I wanted to fly with it. I kept studying, meeting other people who studied them, seeing other dragons. I saw a night-black dragon in the northern deserts; its scales were dusted with silver, and the flame that came out of it was silver. I saw people die in that flame, and I watched the harrowing of that dragon. It lives now on the underside of the world, in shadow. We keep watch on all known dragons. In the green mid-world belt, rich with rivers and mines, forests and farmland, I saw a whole mining town burned to the ground by a dragon so bright I thought at first it was sun-fire arching down to the ground. Someone I loved had the task of tracking that one to its cave, deep beneath the mine-shafts. I watched her die, there. I nearly died. The dragon is sealed into the bottom of the mountain, by stone and by words. That is the dragon which harrowed me." He paused to sip wormspoor. His eyes lifted, not to Ambris, but to Peka. "Now do you understand what danger you live in? What if one year the dragon sleeps through its mating-time, with the soft heat of the suns making it sluggish from dreaming? You don't know it's there, wrapped around your world. It doesn't know you're there, stealing its gold. What if you sail your boats full of gold downriver and find the great white bulk of it sprawled like a wall across your passage? Or worse, you find its eye opening like a third, dead sun to see your hands full of its gold? It would slide its length around the mountain, coil upward and crush you all, then breathe over the whole of the island, and turn it dead-white as its heart, and it would never sleep again."

There was another silence. Peka felt something play along her spine like the thin, quavering, arthritic fingers of wind. "It's getting better," she said, "your tale." She took a deep swallow of wormspoor and added, "I love sitting in a warm, friendly place listening to tales I don't have to believe."

Kor Flynt shrugged. "It rings true, lass."

"It is true," Ryd said.

"Maybe so," she said. "And it may be better if you just let the dragon sleep."

"And if it wakes unexpectedly? The winter killed my father. The dragon at the heart of winter could destroy you all."

"There are other dangers. Rock falls, sudden floods, freezing winds. A dragon is simply one more danger to live with."

He studied her. "I saw a dragon once with wings as softly blue as a spring sky. Have you ever felt spring on Hoarsbreath? It could come."

She drank again. "You love them," she said. "Your voice loves them and hates them, Dragon-Harrower."

"I hate them," he said flatly. "Will you guide me down the mountain?"

"No. I have work to do."

He shifted, and the colors rippled from him again, red, gold, silver, spring-blue. She finished the wormspoor, felt it burn in her like liquid gold. "It's only a tale. All your dragons are just colors in our heads. Let the dragon sleep. If you wake it, you'll destroy the night."

"No," he said. "You will see the night. That's what you're afraid of."

Kor Flynt shrugged. "There probably is no dragon, anyway."

"Spring, though," Ambris said; her face had softened. "Sometimes I can smell it from the mainland, and I always wonder . . . Still, after a hard day's work, sitting beside a roaring fire sipping dragon-spit, you can believe anything. Especially this." She looked into her glass at the glowering liquid. "Is this some of yours, Peka? What did you put into it?"

"Gold." The expression in Ryd's eyes made her swallow sudden tears of frustration. She refilled her glass. "Fire, stone, dark, wood-smoke, night air smelling like cold tree-bark. You don't care, Ryd Yarrow."

"I do care," he said imperturbably. "It's the best wormspoor I've ever tasted."

"And I put a dragon's heart into it." She saw him start slightly; ice and hoar-frost shimmered from him. "If that's what Hoarsbreath is." A dragon beat into her mind, its wings of rime, its breath smoldering with ice, the guardian of winter. She drew breath, feeling the vast bulk of it looped around them all, dreaming its private dreams. Her bones seemed suddenly fragile as kindling, and the gold wormspoor in her hands a guilty secret. "I don't believe it," she said, lifting her glass. "It's a tale."

"Oh, go with him, lass," her mother said tolerantly. "There may be no dragon, but we can't have him swallowed up in the ice like his father. Besides, it may be a chance for spring."

"Spring is for flatlanders. There are things that shouldn't be wakened. I know."

"How?" Ryd asked.

She groped, wishing for the first time for a flatlander's skill with words. She said finally, "I feel it," and he smiled. She sat back in her chair, irritated and vaguely frightened. "Oh, all right, Ryd Yarrow, since you'll go with or without me. I'll lead you down to the shores in the morning. Maybe by then you'll listen to me."

"You can't see beyond your snow-world," he said implacably. It is morning."

They followed one of the deepest mine-shafts, and clambered out of it to stand in the snow half-way down the mountain. The sky was lead grey; across the mists ringing the island's shores, they could see the ocean, a swirl of white, motionless ice. The mainland harbor was locked. Peka wondered if the ships were stuck like birds in the ice. The world looked empty and somber.

"At least in the dark mountain there is fire and gold. Here, there isn't even a sun." She took out a skin of wormspoor, sipped it to warm her bones. She held it out to Ryd, but he shook his head.

"I need all my wits. So do you, or we'll both end up preserved in ice at the bottom of a crevice."

"I know. I'll keep you safe." She corked the skin and added, "In case you were wondering."

But he looked at her, startled out of his remoteness. "I wasn't. Do you feel that strongly?"

"Yes."

"So did I, when I was your age. Now I feel very little." He moved again. She stared after him, wondering how he kept her smoldering and on edge. She said abruptly, catching up with him,

"Ryd Yarrow."

"Yes."

"You have two names. Ryd Yarrow, and Dragon-Harrower. One is a plain name this mountain gave you. The other you got from the world, the name that gives you color. One name I can talk to, the other is the tale at the bottom of a bottle of wormspoor. Maybe you could understand me if you hadn't brought your past back to Hoarsbreath."

"I do understand you," he said absently. "You want to sit in the dark all your life and drink wormspoor."

She drew breath and held it. "You talk but you don't listen," she said finally. "Just like all the other flatlanders." He didn't answer. They walked in silence awhile, following the empty bed of an old river. The world looked dead, but she could tell by the air, which was not even freezing spangles of breath on her hood-fur, that the winter was drawing to an end. "Suns-crossing must be only two months away," she commented surprisedly.

"Besides, I'm not a flatlander," he said abruptly, surprising her again. "I do care about the miners, about Hoarsbreath. It's because I care that I want to challenge that ice-dragon with all the skill I possess. Is it better to let you live surrounded by danger, in bitter cold, carving half-lives out of snow and stone, so that you can come fully alive for one month of the year?"

"You could have asked us."

"I did ask you."

She sighed. "Where will it live, if you drive it away from Hoarsbreath?"

He didn't answer for a few paces. In the still day, he loosed no colors, though Peka thought she saw shadows of them around his pack. His head was bowed; his eyes were burning back at a memory. It will find some strange, remote places where there is no gold, only rock; it can ring itself around emptiness and dream of its past. I came across an ice-dragon unexpectedly once, in a land of ice. The bones of its wings seemed almost translucent. I could have sworn it cast a white shadow."

"Did you want to kill it?"

"No. I loved it."

"Then why do you—" But he turned at her suddenly, almost angrily, waking out of a dream.

"I came here because you've built your lives on top of a terrible danger, and I asked for a guide, not a gad-fly."

"You wanted me," she said flatly. "And you don't care about Hoarsbreath. All you want is that dragon. Your voice is full of it. What's a gad-fly?"

"Go ask a cow. Or a horse. Or anything else that can't live on this forsaken, frostbitten lump of ice."

"Why should you care, anyway? You've got the whole great world to roam in. Why do you care about one dragon wrapped around the tiny island on the top of nowhere?"

"Because it's beautiful and deadly and wrapped around my heartland. And I don't know—I don't know at the end of things which of us will be left on Hoarsbreath." She stared at him. He met her eyes fully. "I'm very skilled. But that is one very powerful dragon."

She whirled, fanning snow. "I'm going back. Find your own way to your harrowing. I hope it swallows you."

His voice stopped her. "You'll always wonder. You'll sit in the dark, drinking wormspoor twelve months out of thirteen, wondering what happened to me. What an ice-dragon looks like, on a winter's day, in full flight."

She hovered between two steps. Then, furiously, she followed him.

They climbed deeper into mist, and then into darkness. They camped at night, ate dried meat and drank worms-poor beside a fire in the snow. The night-sky was sullen and starless as the day. They woke to grey mists and travelled on. The cold breathed up around them; walls of ice, yellow as old ivory, loomed over them. They smelled the chill, sweaty smell of the sea. The dead riverbed came to an end over an impassible cliff. They shifted ground, followed a frozen stream downward. The ice-walls broke up into great jewels of ice, blue, green, gold, massed about them like a giant's treasure hoard. Peka stopped to stare at them. Ryd said with soft, bitter satisfaction,

"Wormspoor."

She drew breath. "Wormspoor." Her voice sounded small, absorbed by cold. "Ice-jewels, fallen stars. Down here you could tell me anything and I might believe it. I feel very strange." She uncorked the wormspoor and took a healthy swig. Ryd reached for it, but he only rinsed his mouth and spat. His face was pale; his eyes red-rimmed, tired.

"How far down do you think we are?"

"Close. There's no dragon. Just mist." She shuddered suddenly at the soundlessness. "The air is dead. Like stone. We should reach the ocean soon."

"We'll reach the dragon first."

They descended hillocks of frozen jewels. The stream they followed fanned into a wide, skeletal filigree of ice and rock. The mist poured around them, so painfully cold it burned their lungs. Peka pushed fur over her mouth, breathed through it. The mist or wormspoor she had drunk was forming shadows around her, flickerings of faces and enormous wings. Her heart felt heavy; her feet dragged like boulders when she lifted them. Ryd was coughing mist; he moved doggedly, as if into a hard wind. The stream fanned again, going very wide before it met the sea. They stumbled down into a bone-searing flow of mist. Ryd disappeared; Peka found him again, bumping into him, for he had stopped. The threads of mist untangled above them, and she saw a strange black sun, hodded with a silvery web. As she blinked at it, puzzled, the web rolled up. The dark sun gazed back at her. She became aware then of her own heartbeat, of a rhythm in the mists, of a faint, echoing pulse all around her: the icy heartbeat of Hoarsbreath.

She drew a hiccup of a breath, stunned. There was a mountain-cave ahead of them, from which the mists breathed and eddied. Icicles dropped like bars between its grainy-white surfaces. Within it rose stones or teeth as milky white as quartz. A wall of white stretched beyond the mists, vast, earthworm round, solid as stone. She couldn't tell in the blur and welter of mist, where winter ended and the dragon began.

She made a sound. The vast, silvery eyelid drooped like a parchment unrolled, then lifted again. From the depths of the cave came a faint, rumbling, a vague, drowsy waking question: Who?

She heard Ryd's breath finally. "Look at the scar under its eye," he said softly. She saw a jagged track beneath the black sun. "I can name the Harrower who put that there three hundred years ago. And the broken eye-tooth. It razed a marble fortress with its wings and jaws; I know the word that shattered that tooth, then. Look at its wing-scales. Rimed with silver. It's old. Old as the world." He turned finally, to look at her. His white hair, slick with mists, made him seem old as winter. "You can go back now. You won't be safe here."

"I won't be safe up there, either," she whispered. "Let's both go back. Listen to its heart."

"Its blood is gold. Only one Harrower ever saw that and lived."

"Please." She tugged at him, at his pack. Colors shivered into the air: sulphur, malachite, opal. The deep rumble came again; a shadow quickened in the dragon's eye. Ryd moved quickly, caught her hands. "Let it sleep. It belongs here on Hoarsbreath. Why can't you see that? Why can't you see? It's a thing made of gold, snow, darkness—" But he wasn't seeing her; his eyes, remote and alien as the black sun, were full of memories and calculations. Behind him, a single curved claw lay like a crescent moon half-buried in the snow.

Peka stepped back from the Harrower, envisioning a bloody moon through his heart, and the dragon roused to fury, coiling upward around Hoarsbreath, crushing the life out of it. "Ryd Yarrow," she whispered. "Ryd Yarrow. Please." But he did not hear his name.

He began to speak, startling echoes against the solid ice around them. "Dragon of Hoarsbreath, whose wings are of hoarfrost, whose blood is gold—" The backbone of the hoar-dragon rippled slightly, shaking away snow. "I have followed your path of destruction from your beginnings in a land without time and without seasons. You have slept one night too long on this island. Hoarsbreath is not your dragon's dream; it belongs to the living, and I, trained and titled Dragon-Harrower, challenge you for its freedom." More snow shook away from the dragon, baring a rippling of scale, and the glistening of its nostrils. The rhythm of its mist was changing. "I know you," Ryd continued, his voice growing husky, strained against the silence. "You were the white death of the fishing-island Klonos, of ten Harrowers in Ynyme, of the winter palace of the ancient lord of Zuirsh. I have harried nine ice-dragons—perhaps

your children—out of the known world. I have been
searching for you for many years, and I came back to the
place where I was born to find you here. I stand before you
armed with knowledge, experience, and the dark wisdom
of necessity. Leave Hoarsbreath, go back to your birthplace forever, or I will harry you down to the frozen
shadow of the world."

The dragon gazed at him motionlessly, an immeasurable ring of ice looped about him. The mist out of its mouth
was for a moment suspended. Then its jaws crashed together, spitting splinters of ice. It shuddered, wrenched
itself loose from the ice. Its white head reared high, higher,
ice booming and cracking around it. Twin black suns
stared down at Ryd from the grey mist of the sky. Before it
roared, Peka moved.

She found herself on a ledge above Ryd's head, without
remembering how she got there. Ryd vanished in a flood
of mist. The mist turned fiery; Ryd loomed out of them like
a red shadow, dispersing them. Seven crescents lifted out
of the snow, slashed down at him, scarring the air. A
strange voice shouted Ryd's name. He flung back his head
and cried a word. Somehow the claw missed him, wedged
deep into the ice.

Peka sat back. She was clutching the skin of wormspoor
against her heart; she could feel her heartbeat shaking it.
Her throat felt raw; the strange voice had been hers. She
uncorked the skin, took a deep swallow, and another. Fire
licked down her veins. A cloud of ice billowed at Ryd. He
said something else, and suddenly he was ten feet away
from it, watching a rock where he had stood freeze and
snap into pieces.

Peka crouched closer to the wall of ice behind her. From
her high point she could see the briny, frozen snarl of the
sea. It flickered green, then an eerie orange. Bands of color
pinioned the dragon briefly like a rainbow, arching across
its wings. A scale caught fire; a small bone the size of Ryd's
forearm snapped. Then the cold wind of the dragon's
breath froze and shattered the rainbow. A claw slapped at

Ryd; he moved a fraction of a moment too slowly. The tip of a talon caught his pack. It burst open with an explosion of glittering colors. The dragon hooded its eyes; Peka hid hers under her hands. She heard Ryd cry out in pain. Then he was beside her instead of in several pieces, prying the wormspoor out of her hands.

He uncorked it, his hands shaking. One of them was seared silver.

"What are they?" she breathed. He poured wormspoor on his burned hand, then thrust it into the snow. The colors were beginning to die down.

"Flame," he panted. "Dragon-flame. I wasn't prepared to handle it."

"You carry it in your pack?"

"Caught in crystals, in fire-leaves. It will be more difficult than I anticipated."

Peka felt language she had never used before clamor in her throat. "It's all right," she said dourly. "I'll wait."

For a moment, as he looked at her, there was a memory of fear in his eyes. "You can walk across the ice to the mainland from here."

"You can walk to the mainland," she retorted. "This is my home. I have to live with or without that dragon. Right now, there's no living with it. You woke it out of its sleep. You burnt its wing. You broke its bone. You told it there are people on its island. You are going to destroy Hoarsbreath."

"No. This will be my greatest harrowing." He left her suddenly, and appeared flaming like a torch on the dragon's skull, just between its eyes. His hair and his hands spattered silver. Word after word came out of him, smoldering, flashing, melting in the air. The dragon's voice thundered; its skin rippled and shook. Its claw ripped at ice, dug chasms out of it. The air clapped nearby, as if its invisible tail had lifted and slapped at the ground. Then it heaved its head, flung Ryd at the wall of mountain. Peka shut her eyes. But he fell lightly, caught up a crystal as he rose, and sent a shaft of piercing gold light at the upraised scales of its underside, burrowing towards its heart.

Peka got unsteadily to her feet, her throat closing with a sudden whimper. But the dragon's tail, flickering out of the mist behind Ryd, slapped him into a snowdrift twenty feet away. It gave a cold, terrible hiss; mist bubbled over everything, so that for a few minutes Peka could see nothing beyond the lip of the ledge. She drank to stop her shivering. Finally a green fire blazed within the white swirl. She sat down again slowly, waited.

Night rolled in from the sea. But Ryd's fires shot in raw, dazzling streaks across the darkness, illuminating the hoary, scarred bulk of dragon in front of him. Once, he shouted endless poetry at the dragon, lulling it until its mist-breath was faint and slow from its maw. It nearly put Peka to sleep, but Ryd's imperceptible steps closer and closer to the dragon kept her watching. The tale was evidently an old one to the dragon; it didn't wait for an ending. Its head lunged and snapped unexpectedly, but a moment too soon. Ryd leaped for shelter in the dark, while the dragon's teeth ground painfully on nothingness. Later, Ryd sang to it, a whining, eerie song that showered icicles around Peka's head. One of the dragon's teeth cracked, and it made an odd, high-pitched noise. A vast webbed wing shifted free to fly, unfolding endlessly over the sea. But the dragon stayed, sending mist at Ryd to set him coughing. A foul, ashy-grey miasma followed it, blurring over them. Peka hid her face in her arms. Sounds like the heaving of boulders and the spattering of fire came from beneath her. She heard the dragon's dry roar, like stones dragged against one another. There was a smack, a musical shower of breaking icicles, and a sharp, anguished curse. Ryd appeared out of the turmoil of light and air, sprawled on the ledge beside Peka.

His face was cut, with ice she supposed, and there was blood in his white hair. He looked at her with vague amazement.

"You're still here."

"Where else would I be? Are you winning or losing?"

He scooped up snow, held it against his face. "I feel as if I've been fighting for a thousand years . . . Sometimes, I think I tangle in its memories, as it thinks of other harrowers, old dragon-battles, distant places. It doesn't remember what I am, only that I will not let it sleep . . . Did you see its wingspan? I fought a red dragon once with such a span. Its wings turned to flame in the sunlight. You'll see this one in flight by dawn."

She stared at him numbly, huddled against herself. "Are you so sure?"

"It's old and slow. And it can't bear the gold fire." He paused, then dropped the snow in his hand with a sigh, and leaned his face against the ice-wall. "I'm tired, too. I have one empty crystal, to capture the essence of its mist, its heart's breath. After that's done, the battle will be short." He lifted his head at her silence, as if he could hear her thoughts. "What?"

"You'll go on to other dragons. But all I've ever had is this one."

"You never know—"

"It doesn't matter that I never knew it. I know now. It was coiled all around us in the winter, while we lived in warm darkness and firelight. It kept out the world. Is that such a terrible thing? Is there so much wisdom in the flatlands that we can't live without?"

He was silent again, frowning a little, either in pain or faint confusion. "It's a dangerous thing, a destroyer."

"So is winter. So is the mountain, sometimes. But they're also beautiful. You are full of so much knowledge and experience that you forgot how to see simple things. Ryd Yarrow, miner's son. You must have loved Hoarsbreath once."

"I was a child, then."

She sighed. "I'm sorry I brought you down here. I wish I were up there with the miners, in the last peaceful night."

"There will be peace again," he said, but she shook her head wearily.

"I don't feel it." She expected him to smile, but his

frown deepened. He touched her face suddenly with his burned hand.

"Sometimes I almost hear what you're trying to tell me. And then it fades against all my knowledge and experience. I'm glad you stayed. If I die, I'll leave you facing one maddened dragon. But still, I'm glad."

A black moon rose high over his shoulder and she jumped. Ryd rolled off the ledge, into the mists. Peka hid her face from the peering black glare. Blue light smoldered through the mist, the moon rolled suddenly out of the sky and she could breathe again.

Streaks of dispersing gold lit the dawn-sky like the sunrises she saw one month out of the year. Peka, in a cold daze on the ledge, saw Ryd for the first time in an hour. He was facing the dragon, his silver hand outstretched. In his palm lay a crystal so cold and deathly white that Peka, blinking at it, felt its icy stare into her heart.

She shuddered. Her bones turned to ice; mist seemed to flow through her veins. She breathed bitter, frozen air as heavy as water. She reached for the wormspoor; her arm moved sluggishly, and her fingers unfolded with brittle movements. The dragon was breathing in short, harsh spurts. The silvery hoods were over its eyes. Its unfolded wing lay across the ice like a limp sail. Its jaws were open, hissing faintly, but its head was reared back, away from Ryd's hand. Its heartbeat, in the silence, was slow, slow.

Peka dragged herself up, icicle by icicle. In the clear wintry dawn, she saw the beginning and the end of the enormous ring around Hoarsbreath. The dragon's tail lifted wearily behind Ryd, then fell again, barely making a sound. Ryd stood still; his eyes, relentless, spring-blue, were his only color. As Peka watched, swaying on the edge, the world fragmented into simple things: the edges of silver on the dragon's scales, Ryd's silver fingers, his old-man's hair, the pure white of the dragon's hide. They face one another, two powerful creatures born out of the same winter, harrowing one another. The dragon rippled along its bulk; its head reared farther back, giving

Peka a dizzying glimpse of its open jaws. She saw the cracked tooth, crumbled like a jewel she might have battered inadvertently with her pick, and winced. Seeing her, it hissed, a tired, angry sigh.

She stared down at it; her eyes seemed numb, incapable of sorrow. The wing on the ice was beginning to stir. Ryd's head lifted. He looked bone-pale, his face expressionless with exhaustion. But the faint, icy smile of triumph in his eyes struck her as deeply as the stare from the death-eye in his palm.

She drew in mist like the dragon, knowing that Ryd was not harrowing an old, tired ice-dragon, but one out of his memories who never seemed to yield. "You bone-brained dragon," she shouted, "how can you give up Hoarsbreath so easily? And to a Dragon-Harrower whose winter is colder and more terrible than yours." Her heart seemed trapped in the weary, sluggish pace of its heart. She knelt down, wondering if it could understand her words, or only feel them. "Think of Hoarsbreath," she pleaded, and searched for words to warm them both. "Fire. Gold. Night. Warm dreams, winter tales, silence—" Mist billowed at her and she coughed until tears froze on her cheeks. She heard Ryd call her name on a curious, inflexible note that panicked her. She uncorked the wormspoor with trembling fingers, took a great gulp, and coughed again as the blood shocked through her. "Don't you have any fire at all in you? Any winter flame?" Then a vision of gold shook her: the gold within the dragon's heart, the warm gold of wormspoor, the bitter gold of dragon's blood. Ryd said her name again, his voice clear as breaking ice. She shut her eyes against him, her hands rising through a chill, dark dream. As he called the third time, she dropped the wormspoor down the dragon's throat.

The hoods over its eyes rose; they grew wide, white-rimmed. She heard a convulsive swallow. Its head snapped down; it made a sound between a bellow and a whimper. Then its jaws opened again and it raked the air with gold flame.

Ryd, his hair and eyebrows scored suddenly with gold, dove into the snow. The dragon hissed at him again. The stream beyond him turned fiery, ran towards the sea. The great tail pounded furiously; dark cracks tore through the ice. The frozen cliffs began to sweat under the fire; pillars of ice sagged down, broke against the ground. The ledge Peka stood on crumbled at a wave of gold. She fell with it in a small avalanche of ice-rubble. The enormous white ring of dragon began to move, blurring endlessly past her eyes as the dragon gathered itself. A wing arched up toward the sky, then another. The dragon hissed at the mountain, then roared desperately, but only flame came out of its bowels, where once it had secreted winter. The chasms and walls of ice began breaking apart. Peka, struggling out of the snow, felt a lurch under her feet. A wind sucked at her hair, pulled at her heavy coat. Then it drove down at her, thundering, and she sat in the snow. The dragon, aloft, its wingspan the span of half the island, breathed fire at the ocean, and its husk of ice began to melt.

Ryd pulled her out of the snow. The ground was breaking up under their feet. He said nothing; she thought he was scowling, though he looked strange with singed eyebrows. He pushed at her, flung her toward the sea. Fire sputtered around them. Ice slid under her; she slipped and clutched at the jagged rim of it. Brine splashed in her face. The ice whirled, as chunks of the mountain fell into the sea around them. The dragon was circling the mountain, melting huge peaks and cliffs. They struck the water hard, heaving the ice-floes farther from the island. The mountain itself began to break up, as ice tore away from it, leaving only a bare peak riddled with mine-shafts.

Peka began to cry. "Look what I've done. Look at it." Ryd only grunted. She thought she could see figures high on the top of the peak, staring down at the vanishing island. The ocean, churning, spun the ice-floe toward the mainland. The river was flowing again, a blue-white streak spiralling down from the peak. The dragon was over the mainland now, billowing fire at the harbor, and ships without crews or cargo were floating free.

"Wormspoor," Ryd muttered. A wave ten feet high caught up with them, spilled, and shoved them into the middle of the channel. Peka saw the first of the boats taking the swift, swollen current down from the top of the island. Ryd spat out seawater, and took a firmer grip of the ice. "I lost every crystal, every dragon's fire I possessed. They're at the bottom of the sea. Thanks to you. Do you realize how much work, how many years—"

"Look at the sky." It spun above her, a pale, impossible mass of nothing. "How can I live under that? Where will I ever find dark, quiet places full of gold?"

"I held that dragon. It was just about to leave quietly, without taking half of Hoarsbreath with it."

"How will we live on the island again? All its secrets are gone."

"For fourteen years I studied dragons, their lore, their flights, their fires, the patterns of their lives and their destructions. I had all the knowledge I thought possible for me to acquire. No one—"

"Look at all that dreary flatland—"

"No one," he said, his voice rising, "ever told me you could harrow a dragon by pouring wormspoor down its throat!"

"Well, no one told me, either!" She slumped beside him, too despondent for anger. She watched more boats carrying miners, young children, her mother, down to the mainland. Then the dragon caught her eye, pale against the winter sky, somehow fragile, beautifully crafted, flying into the wake of its own flame.

It touched her mourning heart with the fire she had given it. Beside her, she felt Ryd grow quiet. His face, tired and battered, held a young, forgotten wonder, as he watched the dragon blaze across the world's cap like a star, searching for its winter. He drew a soft, incredulous breath.

"What did you put into that wormspoor?"

"Everything."

He looked at her, then turned his face toward Hoarsbreath. The sight made him wince. "I don't think we left even my father's bones at peace," he said hollowly, looking for a moment less a Dragon-Harrower than a harrowed miner's son.

"I know," she whispered.

"No, you don't," he sighed. "You feel. The dragon's heart. My heart. It's not a lack of knowledge or experiences that destroyed Hoarsbreath, but something else I lost sight of: you told me that. The dark necessity of wisdom."

She gazed at him, suddenly uneasy, for he was seeing her. "I'm not wise. Just lucky—or unlucky."

"Wisdom is a flatlander's word for your kind of feeling. You put your heart into everything—wormspoor, dragons, gold—and they become a kind of magic."

"I do not. I don't understand what you're talking about, Ryd Yarrow. I'm a miner; I'm going to find another mine—"

"You have a gold-mine in your heart. There are other things you can do with yourself. Not harrow dragons, but become a Watcher. You love the same things they love."

"Yes. Peace and quiet and private places—"

"I could show you dragons in their beautiful, private places all over the world. You could speak their language."

"I can't even speak my own. And I hate the flatland." She gripped the ice, watching it come.

"The world is only another tiny island, ringed with a great dragon of stars and night."

She shook her head, not daring to meet his eyes. "No. I'm not listening to you anymore. Look what happened the last time I listened to your tales."

"It's always yourself you are listening to," he said. The grey ocean swirled the ice under them, casting her back to the bewildering shores of the world. She was still trying to argue when the ice moored itself against the scorched pilings of the harbor.

The Moon Porthole

Fritz Leiber

It was exactly a month after elfin Nerissa Woodvale moved
into the Ultimate Apartments that she was rather unwillingly initiated (but in a deeper sense bravely initiated herself) into the small local society which unpretentiously
called itself the Apartment People, the Apt People for
short, or with a further shortening, the Apt Peops, which
they generally pronounced *Peeps* (like Pepys, a literary
allusion which pleased most of them), except for fat little
old Colonel Buford Hogeston, who idiosyncratically made
it a dissyllable—Pelops without the L.

They were a group of variously frustrated aspiring
spare-time writers, veterans of the rejection slip and creative block, who also shared a keen interest in weird and
ghostly true incidents, either seemingly supernatural, or at
least studded with amazing and mostly sinister synchronicities, though several of them were skeptics of both the
hard-headed and cynical sorts, while only a few of them
admitted to serious religious or occult beliefs of any kind.
Their natural guru and doyenne was the emaciate tall
semi-invalid, but telephonically hyperactive, Portia
Hotchkiss, whose belated first novel *Passage East* had
been published with considerable acclaim seven years
back, though the completion of its sequel, *Removal West*,
had been delayed by a series of mysterious temperamental
and medical problems which the unkind attributed more to
an oversupply of three-star brandy than to an undersup-
ply of red corpuscles. Most of the group occupied apartments at the Ultimate.

One *lunar* month of 29 days, mind you, and little Nerissa
had arrived on the day of a full moon, which was when the
Apts Peops held their regular monthly evening story-
reading or -telling soiree, generally in Portia's spacious
first-floor apartment. Portia firmly believed that her tem-

peramental difficulties peaked on full-moon nights, when statistics appear to show that normal folk as well as lunatics and alcoholics are at their most self-destructively active, and she truly thought that at such times she was most in need of supportive human comradeship.

So anyway, the Apt Peops had a full lunar month in which to ponder Nerissa's suitability for membership in their rather select organization, while she had a like period in which to consider whether they were the sort of folk she wanted to be associated with, and truth to tell, there were times during that month when from the hints she began to get of them, and particularly from one incident that severely shocked her, she thought they were the *last* sort of people she wanted anything to do with, and likewise times when *some* of them, at any rate, considered her the least suitable person they'd ever considered for candidacy.

The way things turned out, her candidacy had decisive majority support by month's end, while she without knowing it devoted the same period to intensive preparation for her testing. After it was all over, old and scholarly Frank Daulby found a certain appropriateness in her having spent the month closely immured in her sixth, and top, floor apartment, the smallest and most isolated in the whole building and blessed with only one window, which was circular and faced north; he'd read of African tribes which shut up their pubescent girls in small, high, lightless huts elevated on long poles preparatory to their initiation into the mystery of womanhood.

At all events, Nerissa's arrival at the Ultimate on one of those hot autumn days that are apt to bake San Francisco after a cool fogbound summer could hardly escape attracting attention, because while with one exception all her impedimenta were contained in two suitcases, a very large portfolio, and a cardboard carton, the one exception was a harpsichord (plus stool for player) that even with its legs removed could not be fitted into the elevator, and so had to be eased up the five flights of stairs by three neatly uniformed professional movers, the thought of whose hourly wage made Rachel Casady shake her head and narrow her ungenerous pale lips still farther.

Rachel was the skinny Germanic wife of the genial apartment manager, an ex-fireman. *He* went off and left the movers to their business as soon as he'd observed their quality, but the two ladies followed them up the stairs floor by floor, taking note of their every movement, Nerissa standing back silent and gravely apologetic, Rachel at their elbows and frequently stage-whispering dire warnings that seemed designed to invite catastrophes rather than avert them. Twice she made hurried little side-trips to hushedly inform cronies of hers among the tenants who chanced to observe them, just what was going on.

Finally they reached their goal, a smallish room and bath (no kitchen) between the elevator shaft and adjacent ventilation shaft and carpeted stairway to the roof, and the hall and the tiled and partly unroofed patio which separated the very big multi-roomed single apartment known as "the Penthouse" from the rest of six and which, with Nerissa's apartment, occupied the whole end of one wing of the L-shaped building on that floor. In a posher era of lower wages it had generally housed the cook-and-maid or couple-in-service tending the wants of the Penthouse occupants.

It turned out, as Nerissa had known it would, that the harpsichord could only be fitted into the room by moving out some of the furniture already there. She opted for the horse-hair sofa and its companion fancy end tables, which were set against the wall opposite the single bed, which in turn rested just below the three-foot-diameter circular window. Mrs. Casady protested that those were the handsomest pieces in the whole building, and when her seemingly timid new tenant persisted in her decision, huffily averred that Nerissa would have to see to their transportation down to the storeroom in the basement. To cut short the fussing, Nerissa arranged with the movers to do that (since the sofa would easily fit into the elevator) before they sent up the harpsichord, though she winced inwardly at the added expense that would mean.

So with further doomful shepherdings by Mrs. Casady the sofa was duly conveyed to the Ultimate's shadowy bowels, the harpsichord deftly slipped into the room, its legs reaffixed, and it was set up against the now-empty inside wall, leaving barely enough space for the door to be opened and closed, as Nerissa also had calculated would be the case. She wrote a check and the movers swiftly departed.

Mrs. Casady lingered, even after Nerissa held the door for her, wondering ingenuously how many visitors Nerissa would have and how much noise the harpsichord would make. Nerissa answered the first question with an inscrutable "None!" and the second with a bland "About as much as a music box," and continued to hold the door open. Mrs. Casady edged out with an injured reluctance. She heard the door shut and then double lock behind her.

Portia Hotchkiss learned about the newcomer from Roberta Roberts, who lived on the fourth floor with two Himalayan cats. Sitting on the edge of the book- and newspaper-piled bed, she enthusiastically told its gaunt occupant, "She seemed like our kind of person. Just think, not a piano, but a harpsichord! And the portfolio—more talents? And especially the predestined way her name fits with yours! When Portia disguised herself as a lawyer, didn't Nerissa play her clerk? Why, she may even turn out to be the person you've been looking for to help you get your *Removal* notes in order!"

Portia doubted that but was intrigued nonetheless, and after Roberta had made her a strong eggnog she got on the phone and stayed there most of the rest of the hot Saturday, asking other Peops about the newcomer or alerting them to her presence, so that by evening most of them were aware of the new arrival.

Buford Hogeston wasn't, although he occupied a four-room apartment on the floor most concerned, the sixth. The Colonel was at the crest of one of his sober cycles, and had elected to spend this fine afternoon (he loved heat) in

Golden Gate Park, mostly at the De Young Museum and the Japanese Tea Garden, cultivating his mind, taming his fierce emotions, and girl-watching with a deceptive tranquillity. Returning homeward in the cool of twilight, he continued the last activity in the rear lobby of the Clift Hotel next to the Curran and Geary Theaters where he chose to take an elaborate tea in lieu of dinner. Replete, he gave his lips a final patting with the snowy napkin, drew on his white gloves, signed to the waitress to slip aside the light table, rose from the richly upholstered seat without aid of his hands (an accomplishment of which he was quite proud; there were some advantages in being short!), rewarded the attentive girl with a dazzling smile, gained the street, and sauntered the last block to the Ultimate, where he ran into Frank Daulby.

Frank was primed on Nerissa Woodvale, for he'd had a good chance to study her while the harpsichord cortege mounted past his fourth floor, been phoned by Portia, and had an inquisitive chat with Jack Casady.

"She's simply a very beautiful girl, Bew, sweet and grave seeming," he finished. "And she *can't* be as young as she looks."

Buford thought, it must be fate. I keep girls at a careful distance all day long, and when I get home I find one has been delivered at my doorstep.

To Frank he said, "She's probably a hooker. The innocent schoolgirl get-up is always the biggest drawing card."

"Come on, Bew! The harpsichord?"

"Respectable cover," the Colonel said without hesitation. "Probably carries her whips and straps and chains in it. If they rattled she could say it was the strings vibrating."

"Jokes, jokes," the other responded impatiently. "No, Bew, you're wrong there. Jack Casady says she's real shy, she even blushes, last address on Crescent Street near Holly Park. What's more, Portia Hotchkiss had the same idea you did, so she called up Dominique Eddy, and she's never heard of her. *And* Dominique got a look at her too and agrees she's no hooker or call girl."

"Okay, Frank, have it your own way," Buford said with feigned indifference. "Far be it from me to set my opinion up against the Ultimate's resident *maitresse,* especially when I haven't even seen this underage paragon."

"That's right," Frank told him, rubbing it in. "And get this, Bew, the Casadys have put her in that little sixth-floor apartment the piano teacher once had, you know, the piano teacher you spotted committing suicide and saved her life. The same room you yourself called the princess-in-the-tower room because of its circular window. You lucky dog."

Buford thought, dazedly, it *really* must be fate. Not just at my doorstep, but practically in my bedroom. Suddenly he was in a hurry to get up to his apartment, but he didn't show it. Instead he said to Frank thoughtfully and a shade sadly, "You're an incurable romantic, old friend." His voice grew sadder still, almost sententious, as he continued, "Ah, youth, youth! whither has it vanished? And whence have come these aching bones and thickening toenails, this short breath? Not for the likes of us, old friend, save in bittersweet reverie, are the sweet slender forms and tinkling laughter, the wildering seizures and poor bewildering minutes of love's proofs and testings." His voice changed, came down to earth, as he observed, "You know, Frank, I've always been aware I've got a big belly, but you're beginning to develop quite a little pot yourself." He lightly prodded the other just above the belt buckle, laughed softly, and trotted off toward the elevator.

Frank Daulby looked somewhat sourly and very skeptically at the retreating figure which for a moment seemed (but what fantasy was this?) not so much that of a fat little old man as a plump, mincing, French dancing master. "You're coming to the Peops meeting tonight at Portia's?" he called after the figure. "Full moon, you know."

"Of course, of course," the answer came floating back, "But later, later . . ." as the elevator door closed.

His dark top-floor apartment held remnants of the day's heat. The Colonel did not turn on any lights but surefootedly made his way into his bedroom, thrust his head out of the open window, and looked sideways along the wall. He breathed a "Ha!" His hand groping across his bedside table found his light-weight ten-power binoculars, and a tiny twist of finger and thumb reduced their focus from infinity to something closer.

Yes, by Zeus! the Fates were indeed busy in his interests tonight. Clotho was working for him overtime! For through the bright circular window he could see the door in the opposite blue-papered wall, part of the keyboard end of what must be the harpsichord, and facing the door, her back toward him, a figure in a softly glimmering grey dress and with blond hair swaying just above the slender shoulders.

But what was she doing? and why didn't she turn around so he could see her face? he asked himself as he 'fined the focus of his binoculars, sparing a brief, respectful, thought for the slightness of the adjustment that had suited them from one sort of beauty to another. He noted that her shoulders were working, as though she were doing something with her hands to the front of her dress, perhaps adjusting the fit of her brassiere. But why did she *keep on* doing it? and in that one place and position without moving around?

She put down what looked like a screwdriver on the harpsichord and stepped aside. He sacrificed a moment's sight of her to scan the door. Above the little brass chain like the one that graced his own entrance, a second and heavier brass chain with a lump at one end had been affixed.

Miss Woodvale surveyed her handiwork for a few moments, turned far enough around so that her neat classic profile was at last visible, and lifting her hands to her throat began thoughtfully to undo her dress, which buttoned down the front.

The binoculars trembled in Buford's hands. This couldn't be happening, he told himself as he steadied the instrument and 'fined down the focus still further, it was too much to hope for the first night! and yet. . . .

As if she'd caught his thought by some defensive telepathy and quite agreed with it, the sylphlike young woman paused in her actions, re-did the three buttons she'd undone, and before Buford could curse himself for his negative thinking (it always came true!), had snatched up a small handbag and a scarf matching her dress and exited from her room into the hall, though leaving her door briefly open a crack while she did something (of course, locked!) to the heavier brass chain from the outside.

Then Buford did act, and with a decisiveness that, allowing for his years, was the equal of hers. He retracted his head out of the night, laid down his binoculars, and hurried into the hall himself . . . just in time to see Miss Woodvale, her blonde locks sheathed by a twinkling grey scarf, disappear into the elevator.

Of course! he told himself, she'd not had to wait for it; it was at the same floor where he'd left it hardly two minutes ago.

His resonant appealing cry of "Please hold the elevator!" coincided with the muted grinding noises of the door of the cage closing automatically as its occupant pushed a button for another floor.

As he listened to the soft sad sound of its descent and the faint thud of its arrival at the ground floor a half minute later, he reminded himself not to give way to despair: there would surely be other opportunities to meet this wonderful and ingenious girl. Perhaps even tonight! Her impulsive manner of leaving had not been that of someone going out for the whole evening, but rather someone reminded of an errand quickly run, say some small purchase forgot and easily made at the small liquor shop and grocery across the street or the hardware and drug store next to it. Perhaps if he just waited a few minutes. . . .

His plotty thoughts were intruded on by the purr of the ascending cage. His heart leaped a little. Could it be that this remarkable girl had returned for him, belatedly reacting in a burst of extreme conscientiousness to his cry of appeal? Stranger things had been known to happen. . . .

The elevator indeed came all the way to the sixth floor and its door slid open, but his well-chosen expressions of gratitude died on his lips, nor did he utter the more sardonic greeting he was next minded to, but only watched with revived interest.

For without once looking in his direction, Mrs. Casady hurried off purposefully in the direction of Miss Woodvale's apartment. He saw her disappear into the other wing, heard the sound of a door being unlocked and then a muted jangling, twice repeated, as if it were being prevented by a chain from being set more than a crack ajar. A grin of gleeful comprehension lightened the Colonel's face. He heard a door slam, but before there was time for Mrs. Casady to reappear, he had retreated inside his own doorway, his mind vastly stimulated by the little scene he'd witnessed and once more fiendishly plotting.

Returning to the office-apartment on the ground floor, Rachel Casady unburdened herself of her grievances to her husband.

"She has no right to shut us out that way," she protested stridently. "And on the first day! What if there's a fire? Or she tries to commit suicide like that music teacher? I think at the least you should report it to Mr. Fang."

Jack nodded several times with dutiful sympathy, then said at last, reflecting on it all, "That makes three tenants have chain-locks now. They don't really bother me, you can always kick 'em open if you have to get inside. I'm more worried by the brace-lock Gene Garson's had put on his door. If he should get trapped in his wheelchair again. . . ." He shook his big head, then continued, "Mr. Fang knows half the tenants have special bolts or locks of one sort or another. He doesn't care so long as the rents come in and requests for repairs don't." He sighed at the world's heartlessness; then a look of genuine puzzlement crossed his honest face. "But you know," he said, "that girl didn't look to me like the suspicious type."

"Hah!" his wife sneered, glad of the chance for some

small retort. "You men are all alike when there's a young and pretty face."

Meanwhile the object of their discussion, serenely unaware of any problems but her own delightfully clear-cut though often terribly abstruse ones, was recrossing the street, just as the Colonel had predicted to himself she might, with a small brown-paper sack containing a pint of skim milk and a box of thin wheaten crackers. She unlocked the outer door of the Ultimate Apartments, surprised at her feeling of simple pleasure at being able to do so (that would vanish soon enough with repetition, she told herself), walked blithely down the long empty hall, entered the empty elevator, and with another secret smile such as had crossed her face unlocking the outer door, pressed the sixth button.

As the cage effortlessly mounted, her mind entered a gorgeous black and white world where her only concerns, blessedly logical ones, were with vast assemblages of musical notes and intricate successions of fingerings—and would have stayed there, too, as the cage stopped and its door opened and she pushed the floor door open and turned left toward her room . . . except that a small and discreetly apologetic cough made her glance to the right . . . and then pause and look and look again at the two-headed hybrid of metal and flesh shuffling toward her through the stuffy gloom, a robot-and-android Siamese being with three straight metal limbs inter-joined with four angled shorter ones and a tubular metal head with a great shining eye peering from beside the other cranium, which was straw hatted. It puffed softly as it moved.

Because Nerissa's own head was in a strange musical world where all sorts of wonders were possible, she was not frightened by this apparition, only astonished and curious.

Rather swiftly the absurd technologic griffin resolved itself into a plump elderly man no higher than herself, wearing a pale summer suit and white gloves and carrying a grey tripod-set telescope equally tall. When they came opposite her, he paused and looked into her eyes. He had a sweet face, she thought.

He said, "M'dear, would you be so kind as to disentangle these binoculars dangling from my neck before they dash themselves against Palomar, Jr., here?"

She studied the tangle of limbs for a moment, then reached in and neatly complied. She asked solicitously, "Isn't that terribly heavy?"

"Light as a feather," he assured her, "but you would win my undying gratitude, m'dear, if you would precede me to the top of the stairs and hold the door open for me, whilst I shepherd little P.J. here out into his proper element, the star-emblazoned night."

"I'll surely do that for you," she told him and went on ahead. Then with her foot on the first step she turned and held out the binoculars toward him questioningly.

"Hang them over the post at the foot of the balustrade," he told her carelessly. "It might wake up his wooden head if he took a look around with them."

She laughed delightedly at the fantasy as she did what he told her and hurried on while he followed at a more deliberate pace, studying not to bump the grey instrument against the steps and low slanting ceiling.

"Are you sure we should be going up here?" Nerissa called in a different voice from the top. "There's a sign in red that says: 'This Door Must Be Kept Closed At All Times!' "

"M'dear," Buford informed her grandly, while not ceasing his methodical ascent, though puffing a little between phrases, "you and I are tenants of the Ultimate. It is our privilege, nay, our right! to resort to the roof at any time and do there what we will, so long as we don't frighten the pigeons or odd passing angel. If Mr. Fang or his minions should seek to bar our way, they would do so in violation of the city's mighty codes, which denominate this as a fire exit that must be kept openable from the inside at all times!"

"Mr. Fang?" Nerissa questioned.

"The wealthy and all-powerful Celestial from Taiwan

who owns this dubious tenement we inhabit," Buford
informed her as he reached her step, "though you'd never
be sure of all that unless you saw him in his silver-black
limousine. I take it you've dealt only with his agents, the
amiable Casady and his Sorrow."

While they were close crowded in the pocket of hot air at
the head of the stairs, he somehow managed to reach a
white-gloved hand out of his tangle and pat her affection-
ately on the upper arm. "And so, m'dear, press bravely
on!"

Nerissa twisted the bolt and thrust open the door and
followed it onto the flat roof, surprised by the rush of cool
wind that washed her. As she held the door wide, almost
clinging to it for security, she felt herself assaulted by the
sudden space around her and the light-crowned tall buildings that marched through it. Dizzyingly high above was a
patch of the telescopic night her companion had spoken
of, its emblazoning reduced to two visible stars, but elsewhere beyond and between the serrated buildings the air
loomed with low white clouds shouldering each other as
they came padding in with outthrust flat heads from the
ocean and the west, like a great horde of silent and gigantic
polar bears. She was seeing the frequent end of the occasional hot day in San Francisco; the prevailing westerlies
sluicing in the thick cooling fog from the great banks of it
that overhung the Pacific in summer.

The sight stirred her. She began to look around at the
light-crowned buildings, the Hilton Tower with its glaring
white coronet, the Sir Francis Drake Hotel with its single
revolving white fluorescent star.

"Where are the pigeons?" she asked her companion,
who was busy setting up his telescope, extending its legs,
attaching its eyepiece, as if there were a whole heavenfull
of stars waiting to be seen instead of a few fog-threatened
ones.

"They sleep at night," he called back lightly, "while the
angels put on their black and silver evening clothes and

masks and their black wings, which makes them a good deal harder to catch sight of."

Gaining confidence, she moved toward him. The door, released, swung to and its lock clicked shut.

"Never mind," he went on, "your front door key will open it."

She felt a surge of power, as when he'd told her the roof was theirs to use. The two-starred black gap was lost to the encroaching clouds, which were especially thick around the top of the next light-topped building she gazed at, a hotel of some fifteen storeys with triangular gables rising from either end of the otherwise flat roof. The one at the front was featureless, but the one at the other end, where the fog seemed thicker, had a large and perfectly round window in it from which pearly light poured. It looked far more beautiful than the Hilton's square-gemmed coronet or the Drake's star, and she felt unaccountably drawn to it, a sharp unexpected yearning, oh! if only she could climb directly there through the cool windy air! and as if in answer to that wish she began to see pearly faint steps or a wide-runged pearly ladder stretching a few feet from her to the strange porthole and somewhat resembling the moon's track in rippling water.

She was about to call softly and wonderingly to her companion when his voice broke in with "M'dear, do come over here. I've got the Ring Nebula in Lyra in the eyepiece, it's a marvelous sight, hurry before the fog cuts it off."

She took a step or two toward him though her eyes were still on her own find, but as she framed her question about the magical eyrie she'd spotted among the other light-capped high rises, he ejaculated, "Oh, damn! the moon's risen over the Clift Hotel. Her light will pale the Ring down to nothing. Do hurry!"

It was weird. At his words the triangular gable vanished and the large pearly porthole window it had held (perhaps the fog thinned there, too, just then) showed forth the familiar mottlings of the full moon. It was as if a minor chord should become a major without proper modulation. It jarred. She was still asking herself what had happened to her mind when she obediently bent down at the small end of her companion's instrument and tried to see something besides darkness in the fantastically tiny eyepiece, while he stood behind her instructing her to hold her eye just so, not joggle the instrument, and so on.

"No, m'dear, you have to squat down a little more," he advised her, his white-gloved hands shifting from her shoulders to her hips. "Like *so*."

Nerissa saw more darkness (there must be a way of looking through these things!) and felt his hands slide gently to her waist.

Behind them the door opened and a friendly voice assaulted them. "Colonel Hogeston, you up here? I thought so! I spotted your spyglasses hanging on the stair-post and brought 'em up for you."

As she jumped up, turning around, Nerissa ducked to one side while telling herself she must stop always acting as if she were guilty of something, especially now she was living alone. The Colonel suppressed the impulse to say "Stop following me up and baby-sitting me, Jack Casady!" and thought, it could have been worse; he could have shone a flashlight on us.

Casady went on in the same friendly tones, "Oh, you've been showing Miss Woodvale the stars." He looked around at the fog. "Or the moon, or something."

"Good evening, Miss. A telescope's an interesting thing, isn't it? I never can see anything through one myself. There's a knack, I guess."

Nerissa nodded while the Colonel said somewhat severely, "The young lady was very kindly, at my request, helping me bring my instrument up here and set it up. Actually we've not even introduced ourselves."

Casady clumsily corrected that omission. The Colonel snatched off his right glove before holding Nerissa's hand for a pregnant moment, his head bent above it. She became conscious of the bag of milk and crackers still in her other hand. Casady guessed he'd done something wrong, and seeking to correct it said enthusiastically, "The Colonel's the hero of the sixth floor, Miss Woodvale, did you know that? A couple of years ago he saved the life of an older lady occupying the same apartment you have who tried to commit suicide by taking sleeping pills."

Ignoring or misinterpreting the Colonel's horrified frowns and headshakes, he went on, "You see, he could see her from his apartment with his spyglasses, through the round window in hers, lying passed out, not like she was just asleep, and he got me and we got in and called an ambulance and got her to the hospital in time to be pumped out."

"I see," Nerissa said. "Wasn't it lucky for her the Colonel was looking? Now I'd better put these things away. Thanks, Mr. Casady, and thank you, Colonel Hogeston, for showing me the roof."

"My pleasure, m'dear," he responded, but his voice no longer danced. "Thank *you* for your help."

"She's a cute little trick, isn't she?" Casady observed when the door had shut behind her. "Here, let me carry that down for you."

"I'm afraid she is," the Colonel agreed heavily. "Did you know, Jack, that cute comes from acute?"

He let the big man take the telescope down for him, carelessly shoving his binoculars into his jacket pocket, their cord dangling outside. Later when he returned them to his bedroom table, he looked out the window, not very hopefully, at his new neighbor's round one. *Already* it was covered with a thick gauzy material that hardly showed even the shadows of anything inside.

The fates on his side tonight? They were strumpets, all! What to do? Well, there was the Peops meeting. But first he'd have a drink. So he opened the brandy and from the refrigerator, one of the bottles of champagne he'd been saving for the next holidays or the start of his next drunk and fortified himself with a couple of French 75s before going down to Portia's.

His arrival there with an opened fifth and a yet-to-be-popped magnum revived a dragging meeting and relieved Ms. Hotchkiss, who took a proprietorial attitude toward the Colonel and hadn't been too happy about Frank Daulby's report of his reactions to Miss Woodvale's arrival.

The magnum made the end of the chapter that Gene Garson read them learnedly from the thin manuscript of his latest novel-attempt on the tray of his wheelchair appear farther from the inevitable bogging-down point than its beginning had seemed. It put more chill into the synchronicities of flight numbers, street numbers, telephone numbers, and room numbers Gunnar Nordgren had accumulated during a recent trip east. ("Those are *fright* numbers, Gun," Saul Rosenzweig observed.) The demonstration of Roberta Roberts', Dee Franklin's, and Portia's ability to improvise short-short stories in the manner of Katherine Mansfield went off particularly well. Dominique read her new ballad "Torquemada on Turk Street" while her big boyfriend Daq Duclose the metal sculptor, who was built like a bear but handsomer, was roused to tell about his season freebasing with the Hell's Angels and how he'd secretly welded his stainless steel figure "Energy as Mischief" to structural members halfway through the N-Judah streetcar tunnel under Buena Vista Park. Portia herself was moved to talk nostalgically of her Calcutta years and ended by trying to stir up sad-faced Essie Furness, otherwise known as Madam Melancholy, who wore silver slave bracelets to cover up the scars on the insides of her wrists, to strike up an acquaintance with the sixth-floor newcomer on the strength of occupying the apartment across the hall from hers. The Colonel heard that and left off fascinating Dominique with tales of mysterious Mississippi and death-obsessed New Orleans, to tell Essie, with whom he sometimes pubcrawled on Geary Street, "If you do get to know her, try to see that the girl has a cross draught, else she'll suffocate all shut up in that stuffy one-window room."

Of the next lunar month it needs be said that harpsichord scales, runs, trills, and occasional melodies *rather* softly suffused the sixth floor and sometimes filtered down to the fifth and fourth hour after hour most days and evenings, that the Colonel's drunk proceeded through its silent, otherwise barely-detectible stage and its voluble and weaving one towards its reeling, stumbling, screaming, who-knows-what? crisis, while October and more heat waves than anyone could remember, reviving recollections of the great "Don't flush the toilet!" drought of 1976 and '77 and shaking the general faith that San Fran was "the *cool* gray city of love."

About the undampened twangy tintinnabulations of the harpsichord, Rachel Casady waited confidently for complaints and when they didn't come in, took to visiting the sixth floor in hopes of stirring some up, adopting her not infrequent role of agent provocateur. What foiled her here was that the Apt Peops were particularly strong and influential in the sector of the Ultimate englobing #607 and while these odd folk differed vastly in their opinions on most topics, they were one and all behind anything that could be denominated as serious art, and Frank Daulby opined (and Gunnar Nordgren, who knew much more, confirmed) that what Nerissa worked on, when it wasn't exercises, was mostly Bach, in particular an interminable cadenza which the Colonel entitled "Big Tin Bird Hovering on a Broken Chord," but which nonetheless unwillingly fascinated him and sometimes made the hairs on the back of his neck rise.

Finally Rachel got ancient Mrs. Drumm on five, her most suggestive crony, to register a protest, but when Jack came up to listen to the harpsichordic din, he couldn't hear anything, not even the low notes that came buzzing down through the walls and up the legs of Mrs. Drumm's bed to stab her in the back.

About the heat, it really was quite intense, especially on

the sixth floor under the roof. At times the Colonel sympathized truly though muzzily with the plight of Miss Woodvale practicing in her little room without cross-draught, though more often as his drunk progressed it was apt to bring on the vindicative thought, "I hope she's sweating like a little pig in there!" but this unfortunately had the effect of bringing on visions that were stimulating rather than disgusting and penetential. Fact was, the Colonel's getting drunk when he did didn't allow him to forget the newcome girl, but rather pinned down and set his sudden November-May infatuation. (Or should that last be April, even March? he asked himself.)

And then one day the Colonel noticed the harpsichord was distinctly louder in his apartment with its open windows, and going to one saw that the round window was no longer shut but open wider than his own and its inner drapes removed. A few feet inside the room, however, a tall hinged screen with posters on it shut off any view of the other side of the room and its resounding instrument and flashing-fingered occupant.

Later the same day he made a trip to the patio garbage chute to get rid of some empties (being still in the early, orderly stage of his drunk) and noted that the door to #607 was open on its two chains, so that while the rather metallic throbbing notes poured out, a perceptible cross draught poured in. Damn, he thought, the girl's a veritable villain, a cunning, cunning fiend!

But why hadn't the Colonel simply continued to press his attentions on the girl despite Jack Casady's unfortunate revelation of his handiness with binoculars, which surely needn't have been fatal to his aims? The answer was, he had; alas, the trouble being that the Colonel's drinking tended to coarsen his always imaginative and reckless style. Finding himself mounting alone in the elevator with the object of his erotic fancy two days after the full-moon Peops Meet, he had inquired gruffly about her health and comfort and then pressed on to say, "And I trust, m'dear, your sex life proceeds satisfactorily? A handsome young female such as yourself should be regularly serviced by two or three vigorous and worthy young males until they're fucked to exhaustion, it not only soothes the ego, gives and dispenses joy, it's essential to health! Come, m'dear, don't blush or turn away, else I'll think you belong to my stuffy generation rather than your own liberated one!"

Lips tightly pressed, jaw set, eyes straight ahead, Nerissa disappeared from the cage in record time the instant it came to a stop, so that the Colonel's move to hold the door for her was a lonely gesture. He stared after her with bleary-eyed disappointment and disillusion. Why did women have to be so ungracious about accepting honest compliments?

After a space of soul searching, Nerissa decided honor did not compel she leave the Ultimate and seek lodging elsewhere; things were getting close and she couldn't afford to lose the time. But she ceased to recognize the Colonel and sometimes used the stairs to avoid him, while the "Big Tin Bird" cadenza quivered with a new intensity and hair-raising desperation.

So the Colonel perforce left off his pursuit of the harpsichordist (unfortunately his thoughts of her, his lubricious visions of her with sweat pouring off her baby fat, were not so readily shed) and a certain hair-raising desperation was added to the usual mounting course of his drunk. He found no relief with his friends and close acquaintants, they'd long ago discovered, even the closest of them, Frank Daulby, Portia Hotchkiss, that there was nothing whatsoever to be done about the Colonel's drunks except to let them run their course.

Only Jack Casady kept closer watch on him the drunker he got, particularly as regards any visits he made to the roof to seek forgetfulness in the stars, and that was pure annoyance. Why, Jack had even tied white rags to the low standpipes and vents so the Colonel wouldn't stumble over them in the dark, and taken down, though not successfully hidden, the little old six-rung wooden ladder that stood against the shack topped by TV antennas that housed the elevator's motor and relays, and how even a child could get into trouble with that was unclear to Bew.

One more thing needs to be said about this troublous time before we explore its triple climax on the full-moon night of the next meeting of the Apartment People. Essie Furness successfully struck up an acquaintance with her new neighbor across the hall—and a good thing that, for even Nerissa mightn't have been able to get through the grueling month without a single person she could turn to. It never got beyond the point of Nerissa dropping in at #608 for a cup of tea from time to time, Essie never got invited to #607, her place was a dreadful mess, Nerissa insisted, but it was a relief to Nerissa to be able to talk limitedly with someone. What created a bond between them was Nerissa's interest in death and sepulchral matters and the melancholy mood (which fascinates quite a few seriously artistic people, especially ones who haven't done much living), and Essie's long history of unsuccessful suicide attempts by sleeping pills or razor blade (most of the scars her silver slave bracelet hid were of hesitation cuts) and her willingness to talk about them.

In the intervals of these rather dismal conversations, Madam Melancholy got in some public relations work for the Apartment People, discovering unsurprisingly that Nerissa was much interested in the supernatural though not addicted to any particular brand of the occult. Essie did not stress Colonel Hogeston's role in the informal organization, his friendship with Portia Hotchkiss, etc., for she'd gathered the girl had a bad impression of him, even though Nerissa hadn't told her about the incident in the elevator.

Essie also learned, on promise of secrecy, that Nerissa normally lived at home with her parents, but had taken an apartment of her own to practice for a trial performance with the San Francisco Businesspersons' Chamber Orchestra, and that the pieces she was working on were chiefly by Scarlatti and Bach, including the latter's Fifth Brandenburg Concerto, which was the one containing the long cadenza she so often repeated.

And there were times as October drew toward an end and the new moon grew through its crescent phase toward full when Essie could have sworn that the girl was on the brink of further revelations and only held back by doubt of her ability to express herself intelligibly or her listener's capacity to understand what she had to relate. She had the abstracted look of one who has blundered into strange realms.

The Colonel, on the other hand, was getting the haggard visage and wild eye-glint that generally presaged a drunk's catastrophe. His well-wishers, though fatalistic, felt a growing concern, an unwilling tension.

And the heat drummed on.

The evening of the full moon was heralded by a break in that, and the fog's belated return, the polar bear clouds nosing in again, chill winds knifing into hot gusts, a feeling of meteorologic uncertainty. The Apt Peops were late in gathering in Portia Hotchkiss's apartment, but they had begun their proceedings, although the Colonel and Essie were both absent, when there came two sharp raps on the door.

Dee Franklin, who was nearest, pushed through the curtain that masked the little entryway and let in Essie Furness accompanied by . . . Nerissa Woodvale. It was apparent even to those who hadn't met her that the latter young woman was tremendously agitated and keyed-up, though fiercely in control of herself—"high," one wise to drugs might have hazarded, most likely on cocaine.

It was also clear that she had something on her mind that preoccupied it and made small talk difficult, though she was doing her best. Portia, after a few covert words exchanged with Essie, asked her to introduce herself and tell them all whatever she felt minded to. Nerissa took a drink of the lemonade Frank Daulby had handed her without telling her about the vodka in it, sat up very straight, and looked around at her audience with an expression of polite defiance, or confrontation at any rate. She took a deep breath.

"I am," she said as the room quieted, "the person who has been making all your lives miserable with my practicing on my keyboard instrument. I like harpsichord music myself—you'd expect that, wouldn't you?—but one great pianist is reported to have said—" (she seemed to brace herself, to put herself on the line) "—that it sounded like two skeletons fucking on a tin roof. I must assume that others may share his distaste, and so I want to begin by registering my heartfelt thanks to you all for putting up with my racket for a whole month without making any complaints to the management, at least none that have been passed on to me."

There was a small round of applause at that, started by Saul Rosenzweig, who was sitting on the floor of the bed next to Portia's feet.

"Thank you for that," Nerissa said, "because there's something just happened to me I'm wild to tell about. You can see that, can't you? Miss Furness has told me you exchange stories about strange happenings, and the way I think now this is the weirdest thing that ever happened to me in my whole life. But first I must give you a little background for it." And she quickly told them as much about herself as she'd told Essie and then went on to describe her visit to the roof with Buford Hogeston, identifying him only as "an elderly gentleman who lives on six," but only insofar as the roof visit involved the illusion whereby the full moon seen through fog had for a few moments become the window of some fabulous penthouse restaurant or skyroom, "or heavenly jewelry shrine or French cosmetics temple," she added.

"Only you've got to remember this fearful yearning I felt to get there, a real pang," she emphasized, "and this very real feeling I had that I could safely, not fly, but *climb* there through the air up the ladder of pearly light below it if only I could reach its bottom rung a few feet above my head, because that turns out to be very important for what happened tonight.

"Two other things I've got to tell you so you'll understand the rest," she went on. "First, early in my stay here, I was terribly insulted by someone who lives in this building." She looked around gravely. "The person is not in this room, so we can talk about it. It was a matter of a sexual approach, purely verbal, but I can't recall anyone ever saying something to me about myself that shocked me as much in my whole life. Maybe I was too easily offended, but I don't think so."

Frank and Portia, and some of the others too, exchanged guarded looks of comprehension.

"That's all you need to know about that," Nerissa told them. "Second is about how I dress for practice. Now you all know how hot it's been the past month, especially on six, under the roof." And she went on to explain the means whereby she'd got some cross-draught. "I had to have the screen, you see," she explained, "because it got so bad in there I'd taken to practicing in my underwear. And then it got so terribly fierce I couldn't stand even that and—" she braced herself, "—I did my practice wearing nothing at all."

Frank noticed she'd finished her drink and insisted on renewing it. Others had hurried refills.

As she resumed her narrative, Nerissa showed no signs of relaxing, seemed if anything still more tense and "high," determined to relate everything exactly as it had happened. "Tonight I began my practice wearing what had become my usual hot weather costume. Everything was going remarkably well, so I decided to run through the whole Brandenburg Fifth without a single error, just as if it were performance night. But I hadn't got very far into it when a gust of hot wind blew the screen over.

"I should have stopped and put it up again right away, of course, but I didn't, I stuck to my decision, I kept on playing without missing a note—or making a mistake either. I told myself that *anything* can happen performance night—a string snap, an instrumentalist take sick and miss passages, lights go out, fire sirens, a fight start in the audience, gunshots, an earthquake tremor—and that this was a very proper test of my ability to meet such emergencies without panicking. I didn't like that big black round of night out there and nothing between it and me in my hot-weather practice suit, but I tried not to look at it too much and concentrated on the Fifth and kept on going.

"And then I began to see, in glimpses, something rising just outside the bottom of the window. At first I didn't know what it was, couldn't imagine, once it looked like a furry little animal, but we were getting close to the long cadenza and I kept on playing.

"But then," she went on, "the thing outside came floating higher and I saw it was—I swear this to you!—the face of the person who had insulted me, staring straight at me while hanging in the dark air (the 'furry little animal' had been the person's gray hair). But now the rest of the orchestra had stopped playing and I was into the big cadenza where I'm carrying the Fifth all by myself. This was the one place where I couldn't afford the least mistake.

"At first I thought the head was leering at me. But then I saw it was more a grimace of frenzy or rapture, I don't know what, or—yes!—in a trance like an ancient witch-doctor or sibyl. I kept on.

"And then came what was, I think, the strangest part of my whole experience. I get the feeling very strongly that the person outside had levitated himself up there, or climbed a ladder of light like the one I'd seen, or thought I'd seen, between me and the moon portal, and was hanging there, but only for so long—oh, I don't know how to make you understand how *certain* I felt about this!—as I kept on playing. If I stopped, or just missed, they'd fall. So now I had two reasons for keeping on.

"As I approached the end of the cadenza, the staring face began, little by little, just as when it had appeared, to float off and down into the night, safely, I prayed. By the time the orchestra joined in with me again, I could no longer see it. I went on and finished the first movement."

She let out a breath. Some others did the same.

"I don't *think*," she continued, "I could have played

through the second and third movements just then, although they're shorter and less taxing for the harpsichordist. I'm not sure, but I don't think so. At any rate as soon as we were done with the first, I rushed over to the window, there's a narrow bed in front of that, and kneeling across it, I looked out and down. I don't know what I expected to see, a body hovering or flying? or one crushed on the paving of the little courtyard below behind the bar next door? but there was nothing at all.

"So I rushed over to Miss Furness', *barely* remembering to grab up my robe, and I started to tell her all about it and got out some, and she persuaded me to come down here and tell all of you."

She slumped back in her chair. But before she could respond to the rather excited flurry of questions and comments, indeed before those were completed, there came a sudden beating on the hall door, a frantic tattoo. Saul, who'd been on his way to replenish his drink, was the first to respond and when he'd got the door open there lurched through the curtain into the center of the room . . . Buford Hogeston.

The Colonel's face was wild-eyed, pale but grimed, and with a four-day pepper-and-salt stubble. His white suit was rumpled and soiled and his white gloves were filthy. He peered around, his eyes alternately bugging and squinting, and then staggered toward the man who'd just emerged from the kitchen.

"Frank Daulby!" he proclaimed, his voice slurring. "You always been after me to write down my hallucinations when I'm having d.t.'s. Well, I want you to know I've just been having some beauties, and I happen to be in the mood to tell you all about 'em." He took the fresh drink out of Frank's hand, drained a third, and saying, "My God, what I been through," staggered rapidly with it toward the foot of Portia's bed and spinning around came down with a creak of the springs on the spot Saul had been occupying.

To his right Portia was sitting bolt upright against the

pillows in her dark negligee and staring at him with an expression in which solicitude and suspicion were mixed, while off to his left Nerissa, leaning forward now, was studying him with an even greater intensity.

He leaned back against the wall, massaging his stubble, then took a smaller slurp of Frank's drink, looked around at everyone again, and began, "You most of you know how I like to go up on the roof nights, when that bastard Casady lets me! in pursuit of my astronomic avocation." The last phrase slurred wonderfully, as may be imagined, but on the whole his speech was rapidly becoming considerably more clear and intelligible than it had been at first.

He continued, "Well, tonight I was up there again, outwitting Jack who's been following me around like a damn nursemaid!—but this time he thought I was out on Geary, making the run. I was up there enjoying the cool breezes, thank *God!*, and watching the fog moving in, when I began having the damnedest hallucinations or illusions or whatever. Maybe relief from the heat was what brought them on. Or maybe they weren't illusions, maybe some of them were really happenings, I can't be sure even myself, you'll have to use your own judgment there."

He took another swallow of the drink, stared up at the ceiling, and said thoughtfully, "You know, illusions are damn funny things, I remember once going to the roof an hour or so before dawn, when most of the hotels have finally turned off their blinding top-lights, damn 'em! The fog was extremely thick—it was one of those nights when it almost gets down to street level—but through it I could see the moon quite distinctly in its proper shape and all (happened to be gibbous phase then).

"But then I realized I was seeing it pretty high in the north, where the moon couldn't possibly be, and the fog thinned a little and I saw that it was just a single window high in the east wall of the Bedford Hotel, all the other windows were dark and the floodlights for that stupid billboard they have on top were off. But for a couple of seconds that window had been a perfect gibbous moon.

"What happened tonight was just the opposite of that. Through the gathering fog I saw the full moon rising over the back end of the Clift Hotel, only I didn't see it as that at all, I saw it as a big round window, softly white, a huge moon porthole, I remember thinking, in a strange temple-looking structure, built by a jinni, I guess, on the back end of the Clift. And below it were short streaks of light, a whole ribbon of them like a moon track on a lake or the ocean, a moon ladder coming down almost to where I was. And I began to feel this awful urge, this yearning, to somehow climb up that ladder and get there to the Land of Heart's Desire, or the Philosopher's Stone, or the Elixer Vitae, or whatever else lay behind that wonderful window.

"Or maybe that was where illusion turned into hallucination, for I began to hear, very faintly at first, a strange dancing music, like a harp but more rapid, a harp with silver strings, I remember thinking, covered with diamond dust. It was a little like de Falla's 'Ritual Fire Dance,' but higher pitched and more spread out. And it seemed to be coming from the sky, or rather from the moon porthole itself, for the silver ladder I saw began to vibrate in time with it, very synesthetic.

"I wasn't paralyzed by all this, or in a trance or anything, for the next thing I knew I'd got the short wooden ladder from where Jack Casady thought he'd hidden it, and set it against the pentshack, and begun to climb it. By that time I know the hallucinations must surely have been started, for that's something I'd never do if I were in my right mind."

He looked at his empty glass and saying, "My God, this yakking is thirsty work," tossed it unexpectedly across the room at Frank, who even more unexpectedly caught it and hurried with it into the kitchen, whence he soon emerged with it refilled, and another drink for himself.

The Colonel took advantage of the pause to reach a hand behind him and pull his soiled jacket off over his head and drop it on the floor, and then strip off his dirty gloves and add them to the pile, explaining, "I got chilled on the roof, but it's still hot down here."

After a hefty slug of his new drink he resumed, "When I got four or five steps up the ladder I reached up and I actually touched the bottom rung of the vibrating ladder of light—more synesthesia, for it not only was palpable, but the music flooded through me from it, filling me with a new icy vitality and making me feel I could do anything.

"As I was transferring from the one ladder to the other I felt a rung suddenly give under my foot. It must have been one of the wooden ones, for the ladder of quivering light sustained me and I completed the transfer successfully, and right away I was going up the light-ladder very fast, a busy little bug—oh, did I have the hots to get to that wonder window!—without getting short in my breath at all.

"That proves if anything does that it all had to be hallucination by now, but God, it was real! The light-ladder would give a little, as if it were more like a rope than a rigid one, but I felt no fear. I remember stopping once or twice to bounce up and down on it and look down at the silly little people and cars in the street, and then scurry on up toward my pearly goal through the very fine cool mist that was gathering around me—I was getting into the fog. Hey, it was *gay* up there!—I mean dancingly delightful, not the homophilic kind.

"By now I was mounting very fast and I think there were beginning to be gaps in my awareness. Because the light-ladder seemed to curve and loop at times and then straighten out again, as though it were dipping into other dimensions and then out again, or as if the moon porthole weren't where it had seemed to be at first.

"And then suddenly I was in front of the round, glistening, mother-of-pearl window. It wasn't as big as it had looked to be from the roof, only about four or five feet across, and yet at the same time there seemed to be a sense in which it was *the whole moon* come down to earth—I can't explain that any better.

"The music was still pouring out, stronger than ever, but now I seem to have lost the ladder, it was more as if a million tiny invisible fingers were holding me up. And I *was* paralyzed or in a trance or something, for although I was only a foot or so from the round window, I couldn't stretch out so much as a finger to take hold of its sill and climb in or whatever, I could only stare.

"What I could see inside, through the general pearly radiance, was a small throne of silver lace-work, very fine and delicate. And on it there was sitting the moon goddess or moon princess herself, clothed in light. She had a very trim figure and she looked exactly like Louise Brooks with platinum hair—you know, *Pandora's Box, Rolled Stockings, A Girl in Every Port.*" He glanced toward Nerissa and said, *"You* wouldn't remember her, you're decades too young and today's young people don't see the classics anyway.

"Across the window between me and her were stretched dozens of silvery strings with rather the effect of Venetian blinds wide open, but much finer. There were other banks of taut silver strings around her set at different angles. And she was making the music by plucking these very fast with her fingers and her toes too, I think—Hell, she was moving so fast that most of the time I couldn't see anything clearly of her but her face; this part of my hallucination gets very spider-webby, and spidery, too.

"Her face stared at me, just as if she were trying to hypnotize me, and I stared back, couldn't do anything else. She had a cruel, solemn, intense look most of the time, but every now and then she'd make faces and sort of smirk and laugh at me.

"And then gradually the music got softer and the million fingers began to give a little, to let me down and draw me little by little away from the nacreous window. They began to rock me gently and everything slowed . . . and suddenly I came to myself sprawled on my face on the roof. I think I must have thrashed around a bit while I was passed out," he added, distastefully examining his grievously smudged white shoes and pants, and glancing down at the heaped dirty jacket and gloves. "I looked up through the fog and saw the full moon about an hour and a half above the Clift Hotel, so I came down here to tell Frank, who's so curious, all about my delirium tremens for once."

Instantly there started a chattering flood of comments and questions directed not only at the Colonel but at Nerissa too, about the remarkable way the stories fitted together—at one point Nerissa said, "No, the face I saw was clean shaven," while at another the Colonel ducked his head comically and lifted his hands over it, as if to shield himself from the deluge—and what explanation could there possibly be: telepathy? the collective unconscious with all its moon-myths? or one more weird effect of full moonlight itself, which was already known to have such strange powers over mad folk, lovers, spawning fish, werewolves, cat goddesses, and dogs.

But this tumult had not got very far, at least not developed its full pitch, when it was interrupted by three heavy knocks on the hall door, the unmistakable bangs of authority. Again it was Saul who went and this time the curtain was swept aside by Jack Casady looking rather hot in his invariable lumberjack shirt. He spotted the Colonel on the foot of the bed and greeted him accusingly, "There you are! I been worried about you the last half hour!"

By then Portia had thought to ask him if he wouldn't please take a drink, and he'd made the inevitable response of, "Well, I don't mind if I do," and Frank had fetched it, and he'd taken a good swallow after an appreciative nod to Portia. He looked around at them all then and said somewhat embarrassedly, "Excuse me, folks, for breaking in on you, but for the past few days I been a little concerned about our friend here," with a polite shrug toward the Colonel.

"I think we understand, Jack," Frank said softly.

The Colonel, looking very chipper, said sweetly, "Thank you very much, Jack, but would you mind telling me what reason you had to be worried about me?"

"I'll tell you why," the stalwart manager-cum-janitor responded, moving to the center of the room. "A half hour ago I found the door to your apartment wide open, and all your lights on, and you not there. Then up on the roof I found these spyglasses of yours—'' He hauled them out of a pants pocket and held them up and shook them, there was a tinkle of glass ''—broken. And I found the ladder—'' He took time to explain to the others in the room, ''It's a short wooden ladder they use to get at the TV antennas,'' then went on to the Colonel, ''And I found the ladder with one of its end rungs broken, lying as if it had been set against the shack and then knocked down. What puzzled me especially was that the break was *inward,* that is, inward from the end.'' Once more he included the room in his explanations, ''You see, if you started to climb a ladder and the first rung broke when you put your weight on it, it would be broken *outward.* But what an end rung broken *inward* means I do not know, except that someone climbed a ladder and tried to do a balancing act on the top rung, and it bust. Anyhow, the full moon reminded me you people would be having your meeting, and knowing that Colonel Hogeston would be supposed to be there, I tried on the chance.''

(Anent these matters, Frank Daulby afterwards observed privately to Saul Rosenzweig, ''I don't know about the ladder, but about the binoculars, I'm sure they're not the pair Bew's using now, but an earlier pair very much like them he dropped on the sidewalk from the fire escape when he was out there looking at something or other with them. As for the way the two stories dovetailed, I know Bew has a key to Portia's apartment from the time they were a little closer to each other than they seem to be now. Couldn't it just have happened that he got there a half hour earlier than he appeared to, and let himself in with that key and heard the start of Nerissa's story, and listened to it all from behind the curtain, dreaming up his own story the while to match it, and then let himself out again and started banging on the door. Yes, when I consider it, it strikes me as a distinct possibility, just the sort of stunt that Bew loves—and one that would have the bonus of making him look romantic to Nerissa. But, as I say, I really have no explanation for the ladder.'')

At the time, on full moon night, there was much wondering and jabbering, but no firm conclusions reached and no further revelations of consequence. The meeting soon degenerated, or flowered, into a drinking party, with the Colonel sitting on the bed beside Portia (he'd moved to its head when she invited him) and fascinating Nerissa (who sipped her third lemonade cautiously, she'd come to suspect them) with his stories about the cemeteries of New Orleans, the crypts, the glass-fronted coffins, brown bones glimpsed through cracks in mausoleums, the grates for burning Chinese bones prior to reverent shipment home to China, all the lovely sepulchral paraphernalia.

Portia asked the harpsichordist if she was at all worried about the performance just three nights away.

She shook her head and, smiling, said, ''After what happened I think I could play the Fifth in a sleep-walk.''

(As a matter of fact, she did very well at the performance, sufficiently well, at any rate. By melancholy coincidence, on the same evening Frank and Saul escorted the Colonel to what he persisted in calling the Alcohol Hospital and said goodnight to him when he was abed in the detoxification ward.)

But on the night of the meeting and party, Nerissa was emboldened to add to her answer to Portia's question, with a smile that seemed just the least bit wicked, ''There's one thing though, after the way I've been practicing this whole month, I don't know how I'll ever be able to do the Fifth to full advantage with my clothes on.''

Fiona looks for a spell to turn
the cat back into Sister.

Contributors' Notes

In the cover letter accompanying the submission of his poem, BELLAMY BACH volunteered the following specifics: he was born in 1963, spent a globe-trotting childhood with his mother in many "often magical, often isolated communes and hippie enclaves," and currently attends Antioch College in Yellow Springs, Ohio. However, when asked for further information he responded: ". . . those were all lies. Don't believe them. The truth is, I'm just a figment of your imaginations." Some write fantasies; some, perhaps, live them.

British author ANGELA CARTER traces the roots of her fiction to "witch blood on Father's side; solid radical trade-unionists on Mother's." Winner of the Somerset Maugham Award and the John Llewellyn Rhys Prize, Carter writes fantasies that are often marked by grotesque imagery and eroticism. In addition to literary analysis (The Sadian Woman), and stories set in Japan, Carter's fantasy includes The Bloody Chamber, The Magic Toyshop, Heroes and Villains, The War of Dreams, and The Passion of New Eve.

MICHAEL DE LARRABEITI is a British author of westerns, mystery, suspense, and fantasy. He is best known in this country as the author of the "Borrible" books, which have become underground cult favorites. Borribles are modern, streetwise, feral Peter Pans who live in the back alleys of contemporary London; the New York Times called them "chilling . . . the offspring of a singular imagination." Of "The Golden Goat" de Larrabeiti writes: "I lived in Provence for a number of years and for a great deal of that time was a travel guide there. Taking American and British trippers up and down the country was a fine education. Provence is a fascinating part of the world and full of folklore. This particular story is *not* a translation from the French, but simply based on one-line mention in a guide book of a Golden Goat that is said to guard a treasure hoard."

RICHARD ENGLEHART has taught high school for seventeen years. He currently teaches English literature, and classes in mysticism and creative writing, but formerly taught drama and mounted school dramatic productions. His involvement with theater is extensive; for twenty-five years he has acted, directed, produced, and designed productions for various southern California theater companies, and serves as a judge for community theater competitions. Writing is another important part of his life; he has sold fantasy stories to several magazines and anthologies, encouraged in these endeavors by his close friend, writer Theodore Sturgeon. "Fiction," Englehart says, "is a great deal more *real* than history. I've been accused of living in a fantasy world; fantasy seems to me to be very important. I *think* in fantasy; I'm a dreamer." Englehart hails from Pennsylvania, and lives with his wife and his twelve-year-old son Mark in San Diego.

ANDREW GLAZE is a dramatist and Southern poet. His first book of verse, *Damned Ugly Children,* won a Notable Book citation from the American Library Association; *A Masque of Surgery* and *The Trash Dragon of Shensi* have appeared since. Glaze's plays have been produced by the New York Shakespeare Festival and the Lincoln Center Library. "The Trash Dragon of Shensi" first appeared in *Atlantic* magazine.

PAUL HAZEL received his B.A. and M.A. from Yale University, and currently makes his home in Connecticut with his wife, two children, seven beech trees, and a borrowed cat. He is the author of a stirring trilogy of dark fantasy rooted in Welsh and Irish mythology. Called "The Finnbranch," the first two volumes are *Yearwood* and *Undersea; Hazel* is at work on the final book. "Cerridwen and the Quern of Time" is drawn from the world of The Finnbranch.

A literary golden age, the T'ang Dynasty (618–907), produced China's four greatest poets, and its most infamous—the "sorcerer poet" or "demon poet," LI HO (791–817). A child prodigy (published at age three), Lio Ho wandered the countryside in a drugged trance, writing notes and scattering them on the ground for a servant to pick up; the notes were used as the bases for Li Ho's poetry. Li Ho earned the name "sorcerer poet" because he rejected the conventions of T'ang verse and meter; worse, he wrote fantasy. In lyrical, imagistic Chinese, a seeming fantasy journey to the Forbidden City (Peking) for a lunch of dragon whiskers and cloud ears (lily buds and tree mushrooms) is really a travelogue; but Li Ho insisted that when he wrote of dragons and faeries, he wrote *about* dragons and faeries. For this, his work was reviled and suppressed for over 1100 years, until Western translators discovered that Li Ho was a very modern poet, a millennium ahead of his time.

Lutenist, Renaissance scholar, collector and performer of folksongs and madrigals, ELLEN KUSHNER has edited fantasy books for two New York publishers, and is writing a fantasy novel of her own. She shares an apartment on the upper west side of Manhattan with another editor and too many cats. "Gwydion's Loss of Llew" is derived from a section of the Welsh *Mabinogion.* The magician Gwydion is unable to save his son from a curse placed on Llew at the time of his birth. As a result, young Llew is betrayed by his bride (a woman made of flowers) and transformed into an owl. Gwydion, inspite of his magical prowess, is unable to find his transformed son, and searches for him through the fields and forests of Wales.

Although the recipient of six Hugo Awards, three Nebulas, and two World Fantasy Awards, many critics feel that FRITZ LEIBER has yet to be honored for his full role in 20th century popular culture and fiction. Persons as diverse as Marshall McLuhan and Stephen King have been quick to acknowledge Leiber's influence on their work. Stage and film actor, one time lay Episcopal minister, philosopher, editor, author, and critic, Leiber has, for forty years, challenged the boundaries of commercial fiction. His work is characterized by a richness of narrative detail and creative characterization. Leiber is often credited with the invention of the contemporary urban horror novel, and pioneered the use of complex moral ambiguities and the self-aware anti-hero in modern fantasy tales, the use of pacifistic themes in adventure yarns, and the use of fantasy and s.f. as symbolic motifs for examination of the author's life. Leiber's fantasy includes: *Conjure Wife; Gather, Darkness!; Our Lady of Darkness; Night's Black Agents;* six "Fafhrd and Gray Mouser" volumes; and numerous short stories. Still active in his seventies, at work on several new projects, Leiber lives in San Francisco, his apartment watched over by portraits of his parents, Shakespearean actors.

The resurgence of modern fantasy is usually credited to the release of paperback editions of Tolkien's works in the mid 1960s. A case could be made, though, that millions of people were really introduced to modern fantasy through the rock and folk singers of the same period—one of the most popular of whom is DONOVAN LEITCH. Musician, songwriter, poet, illustrator; Donovan brings a touch of fantasy to all his endeavors. Magic abounds in the lyrics to his albums, from the haunting "Legend of the Girlchild Linda" to Lewis Carroll rhymes set to music; from the psychedelia of "Sunshine Superman" and "Season of the Witch" to the fairy tale, "The Enchanted Gypsy." "These poems are for youth, that is true," he writes, "but they are fluid in their nature and may be enjoyed by all."

English engineer and aviation scientist R. P. LISTER's comic verse has appeared regularly in *Punch* magazine, *The New Yorker* magazine, and *The Atlantic* magazine (which first published "Haunted"). Lister, born in 1914, plans to settle down and specialize in lyric poetry, come the year 1999.

GABRIEL GARCÍA MÁRQUEZ was born in an isolated tropical region of Colombia, but has lived most of his life in Mexico, Venezuela, Paris, and Spain. His fiction, translated into many languages, such as the internationally bestselling novels *One Hundred Years of Solitude* and *Autumn of the Patriarch,* have earned García Márquez a reputation as a modern master of literature.

Born in Cartagena, Spain, FÉLIX MARTÍ-IBAÑEZ (1912–1972) was forced to leave his medical and psychiatric practices and emigrate to the United States when Franco came to power. A prolific medical essayist and medical historian, Martí-Ibañez also wrote *All the Wonders We Seek: Thirteen Tales of Surprise and Prodigy,* which might be described as a magical tour through South and Central America. This book, published in 1963, was little known in the fantasy field until its rediscovery by anthologists Robert Boyer and Kenneth Zahorski.

The calm of World Fantasy Award winner PATRICIA A. McKILLIP's life masks a driving discipline to master writing and music, combined with, by the author's admission, an often restless wanderlust. McKillip's acclaimed novels include three juvenile fantasies: *The Throme of the Erril of Sherill,* a tongue in cheek (literally, when read aloud) pastiche of Victorian fairy tales, inspired by Middle English; *The House on Parchment Street;* and *The Night Gift. The Forgotten Beasts of Eld* followed, and a trilogy: *The Riddle-Master of Hed, Heir of Sea and Fire, Harpist in the Wind.* Her most recent work is *Stepping from the Shadows,* describing a woman's odyssey through a life of desperate fantasies and realities. Of "The Harrowing of the Dragon of Hoarsbreath" McKillip writes: "Storytelling must have begun around a roaring fire inside a dark, safe cave, maybe with a skein of something fermented passing from hand to hand. Unfortunately, small, safe worlds you invent in fantasy—the hobbit worlds—always seem to invite destruction, or at least a good shaking up. I still can't think about this story without remembering the beginning rather than the ending: the safe world rather than the necessary world."

JENNIFER CAROLYN ROBIN McKINLEY was born in her mother's home town of Warren, Ohio, and grew up all over the world because her father was in the Navy. Other than books, her major preoccupations are grand opera and long walks (both of which she claims keep the blood flowing and the imagination limber), the films of John Huston, and fine horses. She is the author of three highly acclaimed works of fantasy: *Beauty: A Retelling of the Story of Beauty and the Beast; The Door in the Hedge,* a collection of four splendid tales; and *The Blue Sword,* the first novel of an epic work. "I write fantasy," she says, "because I love the stuff—all the wizards, enchantments and mysterious physical laws unlike the ones we're used to; and because, as both reader and writer, I am fascinated by things like Good and Evil, right and wrong, honor and betrayal. It is difficult if not impossible to tackle such things in "straight" fiction, at least not in the video-saturated, bomb-haunted 20th century; and yet I think a good jolt of imaginary black and white helps to sort out the reality of shades of gray."

Poet, editor, and music scholar RICHARD MONACO was, at one time, curator of contemporary music for the Columbia University Library. Since then he has served on the faculties of Mercy College and the New School for Social Research, hosted poetry shows for two New York radio stations, co-directed the Contemporary Music Consort, and been poetry editor for *The University Review.* Monaco's existentialist revision of medieval romance is available in three volumes: *Parsival: A Knight's Tale; The Grail War;* and *The Final Quest.*

The son of George Edward Moore, horticulturalist NICHOLAS MOORE has described his verse as "slightly surrealistic." An award-winning poet associated with The New Apocalypse movement in Britain, Moore stopped writing poetry after 1945.

"In the Very Earliest Times" was once a small part of a NETSILIK Eskimo hunting invocation to the sea goddess Nuliajuk. However, Netsilik belief holds that such magic chants (composed in a secret, nontribal tongue) lose power through repetition. When a spell is defunct, the angakok (shaman) translates it to common language, whereupon the chant may be sung for amusement, or passed along without fear of sacrilege. This one was offered to anthropologists in 1931.

JANE HELEN NEWBOLD is the author of several excellent tales of high fantasy, though "The Ern Queen," which she describes as a "rather gloomy tale of Norse magic," is her first publication. "I am a high school teacher of English," she writes, "much devoted to fantasy and science fiction. I live with my two teenage daughters, three cats, and a dog in the city of Indianapolis and have too little time to devote to writing."

Before being recognised with a 1969 Arts Council Grant, British poet and playwright BRIAN PATTEN managed to "stay alive (by) wandering up and down the country reading poems." "Small Dragon" comes from the pages of the collection *Notes to the Hurrying Man,* and was reprinted in the Penguin collection of Magic Verse.

JOÃO GUIMARÃES ROSA (1908–1967) was a Brazilian doctor and diplomat, serving in Germany, Colombia, and France; he headed a frontier services office for Brazil's Ministry of Foreign Affairs. More important were Rosa's years as a government doctor in the *sertao,* the vast Brazilian backlands and jungles: his experiences, and study of native folklore, inspired a writing style that swung easily from naturalism to surrealism to mythic fantasy—"magical realism." Rosa's influence on Hispanic literature has led translator and poet Alastair Reid to call him "probably the most important modern South American (writer)." Some of Rosa's work is available in English, notably *The Third Bank of the River,* and the novel *The Devil to Pay in the Backlands.*

Although she has won a Nebula award, JOANNA RUSS' political convictions and uncompromising, innovative prose have sometimes prompted ambivalent reactions to her work. When Russ' best-known novel, *The Female Man,* was published as science fiction in 1975, it was sharply attacked within genre and pointedly ignored without: today, the book is routinely listed as a major work of modern American fiction, and as one of the handful of truly important novels directly inspired by the modern feminism movement. "Autobiography of My Mother," a story not without similarities to "The Little Dirty Girl," was chosen for *Prize Stories 1977: The O. Henry Awards.*

A Fellow of the Royal Society of Literature, winner of the Pulitzer Prize, grant recipient of the Guggenheim and of the Ford Foundation, ANNE SEXTON's (1928–1974) poetry is remembered for her vivid, feverish imagery, and confessional tone; the heart-breaking frustrations of her life and suicide galvanized the Women's Consciousness Raising movement of the past decade. *Transformations* was a departure from Sexton's main work; a book of fairy tales reinterpreted into modern narrative verse, it is considered Sexton's most disciplined and accessible opus.

SOMTOW SUCHARITKUL is an avant-garde composer whose works have been performed in more than a dozen countries on four continents. Among his compositions are "Gongula 3 for Thai and Western Instruments," and "The Cosmic Trilogy." His book publications include *Starship and Haiku, Mallworld,* and *Light on the Sound.* Born in Bangkok, Thailand, Sucharitkul has lived in six countries, was educated at Eton and Cambridge, and moved to the United States a few years ago. Of "The Fallen Country," he notes, simply: "This one is for Jay."

Born in 1944, JENNY SULLIVAN lives in Cardiff; "Gran and the Roaring Boys" was found in anthology of contemporary Welsh writers, *The Old Man of the Mist,* edited by Lynn Hughs and partially funded by the Welsh Arts Council.

Poet, anthologist, novelist HENRY TREECE (1911–1966) was a protege of Sir Herbert Read, and cofounder of the Romantic poetry movement, The New Apocalypse. A friend of George Orwell, Dylan Thomas, and Mervyn Peake, Treece also wrote juvenile historical novels, radio drama, and, in later life, vivid adult historical novels, some based on "archetypal Celtic theme(s)," notably: *The Dark Island, The Great Captains, The Golden Strangers, Red Queen, White Queen,* and *The Green Man.*

One of America's most respected poets, and a famed historian, DR. PETER VIERECK won the Pulitzer Prize for *Terror and Decorum,* his first book of verse. Two Guggenheim grants, two Library of Congress lecture appointments, a cornucopia of fellowships and visiting professorships, and many volumes of history, political philosophy, and verse have since been added to his resumé. Among Viereck's works is *The Tree Witch,* a symbolic fantasy verse play.

GAIRD WALLIG is a poet with publications in numerous small press magazines and anthologies. She is also the author of several nonfiction titles, including *A Red Tailed Hawk Named Bucket.* "Bucket lived in our living room," says the author, "and made a nest on the kitchen table out of silverware, plastic roses, shreds of curtains, so that we couldn't use it for four years." Wallig lives in northern California with her husband, two sons, two dogs, a cat, a hamster, and "a few peculiar looking fish. I'm not sure what they are—they might be catfish." In addition to writing, Wallig is a tailor by trade and has held a variety of jobs including phone solicitation for the Arthur Murray Dance Studios and 5-year-guarantee lightbulbs. She is currently devoting her time to writing, and the restoration of a sailboat. "Reading is a special place to me," she says. "Every time life wasn't as special as it could be, I could make it special by opening a door that was a cover of a book."

EVANGELINE WALTON is one of the great figures of contemporary fantasy; her "Mabinogion" tetralogy is among the classic works of the genre. Originally begun in 1936, the first volume was published to little public interest; it was not until the 1970 edition (issued by the Ballantine Adult Fantasy series) that Walton received the recognition she deserved, persuading her to complete the three other volumes. In *The Saturday Review,* Patrick Merla wrote: "I suspect Evangeline Walton knows something about magic from personal experience. Her books are so thoroughly steeped in mysticism that mere anthropological knowledge of Druidic lore is insufficient to explain their authority. Only C. S. Lewis has matched Walton's subtle depiction of the forces of Good and Evil." Walton makes her home in the American Southwest, and is at work on a new novel, based on Greek legendry.

SYLVIA TOWNSEND WARNER (1893–1978) was a Renaissance music scholar, and author of twenty books, including novels whose subjects ranged from a 14th century French convent, to the 1848 Paris uprisings. Her first, and best known novel, *Lolly Willowes*, is a comic fantasy mingling witchcraft with British gentry mores. Her last collection, *Kingdoms of Elfin*, the source of "Visitors to a Castle," has an unusual distinction: these magical fantasy stories, of winged elves and faeries and high sorcery in the invented world of Elfin, first appeared in *The New Yorker* magazine.

THOMAS WILOCH hails from Michigan; he is an editor with the Gale Research Company, a publisher of reference books, and has published fiction and artwork in such diverse magazines as *New Age Journal, Kayak,* and *The Wormwood Review*. Of his fantasy prose-poems, many of which resemble Sufi fables, he writes: "It's hard to say what drew me to fantasy—certainly my admiration for surrealism had been a strong factor, especially the surrealist emphasis on self-created realities. I also enjoy Lord Dunsany's little tales, Zen koans, and Borges."

DR. JANE YOLEN is one of todays most versatile writers of books for young people, equally acclaimed for her poetry, humorous novels, picture book texts, comic verse, biographies, and collections of short fiction, modern fantasy, and original fairy tales. She received her B.A. and Ph.D. from Smith College, where she teaches courses in children's literature. She has been editor of children's books for a New York publisher, and is a critic (for *The New York Times Book Review* and *Parabola* magazine among others) and lecturer. Her latest work is *Neptune Rising*, a collection of fantasy stories and verse about the sea and its denizens. "The magical story is not a microscope but a mirror, not a drop of water but a well. It is not simply one thing or two, but a multitude. It is at once lucid and opaque, it accepts both dark and light, speaks to youth and old age."